# SIPHO SEPAMLA

# *A Ride on the Whirlwind*

**A NOVEL**

**HEINEMANN**
LONDON · IBADAN · NAIROBI

Heinemann Educational Books Ltd
22 Bedford Square, London WC1B 3HH
PMB 5205, Ibadan · PO Box 45314, Nairobi
EDINBURGH MELBOURNE AUCKLAND
HONG KONG SINGAPORE KUALA LUMPUR
NEW DELHI KINGSTON PORT OF SPAIN
Heinemann Educational Books Inc.
70 Court Street, Portsmouth, New Hampshire 03801, USA

First published by Ad. Donker (Pty) Ltd 1981
This edition first published 1984
Reprinted 1985

**British Library Cataloguing in Publication Data**

Sepamla, Sipho
    A ride on the whirlwind.—(African writers
    Series; 268)
    I. Title       II. Series
    823[F]        PR9369.2.S/

ISBN 0–435–90268–7

Printed in Great Britain by Richard Clay (The Chaucer Press) Ltd,
Bungay, Suffolk

*To the young heroes of the day*
*they who now languish in jail*
*who ride the whirlwind abroad*

*they saw the sun go down uneasily*
*while fathers stood heads dipped in despair*
*and made past them in a hurry*

*I salute their bravery*
*which stormed the June winter*
*and shamed lifelong lies*

*they are holloing out there*
*clenched fists their circumcised being*
*for they are heroes coming back home*

This story is fiction. It is based on incidents and events following the outbreak of riots in Soweto and other parts of the country in 1976. The characters are all fictional and any resemblance to real life persons is coincidental.

# 1

Mzi stepped down from the Pietersburg train at Park Station. It was still dark at 6 o'clock in the morning. The winter air was damp and chilly. Looking a youthful twenty-five years of age, tall, broad-shouldered, head poised firmly on these shoulders, he wore a confident air about him. Something stylish about his person was the khaki cap he wore at a cheeky angle.

Park Station in the morning buzzes with a babble of voices. Main-line trains cough out hundreds of commuters; so do trains from Soweto, Randfontein and Springs. The air rings with these voices which tell of their presence but not the complaint that goes with the broad chatter.

Mzi's second-hand military overcoat looked a lightweight on his body. And the calf-length boots added that extra touch of character to his appearance. Swinging from one arm was a huge paper bag. Protruding from the paper bag were glimmering heads of flowers: an artificial bunch. Over the bag was a colourful winter blanket. It was his badge of simplicity and of being a rustic. It wasn't clear whether the paper bag bulged because of the bunch or the other items in it. The whole trip from Pietersburg was made agonising by that paper bag. It contained several components of the deadly automatic rifle, the AK47. With them was a number of hand-grenades and ammunition.

He registered his safe arrival on the platform by going down on his haunches, swinging the loose arm several times. The cold air he breathed in and out was fresh and relaxing. He went over the detail of his trip to the country: this homecoming which was worked out roughly by the office of the Resistance Movement in Dar. The whole trip was an exercise of guts and luck. For to cross the border from Botswana into South Africa fingers were crossed that nothing went wrong. There was Koos van der Stel, a farmer who used, on the Botswana side of the border, South African black labour. In true fashion of a master race, he took everything for granted: the 'boys' required to return to the Republic after their short-term contract had ended would be marshalled into the open truck ready for him to drive off at seven in the morning; the border gate guards cleared him quickly because he carried a group permit for his labourers, whom he recruited from South Africa with the connivance of the local authority. No-one bothered to check the individuals huddled at the back of the huge truck like so many bags of sweet potatoes and pumpkins. Mr van der Stel's black assistants on the farm were not members of the Movement: they shared its spirit because talk in Botswana went something like this: Botswana people cannot be free unless their black brothers in the Republic are free. These assistants helped the Resistance Movement.

Mzi was smuggled into the Republic with the help of van der Stel acting unwittingly. Hopping onto the Pietersburg—Jo'burg train was a right every authority encouraged. He arrived in Jo'burg with a clear and simple purpose: the mission in Soweto. It was to eliminate Warrant Officer Andries Batata of the Special Branch.

The timing of that despatch was clever. Soweto on June 18th was in a state of turmoil: the children's revolution gripped the imagination of many people in and outside the country. The office in Dar acted on the spur of the moment to despatch someone like Mzi to take advantage of the situation. It didn't matter much to the Dar office that the children were concerned with a complaint against the use of Afrikaans in their classrooms. This was read to mean a complaint against the whole fabric of the ruling forces. There was discontent. What more fertile soil was needed for the accentuation of a situation always at boiling point?

Mzi heard the thud of feet on the platform, he saw the movement of human bodies, the gesticulation of hands, and felt the hot, driving pulse of people milling and jostling on the platform. He was home, he told himself several times. Wasn't he part of the crowd of commuters?

He moved up the stairs leading to the concourse. It was narrow, it was crowded. Here the morning crowds moved swiftly. Mzi couldn't be sure that hurried walk meant anything to each of the commuters. Up on one wall of the concourse ticked a huge clock. He thought there was something oppressive in the hurrying of people and the ticking of the clock. At that instant his mind was thrown back to Dar, to London, East Berlin and Moscow. There was hurrying in those places, to and fro and up and down. The people at Park Station had that in common with those he remembered seeing overseas.

His mind turned to the weight on his left shoulder. A heavy winter blanket was slung on his shoulder. It and the heavy coat stamped him an outsider. It was all right on the Pietersburg train. Long distance travellers often went about that way. But on the Soweto train it would be damn odd to wear an overcoat and carry a winter blanket even by hand. And with the paper bag containing a machine-gun, it would be bloody silly to attract attention so obviously.

He went into the loo. The smell was stronger than he expected. Ten years earlier he was in the same loo on his way out to Botswana.

8

The porcelain tiles were then snow-white. On this day they threw at him a piss smell he wanted to shut out with two fingers clipped on the nose. A slimy substance of phlegm hung on the edge of the iron sheet against which men pissed. His whole being was repulsed by the inside of the loo. But he couldn't withdraw yet. He went into one of the two-cent cubicles. He pulled the cistern and the crushing splash of water gave him the cover he wanted: he wrapped the blanket into a fine bundle and shoved it behind the pan. He stood at the door to see if anyone was around to observe his escapades. A man stood shaking his penis nearby. Mzi was satisfied the fellow would be moving out. Mzi lingered at the door and at the moment the other person hurried out, Mzi dashed into a cubicle three moves away and shut the door. Again he flushed the pan just so that he could have the splashing noise once more. He relieved himself of the military overcoat, wrapped it into a bundle and placed it neatly behind the pan. Satisfied there was no-one to give him away, he sauntered out of the place.

He bought a third-class ticket to Dube station. He was about to take a dip into the platform of trains to Soweto when his eye caught the screaming lettering of a billboard:

RIOT TOLL RISES. THIRTEEN BODIES RECOVERED.

He was tempted to buy a copy of the morning paper. But it would have been against the advice offered to him in his brief. He felt a creeping sensation of the skin. And he gnashed his teeth. Presently he disappeared among the many people who boarded the Dube train.

Mzi watched a man seated opposite him. The chattering in the train, the clattering of train wheels, all this noise didn't reach the man. He was dozing, snapping back a head swathed in a balaclava. Tired, tired and drowsy. The man was like a baby in his tiredness. He wore a heavy military coat like the one Mzi left in the toilet. Only with a knobkerrie between his knees. Mzi knew the coat must have been on the man's shoulders for the past twelve hours. For he was a night-watchman. The man's head gradually tumbled forward on a rubbery neck. Suddenly it snapped back and he opened his eyes, smiled with the people around, and shut his eyes once more.

Mzi looked beyond the carriage. He saw the sheer massiveness of the concrete city. Ten years back Jo'burg was not like this, he told himself. All right the tall buildings were there but they didn't look so intimidating, so immovable and so impressive as he saw them on this occasion. The sight filled him with a sense of anticipation.

The train rumbled, the passengers grumbled. What they said was not audible as the train rolled and swayed amidst the clattering of its wheels. In the course of the journey Mzi tried several things: his mind would pick on an item such as the sight of new factories along the railway line, debate the age of each factory and then give up the exercise. Sometimes he pondered over the filling up of spaces he knew to have been empty. A new station was Industria. These were some of the little items to liven up what might otherwise have been a dull and routine trip. The train came to a stop at New Canada station. Several people leaped out of the train, others jostled to sit down on the wooden benches. New Canada was a junction station. The rail line forked out into two from this station as it entered the sprawling city of Soweto.

It was when the train headed for Mzimhlope, daring the vast, empty veld, that an old lady seated next to Mzi braced herself to say: 'Those are beautiful flowers in your bag.'

'Thank you,' said Mzi. He clutched the bag tightly on to his chest.

'How much do you sell one of them?' asked the old lady shifting in her seat. For her movement was not so easy. Her one arm was so huge and fleshy it was an effort for her to raise it.

Mzi chuckled uneasily. He answered: 'They are not for sale.' He touched his military-style khaki cap. The old lady was persistent.

'For your wife?'

'No!'

'Your mother?'

'No!'

'Your girl-friend?'

Mzi laughed. The old lady looked on, her face beaming. More eyes were by now riveted on the couple. Mzi experienced a constriction of his chest. He wanted to scream, to ask the old lady to let him free. Then another idea pressed itself before him: he wanted to move away to another seat. Instead he began to sniff at the flowers. And both his arms went round the paper bag so that he held it tightly to his body. The old lady shifted in her seat. She was in time to hear Mzi say: 'The flowers are mine, ma.'

The train slowed down to stop at Mzimhlope station. The old lady held the upright of the seat for support. She yanked herself up and began to shuffle toward the door. As a parting shot she said: 'Lucky is the person who is going to receive that beautiful bunch of flowers.' Mzi smiled broadly. He couldn't hide his relief. The mask of quiet innocence returned to his face immediately the train pulled off again.

'Dube Station', proclaimed many voices as the train cruised to a stop. Mzi joined the many feet shuffling out of the train, out through the barrier-gates and down the slope from the station into Dube. He walked with a confident step, eyes taking in as much as he could pick on his way. He loved the soft soil on which his feet trod. It was home-soil once more. The paper bag he hugged to him as casually as one who carries a basketful of vegetables from the market place.

He went up to a white-washed little house two streets away from the main Dube street, Mncube Drive. He knew it well because ten years earlier he had spent several days in it on his way out for training. A strange sensation seized him. He couldn't tell what it was. But it bordered on fear, the fear of the unknown. One thing taught in the camps was distrust. Don't trust anyone until he's been checked out thoroughly, was what they were told by one of the instructors. Another point stated was: if three or more Soweto people decide on a campaign, the chances are that one of them works for the cops as an informer. These thoughts crushed him as he waited for someone to open the door. He was hardly a minute knocking but his impatience showed in his dancing feet and the heightened beat of his pulse. He was still waiting when a sudden impulse of fear streaked through his system, sweat pebbles formed on the crown of his head and he was dazed for a second or so. A pick-up van whizzed past the house at a reckless speed. It was enough to upset his balance.

The door opened and he was invited in. Uncle Ribs Mbambo held the door open for him with one hand. A lighted pipe was in the other. Tall, wiry, hair grizzly, nose thin and pointed, teeth fouled by smoking, Uncle Ribs hugged Mzi briefly, nestling his chest on Mzi's strong frame. His face was wrinkled by a smile. Mzi was taken aback by the slight build of this former acquaintance. His own picture of the man was different: for many years he was full of body and vigorous of movement. All that appeared to be the past of Uncle Ribs. Now he got by with the twinkle of the eye and the wrinkles which furrowed his face. Mzi felt saddened by this turn of events. It made him feel a sorrow he least wanted to entertain.

The door was closed and Mzi relieved himself of his sole possession: the paper bag.

'My! My!' exclaimed Uncle Ribs, looking Mzi over. 'You are fit and looks like you could take on two Spanish bulls in one go!' Uncle Ribs returned to puffing from his pipe.

'Thanks,' answered Mzi rather shyly. 'You amaze me, age doesn't look like it ever touches you.'

'Why,' said Uncle Ribs, 'Look at my head, it's all grey.'

'No, Uncle, there are only a few grey strands on that head.'

'You are generous. Camp life has obviously tamed you.' Both men laughed, the younger for a very brief moment only.

'Can I help you with your baggage?' offered Uncle Ribs. He bent to collect the paper bag. 'M'm, heavier than I thought. Well-equipped, eh?' He led Mzi to a room prepared for a visitor.

'Your new home,' said Uncle Ribs.

'Thanks.'

Both men returned to the sitting room and settled down. Mzi took in the contents of the room: three leather seats, a coffee table, a radiogram with a display cabinet full of fancy goods, and a small book case. Uncle Ribs smoked continuously. The room became grey with smoke-clouds whirling round and round. He said: 'You've come in the throes of mad activity. The children are playing a cat and mouse game with the State.'

'Oh,' said Mzi quietly.

'You must have seen the kwela-kwela rushing up the street,' said Uncle Ribs.

'I did.'

'Those chaps are still speed-crazy. That goes on all day long. The cops are chasing God-only-knows-what.'

'Phantoms!'

'Say it again. In all my involvement with the struggle, I've never known the State make such a laughing-stock of itself,' said Ribs warming to the subject. He went on: 'The kwela-kwela will be chasing a boy, a fifteen or seventeen-year-old. As he realizes the law is snapping at his heels, you know what he does brother?' asked Ribs, rhetorically.

'No!'

Uncle Ribs paused, placed the pipe on the ashtray standing on the coffee-table: 'One, two, three the boy jumps low-fenced yards. And he melts into the sameness of the houses.'

'They lose him,' added Mzi.

'Completely,' elaborated Ribs, cutting the air with one hand. And then he brushed his hands together rapidly and said: 'They never find him!'

'Goes to show we can tackle the bastards if we want to,' said Mzi.

'With your kind of training I bet a lot is going to be done.'

'I'm going to give them hell,' said Mzi, boastfully. 'When they shoot along one street, I'll be blowing fuses in the other one.'

'That's the spirit, that's it,' said an enthusiastic Uncle Ribs. After a short silent pause the host suggested: 'You must be hungry, brother.' He didn't wait for a reply but walked toward the kitchen.

'Not very hungry, really,' said Mzi politely. 'Training disciplines,' he continued, trying to put up a brave front. He did swallow once or twice in the process, perhaps from a sense of anticipation.

'The ol' girl is at work,' offered Uncle Ribs. 'You'll have to make do with my poor attempt at frying eggs and a piece of red meat.'

'Is Sis Joyce at Baragwanath Hospital?'

'Ya!' said Uncle Ribs squinting as he held the frying pan a safe distance from his eyes. 'She's some general, as I understand. There's been such an exodus of doctors from provincial hospitals, our girls are having to step in. Saw one little thing dangling a . . . what's the name of that damn thing used by doctors?'

'Stethoscope?' came in from Mzi.

'Ya, stethoscope. I didn't know whether to laugh or cry.'

Mzi laughed dryly. His eye was on the sizzling pan. Presently Uncle Ribs said: 'Come, let's sit down to a men's breakfast.'

It was the first solid meal for Mzi for a long, long time.


Sis Ida Diradikayi sat on a stool looking at her workmanship. Countless bottles and boxes of perfumes and cosmetics lined the dressing-table. At thirty-eight she didn't think she was getting along too fast. But the mirror revealed a sadness around the eyes which make-up couldn't hide. True enough the cosmetics she had been applying hid a bit of her real appearance: dry brown face, watery eyes sunk in flabby bags touched with a whitish cream, broad nose and fleshy lips. Her big bosom heaved up and down as if she had lately engaged in some exerting exercise. In the mirror she caught the doubled-up figure of her daughter, Getty, together with her grand son, Setlogolo. She was very proud of the illegitimate boy, loving and caring for him as if she had carried him for nine wearisome months. She sought the boy in the mirror, saw his outline beneath the blankets. One twist of her neck satisfied her motherhood. And her bosom filled up with a sorrow not clear in the mind's eye. The bedroom gave her a feeling of being cramped. The bed, the wardrobe, the dressing-table and the two sleeping figures were all she could count distinctly. Yet these few items crowded the room. Sis Ida was sorry for herself. She was sorry that she had brought all these worries on her head. Sorry that for four full months she had carried in her bosom a secret hard and painful to share. She never complained of her burden, the yoke of caring for her own children and a dozen more she kept out of charity. There was just no-one she could tell of the pain and the ache she laid her head on every night only to raise it every morning as she faced the day.

She picked a tube of some greasy stuff and daubed it below her eyes. The blue-black skin turned a light grey. It gave her relief. She felt confident to venture out into the world to proclaim her presence to the new day. This woman known throughout Soweto for her outgoing and open heart looked subdued these days. But Sis Ida remained charming in the street and before her guests.

She hurriedly left her stool, picked up a black handbag and moved to leave the bedroom. June 18 was for her another working day. And as usual she bundled herself out of the bedroom on the first leg of her trip to the City. When she reached the bedroom door, she swung it open. It squeaked. Her hand still on the door-knob, she squirmed with regret. She hated to disturb the close-packed sleeping figures stretched on the floor or sunk in the one studio couch standing in the sitting room. Unconsciously she counted eight of them in the tiny room. Huddled together breathing in and out unevenly, none betrayed a care under the circumstances. She loved them all, she told herself as she wangled her way to the kitchen. Her way out of the house was through the kitchen door. Here she was hit by a crushing stuffiness because this ten-by-eight foot cage, always grateful to the sizzling sound of fried meat or onions and tomato, was made to contain four easy-farting youths together with a work-table, a dresser and a coal stove.

She stepped out of the kitchen door. It was a huge relief: the early morning breeze licked her tense cheeks and brought the freshness of a new day full-blast onto her breast. She trudged triumphant to the main street where she would catch a taxi into town. For Sis Ida waiting in the open air was like having escaped imprisonment. Her whole being was washed over by the sensation of floating in space, a cloud rolling and rolling in the open sky. Yet the sensation was short-lived. For suddenly a thought turned on her mind forcibly. And now as in the past she tried hard to suppress it. It brought tears to the brink of her eyes, it brought sorrow to press on her bosom. It was a thought which at once saddened and imprisoned her. For she wondered how long she would manage to flee from the long arm of the law. Often in the quietness of her heart she felt the ache of her unlawful deed: the harbouring of youths she knew full well had committed wrongs against the whiteman's law and were sought for retribution.

A taxi came and she boarded it for the city of concrete slabs.

In the meantime Sis Ida's house, 1041 Mpela Street, Zone 2, Meadowlands, came alive. One of the girls, Bongi, was first to shake her bum and wake up. She was the headstrong member of the group. For a girl she was considered too forward by some of her colleagues. Yet no one dared to say it to her face. She had these big breasts, attractive and intimidating. And as if to give away their price easily, she was in the habit of sleeping next to Keke, sissy of the group. As she ambled up in her sleepy condition, Keke rolled over to occupy the space Bongi had vacated. She leaned over Keke to retrieve a dress lying on the wooden cabinet of the sewing-machine.

'What's the time, Bongi?' asked Keke. His voice was muffled by the blanket pulled up to his face.

'How do I know?' countered Bongi.

'That's no answer.'

'You'll have to teach me,' said Bongi, her voice edgy.

'Hey, baby, I didn't touch you all night, is that why you're so beefy with me?'

'Shurrup, man,' groused. Sello. He was sleeping two removes from Keke. 'Can't a man be allowed a little sleep after a busy night?' He turned to face away from Keke.

'Keke thinks he's smart,' said Bongi. 'He can't bear to have me face away from him when we sleep. He didn't want to know the time. He was announcing to me that he's aware I'm up.'

'You lie! You lie!' cried Keke. He was the baby of the group and expected to be fussed over. 'I am serious. I want to know what time it is.'

'Then why don't you shake your bloody backside and look how high the sun is,' said Sello. There was so much voice going with those words every other person shook off sleep to await what might happen next.

Punkie seemed to take her cue from the silence which followed.

'Opskit. . . opskit bajita,' said Punkie coming into her own among the lot in the sitting room. She saw Digoro wake up and sit on his bum; watched Roy stretch a naked arm and sit up where he was. The room was like a hippopotamus taking a breather above the level of the water. There was heaving and sighing as the youths came alive for the new day.

'Ya, Mzala,' said Mandla Nkosi reclining on an elbow, 'let them get up.' He had a very sonorous voice even as he woke up. He continued, getting to his feet: 'There's a helluva lot of work to be done today.' Mandla was a fairly tall youth, fair-skinned and handsome. His leadership qualities could be assessed from the way he dealt with the other members of the group: fairly and firm. There was also about him an air of arrogance, but above all he was gutsy. Not the so-called democratic vote made him leader, but his initiative, his willingness to stand up and get things done. No wonder some referred to him as the General.

Presently Bongi called out from the kitchen: 'Coffee is ready.'

Sis Ida was obviously caught on the wrong foot by the presence of the group. This became clear at tea or meal-times. On this morning Bongi stirred her own coffee in the emptied jam-tin. Others used cups, mugs and beer glasses to drink their coffee. It was fun for all, this life of revolutionaries in the making. None had bargained for it but most came to accept the realities.

It was breakfast time so each member was free to pick up a slice of thick dry bread from the table. There were no formalities. A person held his coffee and bread in his hands, stood where he was to munch; sauntered over to lounge on the studio couch or the floor in the sitting room; sat on the threshold of the front or kitchen door or in one of the cars standing in the backyard. Sitting in cars was more inviting because the heat of the sun brightened up the spirits of those huddled there.

The winter sun came up lazily and this allowed the human body to unfold gradually to the new day. But for those who watched the clock, time was always flying away. Mandla belonged to the latter group. He moved from point to point to brief certain persons of their responsibilities for the day.

'Sello, you know what to do with that skunk Timothy,' said Mandla to the first person.

'I'll find him buda General,' said Sello, the toughie in the group, 'and I'll show him his mother. Maybe he's forgotten her sight.'

'Boysi you'll be with Snoek when you see the Bishop. . .'

'Tell him we are starving,' chipped in Nkele. She was among the people seated in the sitting room. Her aggressive nature showed up easily on this occasion.

'Say to him,' said Mandla, 'we need more food than he gives to the dog chained in his backyard, bloody liberal bootlicker. Tell him that!' Then Mandla clicked his tongue and said: 'I feel like taking up the job myself.'

'No, bigboy,' said Roy, second in command in the group. He was one chap who came very near to equalling Mandla. Yet he knew how far to go with his leader. He continued: 'Our job in town is bigger.'

'Okay, Roy. I got a bit carried away for a moment. 'Strue's God I'm going to be rough with the Bishop the day I meet him. He never plays ball with us. Why? Sonofabitch!'

'We'll serve him one of our petrol bombs if he doesn't deliver the goods this time,' said Roy.

'You damn right,' said Sello cynically.

Boysi sat moodily listening to his colleagues making pronouncements. Within him was this tense feeling, gagging his throat. He feared to explode too soon as he looked forward to his encounter with the Bishop.

'Who's on stand-by today?' asked Mandla.

'I am,' said Keke. He was sitting in one of the easy chairs and was partially hidden by Snoek who was perched on the arm of the chair.

'You are mad!' said Nkele. She looked angry as she said this. And pointing a finger at herself she said very aggressively: 'I am on stand-by today! It's my turn to do my washing.'

'Okay, Mzala,' said Bongi, 'Let Keke do your washing. I'm sure he'll enjoy looking at the undies.' There was laughter.

'Voetsak!' said the offended Keke. 'I was merely pulling her leg.'

'You lie,' said Bongi.

'Hold it, bajita,' said Mandla. He already sensed the in-fighting which threatened to develop at that time. 'I think everyone is clear about what is expected of him or her. I don't like to see our dirty linen displayed outside. It is enough the neighbours around here call us the Red Army. Let us not give them an excuse to run to the system to say we are threatening the peace. You all know what will happen if the Superintendent of the location begins to snoop at Sis Ida's place. So peace, bajita, peace. Keke teams up for today with Dan Montsho. Okay?'

And so Mandla went on for the morning. Soon silence fell on the house, activity being elsewhere for the day.


At Westend Police Headquarters sharp at 10 o'clock that morning, the top brass assembled for their routine weekly conference. By special invitation another person to attend was Warrant Officer Andries Batata. He too was a member of the Special Branch with a reputation of sorts. Presiding was Colonel Willem Kleinwater, whose superior standing could be read from the way he held up his neck and combed his brown hair, thinning a bit on the sides and cut clean at the back. His huge frame dominated the conference table, his blue eyes seemed to jump off the surface of the table, so sharp were they. They radiated a terror which he always hid with his cloud of pipe smoke. On the Colonel's right sat Major Edmond Hall, the one with mischievous restless green eyes, huge flapping ears, a nose pronounced in its de Gaulle appearance. The man was notorious for his efficient interrogations. He sat looking straight into space — a very deceptive pose.

'Gentlemen,' began the Colonel, shifting slightly in his cushioned imperial chair, 'the situation in Soweto has deteriorated to an alarming degree. And the Minister is furious, to say the least. I tell you when I spoke to him yesterday he was pounding his desk every now and then as he emphasised his point of view. He says we have allowed a children's revolution to shake the economy of the country. We embarrass him in the eyes of his enemies. I've had to promise him results — in your name too. Do you understand? But what I cannot understand is why our friends in Soweto cannot locate the whereabouts of this piccanin Mandla and the people behind him. I've told the Minister that my personal theory is that the members of the Resistance Movement and their fellow-travellers are the real brains behind the whole agitation in Soweto. Of course the Minister holds the view that the real trouble-makers are this new breed in the townships known as Black Consciousness. He has an unfortunate obsession about this consciousness thing. There's nothing I can do about it. What I want to know is why can't all the forces at our disposal stamp out the mischief-makers? Why haven't we had a meaningful breakthrough after all these damn weeks of hard labour? Why?' The Colonel paused at the point where his fist pounded the table. He was quite agitated. His face flushed a bleeding red and his blue eyes were burning into the skin of his colleagues. They cleared their throats one after another. None could tell when their voices developed crocodiles.

Major Hall heaved up his chest and then dropped his broad shoulders. It was clear the situation was for him quite unbearable. He heaved again, eyelids flicked on and off, his face twisted by the strong feeling embedded in his chest. He was a stammerer and under pressure he was overwhelmed by his condition. At last he managed to say something. This gave relief to his colleagues who had been made more tense by watching him struggle to articulate his thoughts.

'Ge - ge - gentlemen, ar - ar - think th - th - th - the point is one ar - I want to meet P - p-pri- nci-pal M - m - m. . .'

'Yes,' cut in the Colonel sympathetically, 'you are right, Japie, Masemola is our man. Andries here,' the Colonel swung his eyes toward Warrant Officer Batata and continued, 'he's been urging me to lock up that man. He knows quite a lot about what the children are up to. Sections 6 and 10 of the Act allow us to do exactly as we wish under these circumstances, whatever we think is in the best interests of the State. I have hesitated because I didn't want to see the situation deteriorate further. However, recent developments indicate caution is totally unwarranted, the balloon has gone up in any case. We have in the process lost a lot of ground.' The Colonel touched his pipe smouldering in a huge ashtray next to him on the table. Before he put the pipe in his mouth he turned to Batata and asked: 'How do you feel about this Andries?'

Andries Batata was himself a very fit and strong-looking man. Nothing he put on seemed to settle well on his body. Always his shirt or jacket appeared to be holding back a chest and shoulders ready to burst out. His face was strong; brown eyes, huge nose and bold lips. He didn't look an old man but his hair grew so sparsely he preferred to clean his head up to a shiny condition all the time. No wonder he was nicknamed Cleanhead.

On this occasion he sat proudly in the presence of his superiors, alert to the delivery and the debates of his colleagues. When the Colonel addressed him, his normally acidic eye sparkled. He replied: 'Mnumzana, what can you do with children who tell their parents that they, that is the children, they are liberated persons. Is that not disrespect? Is that not politics? No, Mnumzana, arrest the man. You'll see, everything will come to order. I tell you I know my people.'

The Colonel nodded in a majestic manner, replaced the pipe in the ashtray and declared: 'All units will have to be placed on alert immediately. I don't want to take chances at this stage. Cancel all leave. The operation must be undertaken with military precision. I want all my men on hand.'

'Yi - yi - yes Co - co - colonel I -I want to question M - masemola my - myself tomorrow.' The last few words were hardly audible. Hall kept his voice down in the hope that the speech handicap would be minimised as much as possible.

'Certainly, Major,' said the Colonel reassuringly, 'you'll get your chance with Masemola.' A pause and a silence followed. Then the Colonel said, after picking up his pipe to suck it once more: 'That's all for now, gentlemen!'

The conference ended on a higher note than had appeared possible earlier on. For police were men of action, gratified by a solution which looked good from different angles. As they trooped out of the Conference Room they smiled, they guffawed and they slapped one another's shoulders. Alles sal reg kom — All will come right!

The long, quiet, shiny corridors at Westend came alive. The thudding of the feet of policemen coming out of the Conference Room

19

reverberated on icy brick walls. They looked like men itching for action.

About the time the police ended their meeting, Uncle Ribs stood on the pavement in a city street. He lit his pipe for the umpteenth time. For almost an hour he had been jiving on that spot, his keen eye on the door of a building on the opposite side of the street. He was scheduled for a meeting in Pharmacy House; a few minutes to go. Instead of coming into town and walking straight into Pharmacy House, Uncle Ribs took the precaution of reading the happenings around the meeting place. It was for that reason he was now tapping his toes to kill time or merely dancing on his heels. Earlier he was in the book-shop nearby, browsing and flipping pages of glossy magazines. All the time his eye remained on the door of the House opposite. As he left he went up to the cashier, produced a twenty-cent piece, placed it on the counter and mumbled something about the meter and a car outside. The small change was dipped into a pocket and Uncle Ribs sauntered out of the shop blowing a few notes of 'Oh What a Beautiful Morning!'

It was while he stood guard, the morning newspaper under one arm, that he saw Mandla and Roy bounce up several steps leading into Pharmacy House. His keen eye looked up and down the street. He fixed his colourful bow-tie into a perfect position, straightened his shoulders and then crossed the street. The city traffic hummed in its usual fashion, cars crawling, others cruising, and buses dominating the scene by their mere presence.

Uncle Ribs knew the House well enough. He dipped into the basement by a series of steps and came into a well lit room. Mandla stood with his back to the door chatting to Ann Hope. Roy sat in one of the easy chairs, his one leg swinging on the arm of the chair.

Ann Hope was a finely sculptured young woman. Dark hair, slightly long face with blue eyes, she had one of the most perfectly modelled noses seen in a city office. Her charm was in her lips and eyes — always at ease and ready for a smile. She was in her late twenties and of her it was said that she had a golden heart which reached readily to other people. Born in Prague, she was brought up in London. She worked for a long time for Oxfam and came to South Africa at the invitation of the head of Kupugani. There was a shake-up in that outfit which left her unscathed. Nonetheless she gave up her administrative post when the Christian Brotherhood advertised for a Director of relief programmes. Ann quickly established herself in the new job. It brought her face to face with the black experience and catapulted her into the hearts of the new generation of Soweto. Her accessibility and concern did for her what the pomp and dignity of General-Secretary of Brotherhood's position couldn't do for Ian Taylor.

'Good morning, good people,' said Uncle Ribs, flashing a not-so-attractive set of sooty teeth.

Ann asked Mandla to excuse her and she took a step forward, extended a tiny but firm white hand to Uncle Ribs. She said, covering the old man with a huge smile: 'Good morning, Uncle Ribs.'

There was something worrying Uncle Ribs. He sensed it in the way Roy merely looked at him once and sat on, almost with an indifferent air. Mandla merely smiled at Uncle Ribs. But it was not a put-on thing: it was a smile which came from the bottom of his heart, accompanied by his well-known boyishness.

Uncle Ribs took command of the situation: 'Brothers and sister,' he said, perching on the edge of one of the many easy chairs in the huge room, 'I've brought some real good and exciting news. Our cargo arrived safely home this morning.'

'Oh! Indeed!' cried Ann, 'How marvellous!'

Mandla smiled broadly. Roy didn't bat an eye but sat there as if he hadn't heard the message from Uncle Ribs.

'He looks fit and strong,' said Uncle Ribs. 'Intelligent, oh yes, he's damn intelligent. Well-trained. He knows everything about the necessary tools of a revolution. And I can tell you this about him also: he just bubbles with self-confidence. Oh yes, I have no doubt whatsoever in my mind the boy will hit the scene with a thumping impact, that's how good he looks to me.' Uncle Ribs thrust his hand with the pipe toward Ann and said: 'I suggest we make use of him to the full!'

'Oh indeed we must!' said Ann enthusiastically. She went on: 'On my side I'm quite sure I can speed up things so that more cash is made available for the programmes in Soweto. I'm sick and tired of the bullying attitude of the police. And let's not kid ourselves, these chaps are going to pounce on all of us one of these days. The sooner we show them where power sits, that is, Soweto, the better. I am all for Mandla and his friends doing more of their thing. Already the economy is taking a hard knock. I know the stock exchange cannot withstand the onslaught of the last two days. My mind boggles to think what Mzi will do in Mandla's company, honestly it does,' concluded Ann. She was all wrapped up in the excitement of the moment. Her mouth tensed and her fist pumped the air.

Uncle Ribs entered at this point with a cool statement rolling out of his lips in an uncluttered fashion: 'The two meet this evening at my place.' He turned to Mandla to ask: 'Will that be all right with you, brother?'

'Ya, Uncle Ribs,' said Mandla, his one eye on Roy. The latter stared back without evincing any sign either way.

'Jolly good show!' exclaimed Ann. She crossed her legs, and intertwined her fingers on her lap. Her face sparkled.

Uncle Ribs lit his pipe and said: 'I guess that's all for the moment from me, brothers and sister.'

'What about Mandla, have you got anything to say?' asked Ann. She kept her eye on Mandla's eyebrows. There was something about the young man which fascinated Ann immensely. She hoped for the day she could voice it to him without fear.

'We are starving,' said Roy. The words were hard and dry. They jarred the spirit prevailing until that moment. Roy sat up in his chair and looked at Ann with burning brown eyes.

'Hold it, Roy,' said Ann, a hand held up to indicate there was no need for Roy to proceed with his case. She turned to Mandla and said: 'I have an envelope for you here.' Ann raised herself slightly from her chair and pulled out an envelope from the pocket of her woollen skirt. 'Our overseas friends have a message for you as well: strength till death.' She handed the envelope over to Mandla and let it be accompanied by a smile that went awry.

Mandla took the envelope, ripped it open and with one hand poking the air in a clenched fist he said: 'Amandla — Power.'

For once Roy responded. With an icy face but a powerful arm thrust into the air he echoed: 'Amandla!'

The meeting broke up in a fairly triumphant note, thanks to the envelope Ann had kept in readiness.

Uncle Ribs allowed Mandla and Roy to bounce up the stairs from the basement. When he was convinced they had cleared out of the building, he gathered his dignity about him — the pipe and the newspaper and the bow-tie — and quickly bade Ann farewell. He was out of Pharmacy House in a jiffy. His alert eye assured him the coast was indeed clear.


Noah Witbaatjie threw the morning newspaper onto the kitchen table and began to blabber. His customers never knew what to make of him. He spoke English, Afrikaans, Tsotsitaal, Zulu, Tswana, the lot. And when something upset him he raved in several languages. He

22

went on: 'Moegies want to tell me what's good for me.' Noah wiped his fast-balding head with a crumpled white handkerchief which had remained folded within the palm of his sweaty hand. He looked at one of his regular customers, Two-by-Two, perched on a stool across the table and himself looking thoroughly bewildered by the shebeen king. Noah stretched a hand toward the paper spread on the table and grumbled: 'Kyk, these children is mal. Shebeens must close to mark the mourning period.' He picked up the paper, dangled it in the air and queried: 'Sê my jy, who's dead? Seriously, who is dead?' He unfolded the handkerchief, shook it in the air with the free hand, wiped his blown-out fat cheeks and dabbed his glistening head feverishly. He lectured: 'laat ek jou weetie, my bra, there are men like Xuma, Luthuli and others, die real manne. They died and no-one said shebeens must close in mourning. Kyk, I'm from Sophiatown, I should know and I tell you nothing like that happened. So?'

'Ya, bra Noah,' said Styles who had been sitting and sipping beer quietly, 'I could agree with you on all that. But times have changed. These juniors have a point, you know.'

'A point!' exclaimed Noah in a bitter manner of protest. 'You want to tell me burning schools, halls and post offices is a point?'

'I don't mean that, bra Noah.' Styles was seated further away from Noah so that even in his quiet way his voice carried well across the room. He was in the habit of being stylish, fond of forming the letter O with two fingers as he made his point. His head would be drawn back, eyes looking out at an angle. He went on: 'I was trying to say the kids look at the cops with different eyes from their parents! I seem to think the kids despise every adult including the cops. Remember, for the first time it's been the blood of the young ones spilt in the streets . . .'

'My bra,' said Noah cutting in, 'I know what you are going to say. But let me tell you this, ek is van Kofifi, I'm from Sophiatown. I tasted all what is happening now long before all these kids. They don't know what they're doing. They are being pulled around with their noses man, it happened in Sophiatown. Who was against the people leaving the slums. Do you know? Do you? I'll tell you. I can see you are not well-informed about township life. Those bloody landlords fleecing their sub-tenants cried most. And who was behind them? The same Movement pulling that junior boy Mandla by the nose. We know the story damn well. No-one can fool around with us any more. Look man, I came here from Sophiatown. I had nothing to my name. Vokall!' As if to show his once impoverished state, Noah shook the handkerchief in the air once or twice and rubbed his entire head with it. Restlessness was part of his nature.

'Bra Noah is rich,' said Two-by-Two asserting his presence in the silence of the heated moment. But he didn't say more. Suddenly there was a huge figure blotting out much of the light in the room. Batata stood at the door towering over the men killing time with drinks. He showed his disdain with the two nostrils of his broad nose trumpeting wildly. One, two steps into the room and he stopped. Trembling, Noah followed him to the sitting room. He could never understand why cops unnerved him so. Like a puppy he stepped gingerly behind Batata. The latter whirled on his toes and commanded: 'Shut the door!' With just a slight squeak the door came to. Batata went on, still on his feet: 'I don't have much time, Noah.'

Noah was at a loss for words. But he managed to grunt.

'Any news?' asked the cop.

'I see the paper says . . .'

'Put away that stupid thing,' demanded Batata just as Noah was about to spread the newspaper in the air. 'I want to know if you have any leads for me,' declared the cop.

'No!' said Noah bluntly, looking puzzled in the presence of the cop. 'Everybody is scared to talk. People tell you the kids . . .'

'Listen here,' barged in Batata, 'I don't want my seniors to raid shebeens. I know things are not that easy for you blokes these days but man, I can't stop them if shebeens like this one serve no use to us. Do you understand what I am saying to you?'

'Straight!' exclaimed Noah nervously. He was looking away from Batata.

'I know your place is busy, you have many customers. Try to get something. Get them to talk, lead them into an argument, a discussion of the present set-up, anything, I don't care what. Ag man, why should I teach you your job?'

'Ek verstaan, Captain. I know straight what you want me to do. Leave it to me Captain, leave it to me,' said Noah apologetically. For him Batata was a senior cop to be addressed respectfully: Captain.

Batata breezed out in the same superior fashion he had entered. Noah remained behind in the sitting room, calling out: 'Seipati! Seipati!' He came up to the door leading into the kitchen. He was met by Two-by-Two's reply: 'Seipati has not come back yet.'

'Bloody bitch!' growled Noah. 'You know that woman gaan my very bad kry.' He wiped his bald head feverishly. He said 'The bitch has been away two hours now. How does she think I run my business, slipshod of hoe?'

'Maybe she's been delayed somehow, bra Noah.' said Styles

24

protectively.

'Delayed!' sneered Noah, 'You are bloody right! All bitches get delayed somehow. Sy ken my nie mooi nie — She doesn't know me. 'Strue's God! I'll throw her out on her ear, bloody bastard!' Noah walked across to the kitchen door and began to scan the surroundings. He returned into the kitchen clicking his tongue profusely.

Styles took advantage of the silence which followed to suggest that they split from the house. At the kitchen door, Two-by-Two asked Noah: 'Is bra N gonna mourn?'

'Ek? Oh please show me some respect. Why should I mourn? I don't care a damn for those kids and their mourning bla-bla!'

'Business as usual?' teased Two-by-Two.

'Try me baby, anytime,' said Noah confidently. He moved into the sitting room as his customers quit the house.

Uncle Ribs returned home just after lunchtime. The way his creased face suddenly warmed up made the lines of tension straighten out, and showed the relief in his heart that he had arrived safely. He put the paper bag he had brought with him on the kitchen table. Mzi came up to the bag and began to empty it of its contents. To an uninitiated eye, the items brought out by Mzi could easily have passed as groceries: a medium-sized tin of Milo, a tin of condensed milk, salt, sugar packs, half-a-dozen sticks of dynamite, copper wire, dry glycerine, sulphuric acid, nitric acid and pieces of iron which looked like plugs.

'Wow!' exclaimed Uncle Ribs as he saw the items on the table. 'What a job it was amassing these items.'

'Beaut!' said Mzi joyously enfolding a stick of dynamite in his palm. 'I guess you had to sweat for all this?'

'Damn Mpondo was delayed on the mine,' said Uncle Ribs fishing for compliments. 'I feared he would never pitch up. But the poor guy made it at last. His relief was late and as the regulations are firm and strict, poor man had to wait for the relief before he could leave his post.'

'You had to wait, I suppose.'

'What an anxious waiting! I was eating my nails with worry. I didn't want one of those do-gooders of mine securities to come up to me and begin his awkward questions.'

All the while Uncle Ribs blew out clouds of smoke from his pipe. The room became murky with the smoke climbing, whirling and tumbling in the little space. Mzi held the dynamite in his hand. He sat down on the stool near the table and asked: 'How do I move into the local scene? My hands are itchy.'

'Damn lucky boy! You've come in the nick of time, smack into the middle of a children's revolution. It seems natural to me that we throw in our lot with the youth running the show.'

'And how's that?'

'Mandla is the star and we can reflect ourselves in his light. The youth is alive, he bubbles with energy. He's got a certain charisma which you can't miss. What he says goes. No resistance to his word, to his authority. A legend in his own lifetime. I tell you, brother, you are going to take to him immediately.'

'When do we meet?'

'Tonight. Right here. It was no problem setting up the meeting. If I know him well, he'll come alone. Clever, cautious. Sometimes it is a heavy strain to work under suspicion. These young ones do not take us for granted any more. They put us under the microscope — always.'

'Are you surprised?'

'Not me, brother. Not me. It's been a hard, harsh track some of us travelled on the political road. And someone might ask: what have you achieved?'

'Nothing!' asserted Mzi. 'Absolutely nothing. Maybe,' Mzi twisted his lips in a mischievous sort of way, 'maybe there's an exception. Nothing is not correct. The jails are full, Uncle Ribs, the jails are full.'

'But not of your kind. You are the new breed. You are the new standard-bearer.'

'I don't understand.' Mzi was not being entirely honest. He wanted the compliment repeated.

Uncle Ribs obliged: 'After you will come hope marching with bitter despair. You see, brother, until the children said 'Enough!' many of us despaired. We stood on the sidelines, arms folded. Sometimes we were swept by the waves of moments of crisis. Now the children cried 'Enough'. So, we have begun to see alternatives; we've begun to echo the cries uttered in the middle of the street, at street corners, in church buildings, at night-vigils and in the toilets of school buildings. Something definitive, something positive rings in the shrill voices we raise when we speak.'

'In other words, Uncle Ribs, you are saying the people have begun to hear what they are saying. Would you say they have reached home?'

'Not yet, brother, but like the cow which moos on familiar ground, we are about to enter home. That's it!' exclaimed Uncle Ribs. He eyed Mzi through the mass of smoke. His whole face was wrinkled by the cynical smile playing around his mouth and nose and strained eyes. For at that moment Uncle Ribs enjoyed immensely the nostalgia engineered by the presence of Mzi for his eye.

'I'm looking forward to this meeting with Mandla,' said Mzi. There was a silence in the room, a total silence between two spirits harrowed in the passage of time. Uncle Ribs recalled the shifting of fortunes over a period of years. In his mind's eye he saw the collapse of tall frames of steel; he heard the harsh cries for the collapse of the economy of the country, and the sombre voice of hope. Yes, there always was hope amid the crushing defeats experienced by the Movement of which he was a member. And it was this hope which churned out the present times and the spirit of the new breed reincarnated in Mzi.

'Look brother,' started Uncle Ribs again, 'I have these past years toyed with an idea. It fits well with your mission to Soweto. I have wanted to root out the policemen's bastion: the police station.' Uncle Ribs chuckled and held the pipe further away from his mouth. 'But tell me, without training, without the slightest idea of putting together the tools necessary for the job, what chance did I have?'

'None!' blurted Mzi.

'You see what I mean? Not only did we lack someone to lift us up to a certain level of operation, but we needed the skills, the know-how, as the saying goes. I can't imagine the impact Mandla and them will have with you in their company. Gods, man! The cops are going to sweat in the furrow of their bums.'

'You think so?' asked Mzi jubilantly. 'I want to put crackers on their toes and watch them jump,' he laughed bitterly.

Very slowly Uncle Ribs declared: 'I saw the panic brought about by our early successes, when pylons were brought crashing down. But you see, the felling of pylons was like the crumpling of a flower in the veld. The ordinary man in the township missed the fun. For him the heat remained. It was at street-corners; at station entrances. And that is where he would have been moonstruck. You come with that kind of hope. You aim to bring down the operations of the system in the midst of the township dwellers. Do it and you'll see. Aim for the police station and you'll have two birds to bring down.'

'You think so, Uncle Ribs?'

'It must be. Strategy, brother, strategy! Here's one shot that can never go to waste. When you aim at the station you are likely to ferret out your target, Batata. Miss him with the first shot, you won't fail to cause him to do stupid things. I tell you he'll do silly acts

27

which will down-grade him further in the eyes of the people. You don't want the guy to die a hero. The people must cry out: "Good riddance! God has answered our prayers." Do you see what I mean?'

'How vulnerable are police stations?' asked Mzi. But quickly he added: 'Not that it matters. If I put my mind to doing something, nothing can stop me. I'm perfectly clear on that one.'

'In the location, brother, nothing is not vulnerable. If a monarch came to Soweto we could lay him to eternal rest. If the call was for that. Here we rule, no matter what the authorities claim.'

'That's it. Give me your first choice.'

Uncle Ribs was silent for a while. The hand holding the pipe went to his scrubby chin. He held it there as he broke out into a mild smile to say: 'Funny how I have always thought Jabavu Station would be my first choice for attack on these stations perched strategically around Soweto. Clever bastards, do you know the sites for these new huge monsters have been worked out so bloody well? Jabavu happens to be where Batata keeps an office in the townships.'

'Lucky him!' said Mzi ironically.

'Oh he's a master of all he surveys.'

'Not for long!'

'Jabavu sits in the heart of the people. That's why it disturbs the pulse of things. It can be reached by several routes. And escape is therefore easier.'

'Not escape, Uncle Ribs,' cut in Mzi. 'We say retreat.'

'Retreat,' said a smiling Uncle Ribs, 'is quite easy. Actually, if the worst came to pass, one merely slips into any of the nearby houses. Some of them are a mere fifty metres from the back wall of the station.'

Uncle Ribs tried to work out the reason for the puzzlement on Mzi's face. 'What's the matter, brother, any problems?'

'Which one is Jabavu Police Station? I've not asked before, because I thought I knew its whereabouts. But I can't place it.'

'It is one of the newer monsters, in deep Soweto. Oh ya, it was built some seven years ago. You wouldn't know it of course. We'll do an on-the-spot inspection of it this evening. How do you feel about Mandla coming along with us?'

'I am easy. I am your hands, not your brains. I don't care either way.'

Uncle Ribs remained silent, his own blood tingling with the jarring sound of Mzi's last words. The young revolutionary was insensitive at times, thought Uncle Ribs. He fitted the classical example of the boy who comes to town and makes good: brash and quick-witted.

'Ya, I suggest we take Mandla with us,' said Uncle Ribs. 'It might just be the right thing to do to enthuse him with your acquisition to their group. We need the hot credibility of the student group at the moment. We have to take advantage of that if we are to seize the initiative from the group. And it's my considered view you will need their cover to achieve your mission.'

'I have no doubt in my mind, Uncle Ribs, I can show them a trick or two.'

'Precisely, precisely!' echoed the old campaigner. 'We can only go from strength to strength as a result of your work.'

'I am going to sit back one day and become a trainer of new recruits right here!' declared Mzi.

'We need that kind of person,' said Uncle Ribs. 'That's been my complaint over the years. I'm so glad you see things my way.'

'Definitely, I'm going to change the course of history, in this country.'

Uncle Ribs looked Mzi in the eye and allowed the silence of the room to carry his mind to glories unattained.


In the late afternoon Soweto began to bend its neck under the mass of a grey cloud of smoke. Fires were crackling in each home; the chill in the air abroad made the long shadows invisible. Workers disembarked from trains only to rush to the comfort of their little homes. They found their hearts beat fast at the sight of kwela-kwelas. For the police patrolled Soweto as if a dignitary was expected. The vans criss-crossed the streets endlessly.

There was a new sight in the ways of the cops: the camouflaged policeman. He moved with shoulders slouched, hands burdened by a heavy army rifle. He was a terror amidst the innocent presence of the ordinary dweller. The people called him the legalised terrorist: he bullied his way into the consciousness of the township dweller. But his arrogance was on several occasions reduced to particles of ridicule like sawdust in the wind.

There was a story told of an incident which took place earlier in the day. Two youngsters had the use of a Valiant car for the day and as fate would have it they cruised in the direction of the Orlando Bottle Store. The store was one of the very few to remain untouched by the rioting of the last two days. A darkie cop stood guard over the place, armed menacingly. Apparently bored and tired after a hectic two-day spell, he just stood there in front of the bottle store watching people and cars go by, to and from the rail station. The butt of the rifle dug into the ground while he held the rifle at the bottom of the bayonet. Feeling the strain of standing, he had only one foot firmly anchored on the ground. The other was crossed behind the upright leg, foot bending at an angle to the ground with the tip of the boot digging the soil. A cigarette was burning from his thick lips and his nostrils were continually trumpeting out a ring of smoke. He had to look important in all ways.

In his self-assured manner he least expected to be the victim of a silly prank. But alas! The young men in the Valiant spotted him and saw the chance to spring a surprise on him, however risky. The car stopped a safe distance from the bottle store. One of the young men tiptoed up to the cop, whisked the rifle away from behind him and sprinted to the car. The puzzled cop wheeled round and saw the car take off. He stood dumb-founded, watching the tail of the Valiant disappear onto the road leading into deep Soweto. It was a long moment later that the cop's feet of lead allowed him to shift his position. He scowled and beat the air with a powder-puff fist.

And so the day came to a close. The air was tense and rumours were wild. Somehow one of the stories doing the rounds related to Baragwanath Hospital. In the manner of attacks on all properties identified with authority, it was rumoured an attack on the hospital was imminent.

A group of students marched from Diepkloof toward the old Potchefstroom Road. Near Baragwanath they came across deserted tools and equipment of a contractor who had been busy for weeks working on the road. Scared by the events of the day before, none of the workers had reported for work. One of the students clambered up the caterpillar roller and switched on the machine. The damn thing began to roll down the road toward the hospital. The boys cheered it on and hollered noisily.

Two guards stood manning the hospital gates. When they saw the roller, now unattended, they must have thought the world was coming to an end. One hurried to the offices to raise the alarm against an attack. Two policemen appeared on the scene and began to blast wildly with their service guns. One actually asked: 'Waar is hulle?—Where are they?' Shown the roller, they aimed at it in full fury. But the damn thing came senselessly down their way. They retreated, keeping up the fire. Suddenly the caterpillar roller came to a halt at the edge of the pavement near the gates. By this time all the guards were in hiding behind the cubicle serving as an office for the security men. They were puzzled to find the machine stop and no-one alighting from it. For a while they waited, where they were, alert to any activity. They were suspicious of the unseen enemy. None appeared. One of the darkie guards was sent up to check if there was a trap in the whole thing. He went cautiously about his mission, and when he was satisfied there was no harm lurking around, he stood back with his knobkerrie swinging joyously in one hand. He called out: 'No danger!'

Soweto laughed at the red shame on the ears of the armed men. It laughed with the students at the result of the prank played on the security men. The laughter reverberated around Soweto as men sat to quaff a drink and women stood to tend their pots for the evening meal.


It was early evening when Sis Ida disembarked from the taxi bringing her back from work. She went straight to her grocer's shop, dragging her wearied body as best she could. The shopping centre was teeming alive: little children hugging packets of sugar and mealiemeal or half a loaf of bread; older boys bending over a few coins in the game of dice. Everyone around curtsied or smiled at Sis Ida. She was their mum, their aunt, their confidant. Tandabantu's store was crammed like a tin of sardines. Ida had to wade her way through to the counter. She was helped by the hearty welcome from Tandabantu himself, who waved his short bulky arms as if to say 'clear the path for the lady of the moment.' No-one grumbled. They made way in good cheer. Arms still raised, Tandabantu cried out: 'Ah, Mistress Ida, how are you today my friend?' There was a discernible note of sadness in his voice. He dropped his arms.

'Fine, tata, fine,' replied Sis Ida, trying hard as always to put forward charm to shield her fateful position, 'I am fine.'

'I see the paper says shebeens must close down for the mourning period.'

'Is it?'

'Ya, it's all in the morning paper. Those children are right, mistress. We must show the ways of our ancestors. Humanism is a thing of our ancestors, it shows feeling for the pain of others. We must show that the blood shed by the children of some people was spilt for us too. That is humanism. Ah Mistress Ida.' Here the shopkeeper raised his arms and dropped them again as a sign of sheer desperation. 'Know something, if those children walked into the shop this minute and asked for one of the things on my shelves I would say: Tandabantu, you have been given the richness of life by the gods. Share these blessings with the children. And I would give them what they wanted.

Mcwi! I swear by my mother who has brought me here, I would.'

Sis Ida felt pulverised by the assertion. But she merely said: 'Can I have a few items tata?'

'On tick or are you paying cash, Mistress?' asked Tandabantu, businesslike.

'I suppose you'll want cash tata. I know I owe a lot already, but . . .' Sis Ida broke off and produced from her black handbag a small handkerchief. She muffled a dry cough and dabbed her wet eyes.

At first Tandabantu was confused. He folded his huge arms across his bursting belly and smiled. He asked: 'What's worrying you, Mistress, can I help?'

'No tata. Nothing's worrying me. I was thinking about our children, I suppose.'

'O-o-o! Mistress you don't know the burden I carry about. I woke up this morning to discover my boy, Fanyana, is gone. Thixo uyazi— God knows! And when the sun stood overhead, beating down like it wanted to scorch the pain in my heart, the police walked into the shop one after another. Six of them came in and stood at the counter and along the wall, as if calling on a criminal. I swear, Mistress. They wanted to know the whereabouts of Fanyana. They said I should know, I am his father. They said I've hidden him. Tell me, where can I hide a child as big as Fanyana, a whole eighteen-year-old? They poured salt into my body wound, that's what they did, accusing me of lies. They have no shame, humiliating me and threatening me as they did in full view of my customers. Thixo uyazi, if I had a gun I would have died with one of them today. Never in my whole life have I been called a liar. By amakhwenkwe — boys! Raa!'

'Shame on them, tata!'

'What should I have said? I know where he's gone to when I didn't? Did they expect me to shit him out? Raa! These dogs!'

Tandabantu and Sis Ida stood looking at each other. Their silence was accentuated by the buzzing activity around them. Sis Ida warded off a number of kids jostling near her. Least did she expect to arrive at the shop when Tandabantu was consumed by a bitterness such as she never knew he experienced. For the events of the three-day-old demonstrations transformed the lives of the people of Soweto overnight and made of them martyrs of all the country.

Tandabantu broke the silence: 'Let me not take up much of your time, Mistress. Take what you want and pay me at the end of the month what you can.'

Ida choked with the feeling of her own hopelessness. She was aware of the man's sympathy. And this is what made her heart begin to pump hard and the blood rush to her temples. She felt sorry her life seemed to have lost the pulse and the vigour which saw her bounce from day to day as if without a care. Now she remained at the mercy of others. Her own life-style was so dependent on the whims of fate. She walked out of the shop her head bowed, her shoulders tensed. She was carrying a physical burden, hiding the larger burden in her heart. Her comforting thought for the moment was the satisfaction the food she had would bring to the children in her care. These same children were hunted by the police, haunted by the fear of detention.

She was greeted at the gate by the sounds of Bob Marley. She entered the house to be met by a warmth she had come to know and enjoyed to indulge. Above the music was activity. There were those who tried to read above the level of sounds; there were those engaged in the unwritten schedules of the group. They walked in and out, from one room to another; in and out of the house to the back yard or to the two cars parked in the yard.

Instinctively Ida asked: 'Where is Mandla?'

No-one gave an answer. So Sis Ida asked again: 'Batho—People, where is Mandla?' For Mandla was more than the sum total of the number of boys and girls staying with her.

It was Roy who said: 'Gone to a meeting.'

Ida had long learnt not to ask many questions. A hint was all she cared to receive. For her it was enough that the family was at home alive and kicking. The house was in order and neat; there were soiled tins standing in a row on the kitchen table. She didn't have to ask that they be cleared. Their contents always demanded it. These mixtures she understood and she feared. For the fear she experienced settled at the bottom of her stomach and held the muscles down there tight, so that breathing became a conscious effort and self-pity stood ogling at her. Funny how intuition works. It told her again and again she was moving inexorably to an end she feared with the totality of her being. She never spoke of this fear. Not even to her daughter. The latter sensed it and hated her own caged-in situation. For her kind understood little of the march of the times and wished for nothing more than a total peace of mind.

It was a jolly family that shared the meal of the night together later.

At exactly the appointed time in the night, Mandla walked into the house of Uncle Ribs, alone. He walked into a presence which overwhelmed him instantly. He felt overcome by the greatness of the moment. For Mzi was to him little short of a god. He envied the revolutionary in whose company he found himself. For was he not a mere boy when all was said and done, a boy blown out of all proportion by the day's mass media? Mzi admired his counterpart immediately. Yet he reserved for himself a sense of self-indulgence, a feeling of self-assuredness. He was superior on all counts, being a freedom fighter trained abroad.

It was left to Uncle Ribs to articulate the spirit of the moment. He said: 'Good brothers,' and his one hand shook the dead pipe into the ashtray on the coffee table, 'this is a great moment in my life and in the struggle. From now on we have to turn your talents to advantage for the people. I can hear the cheers from Freedom Square; I can see signs of hope on the faces of our brothers on Robben Island. This moment gives birth this minute to a marriage of convenience, a marriage destined to change the course of history in the country. God knows brothers we shall take the fight into the enemy's camp. An eye for an eye; a tooth for a tooth. I shudder to think of the outcome of this happy marriage.'

Silence. A hollow silence fell over the room making the ears of Mandla thump hard with conflicting diffused noises. He was swept off his feet by a joyous sensation he could not thumb down. Silence. There was a total silence in the room. The young men sat without showing any sign of having heard their elder brother. They sat there watching him. They were men of action, not so many words. Even as they sat looking at Uncle Ribs, they itched for action. For a moment he clamped his mouth, not on his bony pipe but on an infectious silence.

'Can I see this Jabavu Station tonight, Uncle Ribs?' asked Mzi.

Uncle Ribs turned to Mandla and in a cooing voice said: 'Oh, oh, my little brother, our brother Mzi here thought you might like the idea he has in mind.' Ribs fell back on his seat and began to suck at his pipe. In the process he excited Mandla's curiosity. There was a sparkle in Mandla's eyes, a faint boyish smile on his face. He was eager to know, anxious to share the secret hinted at by Uncle Ribs. He sat bending forward toward Uncle Ribs, his long arms pillared on his knees by the palms of his hands. It was evident he was completely under the spell of the veteran politician. The latter seized the opportunity to weave more of his intriguing schemes around the young associate. He orchestrated the moment, leading to the revelation of the idea with calculated skill. He went on: 'Think of any place you would want to hurt most the vanity of your enemy, a place the police would see bloody red if you laid your hand on it.' Mandla looked stumped. There were so many places which fitted the bill he couldn't take his pick immediately. He hesitated with one name on the tip of his tongue. That pause was enough to allow Uncle Ribs to say dramatically: 'A police station. Any! An attack on one can never fail to raise the ire of the law to unlimited height. For the struggle would be taken to the threshold of their door. Can you see it?'

'Gosh!' exclaimed Mandla, his right hand going up to his chin. The idea came as if from another world. 'It is the most original idea I have ever heard. It never entered my mind. Not once!'

'And I have the material for the job,' said Mzi. He had a hard look in his eyes as his boast escaped his lips.

'We could not tackle such jobs because we lacked the material. I was never happy with the petrol stuff we've been using.'

Uncle Ribs said: 'No, brother Mandla, don't look down on what you've done. It's been a right start. Humble but right. You know something, you've put many of us to shame. At no time before have our efforts gone as far as you have taken yours. What training have you had? Absolutely none! None!' Uncle Ribs did then what he could do with great satisfaction: he blew out a cloud of smoke. It whirled upwards, curled further and further away from him. There was achievement in that little act. He was satisfied. He kept quiet.

'And you have picked on the Jabavu Station?' asked Mandla of Uncle Ribs.

'Oh by the way you don't know our brother's mission: to eliminate that dog, Batata.'

'I've heard he sticks around Jabavu a lot.'

'You see,' said Uncle Ribs with the excitement of a young boy, 'You see. That's what I thought. We kill two birds with this idea of dealing a blow on Jabavu.'

'I see.' There was another of those periodic pauses when each seemed to have his batteries recharged. Mandla went on: 'When do we do the job?'

'Well, well,' said Ribs as if the recruitment of Mandla left him indifferent, 'Mzi here has not been around those parts for ten years. He wants to sort of reconnoitre the area. Do you want to come along?'

'Oh, certainly, Uncle Ribs. I want action all the time.'

'This is a big deal,' cut in Mzi, 'but I don't want many people around.'

'Oh yes, brother Mandla,' came in Uncle Ribs, 'Mzi thinks only two people are necessary: you and him.'

'You know, my friend, I've worked out every detail. I don't want bunglers in my company. I can't afford such people. My life is at stake. No chances, understand?'

'Top secret!' barged in Uncle Ribs. 'There are three of us in this. And we must be a tight unit. Agreed?'

'Agreed!' said Mandla. He didn't hesitate to commit himself. His keenness was overwhelming for he was a man of action. At that moment he didn't have qualms about leaving out members of his group. It was a feeling which would haunt him much, much later in the night. He went on to ask: 'When is action day?'

'What do you think?' asked Mzi cynically. 'Tomorrow!' The last word fell like the stem of a gum tree: hard without vibrations, and was almost buried where it dropped.

'Tomorrow?' cried Mandla. It was an incredible thought. He was gripped by a sense of anticipation.

'It is the right moment, brother. The people will see it as an eye for an eye,' said a serious-faced Uncle Ribs. No doubt the harsh memories of dead kids reported found in the streets and by-ways of Soweto stood in his mind's eye. He went on: 'We cannot waste the momentum of the bloody demonstrations of the last two days.'

'We can't go wrong!' asserted Mzi. 'I've planned the whole thing right. We can't go wrong.'

Uncle Ribs clambered to his feet and went into the bedroom. He wasn't away long and he came back saying: 'The old maid is dog-tired. She sleeps like a baby.' He paused, hand with pipe underneath his chin, as a man in thought does. 'I was going to say there's never a time I have felt as ready to die for the cause as now. Oh yes, I am prepared to go to jail for the cause. Mandla and his friends have re-kindled in me the warrior spirit. I'm prepared to die. I think you two are going to shake us all out of our long sleep. You are going to make us deal a hard blow to our lethargy. For too long we bowed our heads in despair. Now we are ready to raise these greying heads. We are going to stand tall. So? I think we can start out now.' Uncle Ribs led the way out.

The night air was chilling to the bone. The cold cut into the face skin as if about to slice it open. There was a breeze which hit on the body making the sweat around the pores feel like icicles. No sooner were they out of the house than they felt like travellers at the cold arctic pole. They huddled into Mandla's small Austin 11/55 with relief.

The trip into deep Soweto was a study in fascination for Mzi. His excitement was raised high by what he saw done by Mandla and his band; burnt-out buildings in silhouette under the dim light of a myriad stars. These ruins were mere names in that hour: the post office in Dube, the rubble of the municipal offices; the stubborn remains of a beerhall huddled together under the chill of the night. It was mind-boggling for Mzi to hear the story of fire and billows of smoke two nights earlier.

'You've done a bloody good job, brother Mandla,' said Mzi, unable to contain the thrill of the moment.

'I think so,' cut in Uncle Ribs, unmouthing his pipe. 'We have merely to build on this result,eh?'

'We mean to do more devastation,' said a confident Mandla.

'You wait, brother,' said Mzi, 'the dogs will know where the might of this lion lies. You and I are going to tear apart the insides of our enemy. Bona—Look, Mcwi, 'strue's God ndifunga uma—I swear by my mother! What I carry in my head is enough to frighten these boerans to hell and return!'

The little car coughed its way up the incline, stuttering as if about to choke to a standstill. But it journeyed on.

'Gee!' exclaimed Mzi. 'Did you do that mess-up of the hall?'

'Used to be called Mofolo Hall,' said Uncle Ribs. 'Now it is one of the ghosts of our lives.'

Jabavu Police Station came in sight. It was a massive structure in the middle of the open veld. But the ten-foot high brick wall extended far beyond the brick building into the emptiness around. From a distance it looked impenetrable.

The little machine whirred past the front gate at a slow pace. Mzi was able to pick up a very valuable point at that stage.

'Is it always without a guard at this time?' he asked, pointing out the neglected entrance.

'I can't believe it,' rejoined Uncle Ribs. 'You know, I've always taken it for granted there would be a man there holding a baton.'

'Not now!' said Mzi spitefully. He went on rhetorically: 'Who are we? Babies! They think we are without sting. They must be thinking we've never eyed a police station with the bitter, the hurtful eye. We must show them how wrong they are. Teach them a lesson!'

There was a moment's silence. But Mzi said with boyish enthusiasm: 'We'll walk in. We'll hit them hard, this time tomorrow!'

'8.15 p.m.' said Uncle Ribs, eyes on his wrist-watch.

'Quarter past eight tomorrow night,' repeated Mandla.

'That's it! Strike while the iron is hot, Uncle Ribs!' teased Mzi.

'Ya! Ya! brother!' sang Ribs.

'Can you slow down a bit?' asked Mzi of the driver, Mandla. He looked as if a seizure of the mind had taken hold of him. He looked stupefied. He half rose from his back seat to repeat: 'Can you slow down a bit?'

'Sure! Sure!' said Mandla removing his foot from the accelerator. The car jerked and would have stalled, but Mandla fed it just a wee bit; he recovered enough composure to say: 'Silly of me not to have thought of it myself.' No-one appeared to have heard him. There was a silence in the car. Mandla went on: 'How about a drive round the back part of the building?'

'Brother, that's a good idea,' said Mzi, his eye fixed on the massive structure. He added: 'I can see this whole thing coming down in a heap. Tomorrow this time.' Mzi's hand touched the door handle next to him.

'You said slow down, not stop,' said an alarmed Uncle Ribs to Mzi.

'I know but an idea has just this moment come to me,' said Mzi.

'Stop!' cried a pained Uncle Ribs. 'But that would be suicide. Not in front of the police station. You and Mandla are at the moment hot numbers. Tomorrow this time, ya.'

'Oh please, Mandla.'

'Reckless, damnably reckless,' complained Uncle Ribs. But Mandla stopped all the same. Mzi threw caution out of the door and stepped on the soil around the station. The touch of his foot on the ground in that area sent strange vibrations through his body. The feeling he experienced was mixed: a joy born of a sense of triumph; a fear of an unknown force. Mzi told himself it was as well he broke the ice that evening. This was a feeling he always knew might be aroused in him sometime. For there was something about police stations which disturbed the flow of the blood through his body. There was a strong hatred for all stations. And the station within his reach was only a symbol of the other stations he didn't know. He didn't know their shape. They lived in his mind's eye as buildings of fear, of hate.

Mzi walked down the road enveloped in a mysterious feeling. In a way he was elated as if drugged. As he drew near the gate, silent and forsaken as it was then, fear gripped tight on the muscles of his stomach. He told himself he was a freedom-fighter, no harm would come to him. Yet he regretted not carrying the AK47 rifle. By this time the eagerness with which he had left the car had evaporated. His step was somewhat desultory. But he remained alert, he was purposeful. His eye took in the front and the sides of the wall and the building very quickly. He noted the front and side doors in sight; was content the light around the station cast dark shadows in places.

A car went past him at a helluva speed. Mzi couldn't duck away. He was fast enough to touch his military cap only, dropping to his haunches.

Before he retraced his steps, Mzi noticed a number of boulders along one side of the brick wall. He nodded happily as if the dead stones acknowledged his thoughts. Back in the car he showed how his cup of joy overflowed.

'Easy job! 'Strue's God, this is going to be as easy as making a calabash of clay.'

Uncle Ribs merely looked at Mzi. He didn't seem to share the other man's confidence. But Mzi said: 'I've inhaled the hatred born of the place. This will be enough to spur me on this time tomorrow.'

'Dammit!' exclaimed Uncle Ribs.

'Ho-o-o! Uncle Ribs,' said Mzi playfully, 'you are ill-humoured.'

'Drive off Mandla,' said Uncle Ribs. And to no-one in particular he stammered: 'We are being reckless.'

'No,' butted in Mzi, 'I wanted to have the feel of the ground. My training has taught me this.'

'Taking chances, that's all you are up to. You don't have an idea of the strange power the cops have. From nowhere they could spring on us and dash all your over-confidence.'

'They can never touch me,' sneered Mzi, 'Never! I walk with the gods. They are the source of my power. The gods of my father, of his father and his father's father.' Mzi paused briefly. When he resumed talking he said: 'Uncle Ribs is scared. Yo! Uncle Ribs is afraid of the boer-boys!' Mzi began to laugh. Uncle Ribs remained silent. Mandla was amused. The laughing went on for a fairly long drive. And then Mzi said: 'Tomorrow this time I will have the last laugh, eh Uncle Ribs?'

Uncle Ribs was fuming. He grunted some faint sound. He saw Mzi as a stubborn, reckless freedom-fighter and wondered why the Resistance Movement engaged such silly boys in important missions.

The car took in the back part of Jabavu Police Station. With each passing moment, Mzi lived through the excitement of a young boy trying out a new toy: he couldn't suppress his eagerness to destroy that building and with that to dare the guardians of the law.

A little later the threesome landed at Uncle Ribs's place carried on a wave of anticipation. For Mandla the task ahead gave him mixed feelings as he drove back to his old base.

The house was bubbling with activity as Mandla's little Austin glided into Sis Ida's yard to join the small fleet of minis. Pop sounds reverberated through the closed windows and doors. Now and again the kitchen door screeched open and was closed with the same noise. A figure entered or left the house, from or to some point in the back yard. Mandla stepped into the buzzing mood of his colleagues. He went to the sitting room where he perched on the arm of the overladen run-down sofa. Already seated in it were Roy, Keke, Boysi and Snoek. Dan Montsho sat alone in one of the two arm-chairs in the room. It was fitted snug in the far corner of the room next to the cabinet of the pedal sewing-machine. In that place he was slightly cut off from the whole room by the mountain of books and paper work on the cabinet. No-one seemed to miss him because Dan Montsho was by nature a quiet and inwardly-drawn person.

'Bajita, I have news for you,' said Mandla eyeing everyone and indicating he wanted the attention of all.

'Batho-bantu!' yelled Keke into the happenings in the kitchen. He went over to stand at the door leading to the kitchen and spoke almost casually to those in the kitchen: 'Young slaves, the General requires your ears in here.'

Bongi was first to react: 'Who is a slave?' she demanded of Keke. She was standing in front of him now, arms akimbo. She didn't wait for his reply but stepped past him pressing him against the doorframe. 'Eechu!' cried Keke as if genuinely hurt in the game.

Sis Ida appeared at the door of her bedroom. 'Bathung—People, what is happening now?'

'Keke sit down!' said Mandla peremptorily. 'Hi Sis Ida.' The greetings were returned with the kind of charm only Sis Ida could command. She retreated into the sanctuary of her bedroom.

Mandla took charge of the situation as soon as everyone was crammed into the meeting room. 'Bajita, I have news for you, but before I tell you this, let's hear the day's reports.'

'Item No. 1,' said Keke in an affected manner of seriousness.

'Ag! Voetsak man Keke!' hollered Bongi once more, 'Be serious!'

'I am!' protested Keke looking at Mandla. 'I have something important to report.'

'What is it?' demanded Roy.

'I have a democratic right to speak, of hoe sê ek, bajita? Phela, you must tell us if the state has decreed I am no longer a citizen with rights.'

'Okay, bajita,' intervened Mandla. 'Give us your piece,' he demanded of Keke. 'And make it snappy. It's late!'

Keke stood in the middle of the room as best he could. The room was crammed with young bodies tightly filling the space on the floor. Those who could just managed to stretch legs into this same space. Said Keke: 'I was at the gate this afternoon, on the lookout for Sis Ida. Ya, I was doing just that. Here comes this short, well-built guy with a head large and smooth as a river-bed boulder. He comes past me and as he was about to go past he hesitates, you know, misses a step or so. I looked up at him thinking he was in trouble. Nix! He's drunk. I could tell by the way his eyes were red. I could see it clearly the way he blinked. Gots! I say to myself: Africa has gone to the dogs! The guy read my thoughts. He yelled: "Go to hell Red Army!" To me! Red Army he called me. So I laughed. Ya, I laughed, just like that.'

There were grunts in the room.

Mandla butted in: 'Keke, jokes aside.'

'My ma!' exclaimed Keke. He crossed two fingers to signal he stood by what he said.

'Shut up!' cried Bongi.

Keke didn't like that. He winced at Bongi to register his way of insulting her. She retaliated: 'Nyoko!'

'Keke! Bongi!' yelled Mandla. And dead silence descended on the room. Mandla cut into the thickness of the silence: 'Okay, bajita, let's hear Sello.' Sello said he had looked the length and breadth of Soweto; he had walked in and out of shebeens; he had torn into the spirit of fun-lovers in joints and gumba-gumbas; he had bullied and threatened those close to Timothy but nowhere had he found him. But he had leads for the next day.

It was Boysi's turn to report. From a secret inside pocket of his jeans, he produced a wad of bank notes which he started to count so that the whole room stared down at him unbelievingly. 'The Bishop was nice,' said Boysi. 'He never quibbled. Only he complained he was busy but promised to help with more if he could be warned in time.'

'Bloody bourgeois!' said Roy.

'Not bad, not bad at all,' said Mandla. The money was given to Bongi for safe-keeping. Mandla continued: 'Well, bajita, I've just met a great guy this evening. I don't know how to describe him. But I know in his company I felt small. He's a darkie like me but I tell you, bajita, the guy is special.' Mandla paused, he cocked his head on one side, a boyish smile on his face and a sparkle in his eyes. He became sad suddenly as he said: 'He has come back home from military training in 'Zania. He looks good, he talks convincingly. And you

41

know something, he's coming into the scene with a helluva bang.'

'What's it?' cut in Digoro.

'The elimination of a pain in the neck, Batata.' The room growled. There was a creaking of bones as someone stretched or withdrew a leg.

'Batata has been our number one target,' continued Mandla, 'yet he remains alive today. I don't have to spell out why . . .'

'But I —' Roy was about to add his voice when Mandla chopped him down with his own.

'Let's not make an issue of it, bajita. We didn't have the means of production. Petrol bombs scorched the furniture in his house and burned the curtains. Nothing more! Burn baby burn! That was yesterday. Today the language is different. Mzi is for me the embodiment of the new muntu in our midst. I don't know what you people think but I'm all for working with him.'

Mandla's words came gushing out and were laid before the mighty silence of the room. As he ended the room sighed in relief. For the tension was tight and pained. Members of the group sat with heads sunk into their chests as if waiting for messages from the heart.

Dan Montsho shifted in his far corner seat. There was another round of sighs from the room. Dan Montsho cleared his throat. The level of expectation rose higher. He flicked his spectacles backward so that they settled on the ridge of his nose. He clasped his knees with both hands as if about to raise his feet. And asked the room: 'How sure can we be that we are not buying a pig in a poke?'

The room was stirred into a consciousness of its own; one member coughed; another hummed; quite a few uttered emotional ya's. And then there was a spell of quietness. No doubt Dan Montsho had spoken the collective mind of the group. Mandla was caught off balance. 'I don't understand,' he said with his voice quite flat.

'It's simple,' said Roy, 'Dan Montsho wants to know how we can be sure Mzi is not working for the system?'

'Oh that.' exclaimed Mandla with a pained pitch of voice. Then: 'Egh! Egh! bajita, we are making the job of the system easier, 'strue we are. If doubt is going to be cast on every black because he's not known to some of us, then we are finished. That's exactly what the system wants, we must paralyse each other with this doubt placed on everyone's head.'

'But how can you be sure?' asked Dan Montsho.

'I was introduced to Mzi by Uncle Ribs. And who doubts Uncle Ribs?' queried Mandla.

'But mfanakithi,' chipped in Roy, 'Uncle Ribs stands for one thing. And we stand for another.'

'There is a generation gap between Uncle Ribs and us. It means our vocabularies are not exactly the same. But surely that doesn't mean we cannot work together. Take the elimination of Batata, who can say here that he or she won't welcome it? Tell me? No, bajita, I think we must make our arguments sound. They must stand the test of time, always.'

Mandla had spoken. And in the silence of his voice none could creep in, not with any silly point of view.

Mzi scored a victory lying many homes away. Yet he would remain a fancy in the eyes of members of the group. For no-one saw him; no-one heard him. He lived before the mind's eye of the group in the words and spirit of the group-leader, Mandla. But many hugged him in their sleep on that night.

## 2

### NEWS ITEM
SOWETO PERSONALITIES DETAINED. PRINCIPAL MASEMOLA HELD BY POLICE IN DAWN RAID. NO COMMENT SAYS POLICE SPOKESMAN

The chill walked the early morning worker to the bus rank; the air was cold and damp as a number of workers braved the elements and the muggers to the transport points. The red rising sun made no difference to the spell of uncertainty fastening on the spirits of the people. The tension was high; the fears paralysing, but the mood of the people was openly aggressive. It was a mood which would rise with the sun, only to go down with it later in the day. Such was the rottenness of the normally good-natured residents of the township. They were fed up to the back teeth with whitey's bullying stance.

In the house in Dube Uncle Ribs and Mzi sat waiting for the day to disappear. The waiting was long. And the tension gripping the two men was heavy on their lips. They sat in silence with the only noise coming from Ribs's mouth as his pipe perched on one side of it. It was wearisome this waiting which looked like it had been keeping them company all day long. But waiting can have its rewards and so it did for Mzi: action began when the sun went down. First Uncle Ribs went into his bedroom and came back carrying a pouch of tobacco. As he dug his pipe into the pouch he said: 'I'm happy the ol' girl made her own arrangements to come home this evening.' He was referring to his wife, Sis Joyce. She was sitting up which meant Uncle Ribs would normally have had to fetch her from Bara Hospital.

Mzi came in at a tangent: 'I've wanted to ask how the student group manages for transport. I can't imagine how they would have fared without the car Mandla drives.'

'They have a fleet of these little machines,' said Uncle Ribs blowing a cloud of smoke from his pipe. He went on: 'The man in the street shows more sympathy to their cause than he did to ours. Can you believe that these youngsters can walk into this place one minute and the next moment they drive away in my car? They half ask, half commandeer what they want.'

'Is it true, Uncle Ribs?'

'I'm telling you! I heard it only yesterday, a story which left me shaking my greying head: Mandla was almost in trouble on the Soweto highway; he escaped arrest by a hair's breadth. When he reached home he experienced delayed shock or something. Anyway one of his mates, I think they said it was Roy or Boysi, took over the car. It was driven straight to a backyard spray-painter.'

'He worked on it overnight?'

'Exactly! That's how business-like these boys are. No questions asked, no lies heard!'

'I'm amazed!'

'You wait and see.'

Then there was a muffled sound of a car gliding into the driveway. Uncle Ribs hurried to investigate but said as he moved to the outside kitchen door: '7.45 on the dot. Must be Mandla.' And Mandla it was.

'Hey! Hey! Young man, what are you doing to the motor-trade, letting it rocket to the moon?'

'No, Uncle Ribs,' said Mandla laughingly, 'I borrowed this one from the boys. We have three in the yard and I thought a change for the job was the thing to do.'

'Mzi will be pleased with your thinking.'

The words were hardly dead in the cool evening air when Mzi came out carrying a small suitcase. 'Gentlemen, we'll be late,' he said with a slight edge in his voice.

'How do you like this?' asked Uncle Ribs touching the hood of the little car.

'Another one?' cried Mzi. He wasn't giving away his feelings at this stage. He went on: 'Do you think it's better than yesterday's?'

'Today is always better than yesterday!' offered Uncle Ribs.

'The car, I mean?'

'It is,' said Mandla. He was slightly disappointed with Mzi's response. But he didn't allow this to affect his enthusiasm for the mission. He said: 'It has more guts. It moves, you'll see.'

'I'm not complaining,' said Mzi. 'In my game I want to be sure of my weapons. I can't afford to have a mechanical thing jam at the critical moment. Suicide, don't you think so?'

'Bra Mzi is dead right,' answered Mandla.

'Uncle Ribs,' said Mzi turning to the older man, 'there's that paper bag in my bedroom, do you think you could fetch it for me? I can't put this suitcase down, just in case something unhappily happens.'

'Sure! Sure! brother,' said Uncle Ribs hurrying back into the house. He nipped out of the house soon after, a paper bag in hand, the same bag Mzi had brought to Soweto. It was placed on the passenger seat next to the driver. Mzi sat quietly in the back seat nursing the suitcase on his lap.

The car rolled out of the yard. Uncle Ribs waved a feeble hand at the moving machine as it backed out of his yard. For him the tension began at that very moment. The cool of the night air, the shine of the sparkling stars above left him cold. Not even the brightness of the evening star jutting into the eye as if suspended below the galaxy of the countless other stars above could soften the tight grip of the tension which made Uncle Ribs feel weighted down by the gravity of the mission of his two younger colleagues. He had to seek the comfort of the wall and the door-frame to enter the house and escape the oppressiveness of moments outside the house. But how to break the tension worried him. For Uncle Ribs became then a very, very worried man.

He went straight to his bedroom, perched on the edge of the bed and switched on the portable radio standing on Sis Joyce's dressing table. The crash of the music steadied his nerve. The waves of music were carried to the four walls and echoed into his ears. This became a kind of solace, a wish for an eternity which would bring nothing but this dreamy air of classical music, ethereal and sublime. He resolved to wait for the news, to wait for an announcement he feared to contain in his heart.

Meantime the little car whined up the road leading to deep Soweto. Unlike the previous car, it gave no hint of choking and stopping. It glided smoothly in the night air as if impelled by the silence of the two young men. Each was his own voice and ears. For Mzi the ruins echoed the sound of the moving car; they were so imprinted in his mind's eye, it looked as if they were being carried along to form part of the ruins he already saw huddled under the sky where stood the Jabavu Police Station. Mandla was fascinated by the power of the wheel in his hands. It became the power with which the station would be crumbled. In his heart was also a mixed feeling of this joy and the consequences of a mishap. The fear of cops was in him, ingrained by a habit he couldn't easily erase.

Presently Mandla pulled up against one of the houses standing on the street running behind the police station. There was a long row of houses all fenced in in one way or another. He stopped in front of a middle-sized hedge. But the car straddled across two yards where he finally parked. Any casual observer might have puzzled hard about where the occupant of the car might have gone — which of the houses he might be visiting.

They scuttled across the street but slowed to a walking pace on the stubby grass leading to the back wall of the station. Mzi defied the night by fixing his eyes straight ahead. The suitcase was in one hand; the other hand swung freely underneath a hunched shoulder. The military cap was drawn deep over his eyes, giving him a thug's appearance. Mandla tried hard to keep pace with the long strides of his over-confident mate. He had fears of someone watching every movement they made. To ease his own suspicions of the night, he cast his eye hither and thither. This meant he lagged behind and would then hurry to catch up with Mzi.

At the end of the wall Mzi stood suddenly. Car lights blazed on the dark road in front of the station. Both Mzi and Mandla held their breath. It could be a police car or a kwela-kwela. The lights kept an unchanging rate of velocity and soon the car went past in a roar.

Mzi peeped round at the gate: it was wide open and unattended. Good luck! He breathed out and without warning Mandla he stepped onto the beam of light that turned the darkness around the police station into day. It was as if someone jolted his head backward as the light hit his eyes. He chose a shadowy path as soon as he could. It led to a lone kwela-kwela. Mzi nestled in the shade of the vehicle, unhappily. Two things unsettled him: a door at the back of the station building, and the dash he would have to make to the parking bay in the courtyard. For once there he would be lost to the surroundings. There were a number of police vehicles parked in it, with a sprinkle of unclaimed stolen cars. The place looked a metallic jungle in which one could easily take cover.

He made it. As if to show his self-confidence, Mzi pulled up the military cap and felt the night air play around his eyes. It was a relief, short-lived as it was. He was looking at that back door when Mandla joined him. The latter's relief could be seen by the way he sighed, holding a hand on his stomach. The dash for him was tiring.

'I don't like that door,' said Mzi pointing at the offending door, 'it increases the danger points.'

Mandla was still holding the paper bag. He put it down as he said: 'I would have thought it is God-given. A bomb planted there would increase our chances of success. Don't you think so? And if I'm not wrong, there is a table near that door inside. There's always a cop perched at that table doing homework.'

'I'm not worried about the end part of this game. I can't take chances near a door which can open any moment. There's no cover near that damned door. Can you see that?'

'What about using that lone vehicle near the wall? Plant something in it and blast the wall and all the bloody dogs near it.'

'Plant a bomb in it, you say?'

'Ya, why not? We want the blood of that arse-licker, Batata. Miss him, you get another cop. What's the difference?'

'Indeed, what's the difference,' echoed Mzi. 'I like your idea. I can work up something good, something powerful, a thing which can blow the kwela-kwela to high heaven and the force of the device will blast a hole as huge as a grave. See the bastards tumble, see them buried underneath the rubble. Gots! It's a brilliant idea you have just given me. You'll cover me all the time. That means I won't be working feverishly. I'll be relaxed. I'll know that you'll blast any motherfucka coming our way . . . Gots! It is a bright idea!'

'I must say carrying the AK47 like this knocks me out. The feeling of it is an experience all its own.'

Mzi never let up in his movements. The hands were all the time joining little wires and the teeth cutting off or tightening something. But he said: 'Come, we'll lose time. Shut up and keep watch while I fix the goodies.'

The night was quiet save for a car or so passing hurriedly on the road nearby. There was now a slight chill in the winter air. Mzi was squatting on the ground working methodically with the device. Mandla nestled against the body of a car which had apparently stood unused for a long time. It was an old Valiant stripped of its chrome and doors half-closed. Then it happened: the back door opened slowly. Mandla's muscles tensed and he gripped tight the AK47 in his hands. He was ready to blast away. Mzi felt rather than saw the change of mood of his colleague. He was about to say something when Mandla pressed a finger on his own lips to sha-sha him to dead silence. When Mzi eased himself so that he could come upright, Mandla pressed his right shoulder down with his own right hand. At the same time he nudged him with his right knee. Mandla's heart was now racing, his hands were sweating in the cold air. Mzi remained squatting, a little bemused. For him such moments unmasked the drama of a mission. He had turned to watch the face of his colleague for any give-away signs. But Mandla remained rooted at his place, his eyes glued on the two cops emerging from the door.

The cops were in a carefree mood. One carried a file. Now and then it was flying in the air as the man gesticulated in the course of the conversation with his colleague. The two headed for the kwela-kwela ear-marked for the mission by Mzi and Mandla. Mandla's heart dropped to his knees. He raised the automatic rifle instinctively. Mzi watched this movement with disbelief. 'What's the matter?' he asked.

'The bloody swines are going to take the van.'

'Damn fools!' coughed Mzi. He fidgeted on the ground but said: 'Don't do any silly thing either. Change course, that's all it means.' After a short pause Mzi enquired: 'Are the bastards moving or what, I'm tired squatting like this.' It was obvious the tension of the moment ate into the patience of both young men.

Mandla, his grip still tight, his hands clammy, mumbled an answer.

The van roared and went on to screech out of the police station.

Inside the charge-office Sergeant James Ntloko, the man in charge, complained to no-one in particular: 'One of these days, those men are going to break their necks. Why can't they drive out quietly? Why this roar and screech, as if the devil is behind them? Ag! Man!' The Sergeant tucked his head over a pack of cards at the far end of the counter. Two things seemed to satisfy the ageing cop in the police force: playing spoof alone, and drawing smoke from a long cigarette. He was not one of those smokers who cherish clipping the stub of a cigarette. One quarter of the way through a new cigarette, the Sarge would discard it for a fresh one. 'I am no prisoner,' he boasted about this habit.

At the other end of the counter stood Constable Mpedi. Tall, healthy and charming. His shoulders were always sagging as if he was bored by his surroundings. He made up for this bored look and lethargic movement of his body by being pretty likeable. Now he stood near a couple seated on a bench against the wall. It was clear not all was well between the two and Mpedi was the peace-maker. First the woman and then the man stood up. The woman began to move to the exit door. Her man followed, engaged in a tittle-tattle with Mpedi.

Warrant Officer Batata buried his head in some paper work on the table near the back door. For him there was no world other than his own; there were no people around except himself. His expression was a mask of concentration and disdain. He was scribbling copious notes on sheaves of paper. Batata didn't raise his head as the quarrelling couple left the police station. Always self-confident, always an authority, he spoke to the paper-work before him: 'Mpedi! Mpedi!' Constable Mpedi, alert and obedient, answered: 'Coming, Sir!'

Batata said rather officiously: 'Bring me yesterday's Entry Book.' Mpedi didn't say anything. He stepped in the direction of some office away from the main charge-office. In his silence entered his dislike for the mean Warrant Officer. He didn't like the way Batata ordered him around as if he, Mpedi, was a small boy. But, thought Mpedi to himself, Batata likes to show off at the expense of other people. He was a bully. All the same, he would have to find him the Entry Book. Otherwise Batata would be screaming his top off and upset the Sarge. Now that was a sweet ol' man for you. Working the night-shift with him was a relief — always. Never bothers one, never pushes one around. Give him a cup of black coffee every two hours and he'll go on playing his cards and smoking a thin cigarette between two thick, clumsy fingers: a darling of an ol' man, observed Mpedi, standing in front of shelves in one of the rooms in the police station. He was going through a pile of note-books already filed on the shelves.

The grinding of rail-tracks grated the silence of the winter night. It was a late Naledi train heading for nearby Nhlazana Station.

'All clear,' said Mandla. His voice seemed to choke. His own tension had been mounting while Mzi made final touches to the gadget at his feet. For Mandla heard the tick-tick loud and clear and knew the meaning of it all.

'We'll have to leave the thing by the back door and hope for the best. There's no time to debate situations,' groused Mzi. His own patience was wearing thin.

'I guess you are right,' said Mandla. The tick-tick at his feet added anxious moments to his duty as guard. Even his boyish pleasure in holding an automatic rifle in his hands couldn't erase this fear of the night in the courtyard of a police station. He was in a state, perspiring where he should have shivered.

'Ready?'

'Aha!'

'We have two minutes to clear off this ground. That's long enough to say one's prayer but by God I don't want to see what's going to happen to this building and the bloody cops in it.'

'I pray Batata is in,' snarled Mandla in a croaking voice.

'And may his lips be clamped before he prays,' jeered Mzi.

Warrant Officer Batata rose from his seat, his face creased by some tension. Constable Mpedi remained closeted in the records room and Sergeant Ntloko pored over the cards before him. Batata went up to the exit-door and stood on the threshold scanning what he could see of the night.

None of the cops could tell how it happened: the blast hit the police station so suddenly and thunderingly, it rocked every one of them one way or another. It was heard miles away. The force flung Sergeant Ntloko up and across the room. He landed on his huge stomach, prostrate, pinned against what remained of the wall near the front door of the station. Constable Mpedi perched on his bum in the records room, petrified, his hands clasped in the air where the Entry Book should have been. Mpedi was terrified to find himself in a cloud of dust and debris whirling and whirling as if his own head were in a spin.

Batata was the lucky one. He was swept off his feet by a force he could hardly explain minutes later; it landed him on the soft lawn in the foreground of the station yard. Brave man that he was, he waited outside on the ground, long enough to regain his orientation. His thoughts were for the safety of the others. He was attracted by the cries and groans of Sergeant Ntloko. The man cried: 'I am finished! I am finished!' Ntloko was swimming in a pool of dust, pinned down by an assortment of things: wood, plaster, iron and bricks. His voice grew faint as moments ticked by but he kept up a chorus of: 'Help me God! Help me people! I am finished! Oh! Oh! I am finished.'

It was difficult for Batata to reach his colleague. The place was in darkness due to power failure; the place was in shambles. Batata scratched and cleared until his hand touched the limp hand of his colleague. Dead. Sergeant Ntloko died buried by the mess which was once Jabavu Police Station. Constable Mpedi was rescued and rushed to Bara.

By this time crowds of bystanders, curious, affected and some detached, stood watching the frenzied goings-on at the bombed police station. There were countless volunteers lending a hand at this dark hour of the law. For such is the strangeness of humanity.

Mzi and Mandla were nowhere in sight. Mandla gripped the steering wheel with the power of a conqueror. He was almost singing with the wheels of the car as he tumbled back to base. For Mzi there was a sense of failure enveloping his being. He couldn't tell why but a knowing sense told him the blast wasn't what he wanted it to be. The reverberations were not of a pitch he wanted to hear. Something bigger was what he had hoped for. But from the moment the placing of the bomb had become a matter of chance, he knew he had failed. He resolved to work diligently for the success of his original mission. That gave him comfort. He sat back in the car with his eyes shut. It was as if he wanted to hide away from the ruins they would pass, reminding him of the ruins he had left behind.

Soweto went to sleep that night unaware of the nightmare to which it had given rise. It was a nightmare which would linger for many, many nights to follow.

The radio news items of the night made no mention of this important event — not yet!

## 3

'The death of Sergeant Ntloko is to be regretted, gentlemen.' So began Colonel Kleinwater at the conference of senior officers of the Security Branch the morning following the blast. 'But we must look beyond that point. What we must all appreciate is the seriousness of the damage done to a police station. These children have declared war on the State. It is a matter all right-thinking citizens will condemn.' At this point the Colonel, who appeared to have been reading from a prepared statement, raised his head slightly and looked past Major Hall, seated almost opposite him at the rectangular kiaat table. He went further: 'We will have to act swiftly, with ruthless determination. Those are our orders. Our powers are safeguarded by law. What we need to do is justify these with results. Results, gentlemen, are what is expected of us.' He paused, only for that split second, long enough to swallow. The mood of his face darkened and he went over the next parts of the statement sombrely: 'It is absolutely clear to me we need not handle this issue with kid gloves. We must make these people realise they cannot, I repeat, they cannot tamper with the security of the State with impunity.' The Colonel paused again, pulled the carafe of water toward him and poured himself a glass of water. He turned to Major Hall and while sipping from the glass asked casually: 'How's Batata, Major?'

'F-f-f-fairly well, Co-co-colonel.'

51

'I hear he suffers from shock?'

'Y-y-yes, de-de-delayed reaction says the-the doctor. Ba-ba-but he'll be all right s-s-soon.'

'We need that man, Colonel,' added Captain Brand superfluously.

'Naturally! Naturally!' answered the Colonel. He addressed himself to the Major again: 'Has Masemola said anything?'

'N-n-no. Claims he was taken by surprise.'

'Lies!' cut in Brand.

'I think so myself,' said Hall.

'Don't let him get away with it,' put in the Colonel.

Major Hall twisted his lips and declared: 'Oh no-no! These edu-educated mo-monkeys want to give us nigh-nigh-nightmares.'

'We won't allow it!' vowed the Colonel. 'We need to make an example of one of these people.' The threat in the voice was heavier than the words conveyed. The man's eyes, nostrils and lips carried the message round the table. The silence in the room was matched only by the intensity of the cruelty behind the words. The Colonel announced: 'I want Operation 3 to come into effect, immediately! We are dealing with skelms. They must be in league with white communists. I'm convinced of it. That blast is definitely of communistic origin. It is very clear to me some piccanins have been receiving training in these things in the Northern Suburbs of our city. No doubt about it.'

'I've said so for a long time,' Brand butted in.

'No, gentlemen,' said the Colonel, 'we needn't look far, the trouble is right here with us.' Then he sat up and made his point, looking at his two assistants: 'I want every moving thing stopped and checked — thoroughly. We must catch the culprits within these coming days. It shouldn't take us long with the efficient forces at our disposal.' The Colonel raised his shoulders to declare: 'That's all for now gentlemen. Good morning!' He rose to his feet and said as a parting shot: 'By the way, Edmond, keep me informed of Batata's progress.'

'De-de-definitely, Colonel!' Major Hall had hoped to say that quietly and smoothly. Something in his make-up let him down. It was this very condition which influenced his whole behaviour in the force. Failure disturbed him. And the unrest in Soweto was failure. So he hated Soweto with all the intensity his body could summon. But Soweto was his job.

Moments later, and in the days to follow, Operation 3 became the scourge of Soweto; a symbol of one of the most ruthless events to befall that sprawling mass of humanity, so that in a few days Westend Police Headquarters, from where the operation was masterminded, became a swear-word on the lips of the people; a synonym of cruelty. Roadblocks were mounted on every route leading in and out of Soweto. And for the first time the ordinary man came to understand what the initiated meant when he spoke of 'the system'. Also the camouflage riot squad came of age. Working hand-in-glove with traffic cops, the squad, aided by plain-clothes and ordinary uniformed police, descended on the people of Soweto like locusts. Cars were stopped; trucks were stopped; combis were stopped; buses were stopped; just everything on wheels save the trains was stopped. Then began the search: of boots and bonnets; of back-seats and glove-boxes. A cop would come up to the driver and touch the steering wheel as if Mandla Nkosi was perched somewhere round the wheel. Gots! It was sheer fascination to watch these men engaged in a mighty task such as looking for an insignificant particle of man like Mandla. He remained elusive.

Out of utter desperation a police spokesman announced an important decision from that quarter; a reward of R500 placed on the head of Mandla. The people of Soweto sighed with relief. They never expected such news, quite out of the blue, releasing the tension from their lives. They sighed laughingly. Wasn't it ludicrous this reward? R500 indeed, they said. For all the fuss; for all the energies, the tensions. Imagine the effort going into these searches, they argued in their kitchens, their backyards and on the buses and trains. The whiteman is going mad! If Mandla was so important to the welfare of the State could a lousy sum such as R500 be all he was worth to the informer? The people laughed; it was a loud laughter stretching the ear from Soweto to Johannesburg to Pretoria. A police spokesman announced that roadblocks had yielded a number of cars and dangerous weapons — knives and knobkerries! The laughter of Soweto became hysterical. It was maddening, this laughter from the servants of the city.

Operation 3 took on a number of guises: Mandla's home acquired a certain status in the surroundings. A young constable was posted to watch the Nkosi house from the front. What happened was a simple act of authority: the family in whose house the constable was to be quartered woke up in the morning with a knock on the door. Two white cops stood at the door. Behind them was the constable carrying a small bundle of bedding. The white cops tried hard to be polite. They said something about the house having no phone, but that one would be installed in a day or so. They brought Constable Kekana to stay for a few days, or maybe weeks. They couldn't be sure because of the trouble in Soweto. The Makhulubaas didn't say much to them: 'Take Kekana to Mrs Diraditeng,' he had said. Not much really because he was a busy man. Mrs Diraditeng began to protest. She tried a number of angles: she said she had no authority to accept a man into the house without the permission of her husband. The cops answered they understood; she said there was no spare accommodation. The cops answered they understood. Food?. . . . not to worry the State would provide . . . Lodger's permit? . . . not to worry the Superintendent was aware of all that was happening. MaDiraditeng threw up her hands in resignation. Wasn't she under pressure? Wasn't she a Christian? One of the cops offered to go to Visagie Motors and warn Mr Diraditeng about the latest developments. MaDiraditeng didn't know the word 'development'. But she wasn't expected to query that. She understood the words Goed — Good, Constable, as the whites retreated from the house, leaving her with the load of a policeman.

In the silence which followed the rising of the dust as the cops took off in their car, Constable Kekana spoke: he didn't like what was happening but what could they (MaDiraditeng and himself) do, the whiteman was always pleasing himself because of his power over the people. MaDiraditeng said nothing in reply. But she held her hand under her chin just as one does in amazement. It was her final note of resignation to the new development in her husband's house.

Outside in the street the people of Soweto nudged each other, pointing at the house of Diraditeng, exchanging curious signs of being aware of the meaning of what the police intended for the house of Nkosi. These same people continued to laugh as only the Soweto person knows how; they laughed so loudly it carried beyond that street. Then all of Soweto laughed and the laughing was heard in Sis Ida's joint so that Mandla and his colleagues picked up the cue: they laughed and laughed even when Mandla was feeling the load at the bottom of his stomach, even as his stomach tightened because of the uneasiness he was causing his parents.

Soweto was still laughing when MaMotaung answered a summons to appear before the Area Superintendent. Because Meneer Snyman wasn't one of those officials whose natural instincts made them too nice to black women, MaMotaung wondered about the summons. Her heart twitched with fear when the blackjack brought the message from his superior. She was a widow and that was enough to have her evicted from the house she occupied.

The Superintendent asked if she was aware she owed one month's rental for the house. MaMotaung said yes she was aware. He reminded her of municipal regulations. Raising a hand, he pointed a long, bony finger at the woman in black standing before him. She stood looking at the Super with bitter eyes, her face flabby with the sorrow in her heart. Her own hands were clasped in front of her, wringing the helpless anger racing with her body. Her eyes, burning and hateful, stared at the whiteman seated across the wooden table cluttered with regulation papers and the morning newspaper.

Then the Super cleared his voice, dropped his uplifted hand and curled it on the table so that it remained there like the head of a dead snake. He proclaimed: 'I'm afraid you must move out of that house. You people know the regulations.'

MaMotaung didn't cry or wail as sometimes happens when a person in her position is distressed. She merely sighed and raised her arms to her chest to conserve all the strength needed to take the blows hurled at her. She folded her arms across her stout bosom and stared down at the Super. She asked, 'Where will I go with all my property?' The Super's expression was stern when he retorted: 'It's not my business . . . I want you out of that house, that's all. I don't make these regulations.' For the first time the man looked up at the other man planted next to MaMotaung: a blackjack. The uniformed man stood legs apart, hands clasped behind him. He too turned his head only to look at MaMotaung unsmilingly. There was a consuming contempt for the woman showing in his big, fleshy lips hanging open, and in his tired, red eyes. He didn't sigh or cough or shake his head. He just turned his head slightly and looked at the woman as if to wish for her mouth to shut. But MaMotaung continued: 'I lose a man, now you want me to lose a house. What kind of law is that?'

'Don't be cheeky!' warned the Super in reply. 'You know the law says the rent must be paid.'

'I skipped one month only.'

'So why argue?'

'I couldn't help it. My man died and my expenses were high.'

'It's got nothing to do with me. The law says . . . what it says!' asserted the Super showing signs of impatience. His own strength was now sapped. He was bored with his surroundings. He wanted to be rid of the woman. He had wanted to carry out his duties as quietly, as peacefully as his colleagues in the city managed to do, but the nature of his job always conspired to undermine these wishes. He paused briefly. He looked away from the woman. He would have liked to take in the sight of the skyline through the window. But the windows in the hall were set high in the wall. No chance of even spying the blue of the sky. Inwardly he cursed the piccanins of Soweto for the troubles brought on the heads of all white people. He said to the blackjack: 'Tell her I'm going to give her one more chance.' The other man began to interpret. He was interrupted by the woman who said: 'I've heard all that.' She turned her wrath onto the blackjack: 'Sis! You look down on me. You think I don't hear what this man is saying to me.' She let her hands sweep the air in disgust. This time the blackjack stood at ease. He shook his head in disbelief and took a slight step backward and away from MaMotaung. He didn't want to hear what the Super said. In these days of 'power', as everyone referred to the happenings gripping Soweto, the word of blacks mattered more than that of Superintendents, especially as it was said abroad that the blackjacks had to remember they lived in the townships, not with their bosses in the suburbs to the north. The Super was quick to respond: 'Listen, mosadi, that man works for me. He does what I tell him. If you didn't want an interpreter you should have told me. He's got nothing to do with it. Understand?'

But MaMotaung didn't say whether or not she understood. She glared at the Super. He felt the need to be rid of the woman more strongly as minutes went by. The Super dropped his hands on to the table and pulled himself forward on his seat, his shoulders hunched 'All right,' he began, 'I'll tell it straight to your ears.' He shifted in his seat again. 'I am transferring you to another part of Westcliff.'

MaMotaung was about to protest when Meneer Snyman raised his hand and his voice: 'Don't ask me why it is the law. All right it is the whiteman's law but it is the law. I can do nothing about this. The Government tells me I have to do it. So I am doing it. I tell you you must go out of here and begin to pack your things. I'll send one of our lorries to pick up your stuff and carry it to this number.' The new house number was handed to MaMotaung. Snyman stood up and twisted his strained neck. It was tired from looking up at the woman and a few twists of the shoulders would do the trick. 'You may go now,' he said politely. MaMotaung didn't move immediately. She stood there as if rooted by her anger. Meneer Snyman said sternly: 'I said you may go.' MaMotaung turned to go but not before she said under her breath, audibly enough: 'Dinja tsena! — These dogs!' The blackjack heard and understood. He eyed his superior and shrugged his shoulders. Snyman hesitated to enquire after the latest muttering. For him the day was already exhausting enough. He took out a cigarette from the box on the table and lit himself relief.

In the early evening Soweto began to nudge itself again. This time the women slapped their hands together and expressed their amazement. A policeman and his family occupied MaMotaung's house. The people were quick to observe what the law was up to: a policeman at the house in front, a policeman at the house behind the house of the Nkosis. Mohlolo! — Wonders! they exclaimed. Respect for Mandla Nkosi was heightened. The people of Soweto began to laugh once more. The word was passed around that Mandla was great. The word and the laughter spread rapidly to all corners of the place. What was in the boy which made the whiteman so scared, the people asked. Mandla became the talking point. A few said he must be great to have brought down a structure like the Jabavu Police Station. He must be dangerous to the whiteman for his home to be under such surveillance. Then the minds of the people paged back. No-one in living memory had received the sort of attention accorded to Mandla. Not one of the men on Robben Island was a star at Mandla's age. The veneration given Mandla began to acquire mystic qualities: some said he was the reincarnation of Tshaka and Moshoeshoe, others said he was the prophet Ntsikana. Ageing men bestowed on him the mantle of Mandela. They said it openly, that he was the son of Mandela: they saw in his face the face of that great son of the soil. His spirit began to sweep round the country as all youths worshipped his image. The faint-hearted among men found their spirits bolstered by the word Mandla. He was indeed a legend in his lifetime.

It was to smother the legend that Operation 3 extended itself to all activity in the streets. Police began to harass all youth on the streets. Football players in the streets, and on football fields, gangs of youths lounging on yellow grass; dice players scooping money from the ground or any number of boys found standing together were terrorised into fleeing at the sight of a kwela-kwela. These actions of the police changed the complexion of township streets. They angered and embittered the people of Soweto.

Just as the cops in sight wore camouflage, so their vehicles were meshed in wire, acquiring in the process the ghostly look of movie fantasies. So the people of Soweto laughed and laughed in the bitterness of their day.


At Sis Ida's that morning the house buzzed endlessly with speculation. For once the student group joined the general public seeking the who's, when's and how's of the bombing of the police station.

Roy sat on the floor in the sitting room, the morning paper *The World* spread before him. One finger rested on the word he'd been reading when he paused to exclaim loudly: 'Bafo I don't like this!

Listen to this.' He read: 'the possibility that Mandla and his cohorts may be responsible for this latest act of sabotage has not been ruled out . . .'

'Rubbish!' sang Bongi from the inside kitchen door.

'Rubbish or not,' said Roy, 'the point raised here is my own complaint: what has become of the collective leadership? This guy Mzi runs our show. Why?'

Bongi handed Roy a cup of morning tea and said: 'He's one of us.'

'To hell with that!' shouted Roy, his whole body shaking with rage. A bit of the tea spilt on the paper. He yelled: 'D'you want to tell me every black man, because he's black, he's one of us?'

'Of course, yes!' said Bongi who had moved back to the kitchen door. In contrast to Roy, she was calm, she was soft, as if persuasive: 'Mzi has proved himself. He's done so last night.'

Roy jeered at Bongi: 'E – e! Listen to her. No proof but she says he did so last night.'

'She's right,' butted in Keke. He stepped past Bongi from the kitchen and stood towering over Roy, hands in his pockets, shoulders hunched. 'Perfectly right is Bongi.' Looking down at Roy he said: 'You want me to tell you why?' No-one said anything but both Roy and Bongi looked at Keke hard, expectantly. He increased the distance between himself and Bongi, leaning against the out-door of the sitting room. His whole mood was that of mischief-maker. He said: 'Bongi knows Mzi better than anyone amongst us.'

Bongi was stung. 'How do you mean?' Her burning eyes flamed at Keke. 'Are you saying I sleep with Mzi?'

Keke laughed boyishly. 'Oh no, Bongi, I didn't say so. I just meant if you can make claims for Mzi then . . .'

'You are not a revolutionary,' cut in Roy. 'This man is hardly three days here and you are in love with him already. 'Strue's God you are not a revolutionary.'

'In other words you believe that liar Keke?' cried Bongi, hurt.

'Keke you are a troublemaker,' declared Nkele stepping into the sitting room. 'You don't know what you are talking about. You have a big mouth, Sis!'

Keke raised his hands defensively and said: 'I was joking. I didn't mean to hurt anyone.'

'There's no time for joking,' put in Digoro from one of the easy chairs in the room. He looked aggressively at Keke. All the time Roy was glaring at Keke. No doubt he would have liked to lash out at Keke but so many other members were climbing down on the mischief-maker it didn't look like he would survive the avalanche.

Bongi rose to her own level of argument: 'As I was saying, Roy has no right to condemn Mzi. And there is no point pretending we don't know who did the job last night. The thing is so simple really a small child could see through what has happened. For the first time Mandla does not sleep here with us and a bomb blast destroys a police station. Surely we do not need the services of a witchdoctor to know who did the job.'

'Where does Mzi come in?' asked Roy.

'You can't be serious,' replied Bongi. 'You and I know how much Mandla knows about bombs. So?'

'Tell them, girlie . . . tell them,' said Keke beaming from behind the door.

'Shut up!' demanded Roy.

'Some people are funny,' complained Keke.

'Know your priorities, Keke,' said Roy threateningly. Keke laughed, shrugged his shoulders and fell into a silence.

'My point is this,' began Roy, 'we began the revolution . . .'

'Revolution!' chipped in Keke.

'Yes revolution,' emphasised Roy, 'we've been together. We stopped the Bantu Education classes, right?'

'Right!' echoed Bongi.

'We kicked out of school all the sell-out teachers, right?'

'Right!'

'We did all that together. We took the decisions together. We captured the imagination of the people. We made the gatlas — police shit in their pants, right?'

'Right!'

'In comes Uncle Ribs. In comes Mzi from outer space. They climb on the band-wagon, our band-wagon. Why?'

'They are part of the struggle,' retorted Bongi, her voice firm and emotional.

'I am not worried by names. I am not bothered by personalities,' cut in Boysi, sitting up from his cramped position in the sunken easy chair in the far corner of the overcrowded room. 'Mzi, Uncle Ribs, Mandla, Roy, the whole damn lot doesn't worry me. If one or all of these people are up to hurting the system or any part of it, I ask no questions.'

'Who takes the decisions doesn't matter then?' asked Roy, pained by what he had just heard.

'Kyk, bajita,' said Boysi in a quiet tone. He tried to smile behind the words. 'Today we need not worry about words and the people saying a lot of words. Deeds speak louder. For too long we have heard slogans: 'Freedom in our Lifetime'. First those words were said loudly. Today they are whispered behind raised hands. The people who can say them have been silenced. Others are dying.'

'And there's no freedom,' blurted Keke. No-one paid attention to him. There was a silence in the room.

'The question remains,' bellowed Sello, standing with his feet apart near the door leading to Sis Ida's bedroom.

'What question?' enquired Roy.

'Who takes the decisions?' said Sello.

'Oh ya,' said Roy as if waking from a reverie. He continued: 'Mandla is losing out to Uncle Ribs.'

'Uncle Ribs is a sell-out!' declared Keke. He watched the room for a reaction.

'Rubbish!' cried Bongi.

'I didn't say so,' explained Roy. 'I asked why he wants to use us.'

'He is not!' squealed Bongi.

'He's waited till now. Why?'

'We didn't have a face. The blood of Hector, the blood of Ndlovu, the blood of many other black brothers and sisters lying there in the cold tarred and dusty streets, they gave us a face.' The soft brown flesh on Bongi's face wrinkled as she said all this. Her brown eyes became watery as if she was about to cry. Her round, delicate arm stiffened showing the tenseness of her muscles, revealed in the fingers of her hand: they were moving all the while.

'I have always had a face,' mocked Roy. The cynicism on his mask-like face showed clearly. Here was a young man not prepared to give any ground to any so-called outsider.

'Oho!' sighed Bongi in utter desperation. She stood in the doorway ready to shove off to the kitchen. Punkie held her by the shoulder and said: 'No, chom, don't say we were made by the protest against Bantu Education.'

'Ah, Punkie,' breathed Bongi, shrugging the hand of her friend off her shoulder, 'you want to deny the truth?'

'In any case,' chipped in Roy, folding the paper on the floor, 'in any case this point is irrelevant. My question was: who runs our show?'

'Punkie should keep quiet,' urged Bongi.

'Don't be rude, I can't . . .'

'Listen girls,' cut in Keke, 'this is no beauty contest . . .'

'Keep quiet, man,' demanded Roy of Keke. The girls glared at Keke. Their emotions seemed to well up as a result of Keke's jibe.

'Kyk hier — Look here, Keke,' growled Sello who had been quiet all the time. 'I'll throw you out of the house on your ear.' Sello looked angry. His brow was knitted by the determination ringing in his voice. He went on: 'Met my ma — By my mama, I'm going to do it! Nothing for you is serious! Jokes! Jokes! Jokes all the bloody time! When do you grow up?'

'How can he if he runs home every morning to say goodbye to his ma before she goes to work?' teased Bongi. It was a stinging reminder because it was all so true.

'Watch it, bajita,' said Digoro, tugging at the turn-up of his trousers, 'Let's not allow our emotions to carry us away.'

There was a brief silence. The sun's rays streamed into the room, adding a little warmth to the chilled walls of the room. Roy lifted himself off the floor. One hand held the paper, the other brushed the dust off his bum. He said into the thick atmosphere in the room: 'No-one is keen to answer my query.'

Perched on the arm of the easy chair in the far corner of the room, Dan Montsho sprang alive: 'No-one's trying to dodge the query. We are all aware of it. But until Mandla makes an appearance the game of guessing will continue. For me silence is better than that game. Of hoe sê ek, bajita?' He let his voice carry round the room. Several other voices sang a chorus of 'Ya — ya!'

'No winners!' declared Keke.

'Voetsak!' retorted Bongi.

Keke sprang towards her and enfolded her in his arms. She wouldn't nestle in his warmth. Not in her mood and in the presence of the others. She shrugged him off, saying: 'Leave me alone, Keke. You know, one of these days I'm going to slap your face!'

'Why?' said Keke smiling.

'You are such a tease,' said Bongi, backing away from him. The two mingled with the other members of the group. There was a general movement of young energy: to the kitchen, round the room as if in circles, while one or two people remained seated in the rickety sofa or the easy chairs.

Everyone waited for the news. They waited for the man of the moment: Mandla.

NEWS ITEM

SOWETO REELS : HIGH SCHOOL LIBRARY GUTTED BY FIRE
NO COMMENT SAYS POLICE SPOKESMAN

About the time the student group wondered about an explanation of the bomb blast, Uncle Ribs and Mzi held their own post-mortem, as it were. Uncle Ribs sat deep in one of the easy chairs in the sitting room. It was clear from the way he puffed on his pipe that he was relaxed and satisfied. Not so Mzi. He was on his toes, oscillating between two points in the room like a caged tiger. Slapping a fist into the open palm of his other hand, he said: 'I know it could have been better. I panicked. But why? Goddammit!'

'Point is,' answered Uncle Ribs, blowing up a huge cloud of smoke with spouted lips, 'you chaps made history. Something like this never happened here before.' He watched the smoke trail away. He put his pipe on the coffee-table and began to search with his tongue an opening between two teeth in his lower jaw — a favourite game of his. He went on: 'Here you are, safe and sound twelve hours after the event.'

'You know my regret?'

'Oh come off it, brother, have none!'

'We missed the bastard Batata!'

'Mysteries abound in life,' said Uncle Ribs philosophically. 'He must be surprised himself how he escaped injury.'

'I shall live for him. My ma! I shall not rest until I've evened up things with that cop,' declared Mzi.

Uncle Ribs shifted in his seat to say: 'Look, brother, it won't be easy.'

'I know,' chipped in Mzi.

'The man is no fool.'

'I don't care about this!' snarled Mzi.

'I'm not saying it cannot be done. Oh no, it can,' asserted Uncle Ribs. 'Even if the whole army was to look after him, it could still be done.'

'He must come to his family sometime,' butted in Mzi.

'Exactly!'

There was a short pause. Mzi plunged his hands in his pockets as if to seek relief from the tension of the moment. He said: 'I'm dying to know the swine's home.'

'That? No problem.'

It was agreed to reconnoitre the home of Warrant Officer Batata the next time they went abroad. It wasn't a mission to be hurried in the heat of police activity in Soweto.

Meanwhile at Orlando East, life at Morning Sweetheart, Noah's joint, began slowly that day. The shebeen king was with his current flame, Matlakala. He stood looking at himself in the mirror of the dressing table. He touched the stubs of hair on his head and shook it as if disapprovingly. Then he touched the black lapel of his scarlet dressing gown and said looking at the figure reflected lazily in the mirror: 'Opskit — Wake up honey. I've some serious business to do this morning.'

Matlakala appeared to have missed the urgency in Noah's voice. She replied childishly: 'Oh sweetie. I feel tired after last night's session.'

Noah recoiled, stiffening his whole body. His one hand clenched into a fist as if he said within his heart: Bloody bitch! He shuffled out of the bedroom. Presently the sound of curtains being pulled open was heard reverberating throughout the tiny house. Windows were flung open. Noah went to the kitchen, opened and closed the door of the fridge so loudly that Matlakala must have heard it, and yelled: 'Honey! Honey!' The trick paid off. Matlakala shouted back lazily: 'Coming, sweetie!'

She stood at the door leading into the kitchen, leaning against the door-frame, her right arm stretched so that it touched the other side of the door-frame. Her flimsy pink nightie left nothing to the imagination. Because it was by design short on her thighs, the stretching of the arm had the effect of lifting it higher on her torso and that was that. Noah's vision seemed to blur as he tried to concentrate on her eyes. There was nothing he didn't know before, but the impact of that brown supple body framed at the door behind a veil which enhanced its flowing dimensions made his manhood stand upright immediately. He was given away by his voice: a frog developed in his throat so that he had to clear it, he had to re-frame his words and appeared clumsy where he should have been lordly. In place of a command he said apologetically: 'Honey, can you do me a favour? I mean, clear up the fridge. We have to stockpile these days. Business is damn good, as you have noticed.' At this point Noah found the quiet urging of the woman near him just irresistible. He didn't know what to do but he walked up to her, his hands thrust firmly into the pockets of the scarlet gown. He said, standing close to her as she remained tantalising him: 'Those bums who string along with the kids are losing out to us, the big boys from Kofifi.' Suddenly Noah was all over Matlakala: caressing and hugging her, drawing her into the kitchen. He ended up planting a light kiss on her left ear-lobe. 'What's the matter?' queried Noah pretending not to feel the warmth of his woman's soft body. 'Aren't you in the mood?'

'Why?' asked Matlakala who seemed to be just holding on to her man for the moment.

'Ag, don't worry,' said Noah freeing himself of the load likely to weigh too heavily on him at the very time when he needed to be totally free and alone. He stepped towards the sitting room, which way led eventually to the bedroom. As he retreated from her, he said: 'Honey, please don't disturb me for a minute or so. I'll be in the bedroom talking to the gods, you know what I mean mos?' A slight mischievous smile played on Noah's lips. Matlakala was again fooled. She laughed. She went up to the fridge but before she opened it, she put both her arms on it as if to complete the re-enactment of what she had gone through minutes earlier. She remained so for a while. Her body seemed to be indulgent to the coolness of the fridge.

Once in the bedroom, Noah shut the door, locking it in the process. This and the earlier act of escaping from his lover seemed to have drained him a lot. He perched on the bed and pulled from beneath the pillow on his side of the bedding a crumpled, soiled handkerchief, and began to dab and wipe the stubs of hair on his sweaty head. In the coolness of the bedroom at that hour, he found cause to fan himself feverishly all over his upper body including both armpits. He had to clip his fingers on either side of the scarlet gown, pulling it away from his body to allow the slight breeze to float within the ballooned area of the gown. That way, the air reached the armpits as well. Then he looked at the door anxiously, dropped the handkerchief on the bed and clambered on the bed to fetch from the top of the nearby wardrobe a black box. It was as he stood on the floor, elongating the wireless aerial, that the black box revealed itself as a walkie-talkie. He switched on a panel and the damn thing began to crackle typically, as a radio does. Noah shuffled towards the only window in the bedroom and quietly opened it. Enough only to allow the aerial to nestle in the curtains flowing gently outside the opened portion. His face turned anxiously to the door as he listened for sounds from that direction. There was a far-away noise of glass clinking. The bitch was at her post, he told himself. He touched the panel on the radio and the crackling sound increased in intensity. Standing by the window, watching the unseeing men, women and children passing down the street, Noah's mind raced in anticipation to another part of the world as his voice pitched in: 'Calling XWEO1. Calling XWEO1, This is Crossroads, This is Crossroads.' There was that brief moment when a silence descended on the house of Noah Witbaatjie, a silence in which Noah's breathing was the only agitation audible. He worried about the silence of the whole house when Matlakala might be within hearing distance wherever she stood.

'I read you Crossroads,' said a voice at the other end.

Matlakala stood quietly outside the bedroom door. Her curiosity was all-consuming. She held her breath on hearing the mutterings from within the bedroom. She couldn't suppress her own thrill at what she had discovered and the insinuations of the gossip in the street came tumbling before her eyes. She cocked her ear when Noah said: 'Reaction to . . . Mopeli High School not bad . . . believe . . . burning . . . students . . . themselves . . .' Matlakala nearly clicked her tongue with frustration. There were words she missed. She wouldn't permit gaps to exist in her mind. She shouted a few paces from the door: 'Honey! Honey! Are you all right? Did you say something to me?' She waited for an answer with her hands cupping her breasts. The trick had always gained her rewards before. She was sure it would do so at this juncture. She waited patiently.

Noah cursed. He pushed in the aerial, muttering quietly between clenched teeth: 'Bloody bitch!' Aloud he yelled pleadingly: 'Sweet sweets! Please go back to the kitchen. I'm embarrassed if someone listens to what I say in prayer. I'll be joining you just now!' He waited to hear her patter away. She did. Noah dug his teeth into his lower lip and winced. The woman was getting in his hair, he told himself.

'Coming in XWEO1, Coming in.'

'I read you,' said a somewhat impatient voice.

Just then the noise of the door of the fridge echoed across the bedroom as Matlakala vented her disappointment on it. It was a cue for Noah to say: 'Sorry for the disturbance, Meneer. Had a customer knocking on the door. And that's all for now, Meneer. Over and out.'

Noah switched off the panel with a violent start and buried the aerial in the box. He put the black box on the wardrobe, covering it with a few items. He was simmering with anger as he picked up the handkerchief to rub the sweat of rage streaming from his head. He stood in the middle of the room as if contemplating how to handle the woman's latest goofing.

Matlakala stood against the fridge, hands cupping her breasts all over again. Noah appeared and melted his anger in the seductive pose of his lover. She said: 'I am sorry.' He picked up the morning paper and quietly sat himself down, away from her. Not a word, not a sigh escaped his lips. For this time she had won the game of fooling. She resolved to remain in her flimsy nightie even as the sun climbed the eastern sky. Customers would come and they would share with him the curving frame of her torso behind the garment. She wouldn't mind. It made him jealous and that way he would ask her to change into something else. That way his iciness would thaw. And one day she hoped, he would reveal to her the mutterings in the bedroom.

It was in the evening when the streets of Soweto were deserted, the people barricaded behind locked doors, when talk consisted of incomplete sentences because the mind dealt with baffling situations, speculation riding the crest of each conversation, that Mandla's little car pulled into the yard at Sis Ida's. Supper was almost over for many of the group members. Roy was in the kitchen putting away his plate; Dan Montsho in the sitting room slowly picking up the last remains of thick porridge covered with a juicy tomato gravy: clearly the meat was finished earlier, because for everyone the evening meal was pap and vleis. The rest of the group were engaged in one way or another. For the ritual at Sis Ida's was always there, but almost lost to the casual eye.

Mandla breezed in with: 'Hela, bajita, you can still find time to eat? There's work to do, you know.' That was his style. Where some would have expected an apologetic entry Mandla was charismatic, he was brash, and that was how he was accepted. The air he brought in lifted everyone off their feet. But for this evening it was everyone except Roy and Dan Montsho. It escaped Mandla that Roy remained glum. Nor did he note Dan Montsho's cool expression. The rest were activated by his sudden appearance on the scene. It was obvious he had been missed by his colleagues.

He plunged into the stream of things with an assurance few could match: 'Bajita, the system has touched the tiger's tail. They have gone and burnt out our library. We can't let the boerans get away with it. We'll meet violence with violence like we have already.'

'How this time?' asked Roy cynically. He eyed Bongi as he put the question.

'Blast out that Bantu cop from his house!'

'Batata!' cried Keke.

'Who says?' asked Roy with a sneer.

Mandla's expression was that of a puzzled boy as he asked in turn: 'What do you mean who says?' There were times he found Roy incomprehensible. It was as though he wanted the leadership spot at all costs. It piqued him. At such times he couldn't hide his annoyance with his friend. But friend he was and so he would ride the storm fairly easily. Yet on this occasion something rattled Mandla. There was a look of surprise on his face. He watched Roy uncurl himself with: 'The idea, whose idea is it?'

Mandla stood in the middle of the room. The paraffin lamp-light on the radiogram played sickly on his face and showed a slight trace of sweat on his pinched brow. His sharp eye caught the eyes of his colleagues fixed on him as if each were asking for explanations which he had until that moment failed to give. For once he felt a sense of guilt where triumph should have been sitting. He looked at Bongi, he looked at Keke, and when he cast eyes on Dan Montsho and found him unsmiling, Mandla's chest experienced a constriction he couldn't understand. He cleared his voice and said quietly: 'It is my idea.' Then another thought seemed to have struck his mind: 'Bajita, why the questions?'

Bongi sounded silly as she echoed: 'Ya, Mandla, ask them.'

No-one took her seriously. The most she could raise was a querying eyebrow from Sello who was nearest to her. And with his arms folded across his chest, Sello looked contemptuous for a moment.

Dan Montsho sat up in his favourite easy chair in the far corner of the room. Everyone else turned to watch his next move. For there was in the room at that moment a heavy spread of the coolness of the evening air, a feeling of chill in the tenseness of the atmosphere.

'Well, mfo,' said Dan Montsho, 'there was a sort of argument this morning. We were clutching at straws, we were peeling ourselves to discover where we stand in the struggle in relation to the role played by Mzi.'

Mandla spread his hands and began to press them up and down as if the air were a mattress-spring: 'Okay, bajita, I know I've fucked up your mood. I went and did this thing at Jabavu with Mzi without revealing the job to any one of you. It was a success. That's important. Bigger things are coming, that's also important . . .'

'I queried the decision-making,' cut in Roy. 'I mean it's like the old story of whitey telling us what's good for us and not hearing our side of it. It's the same, same old story. Imagine reading a lousy thing in the paper about the group being responsible for the blast on Jabavu Station.'

'And you were not involved,' butted in Mandla.

'Exactly!' exclaimed Dan Montsho.

Feelings began to relax in the silence which followed. Mandla regained his composure. Relaxed. Confident. He said quietly: 'I am sorry bajita. Believe me, I didn't mean to undermine anyone's role. I was caught up in an adventure I saw as part of our thing. Somehow I find Mzi exciting, I find he's got the kind of guts I admire. The idea belongs to Uncle Ribs. Mzi was to execute it and he needed a partner.'

'There you are!' chipped in Keke. The room turned to face him. He shrugged his shoulders, raised a hand and dropped it so that it slapped the side of his thigh exactly as one does in desperation. He had nothing more to say. And the high expectations he raised were dashed immediately as everyone else sighed or smiled knowingly: Keke again. Always, always playing the fool. But his was a useful act. It helped to drop the tension in the room a little further. It gave Sello the cue to say:

'We were in the dark. We turned around several possibilities for explanations. All the time we were trying to fill gaps. Only Bongi here' — Sello swung his folded arms towards Bongi — 'was sure the job was pulled by you and Mzi.'

'Intuition, woman's intuition, neh?' said Bongi triumphantly.

'I think you'll find most of us sensed it,' entered Dan Montsho, 'but we didn't want to cough out our feelings of joy at that victory. We didn't want to be loud about our secret joys.'

'I know,' said Mandla. He said it as one who doesn't feel the words because the mind drifts on faraway shores. Then with gusto and excitement he went on: 'Gots! Last night was a kind of a dream.' The words captured the concentrated attention of his colleagues. Mandla said: 'There was a time I thought, well brother man, you are gone, you are finished. The system will catch you and parade you like a circus act and you asked for it. I saw these cops come out of the police station. They were coming towards us and I had the "machine" in my hands. Just the feeling of the bloody thing excited my fingers. I wanted to blast their heads off. And there was this guy Mzi saying: "Don't do anything silly." Imagine!'

'Softie! Softie!' said Keke.

'Listen to him!' jeered Bongi.

'You would have peed where you stood!' retorted Mandla. This brought laughter all around.

'Bang! Bang!' said Keke fooling around with a finger pointing at different directions in the room.

'Oho!' sighed Bongi contemptuously.

Mandla continued: 'I think I must have felt like Roy at some point along the line. Because I can't understand why I didn't want to sleep at Uncle Ribs's place. All right, I was excited, I was nervous, I felt victorious because I heard the bomb blast away but I just didn't want to be with those guys. I think I wanted to be alone or I must have felt I don't belong to their set-up. So I went up to my granny's place in Phefeni. But can you imagine what the lights of other cars were doing to me? I tell you all approaching cars gave me a scare. They jumbled my head as if I was a drunk behind the steering wheel. And when I drove through the darkened street, another fear gripped me. Man, it was as if I was driving into some huge, deep, bottomless hole which was sucking me in and in. I was bloody scared. How does the mind work? I've never known such fear before. I mean you know we've done things in the last couple of days but I never was scared of cops or whitey. In fact I become defiant every time I see smoke go up from a sabotage building. But last night was nightmarish for me.'

'I suppose it was a relief to enter MaNdlovu's house,' added Dan Montsho.

'Gots! What a bloody relief!' said a sighing Mandla as if re-enacting the experience once more. 'Thank God, she didn't ask too many questions. I guess the joy of seeing me in one piece at that hour was too much for her. MaNdlovu is a darling. At her age, she can be very probing.'

'Oh, yeah!' Sello sang knowingly.

'Mzi is a wonderful guy,' said Mandla dreamily. There was a note of deep sadness in those triumphant words. 'I know the suspicion in the minds of some of you. In your shoes I might have felt the same. But you see, I met him and for me it was love at first sight.'

'A weakness in a revolutionary!' chided Roy.

'A weakness of a human being!' retorted Mandla. He moved to sit crammed with Digoro, Snoek and Punkie on the sofa. It creaked. It reeled as if collapsing from the weight of the four people. Mandla began to rub his hands together and in a contemplative tone said: 'I know I may be wrong, maybe I am too sentimental about Mzi. But —' Mandla paused. For that very brief moment, a stretch of time measurable only by seconds, his youthful mind had gone back many years. Within this brief pause, when his colleagues had their own minds wrapped in the magic fascination he created, his own pictured a succession of stalwarts in the struggle: Dube, Lembede, Xuma, Luthuli, Mandela and Sobukwe. In the days leading to the climax of events in Soweto, the shining light kept alive by the deeds and sacrifices of these great men had been encapsulated for him and his colleagues. And of all these men there was none of the breed of Mzi. None, that is, who had at that early age gone through the fire as Mzi clearly had. For not even Mandela, the personification of a new kind of action-man, matched the do-or-die fatalism of Mzi. So it was with a deep sense of conviction Mandla said to the room: 'Mzi for me is different!' He shut up.

Bongi was first to hum her concurrence. Then followed sighs and grunts. Keke voiced his own: 'Great!'

Mandla echoed: 'The man is great. He is purposeful. One sees it immediately, that there's a new breed on our scene: determination, guts, action. He doesn't mince his words: he hates the boerans. He hates Batata.' Mandla's own voice rang with bitterness and this hatred captured from the trained freedom fighter. The voice choked dry so that he had to pause, to swallow, as if refilling his well of emotions anew.

The room was in silence. Except for a few heads turning to inspect the reaction of colleagues; the creaking of bones as those standing relieved the weight on their feet; more sighs and heaving as tension broke in the silence of the moment. The room was wrapped in the magic fascination woven by Mandla's charismatic presence. Even Roy was quiet. Glum, eyes restlessly searching a number of colleagues, he seemed to have been beaten by this infectious silence sealing the lips of everyone in the room. He was one of those who heaved heavily, tumbling finally into a pit.

Mandla rose from the sofa, said: 'Bajita, there's a job for tonight!'

'I want to be there,' offered Sello.

'Same here!' said Keke.

'Three is a crowd, bajita,' suggested Mandla.

'What do you mean?' asked the subdued Roy.

'The job is too small. I think Roy and I can handle it easily.' Mandla sounded as if they would be going out for a picnic. There was no fear or tension in his voice. He said: 'We'll take one or two Molotovs.' Turning to Roy he asked: 'Don't you think that should be enough? We want to put the jitters into that man's house, that's all. What do you say mfo?'

'Sounds like three is enough: one each on the front windows and one on the front door. That should make the bastard think the end of the world is at hand,' cursed Roy. Roy's words were always deeply felt, frothing with a consuming hatred for those considered the enemy. He moved into the kitchen – the lab.

'Okay, bajita,' said Mandla, picking his way to the kitchen, 'let's get down to mixing.' He turned a second to say to his followers: 'Careful of the quantities in each bottle, okay?'

The house sprang alive as if from a slumber. The unity of purpose among the group was a joy to watch. No-one needed prodding. Each took part like trained workers on a production-line. One picked up a bottle, examined it; another scooped sand from a container standing ready; yet another carried a measure of petrol. So it was. The group operated in the true fashion of a military unit. These were sights which became memorable to Sis Ida. She never ceased to marvel at the discipline of the group on such occasions.

On this occasion she came out of her bedroom at the moment when the group trooped into the kitchen; she saw Mandla, exchanged the usual warm greetings and jokes. Her mind went ahead of the goings-on in the kitchen and in her backyard, because she knew in the deep chambers of her heart that the joy of watching spell-bound the activities of the group masked a little fear somewhere in her being. She had begun to experience this fluttering of fear, as if a leaf was waved by an unseen breeze. There was among her neighbours a chap she didn't trust. Two-by-Two was a won't-work. Not only that, he was a gossip. He picked up an incident from one point of the neighbourhood, carried it to another. And vice versa. Sis Ida wasn't the only person who distrusted Two-by-Two. The women around said he was as free with his tongue as a female gossip — a liar they called him. He bought the liquor he was fond of guzzling with a pack of lies.

Sis Ida watched him pass her house. Lately he was in the habit of going past at a helluva slow pace, as if troubled by his feet. She observed him closely. There was something about him she didn't like. Not a bit. Her dislike of him was mixed with fear. For she had heard the name 'Red Army' applied to the group. The origins of it, she couldn't tell. But she was quite certain Two-by-Two was one of the persons responsible for the tag. 'Red Army': it wasn't a good nickname. The cops hated communists. If the news got as far as the cops (and who could trust Two-by-Two not to speak to them about it), Sis Ida was gone. That much she knew. And it was no comforting thought.

Yet how would she begin to warn these children of Two-by-Two? In whom could she confide her secret fear? For this fear was compounded by the fear of the very nature of the activities in her house. Oh, the agony of living in fear, of living a fateful life whose every turn, every twist was like the devil's pike turning the body of a damned person in the fires of hell.

She recalled two nights back. There was greater activity. Not only that, the little cars in the yard zoomed in and out like ants on a mission. And in the morning she was greeted by the sight of debris on the streets, and the smell of burnt-out smoke. And the word in the taxi was that the 'Red Army' had done it all.

On this night she found herself feeling like a zombie in her own kitchen. Always tolerant, always charming, she gave way to those she saw busy at the kitchen table. She saw they were mixing. For life. For death. Her mind didn't register so well these days. She said in her heart: these children are brave; they are careless. Admiration. Fear.

Then Sis Ida heard the roar of a little car in the backyard. Her heart sank this time. She had picked up the news of the night's mission. She didn't like Batata. Why, she cursed his name every time she heard it mentioned in the house, in the street or in a taxi. Batata was a fool. He killed his own kind, she said. Yet when the car pulled out of the yard, she pictured his huge, heavily-built frame lying there in death, and her heart twitched with a fear she felt deeply.

The roar of the car was soaked in the dampness of the winter night and receded into the distance. It died with the echo of Sello's voice as he said, fist clenched in the air: 'Power! Power! Amandla!'

The silence returned to the night. Those who waited remained with their ears to the ground, as it were, and with bated breath.

## 4

It seemed as if it lasted for days on end for the people of Soweto. They knew no rest from the battering and harassment of the police. Only their resilience, the will that refuses to bend under the might of legalised terrorism, carried them through. The people cupped their hands in prayer, they cupped their hands to receive the dripping of their own blood. For Soweto became the grave which stretched from end to end, enveloped by the deeds of men.

On the fifth morning after the outbreak of unrest, Major Hall sat in his office, his flabby cheeks nipped by the early winter breeze. His brow was furrowed as he sat staring at a photograph before him. Stacks of files lined his desk. There was something engaging about the man whose image he was studying. He raised the picture, turned it at varying angles as if to conjure up at that very moment the presence represented on the paper. 'Mbambo', he muttered to the room. He read a few notes from the man's file: Mbambo was referred to as a backroom boy in the affairs of the Resistance Movement. The police picked up his involvement from the time of the 'March on the Union Buildings', when twenty thousand women descended like locusts on the granite structure in Pretoria. Hall himself was a youngster then, still rising in the ranks of the force. But he remembered vaguely this event. On that sunny afternoon the country stood poised to repulse with all the might it could muster the manipulations of the communists. For communism was the beginning and end of the searing pain ripping the side of the nation's body. So it was said.

Not much was heard of Mbambo after the march. He continued to live quietly in Soweto as if untouched by the day-to-day grumbles and mutterings of the place. Major Hall was deep in thought as he looked at the picture once more. He wondered how the man would look these days. He toyed with the name Mbambo, cursing himself for not thinking about the man's activities during these days of unrest. 'Gots!' he exclaimed, slapping his left hand down on the desk. His hand was moving toward the telephone on his desk when Batata came in.

'Morning Major,' said Batata quietly. There was no cheer in his voice.

'A-a-h! Andries,' exclaimed Hall, 'just the man I wanted! Morning to you. Take a seat, A-andries. I-I want you to-to look at this . . .'

Warrant Officer Batata took his time staring at the picture. He thought he knew the face, but where would he have seen it, he puzzled. Soweto was such a gigantic location, teeming with thousands of faces, one could not distinguish one from the other. And if one could say one knew a face, where would one say the meeting occurred? It was a huge bother to the maintenance of law and order, the magnitude of the place. Wish the dreamers had seen it that way the day they carried out their dream of the place, he thought to himself.

'No!' he snapped. 'I can't place him, Major.'

'Think, Andries,' suggested Hall. 'I-I do-don't know why I want to see the man, something about his thin face, his eyes. Those eyes, Batata, don't they glare men-menacingly at you even in their stillness, do-don't they? . . . Look what they say in the report: once a very staunch member of the Resistance Movement.'

'Resistance Movement!' cried Batata. 'Of course! We must detain him. He could be a loose puppy doing damage in the place.'

'I-I want that man picked up.'

'Of course, Major. The swine want to wipe out my family.'

'I know, Andries. His type is dangerous, using school children for their ends.'

'It's the Colonel,' said Batata in a dejected tone, 'he doesn't want to listen to me. I've long said the Resistance Movement people are a danger. Skelms. They hide behind piccanins. I don't believe the story about the trouble coming from the Northern Suburbs. No, Major, the trouble is right here in Soweto. There are many members of the Resistance Movement pushing the little swine. You know, Major, I nearly lost my wife and children. As it is my wife has taken the children away. They must live with her mother in Vendaland.

'What a shame!' offered Hall. And to prove the pain of the experience wrestling with the peace of his mind he said sadly: 'Three days and three nights I've not had a wink of sleep, Andries. Th-think of it!'

'I'm going to catch one of those bastards,' vowed Batata, his large mouth twisted by a deep-seated anger, 'and I'll break, break his neck,' he concluded frothing at the mouth.

'No-Nobody knows our problems, not even the-the Colonel,' wailed the Major. 'I'm going to act, and explain afterwards. Th-that's all I'm going to do!'

A knock at the door and Sergeant Ndoda Ndlovu walked in.

'Good morning Major, good morning mfo,' said Ndlovu cheerfully. There was a lilt in his step as well.

'Morning Madoda,' replied Hall. Batata grumbled something inaudible. Ndlovu made as if he were unaware of his black brother's sulky response. The issue went beyond that office, he told himself.

'Co-come over here, Madoda,' suggested the Major. 'See this man, Mbambo, know er-er-anything about him?'

A fire died in Ndoda Ndlovu. Slowly but firmly he replied: 'No!' He shook his head, played with his mouth as one does under tension: 'No, Major, I've never seen the face before.' He turned to Batata mischievously and said: 'Do you know him, mfo?'

Batata stared angrily at his colleague, his eyes burning all the time, because there was no love lost between them. 'H'm,' he answered.

The Major threw the picture on top of a file and said very, very casually, as if saying he'd be going for lunch — no urgency, no feeling: 'We're picking him up tomorrow at 4 a.m. on the dot. Same address as of old times, I see on the back of the photo.' Then he stood up on his feet and towered over the proceedings. He announced: 'Well, gentlemen, the-the Colonel went to Pretoria th-this morning. I-important co-conference. As-as you might guess, Pretoria is un-unhappy with all of us. As al-always, po-politicians blame us for all the wrongs they create.'

'That's not fair, Sir,' said Ndlovu, trying to force a smile.

'Nei-neither here nor there, Madoda,' answered the Major. The slight beam on his face was his own contribution to keeping the ship buoyant. 'We'll do our best with the powers in our hands. Grab those we need in the-the er-er-execution of our duties. More than that . . .' The incomplete sentence remained suspended in mid-air. He was looking beyond the two men with him. There was resolve and a consuming force in his voice. He repeated: 'More than that, there's nothing we can do. Can we now?'

'Ya,' said Ndlovu. Batata looked like an overblown frog with the bitter anger sitting on the inside of his cheeks. He didn't utter a sound. Both the Major and the Sergeant saw the anger in their colleague's brown eyes, and they understood. The Major shared this bitterness, but not so Sergeant Ndlovu. His appearance then was a mask covering something deeper. Yet he repeated in a dry unconvincing voice a sheepish echo of 'Ya!'

A silence fell on the room. There was no warmth in it, winter remained drifting around and around so that the little meeting broke up on that cheerless note. Each of the black men went to his own place, each taking what he wanted of the orders of the day.

Sergeant Ndlovu went to sit at his teak table and spread the morning paper across it. He buried his head in it. His eyes merely settled on the paper. His mind roved over a period some ten years earlier. Then he was not a member of the police force. He had worked as a messenger in a men's clothing shop: sealing envelopes containing monthly statements, wiping the shop-windows again and again in the course of the day and running errands for the shop and its staff. One evening he had been persuaded to attend a meeting. He had liked what he heard from the one or two speakers. But it was the presence of a man, whose face he often saw in newspapers, that he carried home in his memory. The man had been introduced as Nelson Mandela. The man was charismatic. One listened to him as if compelled by some inexplicable force, for there was a fire eating into one's soul as he spoke. There was also truth in every burning word he uttered. Ndoda Ndlovu never forgot that first encounter with the Resistance Movement. He would go to the same place again and again. There was a captivating homeliness about the place. He came to learn the hostess was Mrs Nothando September. She was simply referred to as MaRadebe. No, there was no Mr September on the scene. He never got to know what became of him. Such was the hallowed presence of the place. One never asked awkward questions.

It was in the course of activities at MaRadebe's joint that he met Uncle Ribs. Even in those days there was something mystic and mysterious about the man. Slim, cheerful, but definitely not superficial. Many around said Uncle Ribs was deep. He worked a lot for the Movement under cover, shunning the glamour and glitter of the spotlight. In those days Uncle Ribs was marked by one seemingly incurable habit — smoking. He chain-smoked at an alarming rate. And there was even at that time a suggestion of a health hazard, for the man coughed violently at intervals. But behind the cloud of smoke the brown eyes darted and observed detail in an uncanny manner. No wonder they said he was a deep man.

Ndoda watched from the sidelines as the leadership of the Movement was picked up, first during the Emergency leading to the Treason Trial, and then at the time of the Rivonia Trial. Each time it happened he would be concerned for those men in particular with whom he had conversed, laughed and shaken hands at farewell time. One was Uncle Ribs. Ndoda would remain to be agonised by concern until it was confirmed Uncle Ribs had escaped the dragnet.

After Rivonia many of the members of the Resistance Movement went, swept underground like seed in the field. Many would grow to be silent elders; others sprouted from the soil in which they had been buried by force of circumstance, to continue the struggle. He thought he was going to serve the cause from a position of protection by joining the police force. That's how he lost touch with Uncle Ribs. But the man's engaging eyes remained beacons. He couldn't have missed him when Major Hall presented the photo before his eye. A strange metamorphosis occurred in that instant. He became a member of the Resistance Movement and acted as one. It was sheer instinct. But it frightened Ndoda to think what he was into, frightened him because the game of deceit can be fatal in the police force, especially in the Security Branch.

Sergeant Ndlovu turned a page and continued to read for the unseen observer. He was having to hold tight to his sanity. A succession of conflicting feelings played havoc with him. An impetuous thought told him to act immediately. Uncle Ribs must be saved. But a cold, steely voice warned of the consequences should the good act misfire. His body muscles tensed, his brow furrowed, his mouth twisted with the intensity of feeling gripping him. That's it, he told himself. He folded the newspaper, placed it on one side of the table, and picked up one of several files on the table shelves. He didn't think he was hurrying out of Westend Police Headquarters, but he was. Blood rushed to his head, impelling him to act by a compulsive instinct.

A policeman can drive as if the devil is in pursuit of him — anytime. Especially in the discharge of his duties. Ndoda Ndlovu was in an official vehicle, was dashing to Soweto, tearing down the Soweto Highway as if to catch an important witness just at that moment when the last gasp of air was about to leave the dying man. All the way he kept telling himself he was right. Uncle Ribs must be saved. It was his duty to save him. It was for this very reason he had joined the force, many, many years ago. The people would one day know, they would forgive the sum total of the arrests he had made in the course of his duties and thank him, yes, thank him for saving Uncle Ribs. For he might have died in detention. These days anything might happen to a detained person. There were cases he knew . . .

There was a roadblock outside Diepkloof. He slowed down, his eye took in the string of vehicles lined up along both sides of the road. He put his foot on the brake and began to crawl. They would recognise the car as a police one — the lean, spiralling aerial was a give-away. And he was known to many of them. Ndoda was a tall, lean man fond of a grey felt hat which he wore at an angle to his ill-fed face. He was always cramped in the little Volksie allocated to him, but he preferred it to a big car. People were less hostile to small police cars. It might be some time before they reacted to a person in a small car. By then a lot had been gained by an investigating officer if he was smart.

At various points in Soweto he saw more police. They stood at ease, their rifles jabbing the ground. Again he told himself he was right to want to save Uncle Ribs. By now he seemed to have withdrawn from his sense of being a policeman doing State duty. Another feeling entered his being. The people walking in the streets under the watchful eyes of the law were part of this being and he belonged to them. For the first time he acknowledged they were wronged, harassed and terrorised by an unfeeling force.

He stopped the car. He held the file conspicuously as he closed the door of the vehicle. His eye went instinctively up and down the street as he locked the door. He couldn't take a tight grip on his own feelings. He didn't know why, because there was nothing in the street to be scared of. Of that he was satisfied. But tense he was, his head was in a jumble, he felt the beads of sweat pouring out of his skin. He stumbled nervously on, making a show of comparing the house numbers to an imaginary number on his file. All the time he was edging toward the one big house jutting beyond the match-boxes in the neighbourhood. For Dube Village was the bad dream of some official, reflecting ambition tempered by envy. The result was this mixed bag of houses standing cheek by jowl.

Mrs Nothando September sat in the kitchen of her big house supervising the activities of her only servant. In the ten years since he had seen her there hadn't been much change about her: she remained attractive although her light skin had darkened a bit, and she was a little plump. There was something regal about her. It struck Ndoda immediately as they exchanged ritual greetings. For a while she remained distant, unnerving the police visitor. The man wished he could have got rid of the file, but how and when had been his problem. He tried hard to underplay his role of cop by giving Mrs September all the civil respect he could summon. She remained suspicious. Police were no friends in the thrust and parry of Soweto life. They were distinctly disliked. They were the enemy. Sergeant

Ndlovu was aware of it. He bided his time hoping his foolish smiles would seep into the marrow of her memory. He was trying to break down her resistance as he asked: 'Do you remember me?'

The middle-aged lady sitting near the kitchen table, one arm resting on it, the other curled on her lap, didn't bother to rack her mind. Instead she asked bluntly: 'Who are you?'

Ndlovu sat upright on his chair and thrust his chest forward and smiled broadly. 'You mean you don't remember me? Of course it's such a long time since we met.' Then he hooked a finger in mid-air and said knowingly: 'Those days!'

Mrs September remained unbending. But she did withdraw her arm from the table and placed both hands on her lap. This time she said: 'I don't recall a policeman like you in this house.'

'Exactly,' said Ndlovu expansively, shifting on the seat in the process, 'I was not a policeman in those days.' He clammed up suddenly and eyed the maid shuffling hither and thither in the kitchen. Mrs September picked up the cue and said politely to the maid: 'Zodwa can you leave us a minute? I think you can finish up my bedroom, don't you think so?'

The maid disappeared into the interior of the well-ordered house. She closed the door leading to the dining room behind her, in anticipation of the instruction to do so. Mrs September watched her go and acknowledged her civil behaviour with a slight nod of her head. She was proud of her discipline in the house. Then she turned to the cop and hummed, her hands still on her lap: 'M'h.'

'You want to know who I am?' said Sergeant Ndlovu confidently.

'M'h!' repeated Mrs September, folding her arms.

He eyed her expertly at an angle, chewed his teeth and sighed: 'Ndoda Ndlovu.'

Mrs September remained impassive, staring at him.

He melted into: 'Remember Uncle Ribs, Mnyumane and others? One evening Mandela came to address a small group of . . .'

'Aw! Aw!' exclaimed Mrs September as if she really needed all that prodding. 'I can see a young man of your build and complexion. You haven't changed at all. Now I remember!' she enthused. Then she resumed the posture of a sphinx and said: 'What puts you here today?'

'The turmoil in the townships,' blurted Ndoda. 'Uncle Ribs is in trouble,' continued the cop after a pause. 'I don't know if you still see him but I could think of no-one to talk to about this but you.'

'Ewe toro — Yes indeed!' replied Mrs September pensively. She raised her arm, pillared it on the table with her elbow, cupped the hand and rested her head into it as she asked: 'You say he's in trouble?'

'Trouble, mama.' The policeman began to search for words. He was looking into the future when he might be required to account for the words and the act which had brought him to see Mrs September. He was well aware prison gates shut on every human being. And it might well be him. He wasn't being rude when he asked: 'Can I trust you, mama?'

But Mrs September replied: 'What do you think?' She dropped her arm from the table. She was looking the cop in the eye as she said, with an almost detached air: 'It is up to you.'

The cop wilted. Accepting his blunder he said: 'Please forgive me. I didn't mean to offend you.'

'Who is offended?' asked Mrs September with the confidence of a self-assured person. There was an expression of contempt in her eyes as she looked hard at the cop.

Sergeant Ndoda Ndlovu found himself cowering before his hostess's brow-beating. He wished to be rid of the compulsion which had brought him to her. After so many years, he couldn't decide whether or not to trust her. Do I have a choice, he asked himself in the silence that settled on the room. They will say I tried to save Uncle Ribs and was let down. They will say I was treacherous. The two conflicting thoughts pressed the inside of his mind so that he sat facing his hostess uneasily. He blurted: 'The Security Branch will pick up Uncle Ribs tomorrow morning at 4 o'clock. Can you pass on the message. It is in your hands. He is in your hands. I am in your hands.' He was impelled to go on because she exclaimed with shock 'Awu!' as he voiced the first sentence of his statement. Now he looked at her, hearing his own blood pulse heavily through his veins. His whole being collapsed into a sense of hopelessness. But he was relieved by the mere uttering of what had pressed on his chest like the heavy door of a safe, cold and unyielding.

Mrs September, brave, stern and always cool, slapped her hands and sat upright on her chair. For once her eyes roved round the kitchen: the stove was cold. Yet she must give the cop tea. If the news brought this heaviness of heart to her, how was he who carried it from town to township? Poor thing, she said to herself of the cop. 'Zodwa! Zodwa!' she yelled within the confines of the four walls. In that silence her voice jarred the feelings of the cop. It tore off a quietness he wished to retain. But he was a visitor, he was at the mercy of the lady. This regal lady who had been over the years the confidante of many men in the Resistance Movement. Funny

79

that Major Hall had said nothing of her. Or was she also on his short-list? Sergeant Ndlovu was shaken out of his reverie by the creaking of the door as the maid, Zodwa, re-entered the kitchen. He heard Mrs September say lightly: 'Ag, tog, my child, make us some tea. We can't let a visitor go without a cup of tea. Or what do you think, meisie?'

Zodwa smiled and proceeded to begin the ritual. She knew her job well.

After the pause, Mrs September asked the cop in a quiet and con-cerned tone, speaking more to herself than to him: 'What could the poor man have done?'

Ndlovu shrugged his shoulders and said: 'These things happen.'

She replied in her home language: 'You needn't tell me! . . . But don't these people see they are on the way to hell? They must not want to drag us along.'

There was another pause. The silence between the two was broken by the clinking of cups and the flapping of cupboard doors. Sergeant Ndlovu felt the dryness of his throat choke him. A concern for his own survival impelled him to force through the words: 'I am at your mercy, ma.'

He heard her reply: 'My friend, we are all in this mess together. If anything wrong happens I shall be as guilty as you. The blood of Mbambo is our blood. His fate is ours. D'you see what I mean?'

'I thank you. I knew that in you I would be meeting a friend.'

'If I gave away you or Uncle Ribs, or if I failed to pass on this message, I know by the decrees of my people, the gods would give me their backs. Hayi! — No! Trust me, Ndoda, to act correctly in this matter. Mbambo must be saved.'

The tea was a relief to the Sergeant. He was nervous of sipping it with a hissing sound. And when the cup was empty and he stretched himself to place it on the table, he faltered so that it wobbled on the saucer precariously. He dived toward the table to save the cup.

Moments later Sergeant Ndlovu emerged into the street. He felt the glowing spirit of the sunshine and the hugeness of the day. It was as if he had been closeted in the house with Mrs September for hours on end. He tried to put a sprightly foot on the ground as he walked to his car. But there was a feeling of shame whipping his ears and face. Even as he exhibited the police file in his hand for all and sun-dry to see, he couldn't suppress this sense of guilt. Something in him snapped. He felt its sound roar with the engine of the car as it started off. He would remain scared for hours, unable to wipe the lean face of Uncle Ribs from his mind. The die was cast, he told him-self.

It was early evening. The day was long and boring for Keke. It was his turn to do his own washing. For each of the members, going home was ruled out. But for Keke, darling of his mom, Auntie Bettie, the umbilical cord was difficult to snap. More than any other member of the group, he found the time in spite of jittery guts to sneak home in the mornings. Thus it was he remained at base when others went their ways for the day's adventures.

The fingers of the setting sun stretched all over the location. The winter day was as usual chilly and unfriendly. And that made Keke huddle in the sitting room alone, and kill time as best he could. Now and again there was a shuffling sound as he mixed cards for the game of spoof. His lethargic manner of play, his morose expression, these were some of the give-aways of his spirits at that moment.

His mind drifted. It was for him an effort to hold it in focus. He tried hard several times to suppress the unfavourable reflections imposing themselves on his young mind. Hard as he tried, it became futile at some stage.

Seventeen years, he told himself. First year matric. An only son of the family. A family living above the level of the gutter. His father was a senior clerk of long standing at the General Hospital in the city, his mom a Sister at Baragwanath Hospital. They owned a second-hand car of German make. It was a well-kept, well-oiled machine which did the family proud in the neighbourhood. It marked them as 'rich' people. And Keke was immersed in the glory of his family.

It had been in the face of stiff family opposition that he joined the surreptitious adventures of the student group. Bra Baba, his father, decried his son's mysterious disappearances from home in vain. Auntie Bettie was motherly, enveloping her son with warm welcomes, unwittingly feeding him morsels of courage.

When June 16th occurred and the role of the Soweto child displayed itself before the eyes of each family, father and mother were shocked into a new sensibility about the meaning of their son. He was a man, a brave man at that. Bra Baba shut his mouth. Auntie Bettie sang the praises of the new generation. She encouraged Keke to sneak home every now and then for money and a change of clothing. In a way she wanted to satisfy herself of his welfare. She was aware it was a tough role he had chosen, but in fact it was something he had no choice over because of the strong group spirit permeating the whole of his generation in Soweto. Times have changed, she had heard it said several times in the wards of Bara. And she lived to witness the hospital and staff panic brought about by the so-called attack by the students on the hospital. The following day she would laugh with her son as each related the true happenings of that day.

Keke recalled his mother's face. Stretched smooth by the face-powder she used, charming and warm. His own heart sank. He was looking into the bargain of his life from the day he joined the group. He looked at the kind of life they lived. He heard his own voice cry 'Amandla! Power!' And he wondered about that power. Others might see it, but he, at that moment, he couldn't. His vision was blurred, his courage blunted. In his lonely depressive mood he failed to see the gains notched up by the group. He seemed to regret his life of dodging the cops, of sleeping from place to place, of eating the most basic of foodstuffs. It dawned on him that what had been seen by most of the group as a temporary inconvenience had become a way of life for them: he wondered how long the group would hold out. And then it happened. He fancied there was an informer within the group. Nothing tangible to go by but he became convinced there was an informer. What had the informer done so far? Nothing. But that's how they operated.

He stood up from the sofa and wandered aimlessly in the room. He went up to the window, parted the curtains, looked unseeingly outside. Nothing there, only a bare stretch of the earth. He withdrew from the window, feeling the loneliness of the house. He stood upright and let the cards drop from his hand on to the sofa. They did so in a rush of noise. It jarred his ear. It was to escape the noise that he sank onto the sofa himself and sat brooding. The room was empty. The crowded nature of it failed to fill the emptiness he experienced at that moment.

Dan Montsho worried him. He was too quiet for Keke's liking; too upright in his ways. He had an analytical mind. It was able to separate chaff from substance, illusion from reality. He spoke so little. That's it. He said little within the group. Such a man was dangerous. He could be the informer.

Boysi played up the bravado. Keke recalled how the Bishop was said to have been terrorised. These toughies, thought Keke, they are adept in the game of make-believe, but one need never trust them. He concluded he would have to be careful of his words and antics in the presence of Boysi. He could be the informer.

A twitch of real fear touched him. His mind settled on Mzi. Never mind what was said about what he had done at Jabavu Police Station: the man worked for the system. He was dead sure. How come he was not arrested? The cops are smart. They are giving the group and Mandla a long rope with which to hang themselves. They wanted the group to reveal its entire hand. That's it. The group must show the local backroom boys, must show the base of its strength, its master-mind and its links with overseas operators. And then the cops would pounce. They would be lopped off one by one until nothing of the group remained. That's why Mzi and Mandla were not pulled in. The cops were playing a cat and mouse game with all of them, and their man was Mzi. It didn't surprise him, Keke, that no arrest had yet been made in connection with the blast at the police station. It was all a trick. Ya, it was a diabolical scheme of the cops and Mzi. How to warn Mandla? The other members of the group were all right, but Mandla . . . He was in the grip of Mzi and Uncle Ribs. What about Bongi? Another twitch of the flesh seized him. He was convinced Bongi was having an affair with Mzi. One saw it in the way she warmed up to the man's name; how she defended him. No doubt Bongi sneaked away to meet Mzi. He must be fucking her. He knew women. They don't defend one unless they are one's mistress. Every time she claimed to be going home, as he himself did to see his mom, Bongi went to sleep with Mzi. Bitch! The word echoed in the room because Keke said it aloud. It was that kind of word. It filled up the mouth so that the expression of it became an enveloping thing. It was charged with strong emotive charges, demanding an explosion of immense feeling.

He arrested his drifting mind. When he shifted on the sofa it was as if he wanted to sit on the wandering thoughts in his head. He gathered the cards on the sofa and piled them up in one hand. He was exhausted by the mental exercise so he shut his eyes. It was a relief. A break from the forces eating into his young body. There was no explanation for it, this suspicion, this jealousy. It must be fear. He felt it clearly, in the silence of the room. Fear was churning itself like the food he ate, right there at the bottom of his stomach. It was as if it mingled with the food digested in the stomach. How to squeeze it out was a problem because it made him uncomfortable. He wanted to be at ease, with his thoughts, with his colleagues, with his surroun-dings, but there was this fear settled at the bottom of his stomach.

What did he fear? Not Dan Montsho. Not Boysi. Not Mzi. The cops. The cops. The cops. They mowed down innocent children in the streets. A man rushing to the train to go to work, gunned down. A woman standing in her yard watching a fascinating scene in the street, gunned down. What would happen to the group? The charges were galore, armful. For each member death would be slow and painful. For members of the system were said to be insensitive and cruel. Barbaric, some had said.

Keke saw fear in the stillness of the room. There was absolutely no warmth within the four walls encompassing his young body. There was no witness to this fear which intensified with the passage of time. He never knew how it began, but he wished he could be rid of it. He clasped the pack of cards between his hands and tightened his grip on the cards. They became squashed-in. That's how he felt. Fear squeezed him into something like a cage. The feeling was oppressive. He stood up to escape the force pressing him down. Then he threw out both arms and was relieved he still had control of his reflexes. He swung round and round, first one arm and then the other. The cards were in one hand. The exercise was a masterly idea. It helped a lot. It eased the oppressiveness he experienced. But no sooner was he through than the throbbing ache of fear returned. He flopped on to the sofa and sat disorientated, one hand holding on to the arm-rest, one leg crossed over the other. This was the paralysing effect of fear. He would remain thus for a spell of time that he couldn't remember himself.

Boysi and Sello found him in that sorry state.

'Bajita I am worried,' he confessed immediately, changing his position on the sofa.

'How's your mom?' asked Boysi. There was a lot of sincerity behind the question. For Boysi was that kind: hard or soft as the moment required.

'You blow hot and cold too often,' said Sello cynically. He remained standing when Boysi went to sit in the easy chair in one corner of the room.

'What worries you?' asked Boysi sympathetically. He tried to smile at Keke.

'An informer,' blurted Keke. There was no way he could have brought out his fear in bits and pieces. It had to gush out like ice as it thaws downstream.

'An informer?' repeated Boysi. His own face began to cloud. 'Where? Among us?'

'In or outside the group does it matter? If he reports us to the cops we are finished. I am working out the escape route through Botswana. But I have no contacts in Zeerust. If only I knew one person in that area.' Keke's voice was crying, his eyes were shifty and his whole body restless. There was no doubt about his fear of arrest.

'You are a sissy,' said Sello to him. 'I can't believe it, you know.' Sello went to perch next to Keke on the sofa. 'You are a real blabbering sissy. How do we know that you are not the informer?'

'I am not,' cried Keke. 'You know I am not.'

'Okay bajita,' said Boysi. 'let's not run to conclusions.' His voice was hoarse. He was searching for an opening in order to send in an effective blow: 'Who is your suspect?'

'Mzi!' said Keke without hesitation. He eyed both colleagues in turn.

'Aha!' exclaimed Boysi knowingly.

'That guy is a spy,' asserted Keke.

'How do you know?' asked Boysi, his voice now croaking a bit.

'I know. You know. Roy knows. Everybody knows.'

'What are you talking about — Mzi a spy! 'Everybody' knows it. You must be mad. You need your head examined!' said Sello angrily.

'Bajita I know what I am talking about, Mzi is with the system.'

'He can't be!' shouted Sello. And then he dropped his voice slightly as he saw Boysi signal to him. He went on: 'You don't blast a police station to show that you work for the system. You must be bloody mad, that's all. Why don't you run home and stay put there, man!'

'Not so loud, bajita,' pleaded Boysi.

A silence fell in the room. Each of the youngsters kept his thoughts to himself. Each must have been aware of a dimming of a light in his heart, in his surroundings. Darkness was creeping over the room, gradually, unnoticeably. The expression on each one's face was lost in the darkness settled on the room. But agitation showed easily in Keke. He couldn't sit still on the sofa. Something kept prodding him to sit first this way and then that way in search of comfort.

'I want to live,' said Keke, breaking the silence brooding over the room. 'I want to live,' he said again to himself.

'We all want to live,' replied Boysi in a matter-of-fact tone.

'I don't want to live from moment to moment, holding my life in my hand as it were. I don't want to put so much of survival into each moment as if there was nothing else to do in life. I'm bound to hate these moments in the end.'

'But that's life, baby,' said Sello arrogantly. 'We walk with life and death like they are our shadows.'

'And we live to fill up each moment with choices offered us by fate,' said Boysi. 'Life defines itself in those terms. Each moment is filled by us and the sum-total is life. For God's sake pull yourself up! You are depressed, that's all.'

Keke looked brow-beaten. He sat there looking beyond his immediate surroundings. If he had closed his eyes no-one would have cared. The message was sure reaching him. In the pause which followed, he couldn't take it any more. He needed to escape from the flaying he was getting. The alternative offered by his friends was more than he could take in his frame of mind. He stood up, hands dangling at his sides. There was no doubt about it: he had had enough of the conflicting voices reaching the core of his being. He went into the kitchen to escape the oppressive atmosphere of the sitting room.

Boysi and Sello remained looking at each other incredulously.

Presently the house was once more alive. In ones and twos, the other members of the group trickled in. Roy presided over the proceedings.

Boysi and Sello said nothing about the little discussion with Keke. Instead they reported on their mission to see Ann Hope. Sello said: 'The white trash gave us a small sum of bread. She promised something bigger next time.'

'Why we have to depend on whitey for survival makes me damn sick,' added Boysi.

'We can't succeed in every venture,' put in Dan Montsho. 'It's unhealthy.'

The truth of that kept everyone silent for a moment or so. Then Digoro, perched on top of the paper-work on the radiogram, said: 'I beat up that sonofabitch Matthews. I found him hanging around Pillay's shop in Diagonal Street. Something told me to check some disc at Pillay's and there was this bum. Browsing around you know. I said to him: "Brother, I have business with you. Can we go outside to talk?" He wanted to be funny. I gave him a clout across the face and he must have seen stars. He was guarding his face when I held onto his belt and pulled him outside. He bellowed like a bull, he was crying for mercy.'

'The sell-out!' chipped in Roy.

'I blasted him good and solid. I don't remember how I did it but I think it was a right to the jaw: he dropped like a pumpkin and doubled up on the ground. I showed him no mercy. Some charas — Indians tried to plead on his behalf and I told them to keep out of it: it was a freedom fight, I said. Someone blew a police whistle. I cleared off satisfied I'd taught the dog some mother Africa truth.'

'Masquerading pimp!' declared Roy. 'He'll stop using our name in vain. Imagine him collecting money from the people in our name!'

'He must be an informer,' said Bongi.

Boysi and Sello found themselves looking at each other. The word informer was like sell-out. Emotive. Repulsive.

By this time there was general activity in the house. Food was served. Snoek asked Digoro to shift from the radiogram and it began to blow sounds around the room. The waves drifted into the other rooms as well. This made some heads to bop and feet to tap. The centuries-old cry moved young bodies to swing to the compulsive rhythm of a Caribbean band.

Soweto went to sleep. Night-time brought about a certain consciousness among the people — fear, a tight grip on one's guts. For there was no doubt about the uncertainty hovering over the lives of people. Fear was like a mist settling on each house-top and drifting into the hearts of people. But there were those who just didn't care about the cops. They laughed, they sang and they drank the hard stuff as if unaware of the game played by cops and kids — hide and seek. One adult joined the kids to play the game — only he was tired, having exhausted his energy.

Uncle Ribs stood towering over a heap of papers in the kitchen. For hours on end he rummaged through drawers and book-cases sorting out documents likely to cause trouble if the cops laid their hands on them. The heap would soon turn to a bonfire in the backyard. There was a sense of urgency as Uncle Ribs moved round the house. Now and then he would fling out his arm to look at the watch on his wrist.

He stood contemplating the moment. Not much time left, he told himself. Sis Joyce lay awake in the bedroom. Although it was past midnight she couldn't get to sleep. She did cry. She did sniffle. Now she lay quietly on the double bed she had shared with her husband these many years. She couldn't accept that she would tumble over and over it without bumping into him any more. This she couldn't take — the life of a widow while her husband was still alive. Thixo! she exclaimed, and she stared at the ceiling as if God would be somewhere up there. But He was not, so her mind replayed the scene earlier in the evening: she had arrived home to be told by her husband that he must quit the country. No mincing of words, no apologies offered. His mind was made up. He must quit. The alternative was too ghastly to contemplate. These chaps were desperate. They were groping. They were grappling with a situation beyond their direst forebodings. For no-one had ever thought the country would be in the grip of a children's revolution. But it had happened. No doubt about it. The events of the past few days were evidence of a mood sweeping through the vast locality in a fearsome way. And let no-one make a mistake about the meaning of it: a revolution was at hand. There was only one way for the whiteman to stem the tide of it. He had to be ruthless. If it meant he must kill he would do so first and explain afterwards. She tried to coax him out of quitting. He was determined in his decision. Nothing short of going would satisfy him. That was how she received the shock of her life. She answered with tears for she was saddened and bitter. Then she stopped crying because she noticed what it was doing to him. For he was hurt. He was having his feelings twisted in a tight knot by this hurt. Only once before had he been hurt as he was this evening: when they lost the only child she had carried in her womb. That was some twelve years earlier. And she was advised then to give up child-bearing. Her man had wilted like an autumn leaf and for days his mind was a rudderless raft.

Uncle Ribs joined his wife in the bedroom to look for more incriminating material for destruction. For a very brief moment their eyes met. But he contrived to avert his eyes from hers. He understood what she must be thinking and what she must be saying to herself about him. He turned to face her but his eyes looked beyond hers. He said: 'For years a slogan kept echoing on my lips: 'Freedom in my lifetime'. It was a mere slogan until the children called the bluff of the whiteman. Meeting Mandla and Mzi has been a tremendous experience. I can see the words turn to fact. I can feel it in the pulse of my body, the day is within sight. I escape to see the dawn of that day. I want to celebrate with drums and stamping feet and hands clapping that great day. Oh I know you can't believe me ol' girl, but the day is coming. A little more push, just a little more action from all of us, and this huge boulder that's been blocking our path, this lid made of lead that's been sealing our pent-up feelings, shall be heaved away. And we shall celebrate as I say. These boys have shown me the way. The message is clear: all the time we have needed more than catchy slogans at the end of conference resolutions. The voice must mingle with the flames of burning timber and the fumes of petrol. MaRadebe, take heart, we shall stand together on that great day.'

Sis Joyce stared at her husband. She desperately wanted to free him from the chains of her heart. She saw then what she had suspected as soon as she set eyes on him arriving from work: he had aged in that one day; the furrowed brow carried a heavy load in those folds; the wrinkles on his face had multiplied. It couldn't be a false alarm, this raid that he claimed would take place in the early hours of the next day. He believed it with his whole heart. She must sympathise. She must be understanding. He stood leaning on the bed while she recalled his earlier utterances: I hate to go . . . I don't want to be a martyr . . . I am dedicated to the cause of justice . . . we will meet again. She tried to picture Mrs September. No luck. Mrs Xinga she knew very well. They were in touch with her as neighbours. And it was not surprising she had brought the heavy news. There was no doubt about the precautions taken by Sergeant Ndlovu whom she didn't know. But she remained sceptical of him. Just as well her husband planned to go away after ascertaining the source of the warning.

The hour of parting was creeping nearer and nearer. No words were said between the couple. Each sensed the thoughts of the other. Uncle Ribs engaged in eliminating all evidence which might expose his wife to gruesome action by the cops. For the mind of these chaps worked in simplistic fashion. One had to know things one didn't know. The alternatives were cruel. No-one wanted to rot in jail. It was for this reason Mzi was moved to MaNhlapo's house. His mission was incomplete and the hospitality of MaNhlapo was likely to keep him out of jail long enough for him to do his work. Sis Joyce learnt of the arrangement on her return. The absence of Mzi was like a hole blasted on the side of her body: it made her feel hollow, incomplete. But she could accept the absence. Not so that of her husband. He re-entered the bedroom to find her propped up on one elbow as she asked: 'Are you aware we may never see each other again?'

He sat slouched on the edge of the bed and began to rub his hands. He was looking for appropriate words. And the silly pieces escaped his mind at the very instant he needed them so badly. He searched the interior of his mind and could only experience emptiness as he did so. But the words, the right words at that crucial moment remained foreign to his tongue. Sis Joyce waited. She had lost the energy to push him, so she waited. He cleared his throat and said: 'I can never pay back what I have taken from you. I beg you to understand, no, to accept that at no time did I act in bad faith. I know how you feel. I know how I feel. I am having to wrench myself not only from you but from the fatherland. Nothing is harder. I go away with my mind blurred. I am in a mental spin, but I do know that the love I bear for you comes from a source that is bottomless. I love you girl. I shall always love you. I shall always seek to find you in the wilderness to which I go. In my dreams and in the tomorrow I want to build. And I believe, I believe it with my whole being, that we shall yet meet again. I can't see myself going forever. I can't see us parting forever. We must meet. Even if it means we must starve together, we shall meet.'

Uncle Ribs stood up and said, looking at his wrist-watch: 'It is time.' He held out his arms and Sis Joyce flung herself into them. They held tight to the burning sensation of their two bodies, they were inflamed by fires fanned by the meaning of that brief moment. Uncle Ribs grunted. Sis Joyce whimpered. And a fear made Uncle Ribs wrench himself from the blazing fire of his wife's body.

The only light burning in the house was snuffed. Uncle Ribs tip-toed to the kitchen door and was out.

It was a little after 2 a.m. when Uncle Ribs hugged the shadows of his house. Each step he took was calculated by a fear lurking in the meaning of the dark hour: someone waiting there to pounce on him, someone spotting him by sheer coincidence. But his nerves were shattered by an unexpected noise: the mewing of two cats in the middle of the night. The noise tore right into the centre-line of his being, jarring his ears and releasing the pent-up feelings of the moment. Such was the secrecy of his parting from his home.

The opening of the gate to his house, and its shutting; the crossing of the street to walk the tight-rope to the house opposite his, and the entering of the yard, made him sweat in the chilly, almost damp winter night. The stretch across the street was like an interminable mile. Cutting the air from home to the neighbour's sanctuary was enough to make Uncle Ribs age in an instant. It was the heaviness of his heart and the meaning of it all which battered his soul with each step he took away from home. Yet the weals of time torn into his flesh over the years tightened his courage. He was able to reach his goal without breaking down.

Daniel Modise was a much younger man than Uncle Ribs. He considered himself uneducated. He had come to venerate those who had the good fortune to have access to the written word. He worked as a garage attendant and was outwardly content in his position. Yet he was not blind to the meaning of his station in life and the efforts of others to improve that station. One of the people he admired to the point of hero-worship was Uncle Ribs. For there was something about the man which stamped him as a leader among men. As neighbours the two families exchanged more than the pleasantries of the morning and evening. They shared the cost of living as only the location people knew how. A packet or two of matches, a spoonful of tea-leaves and the loan of the daily newspaper, these marked the affinity binding the two homes. It was thus no effort for Uncle Ribs to arrange that Modise's house be the sanctuary he needed for a short spell on this night.

Uncle Ribs tapped lightly on the back door and eased his dislocated frame into the darkness of his neighbour's house. His resting-place was prepared for him in the bedroom facing the street. He would wait there for the descent of the men of law onto the quietness of his own house.

Waiting was a severe strain for both man and wife. Uncle Ribs knew what waiting for eternity was like. All his life he had had to wait: at the bus stop; at the station; at offices of law; in shopping queues in the city; at the doctor's surgery; the lawyer's office. God damn where was it he could say he didn't have to wait, because even at the graveyard he was expected to wait his turn before he conducted the service to bury a loved one. So he waited with eyes wide open. And this waiting was strenuous because it was in the dark. His mind crossed the border into Botswana several times and was tired of that trip. But he refused to let his thoughts settle on Sis Joyce. The pain of it went deeper than anything he knew. So he waited, telling himself again and again he wouldn't worry, Mzi and Mandla would make his own sacrifice worthwhile. He waited.

Across the street Sis Joyce tossed and turned for a long time before her body collapsed under the weight of fatigue. By then her mind was muddled up, she didn't know whether she was thinking or worrying. She experienced a different strain: sleep came as spasms of pain. She was nagged by a nightmare. The setting was a hospital where she was a patient. Her legs were tied to the bed with chains. Now and then she tugged at them to free herself of this bondage. She would begin quietly, her tension registered around her mouth. Pull. Pull. Pull. As she did so the iron screamed with her frustration and the noise rose in intensity with her futile effort. And then she would cry out and as the clamped feelings burst out she would open her eyes with relief. She was no sooner awake than she would sink into a fitful sleep once more. As if by design she would pick up the threads of the nightmare again, and in her sleep experience the curling of her body. Then the aggressive will to be free. And again she would be seized by the nightmare.

The cops arrived in a string of cars — nine in all. Sis Joyce lay fighting for her freedom in sleep. She wouldn't know of the siege on her house until there was a persistent banging on the front door. She awoke to hear the echo of a noise in a hollowness. Her body felt beaten up and much as she thought she was doing her best to hurry up she dragged. The darkness in the room was relieved by the blazing torchlight streaming in through the window. She flung off the blankets, swung her feet on to the floor and began to fumble for her dressing-gown. Even as she took the first step out of the bedroom, her heart hung at her knees. Her whole body was deadened by the fear of meeting the cops at that hour. And she didn't know the time although she guessed it. Far away a cock crowed. Far away a bus rumbled. The earth never went to sleep, she thought.

Major Hall failed to be cheerful. 'Er-er-excuse me,' he stammered, 'I'm Major Hall from Se-se-security. I want to speak to-to your husband. Can I come in?' He walked in followed by a number of his men. And like a fist unfolding the men spread themselves into the three other rooms of the house. Sis Joyce couldn't remember what she said or did to allow the cops to take over the house. But quickly she understood where their power lay, not in the piece of paper the Major was folding over before presenting it to her, but in the cold steel of the rifles in their hands. She eyed them with contempt. In her heart she called them dogs. She felt a certain sense of impotence as they began to rip the house apart.

Batata stood at the door leading into the bedroom and said to the Major who was still standing with Sis Joyce in the sitting room: 'He's not here.' Another cop from the other bedroom stood at the kitchen door and said: 'He's not here.'

Major Hall's face hardened. He asked with an edgy voice: 'Where's your husband?'

'I don't know,' said Sis Joyce stiffly.

'Look man, we are members of the police and you must tell us the tru-truth.' Sis Joyce knew all that, and the noise of busy-bees in the other rooms confirmed it all. She elected to stare at the officer. She was aware he didn't like her stance but she didn't like his presence in the house either. 'Are you going to-to an-answer?' he inquired.

'I keep my own house-key. Last night I used it because the house was locked when I arrived from work.'

'Does he have another woman?' said the officer jokingly. He had to swallow in the process.

Sis Joyce felt a revulsion well up in her system. A compulsion to spit at the officer seized her. In her effort to hold tight onto herself she clamped her lips as well. She was conscious only of the hate in her and the silly tittering of some of the men with the officer.

Out of the small bedroom came Batata. He stood a few paces away from the officer and said: 'Captain, let us take her in. She'll never tell the truth in this house.' Sis Joyce turned her brown, soft eyes on Batata. There was nothing tender in them. Her look at Batata was hard, contemptuous.

'L-look, man, I must warn you, I-I have the necessary powers to lock you up un-until you tell us the truth.'

She continued to ignore the officer. With the hate in her still burning around her eyes, she turned her head to take a look at what the law was doing to her house. On one easy chair perched a cop. He was reading a book pulled down from the small book-case in the room. He wasn't really reading. He flipped through the pages like a child serving his curiosity through a picture book. The pile of books on the floor was rising. The cop didn't seem to have the energy or inclination to return books to where he had found them. Sis Joyce wished to warn the man that she wouldn't have the time to pack the books into the shelves. Her time was already limited in the mornings. But silence was her defence under the siege. So she held to the tightness of her lips.

Another cop came out of the senior bedroom and announced: 'There's nothing in the wardrobe, nothing under the bed, Sir.' That was the cue for Batata to shove off. He disappeared into the kitchen mumbling something inaudible. The cop who had come in with the report turned to face Sis Joyce: 'Where do you people keep the bombs and hand-grenades?'

She didn't answer him but she did sigh. She heaved her breast and took a step toward her bedroom. It was a reckless move. She had ceased to care, for they had nibbled at her heart with little, annoying suggestions.

Major Hall commanded: 'Stand where you are! I-I didn't give you permission to move.'

'I didn't know I needed your permission,' she replied with derision.

'Don't be funny, l-lady,' said the angry officer. 'Y-you'll force me to take se-serious action against you. My men haven't got time to waste.' He paused briefly, then: 'I want satisfactory answers to-to my q-questions, understand? Has your husband slept out before?'

'No!'

'Was he always alone?'

'I don't know.'

'Come on, do you stay just the two of you here?'

'Yes!'

'Any visitors lately?'

Visitors? She had to unhook a curtain in her mind to get to the answer for that one. The safety of her husband and herself was paramount. She shut her mind completely to the existence of Mzi.

'You heard me!' growled the officer.

'No!'

Hall was no fool. It was as if he read the conflict in her mind. He insisted: 'Speak the truth: have you been only two in this house?'

Sis Joyce hid her embarrassment. She looked away from the officer. And remained silent.

'Are you deaf?' demanded Hall.

First she looked at him with eyes appealing for help, then she shook her head. The officer missed the tight grip on her lip. Her mouth was almost twisted because of the tension around it. But she got a fright when he bellowed: 'For Chrissake answer me, have you had no visitor lately?' She shook her head and then her lips burst open to say quietly: 'No!' She braced herself for the worst. She imagined being locked up in jail; she saw them beat her up; heard the screams of the interrogating officer. She was helpless but she was determined not to crack. She would remain protective to the man waiting in the opposite house. She imagined him watching his house in agony. For he was in love with her. She wished the cops would go. But they did not give her a hint of it. The Major looked very much alive, very much alert at that hour of the morning. She didn't know the time but the cocks had crowed so many times she had lost count somewhere along the line. And the movement of vehicles far off seemed to have increased considerably. But that didn't give time: it merely suggested hope. She was comforted by a thought without foundation: that the cops would drive out of the location before many people began to spill out of their homes.

Major Hall tried a bluff. He was quite serious as he said: 'My information is that you-you are keeping young students in the house.' He waited for her reply. She kept silent.

'Is it true?'

'I don't know.'

'How do you mean?'

'I don't know the students. Where are they?'

'That's it,' exclaimed Hall, 'we came to find out.'

She didn't believe him. So she kept mum. She was now fully aware of the pumping of her heart. It seemed propelled by the fear twisting her mind. But the grip of the cops on her remained unyielding. She would have taken courage if she had known of the frustration experienced by Hall. He could only stare at her as if working out whether she was dumb or full of guile.

Across the street Uncle Ribs began to worry. He stood near the window at the very instant the first car cruised up to a standstill in front of his gate. He saw the doors flung open as the cars vomited men eager for action, always. Two cops, heavily armed, ran to the back of the house; two took positions at the two front ends of the house and four stood sentinel at the gate. The whole lot of them were armed. He saw Major Hall, tall and lean, trotting ahead of his men. He was wearing a windbreaker and had one hand squeezed into its side pocket. He was followed by eight men including Batata and Sergeant Ndlovu. Two of them carried R1 rifles at the ready. While one policeman knocked at the front door, another played his torch-light on the windows. Uncle Ribs was disgusted by this act of comedy. He longed for his pipe because all evening he had not used it. He didn't want to leave behind in the house the smell of a man. He watched the cops rock the house in a desperate move to enter. Joyce is a heavy sleeper, he told himself. Then they trooped in like sheep, bumping into each other at the small location door. Minutes ticked by as he waited anxiously. He trusted his wife, believing in her solid make-up. Yet there was always a possibility of her being bludgeoned into submission. Courage, he told himself. So he waited, panting the despair of a man who saw himself broken up by a force whose mindless might he felt impotent to withstand. His house was under siege. And he was well aware what it meant at that very moment: harassment of his wife; wrecking of the peace and order in the silence, and curses on the location people as a whole. Something made him feel sore. It was a throbbing pain which swelled and ebbed as moments ticked by. He wondered how Joyce took it when the presence of the police caused so much hurt in himself, outside their presence. His sense of guilt intensified. He toyed with the idea of giving himself up. Waiting and worrying was like the searing of a pain across his whole being. He didn't realise when it was he first saw the crack of dawn. But when he did, hope flushed through him. It was as if the easing of darkness was the lifting of a burden from his shoulders. The greyness of dawn held relief for him. And then he heard the creaking of a door somewhere in another part of the house. Daniel Modise came to join him. As he took up his position he asked: 'Are the dogs there?' Uncle Ribs replied curtly: 'Ya!' And there was a silence once more in the house. For men knew the meaning of these raids; they deplored their own impotence in the face of them and they cursed the day the last impi was routed by whitey. Each felt the flame kindled in each heart by these raids. Each vowed that the humiliation would one day be paid back in kind. So the two kept vigil together in a brooding silence.

It was a long waiting. Modise wrenched himself from the window saying he had to prepare for work. His movements in the kitchen jarred on the ears of Uncle Ribs. He wished for the silence there had been earlier, as if he could hear the words hurled at his wife across the street. But it was useless for him to worry about the noise, he told himself. For Daniel Modise was in his house doing those things he had to do. It occurred to him that his annoyance with the noise was part of the bigger sacrifice. He would have to accept that a new life was opening before him and the shutting out of the past would not be an easy thing. So he waited, feeling his body tense increasingly as time marched on.

Presently Modise brought him a cup of coffee. The first sip roused his sensibility. He realised then that he had wanted this cup of coffee for a long time. The taste and the relief he gained rushed to his body, and the mind seemed to be rested from worrying. He thanked Modise again and again. Modise joked: 'The police must be drinking coffee in your house!' Uncle Ribs replied: 'They are such terrorists they could easily be helping themselves. MaRadebe will never give a cop coffee in my house!' A pause followed during which the air in the room was clapped by Modise's tongue as he sipped his own coffee. He asked: 'Why do cops come all the way from town in nine cars when there's only one man to arrest?'

'Cowardice!' spat out Uncle Ribs. 'They are cowards, they are bullies.' Then he added: 'They are thugs. You know thugs operate in a gang. Never singly. That's how cops work. They are thugs,' he concluded with bitterness.

Modise sauntered away, still sipping coffee. Again he muttered a few words about getting late for work. To make it, he would have had to leave home at 4.30 a.m., catch a bus at 5 o'clock.

Uncle Ribs remained to torment the moment. He wondered if the police believed the story he and Joyce had worked out together. He worried for her peace of mind. She would be concerned for her job, because these chaps were known to be that ruthless. They might take it out on her if they didn't find him, and cause her to lose face with the hospital authorities. This was how a system became the system. The location people had worked out the equation successfully, he concluded.

Across the street the lights continued to burn. There was one comfort for Sis Joyce. She knew the curiosity of her neighbours was an insurance against the worst. The police might do with her what they wished, but there would always be witnesses besides her man. The people would say they saw the siege on the house by the police, and therefore the law shared guilt with the people who stood by if

96

anything went wrong with her.

Major Hall summoned Batata to his side and said: 'Tell the woman in your own language how grave the matter is. We have nothing against her. B-but if she's pla-playing tri-tricks with me I will not hesitate to take action against her. I want to speak to her husband, I don't want to arrest him. It is a routine matter for the se-security of the State.'

Batata was about to translate these thoughts when he saw the fury of Sis Joyce. She actually turned her face away from him at the very moment when he cleared his throat, raised her hands to her hips and made a hissing sound. Batata understood her behaviour to be contemptuous. He would have taught the woman some African customs but he was made helpless by the correct manner in which the Major treated this educated woman. He clicked his tongue and stared at the back of her shoulders. He said to the Major: 'She's cheeky. Why don't we lock her up?' With that he moved away from the proceedings, telling himself he would yet get even with her.

Just then a cop came up to Hall holding out some document. 'I found this in one of the drawers of the dressing-table.'

'M'm,' said Hall, 'th-the Free-freedom Charter. So your husband was still a Commie,' he said with satisfaction. 'Tell him we want to see him at Westend Police Headquarters noon today. Otherwise we will be back for him.'

The law trooped out like ants. They bumped into each other behind the Major in their eagerness to escape the cramped atmosphere of the location house. In that instant when he waited for his door to be opened, Hall picked up a number of houses from which neighbours were watching the happening at the house of Uncle Ribs. He told himself with relief that the location people were children. Their curiosity was that of the simple-minded. And to register his defiance of them, he banged the door of the car so hard the noise reverberated up and down the length of the street.

It would not be long before Soweto sang the comedy of the house of Uncle Ribs. The people jeered when they heard he had watched the law from opposite his house. They sang what fools, what waste and what utter rubbish that the security of the state should make so many men circus clowns.

Dawn bathed the morning grey as Uncle Ribs walked briskly back to his house. He waited only long enough to be certain that they had left the location. His heart was pounding madly in his anxiety to see how Sis Joyce had taken it.

She sat in one of the easy chairs, legs crossed, and watched him come up to her. Her spirits were low but her strength remained. She was able to stand up and allow him to enfold her in his arms. He mumbled: 'Well done, well done, girl.' He was silenced by her kisses and although his manhood was roused, he knew it was a brief encounter with her.

He wrenched himself from the warmth of her blazing body and darted into the bedroom. He packed a brief-case, taking only the absolute minimum of clothing: a vest, underpants and a shirt. Again he embraced his wife and clung to her smooth flesh, smothering her with wet, burning kisses. He had to suppress all his feelings for the moment, refusing to think of another time like that one. He refused to accept that it would be a long, long time, if ever, before a repeat of that crushing experience might happen again.

Then he took the first step to the outside kitchen door. It was with a myriad regrets that he did. His body began to crumble, his spirits tumbled to his knees. It was an effort to open the door and that light clicking of the locking device touched the very core of his heart. Then his mind was blinded by the hugeness of the morning. He did not see the early workers rushing past his house. He was not aware of his own darting in the street. Like mist he was lost in the rising pink sun.

## 5

NEWS ITEM
BLAST HITS RAILWAY SECTION IN SOWETO. THOUSANDS OF
COMMUTERS DELAYED FOR WORK. NO COMMENT SAYS
POLICE SPOKESMAN

Mzi sat at the bottom end of the bed. The butt of the AK47 machine gun rested on his left thigh. In his right hand was a piece of cloth with which he wiped the rifle. There was a satisfied look on his face. Now and then he would stop the movement of the hand to admire his handiwork.

It was late in the morning and his mind kept drifting to Uncle Ribs and his escape. In the quietness of the house thinking easily turned to worrying. It must have been hard for a man as old as Uncle Ribs to break with his wife and country, thought Mzi. He wondered if Uncle Ribs would remain in Botswana or go to Tanzania. Very likely the latter place was a more useful choice. There was a lot to be done in and out of the country because sacrifice had many faces. When he thought of Sis Joyce a mixture of pain and happiness washed inside of him. He hugged the rifle to his body and felt the coldness of steel on his cheek. She was the kind of African woman to be proud of, he told himself.

The next twelve hours were critical. And it would not be until the next day that the news from Botswana would filter through. Thanks to the telephone. Mzi waited. Then he turned to look at himself in the mirror of the dressing table. He liked what he saw reflected. In particular he liked the military styled cap on his head. He let it perch stylishly at an angle. God made him handsome and it wasn't for nothing. He would get out of the house and do in that black bastard Batata and the sun would shine brightly on his lovable face. It was Batata who restrained his life; he made it impossible for him to mix freely and enjoy the company of other people especially the women folk. He must carry out the mission soon, he must. Batata was elusive. Twice he and Mandla went hunting for him and they had failed to nail him. Yet, thought Mzi, he would get him. A moving target gets hit sooner or later, he reflected. Why, there was that one chance after the blast on the Jabavu Police Station. Batata showed a suicidal carelessness. He stood guard over his house against orders from his seniors. And any marksman could have picked him easily from across the street in the shaded churchyard. Mzi was on that occasion alone and in the heat of police activity the rifle was left in the room.

He stood up and began to walk round the room like a caged animal. Suddenly he doubled up, took aim at the door of the bedroom, his body tense and his facial expression clouded by a simulated hate. He relaxed, satisfied with his reflexes. His training in the bush retained its professionalism. He was quite happy with himself. The four walls did not bother him anymore. They were at that moment a welcome sanctuary. He waited, expecting Mandla to drop in anytime. He packed the machine-gun away. As he scrambled up from underneath the bed, he heard a knock on the kitchen door.

He stood still, made anxious only by the jarring noise known by a man waiting for the worst fears in his life to materialise. It happened for a brief moment but long enough for him to ascertain that Ma-Nhlapo wasn't talking to Mandla, but to someone else. He caught snatches of what was said. The male visitor commented on the damage done to the railway line. Times have changed, MaNhlapo seemed to say. Tsotsis were no longer killing their own kind as in the past; police have taken over terrorising residents; there was a madness in the location which made young ones challenge the law; they died at the hands of police so they might as well die blasting railway tracks . . . The visitor said Malan started the whole thing. Now he was dead and the country was reaping the whirlwind. Pity he missed the children's revolution, said the visitor. 'Umthetho ka Malan unzima — Malan's laws bring hardship,' added MaNhlapo . . .

The two fell into a silence. Mzi was anxious for the man to leave. He heard the door open again and the visitor said: 'I am on my way to Morning Sweetheart.' 'I thought everyone was keeping away from the bottle?' queried MaNhlapo. The visitor replied: 'We are fighting the battle in many ways.' He left. Mzi sighed with relief.

The winter sun filtered through the sitting room window, warming the ash-block walls. Mzi began to fret waiting as he was for Mandla. He found the confinement of the bedroom unbearable. Every so often he would saunter into the sitting room, perch on a chair for a while and then return to his room. Somehow he didn't like such enforced inactivity. The bush life was far more exciting: one learnt a lot out there. The experience was staggering. It changed his life, changed his personality and made him an eternal optimist. Whitey must be shown all the time he lived on false assumptions, time was running out for him. But what he, Mzi, hated about his life these days was its dependence on other people. For one thing he needed a car badly. Mobility was an important part of the mission. Yet there was nothing he could do because he had no car. There was the one Uncle Ribs left behind. But it would be a moving tomb for him. The law would pick him up sooner than later. He blotted it out of his mind as quickly as the thought occurred to him.

Mandla stopped outside the yard in the mini-car. He hurried into the house. The programme for the day was altered slightly. A meeting with Ann Hope at Pharmacy House was arranged. Mzi offered to drive saying he needed practice just in case it became necessary at some stage. Both hurried out of the house.

The thrill behind the wheel shut out the thought of everything else. Mzi said the car did well for itself. On the open Soweto Highway he let his foot rest on the accelerator as hard as it could take it.

The meeting with Ann was short and the two young men returned to Soweto using the same road. That Uncle Ribs was safely landed in Botswana made the trip back light. They were approaching Diepkloof location when it happened: a car picked up their trail. It didn't take long for Mzi to sense that on their tail was a police car. He let go. But it seemed futile. The bigger car closed in on them and tried to force them off the road. He fooled the cops by slowing down but changed his mind at the very moment when a string of cars appeared from Soweto. That brief moment was enough to dodge into the hurly burly of heavy traffic and make for Diepkloof. One sharp turn to the left, another to the right was all the little car could do. The cops made good the gap but lost Mzi. He bolted into the sameness of the location houses with lightning speed, vanishing in one of the yards without trace — thanks to the low wire-fences and the many people milling around the streets of Soweto. Mandla wasn't equally lucky. He sprinted over the fences with agile ease but not before a bullet hit his left arm. His will to survive was strong enough though to make him withstand the initial searing pain of the bullet tearing through his flesh. He vanished out of sight at a point unknown to the cops.

The car was seized.

Mandla found himself a hero in a stranger's house. There was a young girl who whispered his name to her mother. He was given first-aid treatment and allowed to cool off his feet. He stayed for a short while saying he was worried about the whereabouts of a friend with whom he was in the chase. He left.

Presently he reached the surgery of Dr Kenotsi. The medico said: 'You must leave the country. These bastards will kill you.'

Mandla replied he couldn't leave. 'I am part of the struggle,' he said boyishly. 'There's a cop with whom I must settle a score.'

'You mean Batata?' suggested the medico.

'We are going to eliminate the dog,' said Mandla with bitterness.

The bullet wound was superficial according to the doctor. But he repeated his advice: 'Go before we bury you!'

Everyone fussed about Mandla at Sis Ida's place. While his colleagues wanted to know what happened, he was anxious for Mzi's safety and whereabouts. But no one knew Mzi's face, never mind his whereabouts. It was something he would have to attend to as soon as he had rested well enough. Besides, a manhunt for him was likely to be reinforced, resulting in another siege on Soweto. He relaxed to satisfy the curiosity of the group. Later he began: 'It is a miracle I am here. Someone gave Mzi and I away. I'm sure of it!'

'Sell-out,' cried Digoro.

'Sell-out,' echoed Keke. 'I've been saying it.'

'Bajita, the thing is serious,' continued Mandla. 'I don't know how I made it. I just sprinted wildly. I don't know how . . . there was a time I nearly gave up, my arm was heavy, the blood flowing freely and the arm looked as if dipped in a trough of blood. Gots! I told myself: don't let the dogs catch you. Whew! it was a near-miss . . . but how did the cops know our car?'

'Sell-out,' repeated Digoro.

'But where's he operating?'

Roy who'd been seated quietly came up with: 'How can you be sure Mzi didn't talk to someone?'

Mandla seemed to give that one a thought. He replied authoritatively: 'Not possible! Mzi talks to no one but MaNhlapo.' Because no one among them knew this MaNhlapo, the group eyed one another as if to ask the who and whereabouts of MaNhlapo.

'MaNhlapo could have spoken to someone,' suggested Roy.

'An old lady? You want to tell me the old lady could have walked to the fence and proclaimed across it the fact that her visitor was driving to town in a mini-car? Ag, Roy, be your age, fana — boy!'

'I don't know her,' asserted Roy.

'There's a sell-out in the group,' chipped in Keke confidently.

'Don't be so sure Keke,' said Mandla. 'One swallow doesn't make a summer, remember.'

'I know I'm right.' He was thinking of his brooding fear expressed days earlier. He felt the triumph of one vindicated by the passage of time. He continued: 'I knew it wouldn't be long before an informer grew amongst us. He was planted by the system long ago.'

'Sell-out,' snorted Digoro.

'Sell-out,' cried Bongi.

'How can we be sure?' insisted Mandla. He was playing a seeker's game.

'We suspect it,' put in Dan Montsho. 'We suspect it because cops don't park under trees for fun. They do so in ambush. They act on information supplied. It is quite clear someone fed them the info on that mini. Given our way of survival, it is clear to me, the info could have come from either this group or from Mzi. You cancel Mzi. That means the group is suspect. One of us is.'

'I told you!' said Keke as if confirming the second coming. 'We are finished!'

'Prophet of doom!' sneered Sello.

'Oho!' declared Keke in resignation.

'I still think the trouble is around Mzi,' said Roy. 'We know nothing about the guy. We know nothing about MaNhlapo. Those two are a scene unknown to us. Why cast suspicion on the group? We've done our thing all along without any splits. Enter Mzi and what happens?'

Mandla was hit by a sense of crisis. His allegiance to both the group and Mzi tore his young heart apart. For a while he remained silent as did the whole house. He brooded over the next move

102

knowing well the meaning of it. He dare not alienate the group nor could he cast suspicion on Mzi. He eyed several members of the group as if he expected them to come to his rescue. He concluded: Roy is impervious. But he couldn't blame him for being so. Mzi was supposed to be working in conjunction with the group but was never introduced to them in the flesh. He remained a factor. After the sacrifice of June 16th there shouldn't have been any secrets to the group. Yet Mzi's hand was bound in Tanzania. Instructions were that he should keep out of sight at all costs. And to him this meant the group as well. He remained distrustful of the group, fearing all sorts of things. Above all, he considered the group amateurs. He didn't say this loudly but it was his underlying thought. It influenced his interpretation of the instructions from Dar.

Mandla didn't like what he saw: most members bowed down their heads as in prayer. It wasn't a reassuring sign. And with the room plunged in silence, it was an unsettling sight. He decided to move in at a tangent. He said: 'I don't care what happens to me. I will carry on as if unaware there lurks a Judas somewhere thriving on thirty pieces of silver. I don't care a damn. I know my target for the moment: Bantu cop Batata. That one must be eliminated! The informer can warn him. He can tell it to Westend, it means fuckall to me: Batata must go! It is now a question of when not how. The army cannot help him. Too much of our blood has spilled in the streets of Soweto for the man to walk this earth. He must go! I promise everyone including the informer. I am sure, dead sure, it will happen.'

One by one the heads were raised. By the time Mandla finished his say all eyes were riveted on him. That round he won. Members waited for his next move wondering what he could achieve with one arm in a sling.


# 6

For days Soweto hovered between hope and despair, death and life. The people sighed with relief that Mandla had escaped whitey's bullet. The gods were thanked.

But Batata thought otherwise. He was determined to rid the world of Mandla. He said it to whomever was listening that if he died a minute after killing Mandla he would be satisfied with the fate awaiting him in hell. Ever since he survived the blast at the Jabavu Police Station he had vowed by all the gods at his disposal to do just this.

He invoked the name of his grandfather; of his mother; of his uncle and Jehova. Now he went back to the name of his father's grandfather. That's how far he was on the evening he stood in the shadow of a tall gum tree near Club Siyagiya, waiting.

He thrust his wrist violently outward to check the time: 9.30 p.m. Anger burnt in his guts unsteadying his feet. He could do nothing more than roll up and down where he stood. From where he was scanning the night now and then, he could barely see the entrance of the vibrating young people's night-spot. He was working on a tip-off from Noah Witbaatjie: Mandla and Co. were said to be frequent patrons of the joint. He stood waiting for a youth he pictured as tall and somewhat thin. It was hard to go by what he would be wearing. Reports said Mandla was fond of a black beret and a green scarf. His friend was distinguished by his handsome face and a khaki military-styled cap. For Batata the moving devil was Mandla. Had he known a little more of his companion, no doubt a dozen cars and kwela kwela's would have descended on the club.

The next time he swung his arm to check the hour, his pulse hurried. It was after 10 o'clock. His spirits glowed with a sense of anticipation. If it wasn't Mandla's, he could crack someone else's ribs in there. He loathed all Soweto youth. He recalled the night of the first attack on his house. His wife was pale with fear. She was so scared she shrank away from him refusing that he touch her. It was the first time it happened in thirty years of married life. When he asked: 'How do you feel Mamurena?' she remained ballooned by anger. He found the splinters of the petrol bomb. They crackled underneath his foot sending a jarring sensation through his body. That was when he gibbered something about the gods. And that was when he felt so full in his chest he almost cried.

Next day he went beserk. Tore down his street in a blaze of blinding anger and bitterness. He went up and down the street where the Nkosi family lived and terrorised all living beings; shot down every moving dog, cat and chicken. For one whole hour the street was under siege. Even his colleagues quartered around the Nkosi family found themselves barricaded behind shut doors. It was a hair-raising experience for Soweto. No one dared move in the street for fear of a belligerent S.B. agent, they said. Later on no one could recall an incident so frightful. All Soweto said Batata was mad. People laughed because he was maddened by a boy, an unarmed boy almost a quarter of his age.

11.30 p.m. Batata could wait no longer. He told himself the bastard slipped in through a side door. Hero-worshipped as he was by everyone, anything was possible: the club owner or his agents might be in collusion in a conspiracy against the law. They smuggled him in somehow, he told himself. In that case he would go right in and rip the place apart. They'll know me, he cursed into the chill of the night.

The law rested on his massive shoulders. He flexed them as he prepared to raid the place. He didn't know himself, didn't feel the nip in the air as he rushed the door. His huge frame became the door; eyes slits straining out a fiery hatred, his brow furrowed intensely by this hate; his big mouth hung out loosely, his broad nose heaved fiercely. The beast in him came out in grunts as he took in all the patrons. Gradually word went round in whispers and gestures that a freak cop stood at the door, gun in hand. A deathly silence transformed the gay spirits of the club. By this time he was ready to play out the buffoon caricature. He stepped forward into the club, darted towards the bandstand, his eyes sweeping the patrons hunched over the little tables or those milling around entombed in their tracks. At the head of the huge room he stood looking down on the electric scene before him. He could not make out the individuals because the psychedelic lights reflected ghosts. But he didn't seem to know why the creatures in his eyes were so loathsome. He thought it was the hate he brought into it. No one could tell him of his own satanic appearance in that instant. Cat-like he strode down one aisle toward the bar counter. Suddenly he stopped. For he found himself towering over a youth seated alone, and hanging onto the small table. Batata signalled in the dim light for the youth to stand up. There was no response. He tried to raise the young man by the scruff of his neck. The youth threw out his hands. The touch of one on his face was enough for Batata to release the tension of the moment and of days gone by. He slapped the youth with his freed hand and brought the butt of the gun on his head with a crushing sound. Women screamed, men roared disapproval. Just then Batata let the gun shout in the air as a bullet hit the ceiling above his head. As some patrons scrambled to the exit door, he ensured his safety by clambering on a chair. He was at that time a petty thug made degenerate by an authority he felt slipping from his shoulders. From the inside pocket of his jacket he pulled out a baby brown, and with both hands toting guns he let loose bedlam at Club Siyagiya. One shot after another screamed above the patrons fleeing to the door and was embedded in the ceiling. Batata seemed to enjoy the pandemonium of his creation; he was waving his hands wildly, scattering patrons as chaff before a wind, as he yelled unprintable insults at them. The moment belonged to him but he was not to know that the people he squeezed out of the tiny door in the kind of humiliation they knew only from whitey gave birth to a seed for the germination of a nation's hate.

A few courageous patrons remained to witness more of the bullying antics of the cop. A youth sodden with the beer he held in one hand thought the whole scene was a comedy and in true spirit he clambered up on to one of the chairs. He was raising the bottle yelling: 'Amandla — Power!' when a bullet screamed above his head. He didn't only drop off the chair, he was a heap on the floor shattering the bottle with a jarring noise.

In all the confusion no one knew the whereabouts of the club owner, Keith Shabangu. He was simply out of sight, abdicating ownership to the well known bullying cop.

As calm returned to the surroundings Batata strutted to the door. He blotted out the night with his huge body and declared to those inside: 'Tell Mandla I will always have one bullet for him. I'll get him soon. I will!' He receded into the cold night. He went away as quietly as he came leaving the club to regain its own sensibility once more.

The women jeered. The men bowed down their heads in silence, shame flapping round their ears. The women threw back the word coward at their men who were trying to say Batata was a coward.

The women wanted to know how their men could allow one man to terrorise the nation. It was the sense of this shame which weighed heavily on the menfolk.

Past midnight the lights of Club Siyagiya were still burning brightly. But the joy evaporated into the damp cold night. Somewhere in Soweto the heart of Mandla Nkosi continued to beat. He lay restfully unaware of how near death he was at that very instant.


NEWS ITEM
ANOTHER BLAST ON RAILWAY TRACK. TRAIN SERVICE
DISRUPTED FOR LONG. NO COMMENT SAYS RAILWAY
SPOKESMAN


For several days after the shooting episode Mandla lay low. He would wake up early, enquire after the previous day's activities according to assignment, give instructions for new objectives and recede as if from an impending storm. Roy assumed the role of chief executive as he drove one of the remaining cars from one errand to another.

On one morning it was Keke's turn to do the washing of his clothes. In keeping with normal practice, he woke up early and delivered his washing to his mom, Auntie Bettie. With one arm in a sling, Mandla lounged in the sitting room engrossed in a book by Frantz Fanon. Keke thought he would kill time tinkering in the kitchen. There wasn't much to do except fool around with bottles, tins and wires. One certain feature of the group was its adventurous spirit. Normally he would be carrying things, watching brains such as Mandla's, Roy's, Dan Montsho's, measuring quantities of components, mixing compounds and admiring the results of a confident and knowledgeable mind.

He set about achieving something for himself. Nitric acid, glycerine and bottles stood before him on the kitchen table. Outside the cock crowed thrice in the silence of mid-morning. It was a warm winter day and the air was dry. Mandla dozed off in the sitting room, the book on his lap. Unknown to him, Keke was still thinking about the spectre of an informer: picking him up from his feet and then the head, looking at him from the left and then the right as his hands trembled to measure quantities of the ingredients for a deadly mixture. Suddenly an explosion blasted the silence of the room beyond the four walls; the house was rocked at its foundation; the air clapped at will by an unseen thunder. There was a clinking of glass and clattering of kitchen units. Boom! Boom! Boom! rang the air shaking Mandla out of his sleep. For a moment he was stunned, terrified by the shaking of the house. And then it occurred to his befogged mind that Keke was hollering in the kitchen. There was a whirling cloud of black soot enveloping the kitchen. On the floor, pinned underneath the table and chairs was Keke. He was a ghastly sight, bleeding black blood. He lay there helpless, groaning and crying for help from his mama.

Mandla didn't ask questions, for the chemicals strewn all over the floor told their own story. There was a life to save and possibly the need to escape immediately. He was too fuddled in his mind to peel off simple thoughts: such as the pain and damage to his arm in a sling; the pride of Sis Ida destroyed in the blast and the raid by cops on the house.

The explosion was loud, so loud it summoned neighbours to the scene. They came just in time to see a steady cloud of black smoke curl out of the kitchen door and window. It rose in the still air of its own accord and was lost just above the level of the house but not before the hau's and the clapping of hands in dismay and the gibbering of excited voices. For many the explosion answered questions asked for days without number. The people wanted to know what so many children were doing at Sis Ida's. They were a mystery that ran through the house like a subterranean stream. Sis Ida gave them smiles and respect but sealed the mystery from their sight and hearing. She dared not trust anyone for she was sworn to a secrecy she shared with her charge. Even people like Two-by-Two fed their minds on conjecture as they gossiped about the Red Army. The very resourceful neighbours said they had always known Sis Ida was heading for trouble. They said a collection of children signified they belonged to Power — Amandla. The municipality would eject Sis Ida from the house if it was discovered she harboured the 'Power' children. As always, these voices were countered by others. These said there was nothing wrong in what she did. She was a mother like many other people. The children were neglected at their homes and found refuge in her house. Humanism worked that way, they said.

The blast accentuated a debate in the street for hours. Tongues wagged about the activities in that yard.

Meanwhile Mandla struggled to put Keke in the remaining car. He just managed with the help of middle-aged MaMatime, one next door neighbour of Sis Ida's. Her concern was for Keke, and the safety of Ida's house, she said as she tucked Keke's legs into the car. She looked too frightened to ask questions. But she did offer to look after the house until one of the inmates arrived. She would wait for Ida if need be. Mandla was to rush Keke to hospital, she pleaded.

To the curious observers now gathered at the fence of the house, Mandla looked as if he needed the trip to Baragwanath Hospital for himself. He struggled through the pain on his arm, his face grimacing. At that moment he wished there was one other member of the group. He thought of Mzi and the hopelessness of his own position under the circumstances. The pain in the arm was just excruciating. When he chanced to look at Keke he experienced a twitch of fear in his stomach. He couldn't bear to think of death. Yet Keke seemed to be sinking to a fearful bottomlessness. How tragic it would be to Auntie Bettie, to the group and to Sis Ida if . . . Mandla shut off his mind along that trail. He thought of Mzi: how recklessly he drove at times, as if he defied the law on purpose, as if courting the law as he did was an end in itself. For Mzi cops were bums. One needed to behave as if defiant of their presence at every street-corner of Soweto. They didn't bother him because he hated everyone employed as a law-enforcer. It helped to make Mandla drive to Dr Kenotsi's surgery in a reckless, blinding hate.

The medico was in; Mandla sighed with relief. For Keke was unconscious. The bleeding eased off but there was a pool of blood in the car. The doctor was shocked by the sight of a breathless, messed up Keke. No words were said for death lingered about the young person in the surgery. The few patients awaiting their turn to be attended by the doctor groaned an exaggeration of their own pains. They prayed in the silence of their hearts for the safety of the young man's life. Where did it happen? There were no answers. So the patients said the police must have done it. Children waged a war on behalf of their parents and the police were against the children. Again the patients prayed for the soul of Keke. They overheard mention of the name in the surgery. They spoke of the young man's parents. How they would be shocked as they returned from work to learn of this tragedy. Then one female patient said the burden carried by women was of untold magnitude. For a woman carries a child for nine months in the womb, she must suffer the pain of child-bearing and then the pain of bringing up the child under the stresses of life. The other patients joined in a chorus of deep-felt awu's.

Dr Kenotsi and his two assistants battled for the life of Keke. The medico experienced a searing pain through his heart. He was too near the student group to attend to them with a sense of detachment. Always an optimist in his job, he was encouraged to note the face was only superficially injured. No permanent damage would remain in that area. But the chest was badly burnt, so were the hands and arms. It seemed hours without end before the team emerged from the dressing room after they patched up the sorry mess which Keke was. And all the while the medico was aware death stood by.

There were several questions which bothered Kenotsi in these cases. He worried about his ethical code. In the case of Keke his concern was centred around the boy's parents. They would have to be told in time just in case the worst happened. Besides the boy would remain scarred for life if he survived and human nature being what it was, they might drag Kenotsi himself into the case as an accomplice. They would say he shared the guilt of the student group because of his silence.

Kenotsi didn't trust the reaction of Bra Baba and Auntie Bettie. Yet he couldn't reveal his fears to anyone. Later he spoke to Mandla about survival. Didn't he stand to lose a lot as an individual?

'Mfo,' began the medico, 'I want to warn you guys, things are rapidly moving towards a wall. Our backs will soon be against this wall and the fight to the finish will come sooner than we thought. You must remember the enemy is desperate.' Mandla listened with his head bowed by respect. The medico went on: 'Have you given thought to my advice?'

'I have doc,' said Mandla softly.

'And so?'

'I want to complete my mission,' said Mandla with a feeling that ran deep.

'Batata?' said the medico with a smile. Mandla nodded his head. For the name exuded a chorus of feelings known to so many people in the locations. Even Kenotsi showed the signs as his face was twisted in anguish as he said: 'But Mzi claims that's the very reason he's here. Why bother?'

It was Mandla's turn to be cynical: 'I want to make sure it happens. I'm the only person who can help Mzi see it through. There is no one else he trusts.'

'Are you aware a lot can happen before you reach your goal? These chaps are so desperate, they are working round the clock in an effort to find you. Have you thought of the danger of informers? Make no mistake, your close friend, your relative can be an informer. These arrests that are made every minute of the day have a purpose. It may look stupid that the cops take in everyone, even people not concerned — in fact so removed from politics it is ridiculous to detain them: those very innocent ones can be the danger. One of them can yield information, very often unwillingly, and that will be all the cops want to be led to your whereabouts . . .'

'I know doc. I agree with everything you say . . .'

'But you want your pound of flesh from Batata,' cut in the medico.

Mandla was agitated as he said: 'That man terrorizes my family. They are innocent. He makes me feel guilty for the mess I've put them into . . .'

'You want to undo the mess even if you get smashed in the process. . . ?'

Mandla nodded into a deep chasm of bitterness.

'Do you really believe the elimination of Batata will mean the end of the harassment of your family? You should know better.'

'I know I'm faced with a system not just an individual. The removal of a limb of the system won't lead to the destruction of the whole system. Not in a short time. I'm aware doc. But I'm satisfied that elimination will mean something. I see the man as everything diabolical about the system. He symbolises the evil that we need to destroy in the system. He is a breed of policeman we cannot allow to grow in our midst. His kind we hate because it wears whitey's shoes for him.'

'The damage is done,' said the medico resignedly. 'Just as certain things cannot be reversed in our lives so there are those things in whitey's life which we cannot wish away. He's got some of our people by the balls — sorry for the word but it's true, you know. He's got them so tightly our people just dance to his tune. It's just too late to reverse the order. What do you hope to achieve?'

'Discourage more of our people from joining the police force!'

'Never!' exclaimed the doctor. 'It won't work. Our people have come to see the force as work. For them it is like going down the mine, going to a factory, going to the classroom to teach. Why, it is like going into the army to fight their own brothers. It has its rewards.'

'Money, doc?'

'Survival, mfo. The survival of self, the survival of stooges. The police force is a way of survival . . . Have no illusions about your mission. It won't touch the system. The system relates to survival for others while it relates to oppression to some of us,' said Kenotsi shoving both hands into the pockets of his white dust-coat, leaving the stethoscope to dangle freely from his neck. They were in one of the rooms of the house which served as his surgery. All the time he spoke he was leaning on the iron door-frame. He excused himself from Mandla and slipped into the dressing room to take a look at his charge.

He came back looking very cheerful. 'Thank God he's come round,' said the medico as he reached Mandla. 'The boy has made a marvellous recovery.'

'Thanks to you doc,' said Mandla with a boyish pleasure.

Dr Kenotsi began to rub hands and said he must attend to the other patients. He and Mandla agreed that Sis Ida's place was out for Keke. The medico offered a nearby hide-out where he could keep a check on the progress Keke made. But he was nagged by the thought of telling Keke's parents.

Mandla had to return to Sis Ida's place. He was well aware of a feeling of depression weighing him down. Yet there was no way he could rid himself of it. And as his mind turned to the kind of reception he should expect at Sis Ida's, his low spirits sank further down. He made the trip back in a blind haze.

The sun was down, the air refreshing when Sis Ida dropped off the taxi from work. She had no particular reason for her briskness as she threaded her way home. She moved as one tormenting the moment, seeking to put into each minute as much as was possible. There was a kind of compulsion in her hurried step, as if on this occasion a premonition played havoc with her.

She pinned her black handbag underneath her left armpit and was swinging her right hand freely in the slightly chilly air. When the first woman along her street raised her hand to greet her, Sis Ida waved back vigorously, adding the sweetness of her charming face to her response. The second woman did likewise and the response was as mechanical as in the first instance.

MaBoy stood at the gate of her yard as Sis Ida came past. Her arms remained akimbo, her face a mask of cynicism. Ida didn't attach significance to the coolness of this woman. Ever since Boy Difedile landed himself in jail for car-theft, his mother MaBoy turned her bitterness on the community. She hated in particular the leading lights in the street because she claimed the educated people introduced so-called civilisation which destroyed the minds of the young ones such as her child.

Her cold stare at Sis Ida so unsettled the latter, she had to do something in order to ease its effect. Ida pulled the black handbag from underneath her armpit. She held it in her right hand.

When the next woman raised her hand, she found Sis Ida somewhat cool. MaBoy began the chain of enquiry. For Ida there was always a level of existence beneath which lurked the dangers of a woman of kindness. She couldn't say what it was made her think there was a guard of doom waving her on to an act of misfortune. Never before did she find herself such an honoured guest as on this occasion when women stood waving at her from one end of the street to the very entrance of her yard. They signalled something ominous. And as she drew near her gate the number of well-wishers grew so large it was as if she was a corpse in the street round which relatives paid homage, as the custom demanded.

MaMatime looked hard at the approaching figure. She stood on the threshold of the front door. Quite spontaneously she clapped her hands at Sis Ida, as if to say, wonders never cease! By this time Ida was in a state of collapse. She read a lot into the unusual reception and her mind was muddled up by a fear she couldn't pin down in that instant. Yet she was afraid.

Once inside the house, Sis Ida didn't say anything beyond the exclamation: 'Modimo wakhotso — God of Peace!'

The evidence of dismay stared her in the eye: soot on the walls in the sitting room. She dropped her bag on the first seat on her way to the kitchen. For MaMatime led the way into that abyss of darkness. Again Sis Ida invoked the All-powerful. She cried 'Jehova!' She clasped her hands and felt her knees buckle. A myriad of thoughts crushed her in pressing onto her chest. She had this constriction in her breast which made her want to cry. Instead she appealed for help from MaMatime. 'Help me Auntie Sophie, help me I am dizzy.' MaMatime enveloped her with the hugeness of her body and spirit. She led her to the bedroom where she was eased onto the bed. 'Tighten up your heart my child,' she said in her home language. 'Wonders never cease . . .'

The silence which followed was like the void of eternity to Sis Ida. She experienced an emptiness she was convinced was dying. A road suddenly appeared in her mind. She couldn't say where it led but it was a long, lonely stretch which seemed to carry on and on up an incline.

Such had been her life, she told herself. Alarmed by the glaze in Sis Ida's eyes, MaMatime roused her with the words: 'God will give you strength, my child. Take a hard grip on yourself, He will never abandon you because He is no fool.'

From the depths of Ida's silence, rose the words: 'I don't care anymore what happens to me. The police can take me. The women of this street can laugh at me, I don't care! But what will happen to my grandchild, Setlogolo? He needs me. I am his mother.' Indeed she was right. For a number of years she brought up Setlogolo, her daughter's illegitimate boy, as her own child. He was removed only recently when the overcrowding and the activities in the house began to weigh her down and she feared the consequences of the moment now facing her.

MaMatime answered: 'Your child is my child. You know that it is the way of our forefathers. These things we must never allow the ways of the whiteman to trample on. So don't worry about Setlogolo, he'll be all right with us. What has befallen you is our life. Think of the many people who have shed tears in their homes.'

'I know,' said Sis Ida. Her mind continued to drift. She heard the clanging of the jail gates. She felt a gush of cold air breeze along corridors in jail. Then her mind galloped to Robben Island and she saw the youthful faces of the heroes aging on the infamous island: Mandela, Sisulu, Mbeki and then her vision blurred. She would join the men there — the very first woman to do so. How was Robben Island? She wondered.

She didn't know when the tears began to stream down her face. They fell on her hands, on her lap and she tightened her fingers as if intent on holding them as souvenirs. MaMatime stood by, pleading for long suffering. But Sis Ida cried out intoning the names of her father, mother and grandparents.

Then she muttered something about the rewards of kindness. For she was in trouble because she tried to do good. Was it God? Was it the whiteman or simply bad luck that put her in all the trouble? She cried and cried as if the tears would wipe off instantly the problems attending her person. But she felt the knot tighten round her heart. No matter how hard, how wildly she cried, in the quietness of her heart she experienced this tight grip on her heart and she began to fear an end she didn't want to face.

How did it all start, this kindness? she asked herself. The train of her thoughts was disturbed by someone in the kitchen.

'Be strong!' said MaMatime, 'Be strong my child. God is no fool. I will go to the kitchen to find out who has come in.'

Sis Ida remained to compose herself. She must be strong, she told herself, MaMatime was right, she had to be strong. That meant she must open her heart to her charge once more. It was going to be hard but there was no other way. These children needed her. She must not chase them away from her house. She must blot such thoughts from her mind. Then she felt washed out: it was as if the flow of tears was like a steady stream of quietly rippling water washing over green virgin grass. She felt cleansed and mellowed within her heart. And the limpness of her body vanished. Instead her muscles stretched out with a vigour flushing through her. The strength she craved returned even to her spirits. But she remained calm, her ear pricked to take in the voices in the kitchen. It was her group of children. They exclaimed surprise, shock and horror.

The voices belonged to Bongi, Punkie, Sello and Dan Montsho. Although the voices sounded like bedlam, she could pick out recurrent questions, such as Who did it? What happened? Presently the members trooped into her bedroom to pay their respects to her. As if she would know, the inquiries were repeated. And from her quiet negative answers they read fears for their own continued stay in the house.

Dan Montsho was moved deeply by the heavy mood hanging in the house. Somehow his own mind experienced a foreboding about the consequences which would flow from the event of the day. He didn't like Sis Ida's sealed lips as she sat on the bed like an Egyptian sphinx.

Roy and Boysi arrived to find the house in deep sorrow. There was no MaMatime to soften the shocking impact of that frightening sight in the kitchen. She left earlier for her own house, promising to see everybody the next day.

Roy began to piece together what could have happened. The signs of a blast were obvious. He ruled out Mandla as the perpetrator. This he demanded to know from the group. He said he gave no one permission to meddle with chemicals. Also he was incensed by Mandla's absence.

'Where's Mandla?' he asked. There was no immediate answer. No one could tell. Bongi stepped in.

'He must be with Mzi.'

'Balls!' exclaimed Roy. 'How could he drive with one hand? What's so important about Mzi to have forced Mandla to take such chances? He must be mad!'

'Let's not run to conclusions, gents,' said Dan Montsho quietly. 'Mandla has a lot of common sense. I don't see him take the car unless something very pressing forced his hand.'

Roy stood at the entrance leading to the kitchen. In the silence settled on the house, his eyes roved round the kitchen. Suddenly he asked: 'Where the hell is Keke?'

'He went for breast-feeding this morning,' sneered Sello.

'Gone with Mandla,' suggested Dan Montsho.

'Never!' asserted Roy. 'Keke with Mandla, never!'

'Why not?' asked Dan Montsho.

'Keke's too much of a softie. He'd squeal at the first sign of danger.'

'No! Those two cannot be together on any job, I can't see it.'

The matter of the whereabouts of Mandla and Keke and the mystery of the occurence of the day were left hanging in the troubled atmosphere of the house.

Presently Sis Ida went about preparing for the evening meal in an unusual silence. Her deadpan face was like a contagious disease. Everyone else remained silent, brooding over the beginning and the end of an event which puzzled the house. For brief moments, Ida couldn't contain herself. She snapped, she snarled like a terrified dog. Not once did she apologise for a shortage of eating plates, spoons or knives. It was as if she expected everyone to know the explosion took a toll on all her kitchen valuables. But like the soldiers they were, none of the members said a word. Their own faces were as glum as cold mashed potatoes left from the day before.

When the night dragged itself to a late hour Roy broke the freezing atmosphere in the house. For on this night no one wanted to sleep; no one wanted to venture into the streets either. The group sat up as if at a night vigil. Roy said tentatively at first:

'Bajita, you know Keke bothers me. I don't know why I feel he is behind all this mess up.'

'Roy is right. Keke is a sissy,' said Sello. 'But I'm convinced he decided to stay the day and night at his home.'

'Mama's darling!' added Bongi mockingly.

'I'm not so sure about all that. I have this feeling that nags me,' said Dan Montsho, 'The two must be together.'

'Impossible!' said Roy.

'One or the other is injured and help was needed.'

'Keke can't drive!' put in Roy.

'I know that,' answered Dan Montsho. He was seated in the easy chair deep in the corner with his head tucked in and hands rubbing each other. He went on: 'As I see it, Keke is the victim of the explosion . . .'

'What the hell was he doing?' demanded Roy, 'he was never a mixer.'

'Ya,' agreed Dan Montsho lazily, 'who knows, he might have thought of trying his luck. I can't be sure.'

'Impossible, I tell you!' said Roy.

'Keke is still breast-feeding,' jeered Sello. 'I know his kind. He'll be here tomorrow.'

Dan Montsho stood up and said: 'Oh well bajita, I don't know. We'll wait and see.'

The mystery of the day deepened with the winter night.


About the time Sis Ida arrived home, there was at another part of Soweto, Orlando East to be exact, a scene of stirring excitement. Noah Witbaatjie stood in his shirt-sleeves leaning on the door-frame leading from the sitting room into the kitchen. Nearest him and perched on a stool was Two-by-Two. Next to the latter was his friend Styles. And towering over the seated men was Matlakala, Noah's girl-friend.

Two-by-Two held an empty glass in his hand. All eyes centred on him as he related the blast at Sis Ida's as if he was one of the witnesses.

'How far is this place from yours?' asked Noah in a matter-of-course sort of voice.

'How far?' repeated Two-by-Two. He blinked once or twice as if astonished by the ignorance of well-known man-about-town Noah. His face twisted as he said again: 'How far? The Red Army is just two yards away from my home.'

'Red Army? What is that?' queried Noah.

'The children of 'Power'. You don't know them buda Noah . . .

They are there at Sis Ida's place, the same joint of the blast.'

'Jy ken — you know you are funny, Two-by-Two, you've never asked me to your place even for tea but jy weetie — you talk as if I know your place.'

'My home?' asked Two-by-Two as he sat up on the stool. Without a thought he lifted the glass to his mouth to sip its emptiness. 'Ag, buda Noah, my home is easy to find.'

'Easy he says,' said Noah teasingly, 'It's because you drink from empty glasses that you say easy.' That was a cue for Two-by-Two to place the empty glass on the table nearby.

'Ya, buda, it is easy to find.'

'I know you are in Zone 2 or somewhere there-abouts but I don't know the number.'

'Ouch!' yelled Two-by-Two looking into the face of Styles. 'Why do you tread on my corns, man?'

'Ag, askuus — sorry tog,' said Styles with a simulated sense of guilt, 'your foot was too near mine, I couldn't have missed it as I shifted.'

'Jy jee — you lie man!' declared a pained Two-by-Two. He drew his stool away from his friend.

'All right Two-by-Two, don't be a sissy,' offered Noah laughingly. 'He talks too much,' added Styles.

'I'm talking to buda Noah here,' whined Two-by-Two, 'I'm telling him what the papers missed, I'm telling him my address. He asked for it, didn't he?' Styles put a finger on his lips indicating the silence he wanted from his friend. Being both a bit tipsy they looked like a circus comedy act. They didn't seem capable of taking each other seriously. Two-by-Two answered his friend with an unyielding glare for a moment or two.

'You were telling me your address,' cut in Noah.

'This spy,' said Two-by-Two of his friend, 'thinks he's smart. Cut me out, man!' said Two-by-Two angrily. 'Shit man, cut me out!' he repeated.

'He didn't mean wrong,' pleaded Matlakala on behalf of Styles. 'You can see he's been playful. He's your friend.'

'Moegie — bum!' declared Two-by-Two.

'All right, Two-by-Two, you are talking to me, remember?' said Noah in a fatherly tone. 'Your number?'

'1037, Mpela Street,' offered Two-by-Two.' And he added a tongue click.

'This Ida woman, how is her house, I mean with so many kids, it must have its own character, you know ... big, big gate, fancy style . . .'

'Ordinary, it is ordinary; ya — big gate, tall fence. There is always a small car in the yard!'

'Two houses from yours . . . on the right or on the left?'

Two-by-Two stood up suddenly and started to snap fingers on the left hand and the right hand. He declared with confidence: 'On the right!'

'You talk too much!' chipped in Styles as he crossed his legs and turned away from his friend.

Noah Witbaatjie said to Matlakala: 'Sweetie, give Two-by-Two a bottle of beer from the fridge — on the house! Niks! He doesn't talk too much. He talks sense, doesn't he baby?'

Matlakala made no response to the last observation. She did as told, produced a bottle of beer which she hugged to her breast before she placed it on the table for the benefit of the informant.

Two-by-Two helped himself to the drink, ignoring the presence of his friend. Styles merely smiled cynically as he watched his friend go through the process of happily drinking the rewards of being an informer's informant. He sat like one unconcerned by his surroundings. He wondered if Two-by-Two could be so stupid that he missed the motive behind the leading questions by Noah. For Noah was suspect. The Soweto people said it openly in certain places that Noah was a police informer. How could he, Styles, help children at Sis Ida's place? He could not walk into that house and say Two-by-Two, a friend, gave away their whereabouts to an informer. The children of 'Power' were a feared lot. They might set about beating him up. Their mood was known to be ugly. They could petrol bomb his own home, destroy his home furniture and injure his family. Someone might die. Anything was possible. No, he told himself, he would have to steer clear of Sis Ida's place, hope that the worst does not befall the place. If only his friend was of strong character and did not go about shouting his mouth about things he knew so little about.

Styles saw in the haze of his wandering mind Noah beckon Matlakala to the sitting-room. She went out of the house carrying a set of keys which he concluded were for driving Noah's car. A feeling of uneasiness spread through his body. He began to fidget on the stool, with signs of impatience. He said to Two-by-Two: 'Let's go!'

Noah added quickly: 'I'm not driving you away but I feel lousy. I think I need to rest in bed for a while.'

'All right, all right,' said Two-by-Two between mouthfuls of beer. 'I can't leave this gift from the gods.'

There was a silence in the house. Then Noah said to no one in particular: 'It's getting late.'

Styles picked up the cue. He stood up and repeated: 'Let's go.'

Two-by-Two quaffed the remainder of the beer on his feet. He wiped his mouth and smacked his lips. He and Styles trooped out of the house at a leisured pace.

Noah hurried to his bedroom. He was full in the chest: excitement, news. As he brought down his walkie-talkie set, his mind was searching for the words to reveal the information jammed in his breast. None of the words used commonly for the kids captured the imagination in the way he wanted: Children of Power; Red Army; 'student agitators', these did not please him. They were too commonplace. He wanted something special, the kind of words which would be in character with his own personality; words which would be missed by an ordinary mind. Then he thought of his last trip to Durban. The sea held a fascination for him and to celebrate this respect for its vastness and the dangers in its calm water, he thought he would bring it into the metaphor of his information. His hands were unsteady as he pulled out the aerial of the set, standing near the bedroom window. The damn thing crackled sooner than he wanted. It destroyed the peace of mind he wished for before the important announcement. The atmospherics were running riot in the air. He began to wonder whether the message he was moulding in his head would be carried across vividly:

'Calling XWEO1, Calling XWEO1,' he began to whisper, his voice rising as he suspected it was too low to be reasonably heard by the person at the other end. He started all over again, louder: 'Calling XWEO1, this is Crossroads. Over.'

'Come in Crossroads,' said the other voice rather leisurely.

'Is that you XWEO1, is that you?' said an agitated Noah. He was concerned with hearing himself for such was his anxiety at this point.

'I read you Crossroads,' said the voice with firm assurance. Nothing special.

Noah experienced a vague sense of disappointment with the other voice. He couldn't make out whose voice it was. It certainly wasn't a person who valued his acquaintance. The other man's voice lacked enthusiasm as if unaware what goods were merchandised by Noah.

'Listen baas, I have w-o-n-derful news for you. I've found a shark-infested area boss,' he jabbered with keenness.

'Wat se donderste ding is daai —What are you talking about?' came an angry voice from the other man. 'What did you say?' said a pitched voice. 'Shark-infested, the sea in Soweto?'

'I mean the students, boss,' said a contrite Noah. He found himself climbing down from his high pedestal rather clumsily. 'The trouble-makers, the agitators,' he added, desperate to save a situation slipping from his grasp.

'Where?' asked an irritated voice.

Noah gave Two-by-Two's number and a description of Sis Ida's place. In his muddled state he was unaware he was speaking to some-one who had not the slightest idea of the location of the address, let alone the sickly numbering system in the locations.

'Praat mooi — Talk well,' said the other party. This meant Noah was to repeat all over the information given. And to prove his creden-tials he added:'Tell Major Hall quickly, please boss.'

'Don't teach me my job, boy!' jabbed the other man. 'Is that all?'

'Tell Major Hall please,' he pleaded childishly as if he missed the other man's admonition. The relay ended abruptly.

The other man switched off suddenly without the rituals which ended such transmissions. Noah Witbaatjie was left disappointed. He wished he could know the bastard, as he called the other man. Then he gibbered his usual jargon: 'Ek is van Kofifi — I am from Sophiatown! Die spy dink hy's superior — the bum thinks he's better. I'm going to tell Major Hall about it,' he said to the four walls of the bedroom. The sting was drawn from the message. It entered his feelings as hatred for the other man. As he put the walkie-talkie on top of the wardrobe, he swore to get even with the bastard that belittled him.

He opened the door out of the bedroom and found himself staring into the eyes of Matlakala. He stiffened as he saw her relaxed in the easy chair, a cigarette between two fingers. 'The bitch!' he said to himself with tight lips. Aloud he asked: 'What happened, did you bring the stuff?'

She nodded. Her hard look at him was unsettling. He feared what she would ask and in anticipation of it he thought he would bully her into a defensive stance: 'Don't just sit there, man. Have you put everything in the fridge?'

'Aha,' she replied. Her face was twisted in the smoke of the ciga-rette. She seemed intent on pushing him into the wall, to make him yield to her unbroken stare. He thought he read contempt on her face. For a brief moment man and woman gazed at each other in silence. Noah couldn't take it: his sense of guilt was overwhelming. He stepped into the kitchen, opened the fridge and banged the door to. Matlakala leaned against the kitchen wall near the door. She meant to force his hand. 'Sweetie,' she began seductively, 'why don't you tell me a bit about your other business?'

'What business?' asked a sulking Noah. 'Don't interfere in men's affairs, that's all!'

'You don't trust me?'

'Who says? Hell man, who says I don't trust you?'

'You can share the bed with me but you don't want to share your work with me . . .'

He was crushed in, for the nights in bed with her were an everlasting experience. She was the kind of woman he never tired of making love with. Often he wondered how she was created. He wondered where she learned her business in bed. They don't teach sex at school but Matlakala was able to bring out the best in his manhood as if her teachers did one thing clean and good for her: taught her how to handle a man in bed. It was these feelings of careless abandon she roused when she spoke of sharing the bed with him.

'I don't want us to quarrel, honey,' he said in a subdued tone. 'I just think I am a cunt at times but I am working for the nation. I'm doing this for the good of the country.'

'What are you talking about, sweetie?'

'Ag, forget it, honey,' said Noah throwing up his hands in resignation, 'I don't want to talk about this.' And then he added quickly: 'It isn't as if I don't trust you. It's got nothing to do with it. If there's someone I don't trust, it is me. The bottom has been taken away from me. I can't feel myself where I am.'

'This business,' began Matlakala.

'Ag, man, honey,' said Noah, dragging her to the bedroom. He locked the door and drew the curtains. Matlakala clammed her lips. She thought she wouldn't spoil her game by pushing him too hard. She yielded herself to his fumbling fingers. As always he began up on the head. His fingers slipped down to the breast and then down to her hips. He never ended there but at a point which always left her limp with excitement. Soon she found herself spreadeagled on the bed and with the first motions of pressure on her, she had forgotten how it all started.

Noah won that round with ease. He thought he escaped by the skin of his teeth from the curious questions of his 'maid'. For now she gave him all the pleasure he could hope for, shutting off the disappointment he experienced earlier at the hands of the policeman at Police Headquarters. He would have to wait for the outcome of his report. Maybe the thrill of it all would match the thrill of that moment with Matlakala.

It was 10 p.m. on the fateful day, a day which seemed to have seen more events capsuled into a thimble than any other. Mzi and Mandla sat in the bedroom at MaNhlapo's. For hours on end their voices droned in the room like the small home-made drum in a religious ceremony. Even MaNhlapo's shuffling in and out of the other rooms had no effect on the monotones going on in the young men's room.

Mandla arrived from Dr Kenotsi's surgery, revealed the mishap with Keke and so began the war conference in which he and Mzi engaged for hours. For Mzi it was the spark he needed to fire him into action. The time was ripe for the mission to be fulfilled. Things would get worse everyday. They would have to finish off Batata immediately, before the heat in the streets made movement at night impossible, so argued Mzi.

Mandla said he was all right for his part. If he could drive through the searing pains from the moment he left Sis Ida's to the doctor's surgery and then from there to MaNhlapo's, there was absolutely no reason why the mission should be postponed on his account.

It was agreed the job would be done the next night without fail. The two arranged to meet in the early evening of the following day. In the meantime Mandla was to return to Sis Ida's to allay any fears and sort out problems and queries as a result of Keke's accident. He was sworn to secrecy by Mzi who said his reputation as a trained fighter was at stake. Mzi was rather cynical about Keke's misfortune. He said it was evident the fellow was no revolutionary. If what Mandla told him had happened was true, then Keke was an amateur. Mzi declared: 'You must be careful! From now on anything can happen to you or the group.' He went on to say living in a group crammed as they were at Sis Ida's, was not how revolutionaries survived. 'How you have escaped from the dogs surprises me,' said Mzi. 'Soweto is full of informers.'

It was late in the night when Mandla pulled away from Ma-Nhlapo's. His feelings were a jumble. He was disappointed with himself. When he thought of Keke his mind shut off, briefly. For all the curses on the group affected him, not Keke. He was aware his own estimation in the eyes of Mzi took a knock. He was a peg or two down. If only Keke hadn't . . . Mandla didn't know what actually happened. He wondered if he would ever know the truth from Keke.

When he drove along the road leading from Dube to Meadowlands, he realised he had slowed down. At that hour there was very little traffic. Taxis and commercial vehicles took over the roads during the day, he told himself, but the road belonged to the people at night.

It was lonely and quiet on the roads. Why crawl? Then it occurred to him there would be questions asked on arrival. He tried to piece together what actually happened in the morning. He had been reading Fanon. The introduction by Sartre was heavy and long. Keke had arrived back from home and began to move around the kitchen. No crime in moving things in the kitchen. As if the thought was fetched from some rough  terrain, he recalled spells of silence when he couldn't hear any sounds from the kitchen. He should have investigated those silences. But engrossed as he had been in the book, he didn't. Instead he dozed off. At what point, he couldn't tell. Nor could he tell how long. He had woken up to find himself shaking involuntarily because the whole house was shuddering. He heard the cries from the kitchen. And from the haze of his waking state had remembered Keke.

Was he scared of meeting Sis Ida's wrath, and the group's suspicion, or was it something lurking along the road? He picked up speed, his mind alert to the sights around: houses huddled together under the canopy of night, all quiet and asleep. Thank God it was at night. No one saw the grimaces on his face because the pain in the arm jabbed at him now and again. He wasn't far off from base and he drove along, his thoughts jumping from Sis Ida's place to MaNhlapo's. He kept wondering what Mzi would do for the rest of the night.

Mzi lay on his back in bed. Sleep seemed a waste of time. He was concerned for Mandla. He had this nagging feeling that Mandla might run into trouble because of the amateurs with whom he worked. He resolved not to sleep until at least an hour after splitting with Mandla. He thought if anything were to befall his friend he would know in the hour. The AK47 machine gun was ready to blow off anyone's head. They wouldn't pick him up without a fight.

He blew out the candle and waited in the dark. His eyes pierced the ceiling. There was nothing there. He grew tired of it and closed his eyelids. A few moments later he opened them again intent on keeping control over his body. He was aware that a long stretch of time had passed without any development. But he decided he would wait in any case. The body can take it, he told himself. He said it without throwing the bones, as they say. Sometime in the stillness of the night, a night which grew gradually chilly as if the cold wind outside was iced as it hit the walls, he fell asleep. He just dozed off because his body couldn't take the hammering of the day any longer. And when sleep comes that way it drags with it events of the waking state. He slept so quietly it was evident the mind engaged in a dream.

1.20 a.m. The first police car cruised past Sis Ida's place without lights. It stopped a couple of meters away. The second one followed without lights as well. So did the third, fourth, fifth. They halted behind one another in convoy. A total of thirteen cars and four kwela-kwelas lined and jammed the street. Colonel Kleinwater's car stopped almost directly opposite Ida's house, so precise was the invasion of the night.

Sello shoved his penis back in a hurry, and bolted out of the toilet to investigate the strange sounds he heard: first the crunch of wheels as the police cars ate into the debris in the location street, then a series of squeaks as the big American cars so popular with the cops came to a halt. He leaned on the house wall to take a peek at what was happening and he only had to count up to three to be satisfied that it was no social call to the neighbourhood but a fullblast raid. Dressed in his grey trousers only, breast bare, he suddenly found he couldn't go inside the house to raise the alarm, retrieve his shirt and shoes and dash for safety. For a moment he was at a loss what to do. But the urge to survive was strong. As always it brought to the surface of the skin a slight dampness despite the low temperatures in the air. As he scaled the fence into the opposite backyard, he worked out the only thing possible under the circumstances. He was lucky to land near a few dark objects. He picked up one and it was as good as a stone: a piece of coal. He hurled it onto Sis Ida's house. It crushed on the corrugated asbestos roof with a dull thud. The sound on the roof gave him hope, it gave him strength to distance himself from impending jail. One, two, three — Sello found he did then what he'd never tried before — take on the low fences with such ease. One thought and one thought only galvanised his action — to fool the cops once more and continue the cheating game.

Dan Montsho had lain awake from the minute Sello opened the kitchen door to get to the loo. He heard the squeak of braking cars but was held down by some lazy streak of ill-luck. But when Sello's coalstone crushed and rolled down the corrugated roof, he was impelled to investigate the cause. His dash in the dark was just in the nick of time. He saw the cars come to a standstill without lights and that fact registered in his mind. He sprinted to the one open escape route, scaled the fence like Sello and saw his fleeing comrade hurdling over fences a couple of houses away. He didn't have to work out a plan of escape but followed Sello. Only when he was completely clear of Ida's house did it occur to him that he was escaping from certain detention. The idea frightened him and he was momentarily paralysed in his tracks. That was how he lost sight of Sello. But he put in all his effort and kept jumping one fence after another, wondering when the ordeal would come to an end. Then he came onto an open tract of land. Dan Montsho never saw himself as a brave young man. As with many people, open spaces intimidated him. He felt the tight grip of his stomach muscles. It was the fear of the open space. Yet there was no choice for him. His way to Dube lay across that measureless dark space. He couldn't take refuge in any of the houses around because the idea of police collaborators deterred him from seeking help in the area. Telescoping into each other as if in a crash were recent events: the shooting of Mandla on the arm; Keke's whispered mutterings about informers; Uncle Ribs's forced escape to Botswana, and now the overpowering raid on the house where the group lived. He was convinced an informer lurked in the background of the group. The train of thought stopped when he realised he was crouching low and was looking at a darkened figure standing ahead of him flush on the path he would have to take to cross the open space. It couldn't be Sello. His friend would have given him a signal of his presence. A tree? Maybe. Even so the fear of darkness loomed large before him. He wished the damn thing could relay some sound or wave a hand if it were Sello. But no, there was no sign from that end. His fear grew and his body emitted droplets of water.    He was clammy from the fear of the unknown. He went down and began to grope for a missile. He picked up a handful of stones with his wet hand. And the hopelessness of his situation kept him squatted on the ground. Gots, he thought to himself, how does one acquire guts in the dark? He scanned the surroundings. There was not a single sign of life around, houses were in total silence, and dark. These houses with a sameness so monotonous and jarring to the sense of beauty held no hope for him at that moment. When he saw a movement from the object of his fears, at first he thought it was an occurrence in his inner eye, but it soon dawned on him that Sello stood there signalling him to keep moving on.

'Dammit!' he exclaimed with relief. He teamed up with his colleague and said: 'You scared the hell out of me.'

'Those bloody ratlas — police — scared the shit out of me. I've hardly got my shirt on.'

'What's a shirt to a man's life?' said Dan Montsho philosophically.

It turned out they both were thinking of Uncle Ribs's place in Dube for a hide-out. None could even guess the whereabouts of Mandla. And so strong was reliance on him, they expressed the wish to see him for the next move.

Both melted in the dark ways of Meadowlands as they headed for

Dube.

Meanwhile Sis Ida was woken up by the thud on the roof. For her sleep came in spasms for the greater part of the short spell she was in bed.

She rose sharply from the pillow and caught the crunching of wheels and the squeaking of the brakes. When she went to the window to peep, it was to satisfy the strong urge born of her intuitive sense. The dreaded moment had arrived too soon for her liking. She was still dazed as she called out: 'Getty! Getty!' Then she remembered that her daughter and grandson went away two weeks earlier to stay with relatives in another part of huge Soweto.

She fumbled for the box of matches on the dressing table. Instead her hand touched her wrist-watch. It was 1.23 a.m. What an ungodly hour to have to wake up at, she thought to herself. She waited sitting on the edge of the bed looking at the outline of her own frame reflected on the dressing table mirror. She told herself she looked terrifying in the dark. And it was perhaps the fear of herself in the mirror which caused her to cry: 'Police! Police!' She rushed to the door linking her bedroom and the sitting room and repeated: 'Police, batho — people! Mandla the police are here!' Obviously Mandla occurred to her muddled mind.

Roy and Boysi clambered to their feet about the same time. Then they stood still, rooted to where they had been lying metres apart. A knock on the front door riveted them to their places. Roy cursed, Boysi managed to say to the darkened room: 'Opskit! Opskit, bajita — wake up, folks!' His voice was lost as the rumbling of the front door reverberated through the house. It sent a chill down the spine of Sis Ida. Her hand rummaged through the drawers of the dressing table as her search for the matchbox continued frantically. With a weakened voice she cried out, 'I am coming! I am coming!'

'Open up! Open up, it's the police!' said a voice. It was punctuated by the rapping of hard knuckles on the door.

On the dressing table stood the paraffin lamp. Ida picked up the funnel and lit the wick. When she tried to replace the funnel it was an effort: it kept slipping from the base. And with the noise on the door and the threat of voices outside her mind was in a dizzy spin. At last she succeeded. The short walk to the front door was like the long walk to the gallows. The face of the tall officer hit hers with the power of a whirlwind. The man was inside the house sooner than she wanted. An expression of satisfied glee appeared in his eyes as he saw Roy, Boysi and others. Roy was defiant. He wore a mask of contempt as his and the officer's eyes met.

'Colonel Kleinwater,' said the tall man to Sis Ida. And then he turned to Roy and the other members of the group: 'Good morning mense — people,' said the officer mockingly. 'Sorry to disturb your dreams like this.' His head turned to Major Hall on his right hand side. 'Phew! What a catch, Eddie.'

'Ye-ye-yes, Sir,' stammered the Major.

The room was crowded. Police in camouflage, machine rifles on the ready, stood shoulder to shoulder with members of the group. Bongi was dressed in her petticoat only. Her dress was held to her breast. The other girls stood crowded around her and Roy. They were caught napping but they stood up before the law, their young bodies tense with a sense of hate and resignation. For them, the hour had come sooner than they thought. Each one waited to see what the law had in store for them. They loved none of the men of law but were resigned to obey the one word expected at that moment: detention.

'Take them away, Major,' said Kleinwater to Hall. Batata was first to step forward among all the policemen in the company of the Colonel. He'd been standing almost outside the door, so crowded was the place. But when the command to detain was given he elbowed many of his colleagues out of his way to grab at the chap standing head and shoulders above the others. Holding him by the scruff of the neck, he shoved him forward and out of the house. Roy wriggled and groused: 'Don't hold me like that. I'm no criminal!' Batata answered by tightening his grip and shoved a knee on Roy's buttocks. The other members fared no better. They were frog-marched to the waiting kwela-kwelas, hurled into gaping doors and locked up like beasts.

In that dark, cold winter morning the street sprang alive. Behind drawn curtains neighbours peeped; underneath peach and apricot trees men stood watching the happenings at Sis Ida's. Even Two-by-Two kept watch on the house he described earlier in the day. At first he too wondered what might be the matter at Sis Ida's. Slowly and painfully he remembered how loud-mouthed he was at Noah's joint, Morning Sweetheart. He was searching himself when the cars began to take off.

For Sis Ida the agony of the long day had only then begun. She was asked to take a seat. In her own house she was made a stranger. She sat on the sofa and waited for the next move from Colonel Kleinwater. She braced herself for the onslaught brought on her by her motherly kindness.

He didn't know what time it was, he didn't care; he didn't know if he'd been followed, he didn't care; he stood near the window and continued to tap lightly on the panes. His impatient ear was glued to the window and he picked the sound of the squeaking spring mattress. He wondered why no voice came from the room. So he continued to tap on the window suppressing a temptation to add the knuckling on the back door. One thing was certain: he didn't want to proclaim his return at that late hour to all and sundry.

A man's voice growled from inside, so he whispered to the cold winter night:

'Open up, it's me!' He hoped the other person would recognise the voice.

Mzi kept chiding himself for dozing off after Mandla left him. At the same time there was little he could do in the dark. In turns he would doze or sit up on the bed and begin a train of thought: he began by retracing his days with the boys in Botswana; he laughed inwardly as he thought how he outsmarted whitey to enter the country and the way he travelled to Jo'burg. His days with Uncle Ribs were a source of inspiration. Here was a man who humbled himself in order to work for the cause. His dedication was unbending. It inspired those who came into contact with him, teaching them an unusual sense of loyalty and unselfishness. Uncle Ribs was literally a meeting point for the oldies and the young ones such as Mzi and Mandla. And as Mzi thought of his encounter with Mandla he was filled with pride. For a new dawn had broken with the activities of Mandla and his team. They were the real spear of the nation; less talk more action. They pierced the intransigence of whitey's invincibility. The joy of thinking along these lines made him rest his head on the pillow. He never knew when he dozed off. His dreams were in a way a continuation of his conscious thoughts. Only the mind was immersed in an abyss from which waking up wasn't that easy. That's how he missed Mandla's initial tapping on the window-panes. His growl had more to do with the forces at play in his dream than the person standing outside tap-tapping.

'What happened?' he asked Mandla when they reached the bedroom.

'There's a siege on Sis Ida's dump,' said a somewhat agitated Mandla. 'I counted more than a dozen police cars and kwela-kwelas.'

'Didn't they spot you?'

'They would have been owls!'

A pause followed. Mzi said, pumping a fist into the pillow: 'I told you a crowd like that was dangerous. I wish we'd carried out the mission weeks ago. Now everything conspires against it. A bunch of amateurs!'

'Hold it, man. Those are not amateurs. You can't blame us if an informer infiltrated the group. I can't start a witchhunt among folks I've worked with so well for so long.'

Mzi backpedalled: 'I mean Keke is the amateur.'

'It was an accident!'

'Damn costly!'

'So what? We can't condemn the fellow because of one lousy act: an accident.'

'All right an accident. It won't be an accident if the cops knock on the door any minute now,' said Mzi cynically.

'Why should they? Aren't they still looking for me for the blast at Jabavu Police Station? Aren't they still looking for me for the sabotage on the railway tracks — as if I did all that myself?'

'Don't let's blow our tops, man. I know I started it but we are in this together. We'll see it through together.'

Mandla remained quiet. His anger was still simmering. He thought Mzi was terribly unreasonable, full of himself.

They both waited in the silence of night, they waited for the thudding of feet in the yard and the knuckling on the doors and windows. This winter night was a long day.


Kleinwater chose a spot on the sofa well apart from Sis Ida. Yet his heavy breathing smacked her face. She sat there with hands clasped on her knees. She was tensed. For the moment she couldn't tell what the police were up to. Her uneasiness began to choke the life out of her. She saw one fellow slip into the bedroom; she heard cries of glee from those in the kitchen with a scraping of sorts going on and she watched with a strong sense of anticipation one policeman unpacking the pile of miscellaneous items on the sewing machine and the radiogram standing next to each other in one corner of the sitting room. Suddenly she realised the pile would be her undoing: the books and papers consisted of material not to be seen by law-enforcers.

The Colonel sat tall on the sofa, his huge frame towering over Sis Ida who seemed squashed in on this night. She sat fidgeting with her fingers on her knees but otherwise she was alert: to the menace on her person and of the law next to her. The Colonel stared silently down on her. He didn't look aside even when one of his men was rustling paper on the cabinet of the sewing machine. Presently he began:

'Toe nou — Now then, tell us what you have been up to mistress.'

Sis Ida didn't like the mocking tone of the officer. She remained impassive. The Colonel went on: 'What's your name?' 'Ida Diradikayi,' said Sis Ida. She saw another policeman write that down. She hadn't been aware of the mobile secretarial unit in her house.

'Are you the legal owner of the house?'

'Yes.'

'Any children?'

'Yes.'

'Who are they?'

'Getty and Setlogolo.'

'Are they among the ones we found here?'

'No.'

'No?' repeated the Colonel mockingly. 'Do you run a boarding house?'

Ida thought it was her turn to look the man in the eye. His green eyes were hard and unfriendly. His face drawn in and ghostly in that hour of the day. He stared back at her as if intent to cow her. She was convinced the encounter between them was a re-enactment of the many confrontations between Soweto and the men from the other side of the world. The law-enforcer would never understand any explanation of her humanity. So she replied: 'No.'

'How come we found so many children on your premises?'

She clammed up. Completely. Instead she tried to find a part in his eye which she could read with her heart. There was none. The man's face was all steel. He sat there before her as if he had no beating of his own heart. He was like a machine. Duty demanded he be in that house. The law demanded he take over command of the occasion, and that was what he did. He could sit for hours grilling her in her house about what she did in it. So Sis Ida decided to reward him with a golden silence.

The policeman who'd been standing and flipping through the material on the cabinet brought some papers and books over to the Colonel, dumping them in the space between the Colonel and Sis Ida. The Colonel received these things graciously and, in a dignified manner, produced a pouch in which was kept his pair of spectacles. He looked professorial behind his reading glasses. He held up a publication of the Resistance Movement published in London and called *Sechaba*. He said: 'I see you are a good reader, mistress. Have you gone through all this?' he waved the newsletter towards the other material on the sofa.

'No.'

'Did you buy this from the CNA?'

'No.'

'I didn't think so. Who smuggled it in for you, the SACB?'

'These things do not belong to me.'

'Not yours?'

'Those boys read them.'

'In your house, Ida, in your house. That's all the law needs to know.'

More paper work was brought to the Colonel by a diligent policeman.

It was all stuff picked up from the cabinet and the radiogram. The Colonel browsed through it briefly.

'Well, well,' he said, shifting his overwhelming frame, causing the sofa to groan, 'I find you are a competent research worker — a list of local schools! Which of these have you burnt down already? Let me see . . .' The Colonel's hand went up and down the list and he said: 'Yes this, that and that . . .', and picking up another list he exclaimed: 'My Here God — My God! A record of the clinics as well! Tell me, Ida, what kind of people are you who go about destroying your own schools and clinics? Does it make sense to you?'

'Those lists have to do with my job. They are not places to be destroyed.'

'Is that so?' said the Colonel with a sneer on his face, 'we will soon know the truth. We will soon know the whole truth, I swear it!'

Suddenly the Colonel seemed to feel blood rush to his temples. His eyes began to burn anger and with his voice almost croaking he said: 'I'm not going to have you waste my time! I'm not spending my whole bloody night up for nothing! Are you going to tell the truth or do you want to see me lock you up once and for all?' He was himself trembling with this sudden spurt of anger.

'I don't know what you want me to say,' answered Ida in a quiet voice, 'I've been telling you the truth.'

'Who the hell are these children you've been hiding in your house illegally?'

'I didn't hide them. They came for a few days with my nephew . . .'

'Who the hell is he?'

'Dan Montsho.'

'Dan Manzu? Is he among the lot taken away in custody?'

'No.'

'Where is he then?'

'I don't know.'

'Gots! You don't know! What sort of auntie are you? When last did you see him?'

'Last night.'

'Last night!' he repeated, slapping his huge right hand on his right thigh. 'So bloody convenient, eh? Last night!'

At this point the policeman in the bedroom came out carrying Sis Ida's black handbag. He emptied its contents on the floor at the Colonel's feet. Another policeman went down on his knees and began to hand items from the floor to the Colonel.

The other men stood back in glee and watched Sis Ida's face, trying to read her thoughts. The Colonel received six travel documents which had tumbled earlier out of the bag.

Sis Ida thought the Colonel's breathing denied her room in her house. It was hard and fast. His face was a fiery red. He was flipping through the pages of each booklet, his lips twisted at the turn of each page. Now and then he would nod as he looked at the prints attached to each booklet.

'Say, Ida,' said the Colonel with his mocking tone, 'were you also in the big business?' Sis Ida kept mum. He straightened up like a cobra and declared: 'I won't stand your damn nonsense! Understand? I ask you a question and you bloody ignore me! What do you think I am, your Soweto connection or something?'

'I don't understand the question,' said Ida determined not to be bullied. 'I don't know what big business I am supposed to be doing.'

'You know the bloody racket!' shouted the Colonel.

'What do you mean?'

'Every bloody thing you can think of man! These travel documents were to be forged for use by those children, to cross the border into Botswana.' And he added: 'For military training!'

The idea never entered Sis Ida's mind. It never occurred to her that she might one day be accused of involvement with the training of children somewhere across the borders. Indeed her world oscillated between Soweto and Jo'burg City. It was a world of persuading other women to purchase face creams and other cosmetics; a world of long-suffering where her medium-sized frame often lengthened in order that she might assert her own dignity. It was a world of kindness: motherly kindness whose thankless reward was this humiliation. For the law was putting her down for showing love to young ones. She believed in the rightness of her kind heart. So she said:

'I don't know anything about military training.'

'You lie!' said the Colonel, his voice punching a hole in the air, 'you damn well know what it means!' Just as suddenly as he had risen above the level of his natural posture, so suddenly did he revert back to it. It seemed his body was tired of sitting on the sofa. He was slightly crouched as he turned to speak to one of his men: 'Japie take everything you can lay your hands on and let's quit this house. I'm convinced we'll get better answers at our office.'

In a matter-of-fact voice, Japie suggested: 'Are we taking her with us?'

'Natuurlik — Naturally!' declared Kleinwater. He stood up. A policeman appeared on the scene from the kitchen.

'Sir,' he began, 'would you like to have a look over here?'

'Certainly, Sarge. I had forgotten the place.' And as he moved to the kitchen, the Colonel told the scribe to note the exact appearance of the room. In the kitchen he said with a voice full of menace: 'Jong, Ida, if I have to wring your neck I'm going to do so for the truth. You wait and see!'

Sis Ida was hemmed in by policemen. She was suffocating in the heat generated by the cops. But her mind travelled ahead to the cell she saw gaping for her person. She spoke gently to the Colonel asking if she could be allowed to wear a warm dress instead of the night-gown wrapping her body. The reply was curt: 'Do any bloody thing!'

She went into the bedroom. The air was cooler. The men who'd been in the bedroom sauntered out. She was able to take out of the wardrobe an ordinary cotton dress and a winter coat and she wrapped a floral doek on her head. Suddenly the call of nature played havoc with her. She was convinced it would be the right thing to do: a visit to the toilet. Yet the thought of asking for permission from an aggressive officer made her reluctant to ask. She looked into the mirror and saw a face aged rapidly by gathering misfortunes. She blotted fear out of her mind because she believed faith in God would make her survive. But survival at that moment meant a visit to the toilet. More so, she recalled an African saying: Ask me where I've come from, not where I am going. Her mind was made up; she would walk out of the bedroom and tell the Colonel she wanted to go to the toilet. And she did just that. His reply was forthright: 'Do any bloody thing, I said!' As she stepped out of the kitchen door tailed by a policeman, she was assaulted by the force of law: the yard was dotted with policemen, all heavily armed, standing at strategic points. This first experience with the law was traumatic. Never before did she know a woman could be so besieged by cops as she was. She wondered about other homes. She began to understand the meaning of the cry of Soweto: that the location was a concentration camp in all but name. Her relief after the visit to the toilet was shortlived.

When she returned to the house, her shoulders seemed burdened by an unseen load. Her strength faltered and she was concerned that the tight grip she held on her being was slipping off. She began to screw her mouth in an effort to hold back tears. For sorrow overcame her. She was sorry for her lost family, broken up so suddenly and seemingly irrevocably. The meaning of leaving the house at that lonely hour came up to her face. She wished Getty was around. She longed to hug little Setlogolo once again as she used to weeks back. Only weeks back, she recalled, the tone in the house was so different from that night: everyone was laughing, everyone was free.

Her wrist-watch read 3.45. She blew out the paraffin light. As she stepped into the sitting room where the Colonel and his men waited, it was like stepping her foot into a pool of cold water. Her step was heavy. It was heavy because the house ceased to be hers . . .

The Colonel led her to his car.

She didn't see the neighbours peeping at windows. Her mind was too blurred to see all that. Yet she knew in the pit of her muddled mind that they were there: to sympathise and to mock.

She sat alone in the back seat — tense. She sat there resigned to a fate she was well aware could take many turns. She had read of interrogations which ended in death. She heard death was possible in many ways. Alone, holding only to the thought that it was a case of us and them, she expected anything and she told herself it was sensible to take whatever was in store for her. For it was predestined she would die whatever way she did and if they wanted to dump her out of the moving car at a lonely spot, at that quiet hour, they could go ahead and do it. Her body would be a sacrifice. That meant someone would pay dearly some day for eliminating her from Soweto and her family.

Relief came when the car pulled up in front of Westend Police Headquarters. The sky over there was a light pink and a thin grey as dawn took a peek at the world. The long night signalled its own end.


**7**


At 5.00 a.m. the same morning, Mzi and Mandla puzzled over a light tap-tapping on the window-pane of Mzi's room. Mzi pushed his legs into his trousers instinctively: his mind searched the face of the person concerned and simultaneously wandered to the AK47 underneath the bed. He wasn't going to take chances. He looked for a chink in the curtains through which he could make out who it was waking them so early.

Sis Joyce Mbambo stood huddled up on the outside wall in the cold winter morning. His heart did a double step: it was not the thought of a raid on Sis Ida's place but the arrest of Uncle Ribs that gave him a thud on his ribs. He signalled her to the back door and as he went to open it for her he whispered to Mandla: 'Sis Joyce!'

With a finger hooked to hold up his trousers, Mzi fumbled a bit before the door opened. Mandla joined them in the kitchen. For Sis Joyce, the panting and the heaviness of her tidings made her gasp for breath as she told of being woken up at 2.30 a.m. by Sello and Dan Montsho. 'Sello was freezing, bare-breasted as he was in the cold.'

'Mandla escaped by the grace of the gods,' cut in Mzi. 'He almost ran into the raid as he was returning home at the dead of night.'

'Awu!' exclaimed Sis Joyce, her hands held up near her mouth. Her heart pounded her chest as she realised how close everyone was to the tentacles of the law.

'Did the cops pick up everyone?' asked Mzi.

'They must!' put in Mandla.

'Poor Sis Ida,' lamented the woman. 'I wonder how she took it.'

'Was Batata there, I wonder?' asked Mzi.

'I don't know,' replied Sis Joyce. 'The boys didn't wait to see the police.'

'The dog must die!' said Mandla bitterly. He can't have missed that show . . . Where are they?'

Sis Joyce was for a moment too dazed to understand who 'they' were. She queried: 'They?'

'I mean Sello and Dan Montsho.'

'At my place. Sello wanted to come with me but Dan Montsho and I discouraged him. The location is teeming with police. We couldn't take a chance.'

'You did well to wear your hospital uniform,' said Mandla. 'And thanks for keeping the boys.'

'They need better clothes,' added Sis Joyce.

'And we have no money,' lamented Mandla.

'Ann Hope must give!' declared Mzi.

'You can't go into town my son,' pleaded Sis Joyce, 'the police will be all over. By now they know Mandla, Dan Montsho and Sello have escaped the net. Roadblocks will be heavy. Those two aren't that desperate. I've lent Sello one of my husband's shirts.'

Mandla stifled a guffaw. He said: 'I want to see Sello in an oversize shirt.' Mzi remained glum.

'He doesn't look bad,' said Sis Joyce. 'My husband wasn't such a big man anyway.'

When Mzi opened his mouth he was firm and determined: 'I'll take Mandla's car, drive to Sis Joyce's place, pick up Sello and drive to Dr Kenotsi's surgery.'

'You won't find Keke there,' said Mandla.

'I don't want to see Keke. I need to borrow the medico's car and white dust-coat. I'm going to be Sello's chauffeur.'

'Into town?' pitched in Mandla.

'Why not? We need the bread from that woman Ann Hope.'

'It will be too risky, son.'

'They won't touch me! Not me!' asserted Mzi.

'You don't know the system,' said Mandla, moving away from his colleague.

'They don't know me! I'm not in their books, remember.'

'They'll grill the detained. What if one of them squeals?'

'Too bad,' said Mzi cynically, 'too bad. Goes to show we are in this with amateurs.'

'That's not the point. You don't know cops.'

'Yes they are cruel,' said Sis Joyce.

There was a pause. Mzi broke into it with: 'We are delaying. Chances are if we went away early to Ann, we might make it. We must have faith in those people taken in this morning. Don't think they'll crack so quickly. Or don't you believe in them, anymore?' This to Mandla.

'Of course I trust them. But the atmosphere will be too hot to venture outside today.'

'Atmosphere too hot?' sneered Mzi 'Does this mean we chuck up tonight's operation?'

'You want to be reckless,' said Mandla. He threw up a hand as a sign of despair and said: 'I can't teach you caution.'

'Oho!' said Mzi arrogantly.

Sis Joyce stood up from the wooden bench and said: 'I must be going.'

'I'll take you away,' offered Mzi.

'No, son, I'll manage.'

'I do it for Uncle Ribs, I do it for the people trudging to work this early hour.' Mzi was insistent and this Sis Joyce understood.

'It is dangerous,' said Mandla.

'I am the danger,' declared Mzi. 'If I don't dictate my terms with whitey he makes me a coward. He bullies me to remain behind

136

closed doors. I say to hell with him. It is my duty to take Sis Joyce home and I'm doing just that!'

Sis Joyce didn't enjoy the trip home. Mzi drove as if the whirlwind had him in a spin. It was a short distance but he made her feel it was long. She couldn't have arrived home sooner. Once she expressed this uneasiness by enquiring if they were not being followed.

'Don't worry, nothing will happen to us,' Mzi had reassured her. So arrogant, so self-confident — that was Mzi.

Sis Joyce sighed with relief as she was dropped off. Mzi made as if to go but he U-turned to stop by the house. 'I want to see Sello and Dan Montsho,' he said following Sis Joyce into the house.

The meeting was a quiet affair. Mzi introduced himself simply as Mzi. He had heard of them from Mandla and was pleased to be associated with people in the struggle. Dan Montsho lent him a smile but not Sello. There was something about Mzi he didn't like. Nothing in particular, he thought as he withdrew the hand he had extended in exchange.

Mzi asked what the pair intended to do. Sello was quick to answer: 'I don't trust Keke. Where is he now? He gave us away! I want to quit the country! I want to quit before the bloody boerans lay their hands on me.'

'I don't think you are right about Keke,' said Mzi. 'He's in great pain right now.'

'Where?' stabbed in Sello.

'Hiding place.'

'How do you know?' asked Sello cynically.

Mzi eyed him contemptuously and said: 'Mandla says so!' That shut Sello's mouth for a while. He was ashamed of himself, in a way. Mzi turned his attention to Dan Montsho.

'I don't know what to say,' began Dan Montsho, rubbing his hands and wearing his far-away look. As always he seemed to fetch his thoughts from some distant store. He went on: 'I can't see what I can do outside the country. But staying means a rabbit's life. I'll be running, I'll be hiding from cops and their phantoms. There's a chance — always there's a chance — the cops can squeeze the truth from one of our detained brothers.'

'They'll squeeze blood out of them if its the last thing they must do for information. The swine are that bad,' said Mzi.

'That's why I want to go,' butted in Sello. 'I'm sorry about Keke,' he added.

'Keke was badly injured in the blast,' said Mzi. He was cool and quiet about the information.

'Poor guy,' offered Dan Montsho.

'I want to know who told the cops about us?' queried Sello.

'I never liked the idea of a large group of operators in one place. It was a risky set up. Activity must have been cluttered by the large numbers. One or two persons on a job is what I go for,' said Mzi.

'I've always thought so myself,' agreed Dan Montsho. 'Imagine women dabbling with explosives — so unAfrican.'

'I don't want to scare anyone; I don't want to insult anyone but brothers I'm convinced someone in your crowd was working for the system.'

'Damn sure!' swore Dan Montsho.

'I'm not wracking my head about it,' came in Sello, 'I am clear: I go!'

'How?' asked Dan Montsho.

'Mandla must work it out,' said Sello, 'he's the leader.'

'What if he says you can't go?' queried Mzi mischievously.

'He can't say that. 'Strue's God, he can't!' said a determined Sello. 'My life is in my hands, not his.'

There was a silence in the sitting room. Sis Joyce was heard to be shifting things in her bedroom. No one thought of her in the course of the discussions going on.

'I'll drive you to the border,' said Mzi breaking the silence. 'I can do it tomorrow morning. Tonight I have a job.'

'Do you think it is wise for you to do it?' asked Dan Montsho. His concern was deep-seated.

'Why not?' cut in Mzi. 'Mine is a face not known by the system. No one is looking for me.'

'Besides,' added Sello, 'we don't want to broadcast this fact. Can you imagine what will happen if we begin to look for someone else to do the job, the cops will lay up a trap for us like they did in the case of Mandela.'

'What? Do you know about Mandela's arrest then?'

'It is our history,' butted in Dan Montsho. 'It is what every black child should be taught — how Mandela was arrested on a narrow bridge in Natal.'

'Down with sell-outs!' cried Sello.

'We are making them pay one by one,' confided Mzi.

'Are you coming with us to the border?' asked Sello of Dan Montsho.

'Let's discuss it with Mandla.'

'Okay by me,' said a disappointed Mzi. After a brief pause he said to Sello: 'I want you to come with me to town.' By this time some rapport existed between the two.

'Me?' queried Sello. 'Do you think it is safe?'

'No guarantee,' said Mzi bluntly. 'Your guts will decide.'

'What are we doing in town?'

'Buy shirts for you and Dan Montsho.'

'Seriously?' said Sello looking at his own borrowed shirt and touching it here and there. He was amused by his appearance in Uncle Ribs's shirt.

'I am serious,' said Mzi, looking the part. 'I don't visit Ann Hope for tea.'

'Oh, that one,' put in Sello, 'she's our bank.'

'That's what I mean.'

'No problems with me,' said a confident Sello. Mzi was to return later in the morning for the trip.

## NEWS ITEM
### POLICE POUNCE ON A SOWETO HOUSE: STUDENT LEADERS HELD

It was the morning of the big swoop. The curtains at Morning Sweetheart were still drawn. Matlakala stood at the door leading from the bedroom into the sitting room. She looked worn-out. Getting out of bed was very often for her an escape of sorts. For Noah Witbaatjie used her too often even for a person who took kindly to the attentions of men.

The morning paper lay on the coffee table with the latest news screaming at her. She couldn't resist a glance at the paper. And the morning news was big. She caught her breath as she read of the arrests. For those detained were in Soweto. A thought crossed her mind, a thought which struck at her motherliness. It left her spirits low, tugging at a nook of her being and began to nag her persistently. For she'd never been at ease from the moment she spied on him relaying the strange message on the walkie-talkie. And on this morning Noah had been up very early and said only he would be back soon. It was one of those secretive missions he often undertook. Until the moment she read of the arrests she might never have worried about his strange dealings. But the arrest of kids and the use of the walkie-talkie the day before made the whole issue her concern whatever the consequences.

'Honey, honey!' she yelled, sauntering to the bedroom door. She knew she would have to scream at him, for love-making often left him dog-tired, and he would sleep like a baby. She stood at the door and called again.

'What's the matter?' asked Noah as he raised his head.

'Have you seen this thing about the children and the police?' she asked in an excited way. Noah laid his head back on the pillow. His answer came from an impatient voice:

'I did.'

After a short pause she said: 'I wonder how the police knew about the house?'

'I don't know,' he answered curtly.

She watched him closely as he raised his head. He looked unhappy.

'Honey!'

'M'm.'

'Aren't you sorry for the parents of these children?'

'I don't know.'

'How do you mean?'

'Sorry?' he snarled, 'for people whose faces I don't know! You must be joking!'

She lowered the paper in her hands and said quietly: 'You are angry with me?' Noah flung off the bedding and swung his legs to the floor. His brow was knitted by a consuming anger: 'Oh! To hell with you, man! Why should I worry about petty criminals! . . . trouble makers! And — and their stupid mothers and fathers!'

'Criminals!' coughed a scandalised Matlakala.

At this point Noah was gesticulating quite freely. 'They bloody well are!' he snapped. '. . . Moegies! won't work!' Then he paused short of breath. He heaved out: 'Look what they have done to my business: killed it! Killed it!'

'But they never come here . . .'

'Hey, don't talk about what you don't know!' shouted Noah. 'They were nice, they were like little puppies begging for food otherwise, ek weedie jou, met my ma — I'm telling you I swear by my mother, I would have shown them a thing or two. Ek is van Kofifi — I'm from Sophiatown! You don't know me!'

'Cool down! cool down! I never asked for your place of origin, I'm not the Government.'

'Listen man,' said Noah wagging a threatening finger at his girl-friend who playfully dodged into the sitting room and stood on the other side of the coffee table, 'I know the game you've been playing. I'm not blind. You've been trying to spy on me . . . Let me tell you this: I don't care who you tell about me! Jy verstaan — Do you understand? I know those kids, gangsters who terrorise the people about a mourning period, poor people must not drink during the mourning period, kak — shit! . . . For my money they can bloody well cool off at Westend!'

'Honey you surprise me,' lamented a dejected Matlakala. 'Why do you boil so much at me? . . . And you say the most strange things about me.'

'I know your kind,' jeered Noah.

'What kind am I?'

'You . . . oh . . . you'll pere-pere — gibber all over the bloody location about me . . . Man, I don't care! Your bras — brothers won't touch me!'

The words began to jar in Matlakala's ears. He hurled too many insults for her to remain unconcerned. Her spirits sank to her knees so that she collapsed into the nearest easy chair and said in a plaintive voice: 'Noah, I don't know what I've done to you. If you feel you are tired living with me, say so. I won't force myself on you. Don't find all sorts of excuses on the shore and accuse me of things I don't know. I know men are the same!'

'Women are the same!' cut in Noah.

'All right, we are all the same. Throw me out of your house then. After all I won't be the first person you've chased out. You've squeezed the marrow out of the bone that's me. Throw me out!' she challenged.

He stood away from her. As she spoke he gradually inched towards the window facing the street. He was looking at the quiet street because at that hour the morning and the place were as quiet as a grave. Those going to work seemed like mourners to a funeral: they dragged their feet, for something was taken out of the heart of the people. The silence in the street was witness to the incident which the location woke up to. Like a cloud curling itself over the heads of so many people below it, the gloom rested in the street on which Noah's eyes were cast. He spoke with a touch of regret because he spoke to the one woman he knew had meant so much in his love-life: 'It's up to you baby. If you reckon you'll stay here and work for other people . . .'

'Which people?' cut in Matlakala.

'I don't know them. You do. If you work for other people in my house, I'll have nothing to do with you. Nothing! This is my house! I run the show! You have no business to nose into my affairs. I've listened to your questions; I've known where you were leading me to. I don't care for small boys who terrorise the location . . . Gots! I'm no child. Ek is van Kofifi — I'm from Sophiatown!'

'So you want me out of your house?'

Noah flung out his arm; he wheeled himself to face her and with the anger still burning in his eye, the arm mid-air to show her the way out, he said: 'I don't need you here!' — the finger pointed at his toes — 'you can go man!'

Matlakala gathered her gown together with her pride and returned to the bedroom. Then she stormed into the kitchen and brought out from the kitchen-dresser two paper bags marked Checkers and O.K. When she tried to re-enter the bedroom to collect her personal belongings, Noah barred her way and said: 'This is my house. Sit in the kitchen and I'll bring your things there!' Matlakala hurled the paper bags at his feet and swung back to the kitchen. Not to sit. She walked out. He remained picking up the bags to shove her clothes into them. Presently the bundles were an eyeful. The items didn't belong to the crammed indecency of paper bags.

Suddenly Noah's house sprang alive from outside. Matlakala began throwing pebbles onto the roof. In response Noah yelled at the four walls: 'Wat doen daai tickeyline — What's the bitch up to?' The words were hardly out when they were drowned by the splintering of window-panes. For the woman turned her fury to one item she knew would give her a sure audience.

She was brimful of his misdeeds and these she was determined to broadcast to the neighbourhood. She hurled one stone after another at the bedroom windows and when he seemed to delay coming out because packing meant finding her stuff in the room, she mistook this to mean he was scared to face her in the street. For Matlakala was what the location people called a street-girl. In the eyes of the people a woman who lived by enticing a man to her sacred body was no lady: just a street-girl. When the neighbourhood gathered round the spectacle of shame where broken windows told the beginnings and end of a story they came not only to laugh at Noah but also Matlakala, who was by then panting from the effort of her actions. From her mouth she spat out unprintable words. She told of the man's clandestine activities. 'Noah is a police informer, he sold the children of Soweto to the cops!' She was screaming in a shrill voice: 'He sits in the house because he's lazy to work; he sits all day listening to conversations of his loudmouthed customers. They think they buy liquor: it is poison. Noah is a witch. He doctors the liquor with muti. Poor people don't know what they drink. And when they are drunk they spill out information he carries to the police. He is a police informer, Sis! Pooh!'

Noah appeared on the side of the house carrying in one hand the two bundles of paper bags. In the other he clasped a stove-poker. He caught a few words from his estranged girl and was furious. In utter disgust, he hurled over the fence the two bundles, spilling them out on the pavement. He yelled: 'Get away from here you bloody bitch! The grapes are sour because I'm throwing you out of my house. You are nothing but a bloodsucker. Tickeyline you!'

Once more Soweto wondered. While a few people laughed at the sight of lovers fallen out with each other, the majority stood sharing the news about Noah's role as a police informer. A few women egged on Matlakala saying she must break all the windows of the house. They said Noah was in the habit of using women and then casting them out like phlegm. 'Sis!' they spat, 'a police informer.'

The waves of the happening carried beyond Orlando East. They drifted to other parts of Soweto: Noah was a man to watch; a man to curse.

'Go man!' he yelled at Matlakala. The morning sun began to blind him so that he had to squint to look at her. 'Your threats mean fuckall to me! Go!'

Noah Witbaatjie turned on his heel and hurried into the sanctuary of his house. He plopped into the easy chair in the sitting room, awkwardly because his hands were in the pockets of his morning gown — the scarlet red one. His head was hanging as if he brooded. The paper which was the beginning of his unhappy day, stared him in the eye. The big bold print glared at him and the arrest of the students he read mocked at him. He thought Matlakala walked out of the house with his spirits. He remained seated like that for hours because he was on this day so very depressed.


This morning the sun was full of heat as if the night before hadn't belonged to the same chain of happenings, as if the beading of night and day was out of sequence.

When Mzi returned from dropping Sis Joyce he remained silent about his determination to go into town. Mandla watched him retrieve the AK47 machine rifle; he saw him wrap it up with brown paper, a little soiled. The paper bag was shaken from its nook and the bunch of artificial flowers stuck up purposefully.

'Why take two parcels into the car?' queried Mandla, 'the rifle could have fitted into the paperbag.'

'This is a mere precaution. Nobody's going to touch me because nobody knows about me. You see, the gun goes on the seat like this'. (He meant it would straddle both the driver's and passenger's seats).

'The flowers are lovely enough to fix an eye on. Who's so foolish to look beyond the pretty flowers? When Sello comes into the car, he holds the paper bag on his lap and the flowers will stick out for the lovers of beauty. Clever hey?'

'So you are taking Sello with you?'

'Two is company; one loneliness. I work best with company,' said Mzi with his face twisted by his hard smile. Mandla kept quiet. He gave up trying to dissuade his friend from going into town. He had long told himself Mzi was a stubborn man. He thought he should add that he was also a showy man. For why did he insist on taking the machine gun as if he was a gangster intent on shooting it out with cops? In the open no one won a battle with the cops. No one joined the battle on the black side because guns were in the hands of whitey. It was a form of exhibitionism to straddle a gun on the seats and warm it with one's buttocks. No use!

Mandla helped to carry the paper bag into the car parked in the street. He didn't want to be called a coward. They didn't go out at the same time. And this is how MaNhlapo caught a glimpse of the pretty bundle of flowers in Mandla's hand. She stood a while to admire the bundle but said nothing more than a word of praise. There was an unwritten agreement between herself and the boys. She was told nothing, she asked no questions. For her it was enough to have the company of two young men who didn't drink or smoke or crowd her house with giggling young girls. No, MaNhlapo had no complaints about the young men. There was another side to their presence: there was food in the house, the rent was paid regularly and she could afford herself a few yards of the German print material — isishweshwe.

When Mandla returned to the house and looked out of the sitting room to see the little car take off, MaNhlapo didn't think there was anything unusual about it. She failed to notice the heart beat of her one son, Mandla.

As always she might have cooled him down, reassuring him of the safety of the other son, Mzi. For God always protects his creation, especially the underdog, she would have added.

Mzi was after all not unconcerned on his way to Uncle Ribs's house. For he was on the look out. He wouldn't say it loudly but it was for cops. Like many other folks in Soweto, he had come to know how to outfox the law. There were the beaten tracks in common use. On these the cops ran up and down looking for phantoms because the real people were always a jump ahead of arrest, travelling on side streets.

He arrived outside the house without fuss. He blew the hooter once and waited.

Sello settled in the car making sure that he allowed the gun to huddle behind him. He joked: 'We have good company, hey?'

'No guarantee against the dogs,' said Mzi bitterly, 'but the flowers can be a good gift.'

'How do you mean? Are you going to buy your way through a roadblock?'

'The cops understand bribe. I'll say to the first cop: the bunch is our gift to your wife.'

'What if a Piet has no sense of humour?'

'Too bad. He'll see the efficiency of my machine gun.' After a brief pause he added: 'Why show kindness where there was hate?'

It was a mouthful from Mzi. And there was no way in which Sello could go beyond that point. Both fell into silence. It was a silence they used to fill up gaps in their minds; a silence in which each sat alert to the passing scene mindful only of the danger posed by the presence of cops. Strangely, the whole route was free of police surveillance. So they rode on in that silence, the air shaken by the jarring noise of the little car.

Dr Kenotsi sat reading the morning paper when his two comrades-in-arms arrived. It was at that early hour when the surgery was as quiet and eerie as at the graveyard at night. To break the monotony of working long hours at repairing broken spirits, the medico was in the habit of shutting himself behind the newspapers. So when the two greeted him, they had to stand close to him, to jolt his concentration on the paper. It was obviously the shock of seeing them so suddenly which made the medico say: 'You chaps must be mad! How can you be driving around like this when the boer-boys arrested the larger part of your team?'

'We need money from Ann,' snapped Mzi.

'Ann?' queried the medico as if the name was unfamiliar.

'We've got to see her before things become pretty hot,' said Sello firmly.

'They are hot now! What do you mean before they become hot? They are already hot,' he emphasised, unable to fathom his young visitors. He went on: 'Haven't you chaps seen this morning's paper?'

'No!' snapped Mzi again.

'I thought so,' said the medico with a sense of satisfaction. He pushed the paper towards Mzi. The latter merely glanced at it, screwed his face and passed it on to Sello, who read it eagerly. His eyes remained on the paper for a long time and he soon appeared to be insulated from the other two.

Mzi looked Kenotsi in the eye and said bluntly: 'I've come to ask for your car.'

'What?' cried the doctor in an anguished voice. He pushed his swivelling chair backward and sat up to face Mzi squarely.

'The little car outside has problems. I don't want to see ourselves stopping on the way.'

'You must be joking!' breathed out the doctor in staccato.

Mzi kept quiet. There was contempt in his heart. He recalled telling Mandla that all black doctors were bourgeois. They could never be trusted in the struggle against oppression. So he eyed the medico with this sense of deep-seated mistrust and alienation. But he kept his convictions to himself. Pride overwhelmed him at the same time. And he was determined to reveal himself to the doctor.

'I have no fears,' he began tentatively, 'the cops will do nothing to me. They have nothing against me. They don't know me.'

'Don't be naive, Mzi,' said Kenotsi with a voice charged with anger, 'those chaps will dig up your past even if they have to put the ashes of your ancestors under a microscope. Don't be a fool, man. Wait a day or two before seeing Ann. She's not going to skip with all that money. It's in trust for such emergencies as yours.'

'I don't agree with you doc,' replied Mzi. He was looking beyond the medico for there was a chart showing the skeleton of an obese human being with red lines showing off the danger areas. Mzi didn't seem to understand what it depicted but was fascinated by the sight all the same.

'You don't have to. But think of the risk you place on everyone connected with you for your impetuous action.'

'Doc is missing the point: I want to take advantage of a situation which must get worse. The cops will soon be howling at our heels at every street-corner. Sello here can tell you the heat is not yet on. A day or two and things will be bloody bad.'

Kenotsi got to the core of his feelings; he asked bluntly: 'Why risk my car? Those chaps will confiscate it . . . All right, maybe that won't hit me so badly. But what about my practice, my future? I don't have any intention to skip the country. I don't believe in that sort of thing. Please don't create a situation in which I'll find it impossible to offer my services to the people.'

'Doc is right,' came in Sello, speaking above the lowered newspaper, 'let's not expose him. Better drop the idea or let's use the sickly machine we've got.' He sounded lame.

'I'm not dropping anything. Let them arrest me if they can. I'm

146

going to town! How can I restrict myself? Because I think it is what the system wants? I'm not going to chain myself. Let them do it if they can but I'll blast my way through if need be.'

'What do you mean by that one?'

'He's got a machine gun in the car,' said Sello.

The information jolted the medico. He stood up and looked outside the little window of the surgery as if he'd see the gun in question.

He turned to face Mzi and said: 'Tell me mfo — fellow — are you well?'

Mzi said nothing. Didn't smile. He didn't even grunt. He glared at the medico as if he was about to burst with the fullness of his emotions. Again he showed condescension for the medico who was impelled to assert himself: 'I've never heard the likes of this!' declared the doctor. 'I must say the demonstrations have made many of us travel a long way just overnight. What seemed impossible yesterday happens with such ease today it just isn't real. What do you term this Mzi, urban terrorism?'

There was absolute silence in the room. Not even the ruffling of paper was heard. The alienation of three persons so close and yet so far apart from each other was a joyless sight. Mzi felt the pounding of his heart against his chest. His muscles were as tough as biltong chips. Screaming and yelling at that moment was all he wanted to do because he was disgusted with Kenotsi; he felt let down and frustrated in the course of his mission. His mouth was twisted as he looked at the bourgeois in front of him, the thought occurring once more. It was this hopeless feeling which rooted his feet in the room. He needed the medico more than he was strained by a sense of respect for him, otherwise he would have long ago left in a huff. He was settled in his mind: he'd use the little car outside but some form of disguise was necessary.

'Can I borrow your white dustcoat?' Mzi asked quietly, his anger deflated.

'By all means,' said a tolerant Kenotsi. 'There are no markings on it so it could have come from anywhere,' said he light-heartedly.

'Thanks,' said Mzi bringing the coat down from the peg on the door leading out of the room.

Sello broke his silence again: 'How's Keke, doc?'

'Past the danger point. He's lucky to have found me yesterday. The chap might have died. Some burns were horrible. No, the chap was lucky.'

'We were shocked to see Sis Ida's place in such a mess. And we didn't know who did it,' said Sello. He went on to say: 'Keke was too much of a sissy. I don't know what business he had to meddle with explosives.'

'I've always said you chaps don't know what you're doing at times. You depend a lot on trial-and-error . . . Anyway he'll be all right soon.'

'Some of us can never forgive him for what he's done,' said Sello bitterly.

'Wrong there,' chided Kenotsi. 'The boy is too young to be away from home because of fear of cops let alone dabbling with explosives. I can well imagine his spirit of adventure under the circumstances. You must learn to forgive him.'

'We are on the downward trip all because of him,' lamented Sello.

'It shouldn't be that bad,' put in Kenotsi, 'we've all lost the initiative at the moment. It has happened before but it doesn't mean we'll slide down forever.'

'The cops can't stop us,' asserted Mzi leaning on the door. 'They'll catch the small fish but the big ones like me they can't touch!'

The visitors left and Dr Kenotsi sighed with relief. There was something about his association with the student demonstrations he found oppressive. And Mzi didn't make it any better. He was too showy to be a real fighter, thought the medico.

The first patient was led in and the medico's wandering mind checked itself. There's always work to be done, Kenotsi told himself.

The midget car zig-zagged through the streets of Soweto and plunged onto the Soweto Highway. As always there were many cars on the road because Soweto takes the beat of its own heart from the tense activity of throbbing Johannesburg: the butcher, the vegetable-dealer, the grocer, the factory-hand, the window-washer, all these and more hurry into town in the morning and as the day stretches east to west and its shadows west to east Soweto trickles back into its own hole.

Mzi gripped the steering-wheel tightly. Ahead of them was a cluster of trees, and a car standing idly by. Memories of a couple of days back waylaid one another along the stream of his thoughts. He recalled the ambush. There was no way in which he and Sello could run. There was no place to hide. He slowed down and alerted Sello to his suspicions. His comrade needed no prodding because he was himself looking at the same scene ahead as Mzi, and was bothered by his thumping heart which warned of the danger.

'Fix up the machine,' said Mzi, 'unwrap it.'

Sello quickly placed the bunch of flowers on the back seat and pulled up the AK47 from behind him. He let it rest on his lap and undid the paper. He nearly yelled with joy for the experience of handling a brand-new machine gun. He sensed his own inferiority in the company of Mzi and was overwhelmed by awe.

They approached the point of danger, their curiosity rising. It soon dropped again however — there was no danger in the hulk of a forsaken motor-car. The sighs they gave from relief were lost in the drone of the little car as it sped to Jo'burg city.

Pharmacy House was a beehive of activity, tensed groups of workers huddled by gossip. The lamentations heard along the corridors and in the offices pierced the air. It was into this sadness that Mzi and Sello entered, were welcomed with sorrowful smiles and plagued by more questions than they could take. For anxiety was huge within the building.

Ann Hope perched on the edge of her desk, arms folded across her chest as she spoke in whispers with Mzi and Sello. They wanted to believe her concern as she said she was relieved to see them; they wanted to reassure her as she began to curse the police and the system in the country, but their own faith in the white people remained like the two snapped pieces of a string: for the demonstrations in Soweto marked this snapping in the hearts of youth. Necessity made the flapping in the air of the two pieces of string. As long as necessity demanded there would be this tenuous relation between the youth and the white man. But with the gathering of momentum within the whirlwind nothing would remain. It was known to some, lost to many.

Mzi said to Ann in answer to a query: 'They can't touch me!' His faith was in the instrument left wrapped up and hidden in the inconspicuous little car.

Ann concluded: 'It's all so very depressing this matter, isn't it?'

Mzi and Sello kept silent at that point. For them there was nothing depressing. The pain was so profound it didn't begin with the detention of a few of their numbers. The life of the whole nation was cause for depression. Mzi said they needed cash immediately.

'Of course, dear,' answered Ann. She always warmed up to Mzi. And from the depths of womanhood sprang the itch to snuggle in his long, muscular arms. Ann prided herself on being a foreigner, and was quick to remind any newcomer to her presence of this fact. For her it was a natural act that she was attracted spontaneously to Mzi. She would have done anything to know his true mind because his distant and aggressive stance every time they met in the company of others was not him. So she believed she saw the fire in his brown eyes as hunger, contained hunger for a woman; his snarls were of hunger, this same hunger she swore she could satisfy as a woman.

Mzi stood impatient with the slow process of organising the cash. She hurried out promising to be back in a jiffy. But it seemed eternity to Mzi. And to kill time he went once more over Ann's office: the huge, wooden desk shining with the sweat of the cleaner, the soft chair with arm rests; the carpet on the floor in which his foot sank; the Christian's calendar on the wall showing Mary and Jesus; more paper on the wall — schedules and charts.

Ann came back, shoved a thick brown envelope in Mzi's hand, and smiled. Mzi grunted.

'Can you tell me a bit about what happened last night — no, this early morning?' She was again perched on her desk.

'Ah,' moaned Mzi lazily, 'what's there to say? The dogs came without barking and they pounced, that's all!' he said gesturing. He was light-hearted enough to move around the office like a caged beast. For Mzi was confident, condescending a lot. Sello still seemed thunderstruck. For him Mzi was the leader and the brains. His role there was of companion and he played it well.

'How's Mandla?'

'Fine.'

'I wonder how he escaped?'

'He was with me. They couldn't touch him because they don't know me.'

'Must be a relief to live behind a mask, isn't it?'

'Who made the mask? Not me!'

'Aren't you adorable.'

'I don't know what you mean!'

'I like the way you scoff at them, the way your guts defy the very power in their hands . . .'

'Power is in our hands!' said Mzi stiffening the muscles of his face. 'Power is in Soweto. And the guns in their hands. Only for a while. Wait and see.'

There was a pause. Ann sat watching Mzi and then her eyes roved over to Sello. Always the tough one, he looked meek in the presence of Mzi. No wonder, Mzi with every bit of his body so very attractive, so desirable. Ann wished he wasn't involved in the mess of the struggle.

She offered to introduce them to Ian Taylor, the head of the Pharmacy House agency. Mzi said he was not interested in Ian Taylor. The man was a hypocrite professing Christian allegiance. Furthermore they were due back in Soweto soon, before the police mounted roadblocks around the place.

'Of course, dear,' she said retreating into the mask of her official position.

The trip back to Soweto was tense. Menacing figures kept on springing up in Sello's line of sight. He was really jumpy. Mzi was no less tense. It showed in the grip on the steering wheel — tight, so tight the knuckles of his hand were like weather-beaten boulders. Yet as they progressed toward Soweto, Mzi tried to relax. He swung his head from side to side in time with a tune hummed in his throat. And as it became evident the way into the location was all clear his confidence began to bounce off the steering-wheel as he drummed on it rhythmically.

Sello was dropped off at Uncle Ribs's with the understanding that he and Dan Montsho would purchase their shirts at shops around Soweto.

When Mzi parted from Sello he said he would collect them later for the trip to Botswana. His mind was made up on the evening's engagement. It was off.

The desire to save the skins of two endangered colleagues changed his mind. He was the kind of person who never was generous with an admission of defeat. For defeat it was, though for a good reason and a better cause under the circumstances.

Since the hour of departure was still far off, Mzi and Mandla rested their minds separately: one in the sitting-room on an ordinary upright chair; the other in the bedroom on the bed. Their eyes were shut but their minds wandered all over the possibilities occasioned by the galloping of events since the day before.

# 8

It was an awfully frightful first experience for Sis Ida in a cell. Alone. Scared. Bone dry in the mouth. Her mind wandered endlessly from situation to situation. She was kept awake for so long that her eyes felt bulged like marbles. For her the break of dawn never seemed to come; relief was as remote as an oasis in a desert.

The formalities on arrival at Westend Police Headquarters were brief; she didn't remember anything because her mind was in a terrible state of confusion. Caught napping as she had been there was no way in which she might have re-arranged her affairs and her thoughts before the arrest. She didn't recall where she kept pleading her innocence: whether to the cops or her conscience, it wasn't clear. Yet the chorus line of her innocence was repeated as regularly as the sea-water lashes the coastline at ebb-tide. For many times now she heard the turning of the cell key on doors a little distant from hers. That grating sound reminded her of her own loss of freedom. She tried to forget the sound, but its recurrence made it impossible. It became a fact of life.

Her escort disappeared after locking her up, And she remained to call a cell her new home. In the dim, sickly light it was a painful adjustment. The stuffiness in the air caused her mind to be in turmoil. She wondered if she would survive life in a cell for any length of time. She saw the wash basin from which she assumed she might have to quench the thirst rumbling in her stomach. The water was brackish and tasteless. But a sip of it was enough to give relief to her body. Yet the load on her shoulders remained and she decided that to remove the weight off her feet was what she needed badly. She picked up one of the blankets on the floor. Every bit of it felt coarse and spikey. She unfolded it, to spread it on the mats. The stench of vomit and the white streak of a dried substance on the blanket made her recoil with disgust and horror. She let the blanket drop out of her hands, folding it a bit. She didn't know what overcame her: but she was aware of a dizziness about her. She went to lean on the water basin, stood there for a while; arms across her breast, she shut her eyes as if the act would make the present experience disappear. It helped the dizziness because it subsided like water dropping its level in a trough. Sis Ida opened her eyes and found herself reading the scrawlings on the walls: rough, vulgar and with figures distorted. It was a new thing to see the mind articulated on the walls like this. She wondered if this was a women's or men's cell. It looked more a men's habitat. She recalled the grouse of the Station Commander when told she was to be locked up. He had complained the cells were overcrowded and there was no room for new in-takes. But she was a political case, therefore no two ways about it: she had to be locked up.

Her spirits couldn't hold up her body. She persuaded herself to rest on the blankets telling her mind the white, dried coating on the blanket was hidden out of sight. She collapsed on the bundle. No sooner was she down than she experienced a disturbing sensation: her whole body began to itch as if unseen insects crawled on her skin. This she tried to suppress, aware that if she allowed the thought of lice to take command of her, she would have no way to remain in the cell in a sane mind. But that didn't stop the creeping feel of her skin even as she rubbed hands along her arms. She clasped both arms with hands crossed and contemplated her position. In the process her mind drifted to her house, her daughter and her grandson.

It was many moments later when she realised her mind settled on various situations beginning with the irony of the rewards of kindness: her house furniture fell apart because of overuse; her bill with storekeeper Tandabantu hung on her neck as if the gods placed the necklace of mishap on her alone; the kitchen was in ruins from the cause of a blast no-one seemed to know anything about. For days before her detention she debated with herself whether to approach sympathetic persons in Soweto for help or go straight to the Council of S.A. Churches for it. She hesitated for fear of bringing into the public eye her harbouring of young people on the run. She was always checked by suspicions of the next person as indeed everyone in Soweto was suspicious of his neighbour. For the first time Sis Ida saw just how dangerous her life had been for a long time. She was thinking in that vein when she dozed off. Like a child she went to sleep in the awkward position of her sitting on the floor.

The break of dawn came bringing with it the heavy activity of prison life. The gates grated and screeched open and it was to these eerie sounds that Sis Ida woke up with a pinch of hurt in her bosom. A vague feeling seemingly without origin, only regret. The cell was by degrees becoming a burning inferno and there was for her no way she could ask for relief. She ambled up on her feet; was pained by the stiffness of her frame. How she slept and for how long there was no way to tell except by the measure of this hardness of the muscles.

Hunger pangs began to groan in her stomach. At home she could scrape something together but here there was no way. The law stripped her of the freedom of the house and the sense of belonging at the very moment when the police descended on her. She could never forget that crucial moment. And now she experienced it all over again because she was so hopelessly hungry.

She let the tap run and cupped her hands for water: first to rinse the lousy feel in her mouth and then to sip a bit of it for strength. She looked forward to the prison meal although without relish because she didn't have the slightest notion of what prison food was made of.

It was late morning. That much she was certain and she checked herself trying to work out what she would be doing if abroad. But she did piece together the strange happenings in her new surroundings and found it a frustrating exercise: the grating of prison gates; the crush of footsteps on interminably long corridors. It was never clear where they ended.

Suddenly a key turned forcefully in her door. Her excitement climbed and dropped; her eyes fixed on the door, her mind alternately wishing for and being against the newcomer.

A white female warder sneaked her head in and said: 'Are you all-right, mosadi—woman?' Always mocking these people are, thought Sis Ida. So she nodded heavily. She added: 'I am hungry.' 'Did you sleep well?' she was asked as a counter-punch. She kept mum. For how can anyone living on the level of the gutter be asked if she slept well in a prison cell. The wardress retreated after mumbling about a meal. The grating of the key jarred Sis Ida but she was left with spirits slightly repaired.

Again she thought of her job: she would be smiling, a packet or a cosmetic bottle revolving in her fingers, as she explained to a beauty conscious female the advantages of the doctored liquid.

Her door re-opened and the wardress placed the plate of food at the entrance and let it slide towards Sis Ida. Two glum eggs rested on the edge of the plate. So did two slices of brown bread. She had to collect the mug of black coffee from near the door. She lifted it to her mouth and almost spat out immediately because it was cold and oversweetened. So watery was it, she wondered why it was referred to as coffee. Another sensation churned her stomach: there was a grumbling and a grumbling and she feared poisoning. This brought about a new thought of how she would survive hunger. For now the food meant little to her body since she was not prepared to risk eating or drinking. It was after some time that a key rattled in the door once more. She became alert. They must not catch her napping; they must not intimidate her into touching their food. Sis Ida looked up at the spy-hole and wilted with frustration. She couldn't make out the party on the other side. But she was aware of a paralysing fear. For prison has its own sense of fear. She braced herself against an onslaught. So she waited for the door to open.

Sergeant Ndoda Ndlovu was brief, his face stern: 'Come with me,' he said and began to lead the way in that officious manner typical of persons of the law. Even as he tried to avoid her eyes, she was convinced she knew the policeman. She hurried to catch up with him but remained on his heels. She offered him her open heart and said: 'Good morning.' He answered by humming: 'M'm.' She was disappointed, and resolved to keep her peace. But the thud of their feet along the corridor bounced off her chest. She wondered where he was leading her and was fearful because his attitude was cool and distant, always an ominous sign.

They entered a huge, bare and lonely room. A teak table and two chairs were all it contained. Sis Ida worried about the fact that she was going to be alone with the policeman, a black policeman who seemed unconcerned and unfeeling.

The cop offered her one chair and went to sit on the other. She was of mixed feelings now, but vowed to keep her guard up. She didn't like his grunts. He appeared unwilling to open his mouth. It bothered her because how was she supposed to gain his confidence? She said bluntly: 'I know you.' He looked at her as if sizing her up, his face contorted by what Sis Ida thought was revulsion. Bravely she went on: 'I saw you at Mrs September's place.' Sergeant Ndlovu was jolted by his own fear. He thought of his last visit to that woman's place. Where might this thing end? Would he be revealed before his officers? He didn't know what to make of this woman but was determined to know more about her without giving anything away himself.

'Who are you?' asked the cop.

'Ida Diradikayi,' replied Sis Ida.

'And you say you saw me at Mrs September's house?'

'Yes, those days you were not a policeman.'

Sergeant Ndlovu beamed her a smile and said 'So you know me.' There was no doubt of his relief. For the fear of being revealed as a double operator receded immediately. 'How do you know Mrs September?'

'She's my friend,' answered Sis Ida.

'I want to worship your gods,' said Ndlovu.

Sis Ida felt flattered. What crossed her mind was something which didn't belong within prison: the cop roused in her breast the kind of warmth so many men did every day at work. She suppressed what could have been a loud laugh.

The cop said: 'Don't laugh because I'm serious. Your case has been referred to us of the Resistance Movement Section. And you are the first person they are doing this to.' Sis Ida's face became clouded; she was puzzled being without the faintest idea of what the cop meant. For her, cops were cops, and they dealt with law enforcement one way only: detention.

'I can see you don't understand.' said Ndlovu. 'We operate two divisions: one deals with Resistance cases, the other Black Power matters. The material found in your house and the charges facing the suspects in your house, these things alone could have placed you in the hands of the Black Power division.'

Ndlovu lowered his voice and his head to face Ida across the table and spoke forcefully: 'I tell you, you would be vomiting blood by now! Thank your gods for the transfer to our division.' Sis Ida thanked him in turn for the information.

All the fire in her body was snuffed. She began to fear what was in store for her since she had heard of the barbaric treatment meted out by cops in political cases.

Ndlovu stood up and said: 'I brought you here to tell you this. I don't know you but I admire what you've done for the nation. Don't let the people around here frighten you. Tighten your heart and have courage.'

Sergeant Ndlovu led Sis Ida out of the strange room and along the corridor again. Their feet sounded like a hammering on the inside of a huge barrel. Sis Ida found the thudding of their feet going to her heart and unsettling it. But she was a brave woman, a person of faith, born of the hardships she lived.

No words passed between them. He knocked gently on one of the closed doors at one end of the long corridor, and let her enter the room alone.


For Boysi time ceased to matter. Nor was there for him a way to know how long his ordeal lasted. Ever since he had been separated from the other members of the group, he had been made to stand in the centre of a huge, bare room. There was only one wooden table and a high stool. A forlorn, covered electric bulb gave out the only light. And for long stretches, measured by the pulse of his body, he stood alone without any humans in sight, without any sounds outside the room. It was a lonely feeling, so lonely it made him curse and click his tongue now and again. As yet there was no way he knew how to react to his first experience in jail. Nor did it occur to him he was being manipulated, to wear down the resistance they would want out of the way when interrogation began.

The door of the large room opened. He braced himself for an attack in some way. His defiant spirit told him to look away from the door. But when he heard a low whimpering and a shuffle of feet as if someone was being dragged along, he gradually turned to look at the new scene in the room. The remains of energy sapped through long hours of standing permeated his body and he felt an impulse to shoot forward and rescue one of his team-mates. Bongi's face was contorted by her wish to survive. She was fighting off her captors who held her blouse in a vice-like grip. Part of it was ripped off exposing the breast in a vulgar way. Boysi's anger knew the treatment given to Bongi was mere humiliation. The two men bringing her in seemed to enjoy her plight. One wore a cynical smile; the other masked his face in simulated anger.

Boysi dropped his eyes. A voice yelled at him: 'Kyk haar—look at her!' All the time the shuffling feet went this way and that way in the room. He remained defiant. And the command was repeated: 'Kyk jou donner—look you bugger! Sy's jou cherrie, kyk—she's your girl-friend, look!' With that Bongi's frayed bodice was ripped off exposing the fullness of her turgid breasts and pointed teats to the beastliness of the two cops. One of them turned the light on Bongi's breast. She couldn't shield herself because the other man stood by and commanded, raising one arm of Bongi's: 'Pick up your arms!' She tried but the inhumanity of it all overcame her so that her arms collapsed on her sides. The man next to her held both arms and raised them forcefully above her head. He said: 'Keep them up there!' Bongi's eyes blurred with tears, her head sagged visibly and she barely resisted a scream.

For a brief spell Boysi's and Bongi's eyes met in a moment filled with bitterness and a sense of impotence for Boysi. Yet he saw in her eye mocking laughter, bravery displayed effortlessly. He knew he would have to tighten his heart and not yield to whatever suggestion the cops made to him. How strange, he thought, this changed encounter between them and the hands of the law. Not so long ago they would have been taking each other for granted, teasing each other and not concerned with each other's feelings. But now every minute held pain for both. The empathy between them was so strong it placed their young lives in jeopardy. Their sense of purpose was enough to make them careless of the consequences at the time.

From a drawer on the table, the cop near it brought out a pair of small pliers. He held the tool in the air as he approached Bongi. She clenched her teeth, vaguely aware of the meaning of the instrument in the hand of the cop. Boysi was horrified even as he wondered what the game ahead was. For the one conviction in the hearts of the young detainees was the knowledge of the insensitiveness of their captors.

The moment when the pliers pinched on the little dark brown nipple on Bongi's breast, her pained yell pierced the quietness of the air; Boysi's heart thudded twice in quick succession as shock seized him. He shut his eyes tightly, his face bloated by a rush of blood, hateful blood.

Cold-bloodedly, the cop undid the pliers on the one nipple and placed them on the other. Bongi screamed, tears pouring down her soft brown skin. She tried to wriggle free of her tormentors but her moves served to increase the excruciating pain caused by the pliers.

The man gripping Bongi's upheld arms yelled at Boysi: 'Jong, ek moer jou nou, kyk donner!—Fellow, I'm going to beat you up, look bugger!'

When Boysi opened his eyes slowly, he was in time to see the cop wrench the pair of pliers from Bongi. She yelled a shrill cry and was dragged out of the room sniffling, her mouth twisted by pain and bitter hatred.

Boysi remained standing in the room. His tormentor sat on the stool, arms folded across his chest, and after a pause he said to Boysi: 'My name is Sergeant De Bruin. You can tell that to the people at *The World*. It is mos your newspaper. Well, I don't care, my boy. There's nothing you or *The World* can do to me.' De Bruin stood up and began to pace the room like a restless animal. Suddenly he stopped on his tracks and said bluntly: 'You are dead, man. I'm looking at a corpse right now . . . A policeman was murdered, a police station was bombed. D'you know what it means? You are here on a murder charge. Hoor?—Hear? . . . Ya, we'll let the whole lot of you hang for the life of one policeman. Hoor jy?—Do you hear?' He dropped his voice and a certain warmth seemed to enter his tone: 'I want to save your skin. Save you from the gallows. Come straight with me and I'll do wonders for you. Believe me if you speak the truth . . . co-o-p-e-rate with me, I'll see to it that you go scot free. Hoor jy jong—Do you hear fellow?'

'I understand,' said Boysi unbelieving. The pain from Bongi's breast lingered in his body.

Sergeant De Bruin went to the table to sit and produced pen and paper. Bang went the first question: 'Who is the leader of your group?'

Boysi hesitated. He looked at the cop; he looked beyond him. During the hesitation, the cop brought down his fist on the table twice. Its thudding reverberated throughout the huge room as he yelled: 'Didn't you bloody hear what I asked you?'

'I did.'

'Shit: answer me man!'

Boysi shifted his weight from one leg to the other. De Bruin shot up and cried: 'Ek is die baas—I am the boss! You must answer me!' He sat down and asked once more: 'Who is your leader?'

'Mandla Nkosi.'

The name was acidic in his mouth. He said it because he believed the man knew it already. He was made to say it to fill his mouth with foulness. So he had to fight against this foulness and to clean his mouth he clamped it full of disgust for the cop.

'Where is he?' asked De Bruin, his eye fixed on Boysi's eye.

'I don't know.'

'Kak—Shit! You don't know! Are you going to tell me the truth or do you want me to wring the bloody thing from you?'

Boysi said Mandla went missing from Sis Ida's place now and then and he, Boysi, never got to know where Mandla went on such occasions. He added no-one knew where he was when the cops pounced on the group. Boysi finished off by saying everyone in the group thought the accident in the kitchen involved Mandla and he was thought to be lying low somewhere injured. He was relieved to see the cop nod almost imperceptibly with what Boysi read as satisfaction.

'Who gave you money to live on?'

'I don't know.'

De Bruin stood up slowly and went to perch on the edge of the table facing Boysi. His hands gripped the edge of the table as he spoke: 'You are breaking the agreement. I said tell me the truth and we will work together in peace. I treat you as a sensible adult, show me respect . . . who gave you money?'

'The Bishop . . .'

Boysi cast forlorn eyes at the cop leaving him to complete the answer for himself. The officer said: 'We know all about that political predikant. One of these days he gets it in the neck. Wait and see!'

Boysi didn't even grunt. He remained silent, eating into himself, wondering why he yielded so easily to the pressures of the cop. His mouth became dry; his interest in the surroundings evaporated; he thought his legs began to wobble and he heard himself complain: 'I am tired.'

The cop didn't look up as he replied: 'Wait for orders boy.' He was scribbling on the table filling page after page with material he composed himself because Boysi gave away very little, most of it monosyllables. De Bruin put his pen on the table and looked up at Boysi. He said: 'Here's one more thing I want to know. And listen here don't beat about the bush. I want a straight honest answer, hoor—hear?'

'M'm.' Boysi mumbled.

'Nou ja—Now then: you people did the job at Jabavu Police Station, isn't it?'

Boysi spoke quietly and confidently:

'I wasn't there!'

He couldn't tell what went wrong but his voice grated on his chest. There was something hollow about the words. He regretted the answer himself. So he wasn't fully surprised to see the cop push his stool backward. He noticed the man remained on his seat but the face was flushed, eyes burning, mouth twisted by words left in mid air: 'I didn't ask that bloody question! Didn't you hear me? I said you people bombed the police station, killed a policeman! That's all!'

Boysi didn't open his mouth. His eyes met those of the cop and remained riveted on him. Within his chest was consuming bitter desire for vengeance.

'Hoe kyk jy my?—How are you looking at me?' asked De Bruin. He glared back at the detainee feeling the urge to break the defiant stance of the youth. He rose from the stool and stepped towards the door and bellowed in the large room: 'Follow me!'

At that point Boysi's shoulders sagged. He followed behind the sergeant. Their feet thudded on the long passage. There was a discord in their step, it bounced off the walls on either side of their way in a manner suggesting the differences in the hearts of the two persons. Its lonely ring echoed on Boysi, sending a cold chill down his spine because he didn't know where he was going; he didn't seem to care now, any eventuality was welcome to him even so. He wondered if he was walking to his end, and as this thought recurred like a worry something in him snapped.

He was both surprised and relieved to be handed over to one of the warders wandering in the area of the prison cells. Nothing was said to him. It looked all right because the ordeal with the cop was over, at least for the time being. Disappointment seized him when he realised splitting from the cop didn't mean release from detention, there would surely be a next time for which he must keep up his guard.

The clanking of the prison door slammed into his ears like the blast of a dynamite charge. Wow! it was a noisy relief he experienced — the end of his first tortured encounter with prison conditions, none of which he liked one bit.

Inside the cell it didn't take him one minute to be hit by a tantalising smell. Where nausea due to a stale and stuffy smell should greet him, he found the air permeated by the fresh juicy smell of fruit. Fruit trees in a prison cell? — That he couldn't fathom.

He searched the room for the source of the smell. And as surely as he was his father's son, he saw in the dim light of the cell, a bowl of fruit on the floor. He exclaimed to the four walls: 'Bananas, apples and oranges! Gots! what's not happening?' He was in a way happy he could still talk to himself aloud — sane! Next to the bowl was a bottle of orange squash and a clean mug. The water he could get from the washing basin. But what was the meaning of it? No one had warned him of such slippery paths in prison. Now he thought of Mandla. How would he have reacted to all this, he wondered. His own mind and body were too tired and his feet too aching to allow him the energy to contemplate the new turn in detention. As time progressed he came to realise just how new a pattern to the country's life the group had given. For no one in the past experienced the sort of things open to the group: the way they lived as rabbits running from the cops all the time; the kind of treatment meted out to Bongi; just everything about them and their encounters with the law was new.

A voice clapped the air around his head as if saying: Beware broer—brother, it is a trap! He went to the wall on one side of the cell, leaned on it and thrust both hands in his pockets, shoulders hunched. It was a self-reassuring pose; he could take stock of his surroundings in confidence: what was happening to him? . . . what was the system up to? . . . what did they take him to be? . . . why him?

He made up his mind.

He looked through the only window on his cell. It seemed dawn was about to break. This meant he never had a wink of sleep all night. His body began to show the toll taken in the past hours. He was tired, too tired to keep on his feet, too tired to keep his eyes open.

The bowl and squash bottle made things lousy for him. He resolved not to touch the trap by keeping a distance from it. This reduced the size of the cell.

He tumbled to the floor, knees propping him up for a short while. In that position he was able to prepare his bedding where he soon doubled up for snatches of sleep. It was his very first experience of sleep in a prison cell and it wasn't totally without its nightmarish touches.


**9**

NEWS ITEM
SOWETO WEEPS PRINCIPAL MASEMOLA REPORTED
DEAD IN DETENTION


When the first two police cars came to a standstill near the Diepkloof Military Base, a sedan zoomed past them on its way to Soweto.

There were two persons in the sedan, the driver and a passenger. The passenger asked where a bank robbery might have occurred for the cops to have to waylay the culprits at that spot. The driver replied: 'They must be looking for Mandla.'

'That small boy?' whined the passenger.

'Boet,' said the driver shifting his huge body slightly on the seat, 'the small boy is bigger than you or me.'

'Never!' declared the passenger.

The driver raised both hands in frustration. The car veered just a wee bit off the road whereupon he swung it violently back in line and said: 'You don't believe me, hey? Take a look at today's paper. Or maybe you saw yesterday's? The news is Mandla, that's what the papers sell because people want to read about the small boy. Small boy?' scoffed the driver.

The passenger leaned his bony arm on the door-frame allowing the quick breeze to whip his moustached face and said: 'I swear by the gods of my father and his father's father, I've never heard the likes of what you are telling me!'

'This is iGoli!' said the driver as if he ought to have said that one before because it summed up the world at once. He went on: 'Papers can pick you as you sail out of your mother's womb and sell on the birth process. Papers are like the wild beast, always hungry for news.'

A kwela-kwela appeared. It turned into Diepkloof near Baragwanath Hospital. The driver found something new to enthuse on. He said, bluntly: 'I bet the kwela is on Mandla's trail.'

'You lie!' swore the passenger.

'I'm telling you!' said the driver as if his word was the law. The passenger kept mum, looked out of the window and waited as if to hear further pronouncements from the driver. The car rambled on along the old Potchefstroom road. The driver said: 'The police waste their time. Soweto is so big — where does one begin to look for a runner-away? I'm sure the police chief must be cursing the man who first thought of building Soweto so huge. It is a monster. It is a wild beast, this Soweto. That is why it growls, it snarls and bares fangs even for its own kind. It is seeking sanity because so much of its personality has been destroyed, so much.'

'M'm,' mumbled the passenger. By this time he was fighting off drowsiness.

A small car whizzed past them at high speed. Two persons were in it. They looked like youngsters.

'Hey! hey!' exclaimed the driver roughing up the passenger with his left hand, 'those boys, did you see them?'

'No!' and then 'Yes!'

'I would have sworn one of them was Mandla.'

'Mandla?' repeated the passenger blinking his eyes. The driver saw the man's lethargy and slapped him hard on the thigh.

'The same Mandla I've been telling you of, man!'

'The same?'

'Ag!' declared the driver in desperation. 'You are a fool!' The car lurched forward in full throttle. The driver tried to chase the midget ahead of him. He saw it rise on a bridge and deep down on the other side. By the time he reached that point the little car was not in sight, only a cloud of dust told him it was heading for Kliptown on the dirt road at the foot of the bridge. Taking off the pressure on the accelerator, the driver said; 'How can the police catch those boys? . . . They can't . . . They can't!'

His own sedan was swallowed up by Soweto, by which time his passenger was himself completely fast asleep. The deeds of Mandla were just too much for him to comprehend eyes open.

# 10

The sun was past its zenith, shadows stretched longer and longer from buildings and trees, fingering the brown earth; the breeze beneath the peach and apricot trees whispered past and around the men seated under the trees to measure the day, to examine the turmoil brought about by those who toyed with phrases such as the maintenance of law and order. It was at this late hour that Mzi and Mandla saw fit to begin the journey to Botswana.

The timing was precise since it allowed for time to study moves by the cops and a possible escape through the police dragnet.

On the way Dan Montsho and Sello were to be picked up. Mzi's view prevailed: the two were a terribly weak link in the mission to liquidate Warrant Officer Batata. Mandla asked about Keke's fate. Mzi said it wouldn't be a bad idea to collect him as well.

Going to Botswana into exile was like going into Jo'burg city to buy a ticket at Computicket. No luggage, only a bit of cash in the pocket was all one took. There was no one to bid farewell since Sis Joyce was away at work. Yet the sadness of parting with one of their homes overcame the two young men. Dan Montsho heard the squeaking of the kitchen door as he shut it. It was as if the sound would ring in his ears for ever; his mind galloped to the same squeaking made by his father's kitchen door; the location houses have so many properties in common, especially those properties which mark them as second rate products.

The trip to Dr Kenotsi's surgery in Orlando East was short and uneventful. But all four occupants in the small car remained alert because they were not ordinary persons riding in an ordinary car. The day marked them revolutionaries and they lived the style of law dodgers. It was always a relief to reach a destination in their many-sided programme.

Dr Kenotsi's reaction to Keke being driven out of the country summed up his view of the whole gamble at that hour.

'No, chaps, no!' said the medico in a plaintive voice, 'that's suicide!' Pointing a finger at Mandla he continued: 'You want to tell me you are driving all the way to Botswana in broad daylight? You must be mad! Those fellows will pick you up like ripe fruit from a tree, man!'

Mzi sat leaning on the examination couch. He wouldn't face the medico.

He seemed so much unperturbed by what the doctor said, he looked bored. But no sooner was the doctor through with his point than Mzi was up in revolt: 'They won't catch us! I've studied the cops. They like the old Potchefstroom Road and the Soweto Highway. I know their mind. The Dobsonville road is safe.' He added: 'They'll catch us only if an informer gives us away. That's all!'

Everyone was quiet for a while. The medico broke the silence. He turned to Dan Montsho: 'How do you feel about the whole scheme?' Dan Montsho made pronouncements like a hippo taking its breather above water-level. It was a long, calculated process as if thought must germinate and then sprout in full view. He said: 'Going away makes me feel bad. I'm like a wet dog, I hate it. But I've asked myself what use can I be under the circumstances. The group has begun to crack.'

'Has cracked!' chipped in the medico.

'Oh I feel terrible. Things have suddenly gone out of hand,' lamented Dan Montsho, 'the show is no longer ours . . . We are no longer the nut-crackers I thought I saw in the beginning.' He shot up, fist clenched in mid air: 'We shook the system by bringing classes to a halt; burning municipal offices and wrecking beerhalls.' He resumed his seat and continued: 'Then we were in the thick of things as one man . . . but now doc, we are drifting . . . I have ceased to know what we are doing.'

'And you think you must skip at this hour?' asked the medico

164

sadly.

'I don't wish it very much but again I don't know why I'll be staying.'

'We are going to be involved in the struggle from outside,' bellowed Sello in a rich deep voice. 'The freedom of Botswana or any country for that matter is not ours. There we will still be in bondage because our roots remain in this country.'

'How much can you do outside the country?' asked the doctor.

'A lot!' said Mzi, 'Too much!'

'I'm not so sure,' answered Dan Montsho. 'I suggest there will be limits which chain one country to another. These always threaten the freedom of the small man.'

'Precisely!' exclaimed the medico.

'A fighter can never be chained,' said Mzi. 'If he is determined to achieve a goal it is do or die for him. How can anyone control such a person?'

There was no one to reply. The doctor seemed to accept that argument with Mzi was always futile. He pitied the young chaps in the spell of the trained freedom fighter. He began to be fidgety and this gave Mandla the cue to ask:

'How is Keke doc?'

'I beg you chaps, leave him alone.'

'The question is how safe is it to leave him behind?' queried Mzi. 'He's going to be a target like Mandla.'

'You mean you don't trust the people picked up this morning?' asked the medico, eyes enlarged.

'I don't!' said Mzi bluntly.

Mandla looked at him and said: 'You don't know Roy and Boysi.'

'What about Sis Ida?' asked Mzi. He began to tap a hand on his knee.

'I can't speak for her. But she was like a mother to all of us.'

'She's not a revolutionary! Under pressure she'll crack; she'll want to survive, won't she?' said Mzi sneering.

'She's a human being,' answered the doctor. 'We must expect from her only what a normal person can endure.' Dr Kenotsi stood up. 'Well chaps,' he continued, 'I can only wish you good luck.' From the back pocket of his white trousers he produced a thick wad of green bank notes. He gave a sheaf of them to Mandla. As he led the way out of his consulting room he said: 'I don't want to be in your shoes, chaps. But good luck all the same.' He shook the hands of Dan Montsho and Sello and seemed to lose interest in the foursome. For quickly his eyes turned to the patients huddled on benches in the waiting room.

It was late afternoon when the four youths pulled out of Soweto into Dobsonville. As the car passed Dobsonville Police Station Mzi exclaimed teasingly from the back seat: 'Bye, bye! Batata!'

Mandla was next to Mzi, he added: 'Dinokana here we come!'

The trip meant a definite postponement of the engagement with the target cop. Luck held for the small car. It rattled on through Roodepoort, Witpoortjie, Luipaardsvlei, Krugersdorp West without incident. But the four were all the time alert. The tension in the car could be gauged from the sighs of Dan Montsho and Mandla. As for the driver, Sello, he made the car speed and crawl by turns without apparent reason. At one stage Mzi scowled: 'Why crawl man?'

'T.P.A. I'm worried about the Transvaal Provincial Administration traffic cops.' Outside Krugersdorp West the car dropped from a ridge and for a long stretch the eye could catch the winding road spread before it as the car dipped, wound and rose in the open veld. After a short silence filled only by the purring of the small engine Sello said hesitantly: 'I see a stationary car ahead. Those two reflectors belong to a car. Could it be them?'

'Oh fuck them, man!' said Mzi straining his eyes to see all the same. 'We don't owe them anything! The car moves all right so what would they want with us?'

'They'll waste our time,' said Mandla uneasily. He wore a worried face.

'We don't want to arrive late in Zeerust,' said Mzi.

'Zeerust?' queried Mandla, 'We can't make it. Look what the time is, 7.15.'

'Another hour and we would be saying: this time tomorrow. Remember that one?'

'Like hell!' answered Mandla. The words belonged to another night. They sparked the nostalgic remembrance of another event, and with the memory of the bombing of the police station Mandla recalled a whole series of events which marked his life: the march of thousands of students down one street in Westcliff, the gathering of a storm which turned into a torrent of angry might that lashed and lashed on the granite wall of an uncaring authority . . . The run down the lonely stretch was another ripple of that march and he recounted the consequences to himself: near detention; escape from death — all in the brief spell leading to the stationary car. Aloud he said to Dan Montsho: 'You know I liked your image, calling us nutcrackers.' He turned to Mzi, 'Hell, don't you think we are?'

'Ya,' said Mzi frowning a bit: 'I agree except that my nut has not

166

cracked yet.'

'Batata?' queried Mandla.

'Ya. He's got to go before I can claim to be a nutcracker.'

'But the Jabavu Police Station was part of the system. That blast made you a nutcracker. We are all nutcrackers,' concluded Mandla.

The car approached the source of anxiety. It turned out to be an abandoned husk so common on the country roadside. Suddenly the small car swerved out of the road, it skidded in and out of the road for a couple of meters before it jerked to a standstill.

'What the hell?' yelled Mzi, shaken. The other members echoed his concern with curses and grunts.

'That bloody rabbit shot into my way,' said an equally disturbed Sello. 'I should have killed the bastard!' He relaxed his stiff hands on the steering wheel.

'A rabbit?' asked Mandla mischievously.

'I saw it,' said Dan Montsho.

'Ya, but you mean you nearly broke my neck because of a rabbit? Gee that's being damn expensive,' clowned Mandla.

Mzi bolted out of the car, went round to the driver's side: 'Come let me take over. I don't trust you with my life.'

Sello moved out saying: 'Sorry folks. I didn't mean to harm anyone.'

'You nearly killed us,' said Mzi restarting the car.

'Just to save the life of a rabbit, whew!' Mandla began to laugh. His boyish glee spilled over.

There was nothing amiss with the little car. It stretched the beams of its headlights into the dark lonely veld. The trees along the way looked like devils in ambush. For Dan Montsho in particular the dark menace in the veld reminded him of how he escaped arrest the night of the siege.

Conversation in the car was nil. Everyone seemed to be gathering strength after the shattering of nerves from the events of the past days and the experience with the naughty rabbit. Only the noise from the car clapped the wind around. If it wasn't the drone of the little engine, it would be the choir of crickets in the unseen bush and grass along the road that was heard. Occasionally a sparkling green light appeared in the ground and whoever saw the glow worm screamed 'I saw it first!' just as they would have done as very young boys in the good old days.

The stretch of road to Rustenburg can be challenging around Magaliesberg. Those who know these things say this forms part of the Witwatersrand Range. It looks different because it has been less

167

tamed along the Magaliesberg mountains. The road rises and dips, it elongates along smooth straight stretches, then bends and winds around a ridge and runs through gorges at times, which make it leap out like the tongue of a tired dog.

Outside Rustenburg in the midst of bush and a cluster of thorn trees stood the Dutch Reformed Church Mission's school for the blind. The man in charge was Reverend Immanuel Pooe. Mandla had come to know him in the course of his organising work for the student movement. It was to this priest's manse that the little car was directed.

The four youths arrived at the dead of night when the mission was shrouded in darkness except at Reverend Pooe's manse where a harsh electric light burnt in the surrounding pitch black night. A chorus of crickets welcomed the four as they came out of the car stiff with cramped muscles.

## 11

NEWS ITEM
MRS MASEMOLA TAKEN BY POLICE TO SEE HUSBAND
MASEMOLA REPORTED WELL BUT SOWETO REMAINS
SCEPTICAL

About the time Mzi, Mandla and the others left Soweto, Sis Ida found herself standing in the room in which Colonel Kleinwater sat, seemingly bored, behind a table. For hours on end she stood waiting with nothing happening, no one speaking to her. There were several people who came apparently for consultations and left. Except for a mocking greeting such as: 'Ya mosadi — woman!' no one said a word to her. She was made to peel off her mind, in strips. Her spirits were broken at the very first instance when she entered the room where she found two tables both strewn with a number of incriminating exhibits. Her spirits spluttered in ruins when she saw the books, posters, lists and other items confiscated from her house. The Colonel spent some time looking over these items. In the process he would cast his eyes up at her and return them to an item in his hand. Otherwise silence reigned. In the end he sat back and scowled. The subterranean streams eating into the gorges of his mind were sensed rather than seen by Sis Ida.

The Colonel put the cigarette he'd been smoking on the edge of the table so that it continued to burn without doing damage to the wood. He began: 'We've been talking to the boys and we know a lot about what was happening at your house. So I'm warning you: I want the truth from you, nothing less. Understand? Nothing less! You must tell me everything about yourself, where you were born, schools attended, your family, friends, everything . . . Toe nou— come now, start!'

Sis Ida cleared her throat and made sure she stood upright. It was a conscious effort because her muscles were tired. What she did without giving thought to it was to clasp hands at the back. 'I was born in Fitas.'

'Fitas?' queried the Colonel with an expression of revulsion: 'What is Fitas?'

'Vrededorp.'

'O, ya say so then . . . Vrededorp just outside town.'

'My mother worked a long time for a certain old lady.'

'And your father?'

'He worked on the mines, Crown Mines. The old lady didn't mind my mother living with my father in the backroom.'

'One of those Jewish liberals, eh?'

'Mrs Bosman was Afrikaner . . .'

'Toe nou, carry on . . .'

'I was the only child in the family.'

'Your father must have been lazy.'

Sis Ida paused. Her look hardened, her muscles twitched but she realised her hopeless situation which she resolved by biting her lips in silence.

'I said carry on,' urged the Colonel coldly.

'I grew up in Vrededorp, attended primary school in Sophiatown.'

The word Sophiatown was wholly emotive. Even in the Colonel's mind it struck a gong and in the midst of its vibrations he repeated: 'Sophiatown!' He repeated the word as if he wished to clutch at it at the very moment when it was receding away from his grasp. 'Go on,' said the Colonel.

'I went to Pietersburg for the Teachers' Lower Primary Certificate. I never liked the classroom so I've been doing various jobs.'

'What are you doing now?'

'Demonstrations. I show the public how to use face cream.'

'O! My Here God! So you are one of them. You think black people want to be white.'

The idea seemed to have sapped his strength. He picked up the cigarette from the edge of the table. It was dead so he produced a lighter from one of his pockets and lit it.

'So you are a Communist?'

'I am not.'

'Why read such stuff?' A book was in his hand.

'I did not.'

The Colonel dropped it on the table and picked up another: *Violence Begets Violence.* He said: 'I suspected it: you wanted to overthrow the lawful government by violent means, eh Ida?'

'I did not.'

'You are a Communist, Ida.'

'I am not.'

'You read Communism!'

'I did not.'

The Colonel shouted: 'Don't bloody bleat "I did not! I did not!" all the damn time. Tell me how these things came to your house. They didn't just walk in, did they?'

The Colonel's hair became dishevelled. He threw down the cigarette and crushed it and threw back his head, lifted a hand to repair the damage done to his hair. In the meantime Sis Ida sighed in despair but kept quiet.

'I'm asking you, man?'

'They did not walk in. They belonged to the children.'

'Whom you hid from us. Are you aware we are about to charge you for being in possession of banned literature; of defeating the ends of justice and of being an accomplice in all the blasts that have occurred in Soweto up to now? Are you?'

It was the first time someone spelt out the charges facing her. Their magnitude didn't strike her then as overpowering but they did a lot to burst the limits of her strength. She became frightened even more and was utterly confused by fear.

The Colonel went back to his seat. He picked up the packet of cigarettes and helped himself to one.

His first draw was long. Through the clouds of smoke whirling up and about between himself and Sis Ida, he asked quietly, and almost casually: 'Where is Mandla?'

'I don't know,' said Sis Ida. The answer came out of its own volition; she was weak and muddled. For a brief moment she faced the Colonel without knowing how she managed. Nothing seemed to belong to her anymore: body and mind. Fatigue and the bombardment by the Colonel played havoc with her.

'Listen, there is a murder charge hanging over your head; there is a treason charge relating to explosives resting on your shoulders and a string of other charges on you. Do you understand?'

'I understand,' said Sis Ida softly. Her voice choked with emotion. Her legs became unequal.

'You must tell me where to find Mandla,' emphasised the Colonel, 'It is your only chance.'

'I don't know. I was away from home all day. I don't know what those children did in the house.'

'Kak—Shit! That's all bull you're telling me. The Police Station was bombed at night. The people concerned must have left your house after sunset, in the evening that is. Don't talk bull!'

Sis Ida's lips remained sealed. Her mind galloped to the night of the blast. Mandla wasn't home as she recalled. Other members of the group flitted in and out of the kitchen door, as always. There were those who lounged about in the sitting room, as always. There was not a single clue to any unusual happening to which she could hold. But how could she convince the Colonel of this? Silence was her strength.

'Well, are you going to tell me something or not?'

'I don't know what to say.'

'The explosion in the kitchen, who did that?'

'Those children.'

'Don't be stupid! None of those children was hurt. They couldn't be involved.'

Sis Ida was at a loss. She puzzled how to deal with a person as adamant as the Colonel. He was hard to shift from a viewpoint. How to tell him of the speculation she overheard at the time of the incident?

'Keke? Where is he now?'

'I don't know.'

'Look, you have to tell me the whole truth. I know you know the truth. We've tried Baragwanath Hospital, the clinics and all the Soweto doctors. No one treated a patient with burns. He must be lying low somewhere. He's not at his home either. Where is he Ida?'

'I don't know,' said Sis Ida with a sigh of resignation. The search for Keke at his home meant the police knew a bit about the missing victim and her innocence in this case.

The Colonel pulled out another cigarette from the pack. He knocked both ends of it on the table and placed it in his lips. Sis Ida watched its smoke curl up in the room. She seemed to be floating in space when she heard the Colonel say: 'A number of travelling documents found in your bag belonged to foreign blacks. There's a suggestion that you know more than meets the eye. Is this true?'

'I don't understand.'

'You cannot fool me. You damn well know what I mean. You were up to fraud and forgery with those travelling documents weren't you?'

'No I wasn't. I knew the owners. They trusted me and asked me to keep them. They said my place was more safe than theirs.'

'Rubbish! That's a lot of bull you are telling me. How could your place be safe with so many people living in it? Pure rubbish!'

Sis Ida felt battered. Yet she had to defend herself: 'There was only one document of a foreigner,' she said calmly.

'Your boyfriend!'

'Lemon Banda is a family friend.'

'You'd better give me his address if you know what's good for you. You lie like an old clock I must tell you.'

There was a pause during which the Colonel stared at Sis Ida. She felt the contempt of the man's eyes. Presently he said: 'The law allows me to keep you in custody as long as I feel your answers are not satisfactory. I want you to think over your position carefully. I don't care if you grow grey in jail. Know that!'

The Colonel stepped out of the room. He left Sis Ida to wonder about the meaning of her detention. She felt very hopeless even as she wished to beat her fists on the door as it shut her in. And as the Colonel's footsteps receded into the interminable length of the corridor, her heart sank with the sense of desperation. She became acutely aware she had lost her life somewhere outside the prison.

A warder came for her and she was led to her cell. The strange thing was the relief she felt as her cell door was locked outside.


The sun was long past its high point when Mzi and Mandla headed back to Soweto. Dan Montsho and Sello remained with Reverend Pooe who persuaded Mandla to rely on him to conduct them safely to Dinokana. Mzi was only too happy to accept the offer. He argued that their presence in Soweto at all times was of paramount importance lest they lose track of events.

The little Austin pulled out of Roodepoort town without incident. Ahead lay Dobsonville and then Soweto.

The approach to Dobsonville drops for a fairly long stretch so that the eye catches a glimpse of Dobsonville and Meadowlands quite a distance away. Mzi, at the wheel and Mandla with his eyes constantly alert, sat quietly in the car. At the very instant when the car tumbled down toward the outskirts of Dobsonville, at a point where

172

the road from Meadowlands formed a T-junction with the Roode-poort-Dobsonville freeway, Mandla's eye picked up a stirring and a shimmer. The spotting of the activity down the road hit Mandla in the chest as if a hard punch had jolted him back. He held stiffly on to the dashboard with his left hand while his right fumbled to grip Mzi's shoulder.

'Jee-weez, what's the matter man?' said Mzi annoyed with his friend. The car slowed down.

'Ratlas—police!' cried Mandla. 'Can't you see them? We won't make it mfo!'

'Don't get excited, man!' The car pulled up by the side of the road, Mzi went on: 'We can always work out a plan.'

'I'm not excited,' said Mandla in self-defence. 'I knew the dogs would be waiting for us at that spot. It's a favourite every time there's a blitz.'

'What do you suggest? I want to take a chance.'

'You can't do that!' squealed Mandla.

'Why not? They don't know me. This car is like many other little cars.'

'I don't want to be a martyr. A whole house of friends is in detention. How can we be sure no-one has told the cops of this Austin?'

Mzi's lips remained shut. His eye was fixed at the scene down the road. From where they stood nothing was clearly visible except for a string of cars along the side of the road.

Mandla's hand was on the door handle as he said: 'My face is well known to all those dogs. I'll cut across the veld into Meadowlands. Hopefully we'll meet at home later today. No chances for me!' As Mandla stepped out of the small car two taxis whizzed past them in quick succession. He turned his face away lest someone in those cars recognise him.

Mandla's salvation lay a few meters below where they stood: it was a footpath used by pedestrians too determined to save on trans-port costs to want to use buses and taxis to return home from work. Nearby were a number of factories from which they trudged home every day. Mandla would join the path and disappear into Meadow-lands and the safety of MaNhlapo's sanctuary.

Mzi remained in the car, tense but determined not to be taken by the cops. A wry smile played on his full face as he thanked the gods for safe carriage all the way. Even at that moment he was aware that danger for him was not in his identity because not one of the detained members knew his face or his trademark: the military styled khaki cap. To them only a faceless name was revealed and Mzi could be one of a hundred blokes.

He tried to scan the scene ahead but gave up because it was too far away and faint and because his mind looked beyond the roadblock. It settled at MaNhlapo's, in his room, underneath the bed where a Russian-made AK47 automatic rifle was wrapped and cushioned on the floor. At that moment he regretted his own folly of leaving it behind. He would be working out a plan to blast his way through if it were not for that folly. The problem was how to escape arrest.

When he got out of the car an instinctive impulse told him to follow Mandla's footsteps. But pride was greater. It led him to the bonnet of the car. He fidgeted with the rotor and the points. He went to the starter, touched it and heard the engine grumble endlessly. That made him thank his tutors at Dar. He moved down the road, leaving the bonnet gaping.

His eye looked down the road and he was happy to note no interest seemed roused from the gang at the roadblock. Presently he flagged down a passing taxi and climbed in.

Inside the taxi he removed his cap, using it to fan himself once or twice as if he really needed to. It disappeared into one of his pockets. No sooner was that done than he was seized by doubt: was it right for him to take the chance past the roadblock?

Constable Phineas Matlala flagged the taxi to stop. Humble looking Matlala was a duty-conscious cop. But he didn't break his back to earn his wages. He knew the body aches that resulted from an over-zealous worker. It was to avoid their assault that he allowed himself breaks in between searches. In the course of such a break he saw the distant car stop, a figure emerge and walk to the front. From this distance he couldn't tell what was happening around the car. He had seen the figure climb into the taxi and it was thus with this knowledge that he asked broadly from those inside the taxi: 'Whose car is that?'

'Mine,' said Mzi without hesitation. He added quickly: 'I'm going to the garage down the road to fetch a mechanic. There's just a minor problem with it.'

Down the road stood a Mobil garage. Matlala's brief was to search the boots of cars and be on the lookout for Mandla, whose vague description was inscribed on his mind. It was beyond the brief to help stranded drivers or offer services to such people. They could never constitute a security risk!

The taxi was allowed to pass through with its full load of passengers.

Half an hour later the Austin stood nonchalantly and grey in the fading winter light. Matlala became uneasy about it. Suddenly it was his concern. He knew the tension pulling him apart would cease only after he looked at the car inside out. But orders were orders and that meant he could not leave the checkpoint without the express permission of the officer in charge.

Captain Brand rarely smiled. In a way this made him inaccessible except to the very few who came to know his nature. To Matlala he was Makhulu-baas. All police below him referred to him as such though with varying meaning. To approach Makhulu-baas on a seemingly insignificant piece of news such as an abandoned car was unthinkable for Matlala.

Next in command was Sergeant Strydom. The man was touchy, he could explode a backslap on a target's face as quickly as lightning. Matlala worried how he would put it to him in a voice and a manner unlikely to cause offence.

Minutes ticked by and Matlala's uneasiness about the Austin increased. His position was complicated by the long interval it took him to make up his mind about what to do. He wished very strongly that Strydom was a simpler man who could be trusted to say quietly: 'Ja, Constable, gaan kyk maar—go look it up.' Knowing the man as he did he thought it wise to keep his peace.

It was another half-an-hour later before he summoned enough courage to approach Strydom. At the time the Sergeant's head was dipped into the boot of a car. His safari jacket flapped up at the single vent on the back revealing a skin akin to a well-kept pig. The effort of searching the boot was no joy as could be seen from the way he flung the many parcels in the boot hither and thither.

'Askuus tog baas Strydom,' said Matlala politely in a very self-effacing manner. He said it twice before Strydom raised his panting head and splattered: 'Ag man Matlala, kan jy nie jou bloody bek toe hou—can't you shut your mouth? Can't you see a man is busy?' Matlala drew back, folded his arms and stepped as far away from Strydom as he possibly could. He resolved not to worry about the small car.

He told himself he would not even look at it again. Captain Brand was in fierce conversation with another officer and for Matlala that was that.

Minutes later the scene was quiet. Matlala caught the eye of the Sergeant. He was beckoned to the presence of his senior. It was a glum constable who stood near the sergeant.

'Ya, what did you want?' said Strydom hoping to lift his broken

175

spirits in the process of talking to the other person. Fatigue showed in his crumpled police uniform.

'That car baas,' pointed Matlala.

'What of it?'

'It's been standing there for a long time.'

'Go and check it, man.'

Matlala found the trip up the road exhilarating. There was something about duty on roadblocks he found unpleasant. For one thing it was a function he found confusing, this looking for a needle in a haystack. He did it because it was a duty.

The car was empty. That was the first cause of his disappointment. He flung all the doors open. Only the unseen wind flew out with the sound of squeaking, ungreased doors. Matlala looked at the inside twice, thrice as if he expected Mandla in one form or another. There was nothing he picked out for evidence against the car or the driver. The bonnet was open and he scanned the engine. It was all iron and steel and gadgets — mind-boggling.

Matlala banged all the doors to in utter desperation. The reverberations clamoured down the road to where Brand, Strydom and others stood. Brand merely looked at his assistant. The look was enough to galvanise Strydom into action. He hurried up the road and found Matlala struggling to open the boot of the little car.

'Can't you damn well see die donderste ding is locked up?' shouted Strydom after shoving off Matlala and trying the boot himself. 'I asked you to check up the car, now you are busy housebreaking. Kyk—look Matlala,' said Strydom taking his turn at checking up the car, 'I'm tired man. I want to see my children.' He stood with hands on his hips and said: 'Ask the Makhulu-baas to lend me the list of stolen cars.'

Matlala hurried off to Captain Brand. Japie Brand was proud of his meteoric rise in the police force. He put it down to doing an honest day's work. It was for this reason that when the request for the list reached him he elected to see for himself the car in question. As he approached the little car his heartbeat raced inexplicably. There was a disturbing fascination about the car which made him stretch out the list before Strydom asked for it a second time. For the description of it matched the mental picture he took away from police headquarters. One look at the piece of paper in his hand was enough to make him cry: 'That's it all right. Sarge we've been looking for this car. Where are the occupants, I wonder?' The words came tumbling out of his mouth without thought. At the time he was also counting his losses as a result of the discovery. He turned to

Matlala: 'Did you see anyone leave the car Constable?'

'Yes sir,' stammered Matlala.

'Who?' The one word said a lot about the anxiety of the officer. Matlala didn't miss that one.

'The man who came out of it took a taxi past the roadblock.'

'What sort of a man, Constable?'

'I stopped the taxi . . . the man looked young.'

'That's it Sarge,' declared the Captain even before Matlala's words died in the air. He took a few paces round the car: 'We've let the bird fly from right underneath our noses.' After a pause during which he played his official baton on his open palm, he stopped in his tracks and said sternly: 'Why didn't this man report the case to us immediately?' Strydom heard the threat in the Captain's question. He took a step away from where he'd been standing — he wouldn't allow himself to be engulfed by the threat. He turned to Matlala: 'Jong praat! You hear the Makhulu-baas. Answer man!'

'The baas didn't want to talk to me that time . . .'

'Jong, jy lieg—you lie!' cut in Strydom. 'I can tell you what happened . . .'

'Well, oh well,' butted in Brand. He looked let down so that he didn't wish for a dialogue or argument at that point. He led the way back to the roadblock and said: 'Let's see if we can still rescue the situation. We've bungled this matter.' To Matlala: 'More or less how long ago was it when you saw this young man?'

'About an hour ago.'

'That long?' exclaimed Brand. He blew a whistle. He turned to Strydom: 'Assuming he dropped off at the circle down the road, he could be two miles into Soweto already.'

'Maybe he was coming into Dobsonville, sir.'

'Mandla is too smart for that sort of thing. He wouldn't dally on the way aware the heat was on. No Sarge, he's given us the slip all right . . . Post a reliable man to keep an eye on the car and radio for reinforcements. We'll comb the area. Let's limit ourselves to a small area of Dobsonville . . .'

'The surroundings of the circle?'

'Yes that and a few houses in Soweto itself. Who knows we might just be lucky to flush out the little devil! . . . Sometimes I wish these townships were enclosed in fences like the good old days. It would make our work a lot easier.

'Yes, sir.'

After a pause: 'You've got the picture all right Sarge?'

'Yes, sir.'

All the same as a parting shot Brand said: 'You may be right. He could have headed for Dobsonville thinking he'll sneak out under cover of darkness. We'll spring a surprise on him, the bloody bugger!'

Suddenly, the check point took on a new complexion. Captain Brand began to gesticulate orders left, right and centre, everyone working on the double. He lingered long enough to make sure everyone was hawkish in his search duties. Then he went over to his own car and dropped on the back seat. It was a relief for his battered body and soul, for he was a dejected man. 'What a loss! What a loss!' he kept repeating to himself. He thought of the distance between himself and Major Hall. The gap was closing in fine until then. Missing Mandla on that occasion was a terrible loss. He held his eyes tightly closed and ran one hand over his face. The crackling of the two way radio in the car jarred his ears as its intensity increased. The screeching turned into a human voice: 'calling Car One-Five, calling Car One-Five.' Brand raised his tired body and went to the radio: 'Come in XWEO1.' The voice went on: 'Reinforcements on the way. Major Hall in charge, over and out.' He cut off the radio and declared: 'Bloody bastard!'

Meanwhile Mandla dodged in and out of the narrow dusty streets of Meadowlands, giving Sis Ida's house a wide berth. He crossed Dube Station and landed safely at MaNhlapo's. All this was possible for him because Soweto is a giant always alive, always on the go. Hundreds of people walk the streets, workers mingle with the unemployed; here people have become one man — he zig-zags the streets in search of himself, in search of that which is his taken away by one law or another. This person must at all times lift his carcass off the streets. He has no time to pry because each moment fulfills itself quickly and can sweep anyone into a trap. That was how Mandla found his passage to MaNhlapo's unimpeded.

MaNhlapo was very happy to see him. She said she began to worry earlier in the day when both he and Mzi didn't show up.

Mandla understood what the old lady said. He was not only a son in the house but a father, for MaNhlapo lost her husband many years back.

When she wanted to know the whereabouts of Mzi, she was told he would be in the house any minute.

But when he went into their bedroom, Mandla realised what living with Mzi meant for him. He became deeply concerned for his safe return. He began to take himself to task for splitting with him in the manner he did. Many thoughts occurred to him as he lay on his back waiting. Sleep would not come although his body was fatigued.

178

Mzi dropped off at the circle past the Mobil garage, joined the many pedestrians who trudged up the road to Ekwezi Station. He was thrilled by the rhythm and pulse of crowds milling around the station. The area held a certain fascination for him which he couldn't miss even under the stress of cops: buses, taxis, vendors and of course the crawling, the rushing and the jostling people. The railway police in sight were for him part of the crowd. He ignored them completely.

He tumbled down Mofolo North to Dube. The hurrying of a kwela-kwela on the same road held no scares for him. He lived behind the mask: no policeman knew his face, no records room housed his name.

A strange thing occurred to him: the face of Batata loomed before his eyes as clearly as the face of a man on the huge bill-board advertising a brand of bottled beer. Mzi read the vision as a solemn reminder of his mission. In a way, he thought, the detention of members of the student group could be said to be a blessing in disguise. The struggle was cluttered with the possibility of many persons being destroyed in the cross-fire between them and the enemy. The way was now open for him and Mandla to get on with the job. Of course there was the other possibility: one of the detainees might sing and sink the ship. 'But the cops won't touch me,' swore Mzi. His faith in the invisibility of his shape in the midst of the goings-on gave him strength.

He entered MaNhlapo's yard looking into the details of his next step in the Soweto saga.

**12**

NEWS ITEM
STUDENT LEADERS SKIP TO BOTSWANA
NO COMMENT SAYS POLICE SPOKESMAN

It was the second day of detention for the group but Roy wasn't sure of this. They had made him stand on two bricks from the time everyone else was thrown into a cell. The room was bare but for a hard wooden table, a stool and a light hanging from a long cord. For all that time he was starved. For all that time he walked once to the loo because after that one trip a bucket was brought for him to urinate into and as fate would have it every time he held his penis to pee, he first farted roaringly and then droplets came out of his thing. He didn't like what the cop watching him shouted at him as he farted: 'Passop my boy, jou broek baars—look out boy, you'll rip your trousers apart!'

There was something demonic about the man watching over him. Twice Roy asked for water to drink. Each time the man let the mug stand on the table for a long spell before giving it to him. Once Roy was tempted to challenge the man. He felt like stepping down from the bricks to fetch the mug from the table. He didn't because he thought it would have given the man a chance to use the butt of his rifle on his head.

Roy stood on the two bricks, hands raised above his head. His body tended to sag. He was convinced something of his personality was wrong. And it was this very thought which made him resolve to fight off the sensation creeping into his weakened body. He was a man; he would stand by Mandla, he wouldn't give the cops anything likely to jeopardise Mandla for what he stood for. Roy tightened his muscles, folded his fingers into fists and stood stiffly upright. At that time he became aware of how much he had lost control of his being. How he didn't collapse where he stood was a marvel.

Disorientation: he tried hard to pin his mind on one single thought, like how the cops had caught them napping: what had happened that night? They had been to Dube for a private showing of a film on Moral Re-Armament. For some reason their return to base was staggered. He and Boysi were early and they turned in early. For this reason he didn't know what happened to the others including Mandla. Roy winced at this point because he felt a jabbing pain on and below the right shoulder — a result of the baton hitting constantly in that area. Every time the left-handed guard hit him Roy thought left-handers were more deadly than other hitters. His mind was sinking into an abyss. He would have to fight back the crippling, dissipating dizziness about to overwhelm him. Defiantly, he dropped the bothersome right arm. The guard shifted on his seat. As it happened the arm went down and up again before the guard opened his mouth or did anything serious.

Roy saw the man slide down from his high stool. This time he was jabbed in the heart by fright. He realised he had prodded the hornet's nest. So he braced himself for a blow — first on the right shoulder and thereafter any part of the body. Instead the guard walked to the door stretching his stiffened body. It was clear that walking so slowly in the room gave him relief. Roy shared the relief. It was as if the man's physical relief was his own, only his was a mental one. This same relief enabled Roy to lengthen his withstanding of the torture meted out to him; that one brief moment became hours during which he recharged his own batteries in order to withstand more of the pain of detention. It was murderous to endure the strain of waiting to be spoken to; to be asked a question, a question of who you were, why you did what you did and about the people supposed to make it possible for you to indulge in the things you believed needed to be done. And the questions never came and nobody spoke to you except in blows rained on your body.

Batata did just that once or twice. In the time Roy stood in the room of torture he saw cops come and go. Their visits appeared innocent until Roy was visited by Batata. As with others, he lifted his eyes to see who came into the room. It was enough to infuriate Batata: 'How do you look at me?' said the black cop, 'Do I look like the man who slept with your mother last night?' Roy merely grunted, his own heart filled with hate for the other black man. The cop charged at him. It happened so suddenly, so quickly, poor Roy never had the chance to drop his tired arms in time. The black cop landed a blow on the stomach. His massive hands carried so much power the blow felled Roy. He was bundled up at the cop's feet not before being smacked on the cheek, punched on the stomach again, chopped on both shoulders with karate blows so that he sagged on his knees. Just as he went down on one knee, one blow beneath the chin knocked his half-open mouth shut so that he bit his tongue. The pain made him scream for mercy. He lay at Batata's feet, doubled up by impotence. The guard came up to Batata restraining him from further attacks on Roy.

On another occasion Batata was raining blows on Roy and saying in the process: 'I'm practising for Mandla. Next time I'll be knocking sense into your friend's skull!' The menace in the man's voice remained with Roy longer than the pain inflicted on him.

Everytime Roy received a beating the guard laughed in his face. Once he said to Roy: 'Batata is a black man, he's just showed you what is meant by black power. Mos, you belong to the Black Power Movement.' Another time he said: 'Why can't you ask your Black Power brothers to help you?' Roy came to accept the guard as the salt of his body wounds.

The cop lingered at the open door long enough to make it tantalising for Roy to wish he could walk out of the room. But he was a detained man and detained people know nothing less than humiliation. Bitterness filled him up to the gullet. He swore he would yet get even with this cop and all the cops crossing his path in life.

Moments dragged by. There was no end to his torture. He waited without seeing the end of his tunnel. These same moments tele-scoped into each other, making of time one long drag.

A new experience became a familiar happening: he heard bashing as if someone was being lashed. Screams rent the air at intervals. It wasn't long before he identified the victim — Snoek. There were long spells when a voice spoke and then came yells of anger. Snoek was not being co-operative and the lashing was to persuade him to see the light. The interrogator was loud and harsh. Roy could tell this even as his own receptive powers were diminished; he heard the cop yell at Snoek.

He couldn't say how long the interrogation took place but it seemed hours according to the weakened condition of his body. Sometimes he wished to be in Snoek's shoes. His waiting in silence was more deadening than the physical onslaught experienced by his friend.

A long piercing scream from another room. It was a female's cry which he thought might be Punkie or Nkele. It was a fearful cry of 'ma . . . ma . . . we!' as in danger.

Nkele's hands were being held behind her back, her breasts bare, dangling like over-ripe fruit, for she was a freedom child in the modern sense. Her eyes were enlarged by fear, a fear of an uncoiling slithering snake. At first Nkele had thought they were playing havoc with her nerves, and were merely trying to frighten her so that she would say things they wanted to hear. But when the damn thing kept sailing toward her, its head raised or down, eyes blinking and the forked tongue flicking out menacingly, she realised it was no joke. Survival meant she must scream, she must begin to do more than just whimper for mercy. But with bony white hands holding hers in a vice she was immobilised and could only cry out for all the gods to hear, for all the right-thinking persons inside the police headquarters to hear and have her pain pierce their hearts.

The snake nestled at her feet; she began to wriggle, to dance away, twisting, yelling and kicking. It did not bite her but it did shake the roots of her hair out of position . . .

Time dragged on and Roy remained on his feet. Every bone in his body was a grain of aching, it became so bad he was near collapsing. Gradually the voices he heard sounded far off, as if they were echoes in the wilderness. He found himself slanting his upper body forward, one knee bending and heard the guard command: 'Stand up straight!'

A thought which nagged him like the tick of a clock was the intention of the cops with him. No interrogations, no food, no water but this endless standing. He wished he'd rehearsed his detention.

But how does one rehearse torture? There was one thing to hold to at all costs — his sanity. He was convinced they wanted to drive him mad, they were leading him to a foolish point where he might do something silly and give them the excuse to let him tumble down a flight of stairs, break his neck and be dead. Suicide, would say the records. He had no wish to die. Not yet.

Roy passed out at the point where his lips were curled by a swear word. The guard jumped to where the human heap lay.

<br>

NEWS ITEM
MANDLA BECOMES BLACK PIMPERNEL
REPORTED SEEN IN DOBSONVILLE
NO COMMENT SAYS POLICE SPOKESMAN

Two days after the big swoop on Sis Ida's place, Soweto was still groggy from the event. House lights remained burning at many homes past midnight because no one knew the hour when police might call. Mothers held hands to their hearts, fathers spoke in whispers. Of all people expected to be disturbed by the heavy hand of the law, MaNhlapo was the least concerned. She was up early, went about her house chores as usual and looked forward to the hour of 9 o'clock that morning with some measured thrill. In typical religious style she went about dusting her pine-wood side-board in the sitting room, spirits lifted on the wings of her favourite hymn: 'Lead Kindly Light'. On pension day she always rose to the occasion with one of those plaintive songs as if in lament for the meagre pension received by location persons of her age. Then she muttered at the end of the chorus: 'Beggars cannot be choosers.'

Mandla stood at the door of their bedroom, barefoot. He held his trousers with one finger hooked on a loop, his shirt hung loosely. 'Hi, mama,' said Mandla, 'going places this morning, mama?' His face lit up in his usual boyish fashion.

'What places, son? I'm going for my pension. Peanuts, my son, peanuts!' bewailed MaNhlapo.

'Don't worry mama, we are going to take over everything. And we'll pay decent pensions for a start!'

MaNhlapo couldn't make out whether Mandla was serious or joking. So she shook her head in disbelief.

Presently MaNhlapo shuffled out of the house on her way to the pensions pay point. Mandla remained to ponder the meaning of life: MaNhlapo was unhappy because her pension, the sustenance of her being, was so little; he was living the life of a rabbit because the law made him unhappy, made him run always.

When he returned to the bedroom he found Mzi's eyes wide open, staring at the ceiling, grey, criss-crossed by dull mouldy cobwebs. For Mzi worried about his connection with the student group. Mandla would have been disappointed to know his friend actually questioned his association with the student group. But acceptance of the arrangement was not of his making: the office in Dar and Uncle Ribs sold him the idea. And this had resulted in the slow progress of the mission for which he had returned to the country.

'Hi,' said Mandla.

'My hand itches,' said Mzi in reply.

'Money?'

'Trigger!'

Mzi sat up on the bed. There was no mistaking his mood: hard and ugly.

'I wonder how the dogs are treating Roy and others?'

'Feeding them fists and sjamboks,' said Mzi bitterly. 'Why do you think my hand itches for a trigger?'

'I am feeling the loneliness of their absence.'

'Blame it on Batata!'

After a pause: 'When do we rid the world of the venom?'

'Tonight!' The word fell flat on the floor.

Mandla wished he could agree but wasn't so sure. He asked: 'How can we do it without transport?'

'I've already thought about it.'

'And so?'

'We'll borrow Kenotsi's car.'

'Forget it!'

'The man's got another car for his business.'

'Oh, were you thinking of his Mercedes Benz 350?'

'I don't care for names. I need a car!'

'Ag Mzi, have a heart. The medico's been most helpful. How many other men who could help have done anything?'

Mzi shot up, threw out a hand and declared: 'Time is running out. You and I just made it the other day. But for how long can we hope to escape arrest, especially you. Man! Let's be done with this thing once and for all. Batata is our target, let's take him now!'

'I agree, ntwana, I agree,' said Mandla sympathetically, 'I can't argue against that but let's look at facts. Suppose we take Kenotsi's car and something goes wrong on the job, we have to bolt, leaving the car behind, what do you think is going to happen to the poor

184

man?'

'Poor man,' sneered Mzi, 'a whole bourgeois like him! Nothing will go wrong. I trust my training. We'll do the job and come off clean.' He resumed his seat on the bed and went on: 'Look sibali, we've planned this thing for days, how can we goof it? Not me!'

Mandla was perched on MaNhlapo's dressing table. His whole mind concentrated on the issue at hand. His one hand cupped underneath his chin, thoughtfully. He worried about all that was said in the discussion. Suddenly his looks lighted up as he said: 'That's um, I've got it!' He stood upright.

'Oh, ya?'

'I'm going to see Papa Duz.'

'Who's he?'

'Papa Duz? A coal merchant; a dirty rich black man.'

'Another bourgeois!'

'It doesn't matter. Point is what does he do with his means. Papa Duz has a fleet of cars including VW's and Cortinas. And he's helped us in the past.'

'To clear his conscience?'

'I don't know. I don't care. What I like is a bourgeois who comes to our rescue. We need more of the kind.'

'Wrong there!' said Mzi. 'There's always a danger if a struggle depends on that type of person. The strength of any movement is in its grassroots. Gain the confidence of the ordinary man and you are made.'

'How does that one relate to the car we need for running the movement and doing jobs similar to eliminating the Batata's?'

'You don't understand. Once the people are for the movement, there's no need for cars. For instance in a job like tonight's, we do it and disappear in the surrounding houses. Why run away, where to? If we say we act for the man in the street, we must run to him, surely.'

'You oversimplify.'

'It is the meaning of grassroots.'

'U-huh!' Mandla found words were hopeless. He walked out of the room. At that very moment he needed fresh air very badly and the sitting room was good enough for him.

Mzi remained in the bedroom. He stretched his arms, flexing his muscles as if for immediate action.


The door of Cell No. 6 creaked open. Willie Meyer the warder, stood at the open door scanning the inside of the cell. He squinted once or twice in an effort to locate the prisoner inside.

Boysi stopped the movement of his arm at the very first moment when he heard the key rattle in the key-hole. His back was to the door so that when the door opened, he didn't bother to turn to see what stood at the door.

It was the third day in which the air in his cell was filled with the tempting smell of fresh fruit. The bowl of fruit stood in one corner of the cell, untouched.

'How are the bananas today?' asked Willie stepping forward, leaving the door ajar. Boysi remained motionless, saying not a word in reply.

'I asked: how are the bananas?' said Willie. He let the bunch of keys in his hand jangle noisily.

'I don't know,' replied Boysi still on his knees on a folded blanket. He was in no mood for conversation and he hoped the cop would read this quickly from his cold manner. Boysi told himself: he wants to ferret out my soul. He felt his muscles stiffen as if in anticipation of whatever the warder planned for him.

Willie Meyer strolled toward the bowl, picked up a banana and began to peel it. He bit a mouthful and began to chew noisily. Through an overloaded mouth he said: 'Pride never gained anything for anyone, Boysi. I think you are a fool not to use the advantages at your feet. The Major is a kind man. He is a patient man. But he's human like all of us. He can't give you all the goodies forever. Maybe you think there's a trap somewhere. Well let me tell you I know of none. Daar's niks aan die kant—nothing on the side!' Willie thrust a hand forward over Boysi's shoulder. The tantalising whiff of a banana reached his nostrils with a crushing effect: his mind wrestled with the grinding routine of prison life — bread and tea, pap and tea, bread and tea.

The warder was right, pride gained no-one anything. He could eat the fruit and ward off the cops at the same time. What's wrong with that? His mind raced over these things until he found the reason for his aloofness. The warder was crude. He came into the cell, played on his mind with the fruit as if he was dealing with a simpleton. That's it, he was no-one's fool. He was saying this to himself when he heard Willie say pleadingly: 'Why don't you eat your fruit?'

'I don't want my stomach to get used to things I can't afford.'

'What do you mean?'

'Prison life and fruit don't go together.'

'You want me to tell the Major all that?'

Boysi remained silent. Willie insisted. 'Is that what you want?'

186

Boysi mumbled angrily: 'Suit yourself.'

'Kyk jong—look fellow,' began Willie, going past Boysi so that he could look him in the eye: 'the big people want to make friends with you. Can't you see?'

'How can police be friends with a prisoner?' Boysi asked contemptuously.

'Don't be funny. You are stupid. You forget your whole life is in our hands — my hands. What if an accident happened and you left this life, this struggle, this Black Power rubbish? You think the howling of the whole world will bring you back to life? D'you think so? Never! Never! D'you see what I mean? Grab this chance, man. I don't go about trying it to all prisoners. Grab it with both hands and see.'

'Be a sell-out?'

Willie stamped his foot on the floor and let the thud reverberate around the cell walls. He declared: 'We don't use dirty words in this place. I can now tell you are a deceived young man. Jy's verloor—you are lost! The devil has taken charge of your soul . . . Look around you . . . Ask yourself what happened to Mandela and Sobukwe. I tell you those men lost. They believed the people were behind them. They thought one magic word said by them would raise the country behind them. They were deceived. Fed wrong ideas. Given wrong reports. Their lives lie on the ground as a result, shattered.' Willie moved toward the door leaving Boysi facing away from him. He went on: 'Who will pick up the pieces of those men? Not the adult people. No! Their children, like you. Kyk ou seun—Look old boy, there's still time for you to go straight. I can tell you this: the Major will do anything for you if you will help your people and the country. My people are all right. It is your people who worry me. Listen man, I am not talking for myself only. I know many friends who think as I do. We don't agree with everything the Government is doing. But you must understand it is the Government and therefore we must obey the law. But that doesn't mean I have no feelings for other people, because I do.' Willie sighed as if to indicate that too much escaped his mouth. So he clamped it hard.

Boysi clambered to his feet. For the first time since Willie Meyer came into the cell he turned to face him. In a somewhat quiet voice he asked: 'What do you want me to do?'

It was winter time but the heat in the cell was high. Even the slight breeze edging in through the ajar door did little to mitigate the temperature. Boysi's body hungered for food, it hungered for the quenching of its thirst. He was tempted to ask for time to satisfy these needs. For him even at that hour there would have been no problem, fruits were available, water with which to make himself a mugful of squash was within reach. A bottle of squash had stood next to the bowl of fruit all along.

Boysi was no fool. He was all the time well aware of the special treatment. The question he asked was therefore not entirely without motive.

Willie Meyer leaned on the wall next to the door, dropped his shoulder and brought both hands in front of him. The keys jingled. He twisted his mouth, biting the lower lip. His tone was calm: 'I'm going to be honest with you. I hope you do the same with me. You know, ons die boere, as you people call us, we are straight people. We believe a person gets better results if there's honesty in his heart. By the way you can call me Willie, Willie Meyer to be exact. I know you are Boysi Ma . . .Majola. Am I right?'

'Yes, you are.'

'Shake hands on it,' said Willie thrusting a hand forward, chuckling. He pumped Boysi's hand like train-wheels shunting. Then he resumed his earnest stance. 'Look, Boysi, nobody wants to destroy you. I'm certain of it.' He punched the air to emphasise the point, thereby causing the bunch of keys to jangle. The noise jarred Boysi's ears. But he was able to ask: 'Why am I here then?'

'Exactly! That's a good question. I'm glad you've asked it.' Now Willie stood upright in the cell and after stealing a glance at the door left ajar he said: 'Sometimes we destroy ourselves by the associations we make. Ask yourself how many things you did with the student group were of your own mind.' For an answer Boysi's face softened. The strain on his emotions was lightened so that his dark expression became smoothed out. He told himself he would listen to what Willie was saying.

The warder said 'Did you really want to kill the Bantu Sergeant at Jabavu Police Station? Ask yourself honestly.'

Boysi heard himself say: 'No, I didn't. I wasn't there.'

'Exactly! . . . All right, take the municipal offices, the post offices, banks, clinics, was there sense in burning and destroying those public places? Do you honestly believe your people want to live in their houses without paying rent? What about such services as water, electricity, sanitary removals, don't they enjoy them? Don't they want them?'

'They do. The people did what they did to bring their grievances to the notice of the authorities.'

'By burning?'

'Demonstration . . .'

'All right, demonstration, if you want to call it so. Was it your idea?'

'No! But I was part of the movement.'

'You want to tell me in your heart is only evil? You can't deal with the next person unless you show him this evil?'

'I am not evil.'

'Why destroy? Was there no other way to show your grievances?'

'I suppose there was, but . . .'

'You followed the lead of others,' butted in Willie.

'One needs to identify with others.'

'Even if this meant you were throwing away something of yourself?'

Boysi was tentative as he said: 'We acted in self-defence. Blood was spilt by others and we stood up to stop more blood spilling.'

'You dirtied your hands, trampled on your will, your soul. Listen, Boysi, man is made in the image of God, not Satan's. We are supposed to do good at all times.'

'I don't know good.'

'Take a mirror, look at yourself in it and tell me if you don't see good in yourself.'

'But you are asking me to look beyond these prison walls. How can I?'

'It's up to you.'

'How do you mean?'

'The Major wants to have a chat with you.'

'Oh.'

'I came to tell you but I delayed. I thought you'd do with some home truths.'

'Such as?'

'Life must be lived. You are too young to be wasted in jail. Your people need you. The country needs you.'

'To tell on the student group.'

'I don't know. Meet the Major, he'll tell you what he wants of you. He doesn't want to know what you don't know, that's all.'

Willie stepped out of the cell and waited for Boysi to follow.

The prison door was closed by the warder but it was Boysi who stepped ahead to the Major's office. His mind was in confusion. It was a relief to be outside the cell but the purpose of the visit to the Major gave him no joy. Even as he stepped on the neat, long corridor he heard his heart thud inside his chest as if the act of betrayal was behind him. Yet it was only Willie Meyer, the smart persuader, who echoed his step.

Boysi wished the corridor would lead to no end in particular.

Sis Ida heard the eerie sound of feet thud on the corridor. She wondered who could be joining her at the grilling chambers. She sat watching her interrogator. For a brief moment she fumbled with her train of thought, disturbed by the feet outside. She was anxious for the conclusion of her interrogation session, hours and hours of it.

The man seemed to have paused for some reason. This allowed Sis Ida to go over her routine of the morning: a short prayer as she scrambled to her knees. Invariably the words of her prayer were: 'In this hour, O Lord, give me strength and give my charges strength. Amen Lord! . . . Amen!' Next came the folding of the two coarse and stinking blankets. The heap was used as a seat in the daytime.

The visit to the ablution block was a very welcome form of exercise. The feeling of walking, treading the stretch of a few meters away from the cell gave joy and a thrill no-one except another detainee could ever understand. Years of ageing were restored and she felt ten years younger.

There was no-one of her kind she met on the way, no-one she could exchange a smile with but she did feel the exhilaration of the heart in the short stretch. Prison life is desolate; it is depressive. But the short walk to the ablution block had none of these qualities. Instead she saw the cars parked in the courtyard, cars racing on the highway, at the back of the building, and saw the neat blue skyline. Her spirits soared with delight for the brief distance.

Her interrogator yawned and scratched his head. It was the umpteenth time he scratched his well-kept hair. As if for the first time Sis Ida saw him scribble on the pad: the head of the pad was nearest his chest and the bottom faced away from the man. Then it occurred to her this was how left-handed persons wrote. The letters were as readable as if any other person used the pad.

She worried about her loquaciousness. The other day she was standing and very little escaped her lips. On this day she was offered a seat straightaway and the result was her control over her mouth left much to be desired. She was chattering away like an agitated parrot.

Her interrogator was a young man, though hugely built. Ida told herself he was a baby, 'n melkpens. He made her relax — 'feel at home,' those were the words he used at the outset. The result was she spoke of her trips to Botswana and Swaziland. So the youngster suggested she was a courier. She denied this. But she recalled that her very last trip to Botswana took her to the refugee camp on the outskirts of Gaberone. On that occasion she brought back a letter to one family in Soweto from an exiled daughter.

A twitch of fear seized her as she remembered her loose tongue.

'Toe nou, tell me about the meeting you attended at Mrs September's.' And when Ida showed signs of puzzlement the young man said: 'Don't tell me you don't know Mrs September.'

Sis Ida smiled dimly, sat up on her chair and placed both hands on her lap. She felt her world collapse further into a deep abyss. Her spirits sank into gloom because she couldn't well say she didn't know the lady in question.

'Yes, I know her. Many people know her,' she added.

'About the meeting?'

'Meeting?' she asked with disbelief. She puzzled about the cop's knowledge. For it was one meeting she did not want to recall, least of all at West End. She saw the charming face of Nelson Mandela. He sat deep in the easy chair made of leather, those days when leather was an item of exclusiveness. His voice boomed around the room for the selected few members of the Organisation trust-worthy enough to meet him. And Mrs September had invited her as a friend. Now the young cop wanted her to recall all that over again. Her brow frowned to impress the cop with her anxiety to remember. Only it looked as if the frown would fossilise. So the cop came to her rescue: 'I am talking of the Resistance Movement meeting you attended with several men at Mrs September's place. Tell me about it.'

At this point Sis Ida felt sorry for herself. The cop paged back fifteen years in her life. Like so many other black people she looked in through several organisations in the course of her life. Mrs September introduced her to the Movement; she joined with great expectations, was disillusioned by the uphill nature of politics, disenchanted by slogans, and withdrew to join another organisation engaged in the cause.

She wished the man would ask about why she was in and out of the doors of so many of the organisations. Why didn't he ask about her sojourn with M.R.A.? She would tell him her society allowed no convictions to take root in one. Instead illusions were pocketed as beliefs until one realised in the glare of the sun that the belief was as shiftable as a chair to be replaced by another. It seemed to be something to do with survival. Sis Ida said the meeting was so long ago she couldn't remember details of it. Yes Mandela was there. She couldn't recall his words.

'Tell me,' said the young cop eyeing Ida sympathetically, 'does your job take you to many places?'

'Yes, it does.'

'Botswana, Swaziland and so forth?'

'Pretoria, Vereeniging, Springs and Randfontein.'

'In other words, only around here?'

'Around here, yes.'

The cop scribbled endlessly. His huge body spread all over the table, covering the pad. His chin hung over the pad like a lampshade. 'Tell me, how many meetings did you attend with these men at Mrs September's place?'

She scratched her memory for an answer and came up with: 'I think one.'

'Sure?'

'I think one.'

'You met Mr Mbambo at the meeting?'

'Mbambo? I don't know him.'

'Sure?'

'No, I don't know him.'

'Remember any men?'

'I don't. It's so long ago.'

'Jong, you'll have to give me some names. I'm not in a hurry. Think! I'm not pushing you because we have the whole of today to do the job.'

Ida was disappointed. She said: 'I don't think it will help.'

'With a bit of luck, who knows what can happen?' After a pause the cop said: 'Oh yes, I understand the people in Soweto call you mistress. Are you a qualified teacher?'

'Yes, I am.' Ida thought the cop revealed a part of her life she gave little thought to: the role of her neighbours. She was convinced the little pieces of information disclosed showed up some neighbour as a busy-bee. Who spied on me? she kept asking herself. The query remained unanswered.

The cop said mockingly: 'Mistress Ida, how does it feel to be in prison?'

The woman in her revolted. She told herself she wouldn't knuckle down under his humiliation any longer. He's kept me for hours, asked stupid questions about my past, threw me around with these silly rumours and now he mocks at me. Sis! a small boy like him! What's he up to, to crumble me like a raisin in the sun? He wants to waste me away with worry . . . enough! He can kill me. He can kill me now, I don't care! Ida began to sulk, it showed in her swollen lips and blown out cheeks. Her whole face was masked by anger.

The cop reacted swiftly. He banged the table, shattering the peace in the room. His left hand pushed the pad aside as he declared: 'I joke with you, you get angry with me, what do you think you are — Queen of England? Jong, I don't care whether you are educated or not — jy's sommer 'n tiekie-line. You sit there met jou bek vol tande. I ask you questions related to the security of the State and you get cheeky. Gots! Jy's snaaks—you are funny!' After a pause the youngster went on: 'Do you know who am I, do you?' He paused again as if expecting a reply. But Sis Ida clamped her lips defiantly.

'I am not one of your kafferboeties, look at me properly!' Sis Ida raised her head slightly to look at the man squarely. He raved: 'Wat kyk jy my—why are you looking at me? I didn't sleep with you last night! Hoor jy—D'you hear me? . . . Bloody communist hoermeid—whore!' he ended it with a long click of the tongue; stood up and hurried to the door. He went out of the room leaving Sis Ida to ponder the why and wherefore of the harangue.

She waited anxiously for his return because it became clear he was standing outside the door. Her waiting was an eternity, it was like the moment in church when one of the marrying partners waits for the other. The thing worked on her nerves. Much as she told herself she was to keep cool and not allow the young man to upset her further, she worried about his non-appearance. Her concern grew in intensity as moments ticked by. She waited. Strange this waiting, as if indeed he was her lover for whom she had to wait.

He came back quietly, walking casually. He seemed calm as if rid of something. He spoke in a low, deceptively polite tone: 'Ida . . . Ida,' he said pleadingly, 'what have you got against me? Do you hate me? Do you distrust me? Have I done you wrong because if I have, I apologise. If I've hurt you, I apologise.'

Sis Ida didn't know what to make of her interrogator. She answered simply: 'I am tired.'

The cop went on as if she hadn't spoken: 'Believe me, I can't do anything evil to you. I must have lost my head just this past minute, I'm sorry.'

She looked at him and saw in him another man. So she felt moved by his admission. She became more motherly towards him because at that very instant it occurred to her the young cop was sick like so many other people she met in her daily work. He revealed before her that he lived with subterranean streams in his make-up. These were like little devils exploding into the open at awkward moments. In other words he suffered from dual personality. The nature of his work was such that to survive he developed a split personality. 'I'm about to let you go,' he said, 'but before I do can you answer this one: who blew up your kitchen with a bomb?'

Ida's eyes softened as she replied: 'I don't know but I suspect it was that small boy Keke.'

'Not Mandla?'

'I don't think so.'

'Where's this Keke now?'

'I don't know.'

'Who would know, any of the detained gang?'

'I don't know.'

'Maybe Mandla?'

'I don't know.' Sis Ida was showing signs of tiredness.

'We missed him.'

'Who?'

'Mandla.'

'Where?' Her spirits were lifted briefly.

'Dobsonville.'

The cop related what had happened at the roadblock. This kept Ida's chest tight. She relaxed only when the cop said Mandla was as slippery as an eel. He swore: 'We'll yet catch him. I'm dead sure of it! You can see the net is closing in on him. You wait.'

It was late afternoon when Sis Ida dragged her tired body into her cell. For her even that hell-hole was welcome after the harrowing experience of the interrogation.


When the winter evening settles on Soweto, it does so like a heavy boot. A grey, thick cloud of smog broods above the houses until darkness swallows up everything. Daylight is shut out quickly. The child hurries to the shop; mother hurries with the evening meal and father takes the shortest route from the station or bus stop to home. Because there were still outbreaks of rioting, thugs joined militant students; pickpockets moved to the city centre and the cries in the location were in fact reverberations of June 16th: Power! Power! Power!

Papa Duz (short for Dubazana) stood outside his coal-yard like a man on inspection. Night fell fast in winter. He strained his eyes to make out the youth descending on his property about closing time. When he saw it was Mandla his joy was subdued by a sense of caution. There were few persons he trusted, least of all his own servants. Once he discovered one of his men worked for the Special Branch. He did not fire him outright. He confronted him one day and the next day the man failed to pitch up for work. He never saw him again.

Papa Duz was his own history. During the long period of Emergencies he was in and out of jail. A former member of the banned Communist Party, he flirted with the Resistance Movement for a while, remaining on the wings all the time. Once he said to Uncle Ribs: 'You chaps suffer from indecision. You don't go the whole hog in the game. I see you marking time as long as you compromise yourselves with your capitalist bosses.' Luck smiled on Papa Duz, however, and he became a capitalist without shame!

He considered himself too old to join hands with the student group but was fascinated by what he termed their reckless adventures. One of the cars used by Mandla and his colleagues came from Papa Duz's pool. When police were about to capture it, the group set it alight to destroy all traces of it.

'Hungh,' grunted Papa Duz leading Mandla to a shack serving him as an office inside the coal-yard, 'long time no see. Where've you been hiding, son?'

'Around Soweto, Papa Duz,' said Mandla cheerfully.

'They don't seem to be catching up with you, these boer boys?'

'I'm Sunlight soap, pa. I slip through their hands at the very moment when they think they've got me.'

Papa Duz laughed loudly. He said: 'The gods must be with you.'

'All the way!'

There was a silence in the shack. Papa Duz began to light up an oil lamp standing on a small but cluttered table. Suddenly he laughed aloud again and slapped his thigh. He looked comical in the lighted shack because part of his face was black with soot. 'What can I do for you, son?' he said settling in a rickety chair which groaned from the load. Over the years Papa Duz had been putting on weight in a fearful way. As a result he looked shorter than he truly was and as heavy as an elephant. His movements were slow, as if well measured. His eyes were searching, piercing into the flesh of anyone with whom he was in contact. Mandla was thus compelled to come clean with his mission immediately.

'Mzi and I need transport, Papa Duz.'

'Mzi?' repeated the coal merchant. 'I've never heard of the name. Who's he son?'

'The Jabavu Police Station man,' said Mandla proudly.

'Is the fellow still around? I thought he would be in Swaziland, or Botswana by now.'

'The police are looking for me for the job. So he can do more jobs . . . you know Papa Duz, I gave them the slip the other day . . .'

'Where son?'

'Outside Dobsonville.'

'I heard of it. You left your car and slipped into Dobsonville. Oh my God! Ha! Ha!' roared Papa Duz. Again he slapped a thigh. 'You boys make me green with envy.'

'I am the Black Pimpernel. They won't catch me easily, I swear by the gods of my father, his father and their fathers.'

Papa Duz was laughing as he stood up from the chair. He went to the door, peeped outside, looking to the left and to the right. As he shut the door to resume his seat he said: 'One can't trust these monkeys prowling in the dark.'

After a pause he said: 'You boys bring back the good old days — the miners' strike of the late '40s, the May Day riots along the Reef and the big coastal towns. In your deeds I see walking upright once more Mandela and Sisulu, Govan Mbeki, Clement Kadalie and all the great sons of our fatherland. Your cry of Power! Power! reminds me of the resounding echoes of Mayibuye! Mayibuye! heard in Freedom Square, Sophiatown. My God!'

He rolled the loose sleeve of his khaki shirt back into position. In the bright light of the shack his face was beaming, the wrinkles of care and age smoothed out. He looked across at Mandla perched on a wooden box: 'I have two cars for your choice: a Volksie and a Cortina. But I think the Cortina packs a lot of power. You can have that if you wish!'

Mandla jumped to his feet: 'Oh! Papa Duz!' He was choked by joy and had enough thought only to shake the hand of Papa Duz. Words were inadequate on this occasion.

Soon he was lost in the darkness enveloping the coal-yard and its owner.


Mandla rode back home in fine fettle. Although the Cortina was a second-hand car over and over again, this didn't touch him. The wheel in his hands felt good and it seemed the car glided in the air, so smooth was the ride.

His mind was occupied by other matters such as the spray-painting of the car. After the job earmarked for later in the night, he thought it would be wise to give the car a new life. This was something they had done before. Earlier one medical man who gave them a car formerly used by his wife suggested a new appearance for the gift. Mandla and his colleagues thought the idea was excellent. They were lucky to find an Italian spray-painter in Booysens, a suburb of Johannesburg, keen to dispose of equipment no longer in use at his business site. Thereafter spray-painting cars became part of the struggle.

The thought of Mzi crossed his mind. He anticipated his sardonic smile of satisfaction. For Mzi was a hard man to please. Anyway with the car in hand it looked like the night's mission was a reality all over again. He could see nothing ahead to postpone the elimination of Warrant Officer Batata. Thought of Batata raised his blood tempo and he found himself pressing hard on the accelerator and emitting an agitated tongue-click.

From deep Soweto at least five roads led to Dube. Mandla's choice cut Mofolo Park in two. With the grey grass stretching far into the dark, and the pine trees dotted around the park like sentinels along a security fence, the sweep through the park made driving a jolly-heart's delight.

Past the Assemblies of God Church and Sizwe Stores there was not much unusual. He was looking forward to meeting Mzi, and his heart was light at this point. Near the Salvation Army Mission in Mofolo on the right hand side of the street, he saw a car which raised his pulse. About the same time he felt the hard dynamite stick inside the lining of his black lumberjacket. He always said he wanted to be ready for what he termed an emergency. It seemed the car he saw was a kind of an emergency. And the stick would be handy.

He stopped the car, reversed to check the other vehicle. It was definitely a police car. The give-aways were there all right: a lanky aerial and the massiveness of its body. A look at the number plates gave him another jolt. Batata's car bore similar numbers. He wasn't too sure of this point but a sneaking feeling told him he was right. He moved forward a safe distance and parked along the high fence of the Mission. The core of an idea had already jelled in his head: Batata must be eliminated at all cost. He would explain later to Mzi what had happened because the opportunity was too tempting to postpone.

House lights were still burning at many houses in the neighbour-hood — too bad. He couldn't postpone the chance given to him by the gods in such matters.

As he neared the police car he became convinced the driver must be Batata — the model and the shape of the car were exactly like the one Soweto had come to know so well. By this time he was floating in space: the excitement and the anticipation of the coming event were overwhelming. He moved as much as was possible in shaded spots to the house in front of which the car was parked. His mental turmoil blinded him to all other considerations, such as being spotted by an onlooker or the collapse of the scheme should the driver come out of the house any moment. He was himself driven by a demonic force which crushed in his young body making of him a little robot bent on destruction. In his ear rang a stock phrase: the end justifies the means.

In the house in question, the owner, Charles Mthembu, sat with his visitor, Sergeant Phineas Rampa of the C.I.D. From time to time both laughed heartily, propelled by the fire of the bottled beer cluttered on the table. Apart from frequent visits to the loo in the backyard both men sat as if the drinking spree would never come to an end. There was nothing unusual when Mthembu slipped out of the room. It looked as if he was going to pay his respects in the backyard as usual. However he picked up one or two empty bottles in the kitchen and walked out. He scaled the fence in the backyard to buy full bottles at the nearby shebeen.

Sergeant Rampa was a very dark and stockily-built man but was able to carry his hugeness with ease. When it seemed like his host was taking a long time to return from the loo, he stood up to take a look at a drawing on one of the walls. He smiled to himself because before him was a figure of a black man seated majestically on a rock, a spear planted in the ground next to him. Chaka, said the inscription at the bottom of the frame.

He was about to resume his seat when he felt an urge to take a look at his car outside. One look was enough to reassure him. In his befogged mind, he didn't seem to think much of a figure of a human being entering the gate as he withdrew from the window. Nor did Mandla behave untowardly when he saw a man's figure appear at the window — curtains parted briefly. In that flitting moment he saw before him a figure equalling in size and appearance the hated Batata and he was fired by the zeal to complete the annihilation of the man.

There was a shattering of broken windows, there was a thunderous boom as an explosion ripped Mthembu's sitting room apart. The suddenness of it all and the power of it were such that Sergeant Rampa died painlessly under the force of debris. He died with the chimes of an ordinary home clock ringing in his ear.

Charles Mthembu, like the people in the neighbourhood, raced to his doomed house. He was too late to help Rampa but was in time to whisk his wife out of the wreckage of his fine house.

Mandla disappeared from the scene but not before he was spotted darting to his parked car. Luckily he knew the lie of the land well enough to race off in the dark. Beyond Mofolo Park the road blazed before him and he was much relieved.

No one followed the fleeing car.


Meanwhile Mzi stood in his room, feet planted apart, knees bending forward, body crouched. In his hands was the AK47 automatic rifle held in readiness for firing. His whole body was tense from the concentration required by such an exercise. He relaxed only as he saw Mandla hurl himself face down on the bed. From the manner Mandla's fingers gripped the bedding, Mzi became concerned.

'What's the matter, are you sick?'

Mandla remained silent. Mzi walked to the edge of the bed. He asked in an emotion-filled voice: 'What's wrong?'

'The car is outside,' said Mandla quietly, words muffled by the bedding, 'please leave me alone!'

For the first time since they began to team up Mzi heard his colleague's words with disbelief: curt and edgy. Mandla seemed out of reach and Mzi was taken aback. Holding the rifle in one hand, he leaned over his friend and touched his shoulder in a show of compassion. He said:

'We are in this together, mfo.' Mzi's voice seemed to choke with feeling as he continued: 'I know sometimes it isn't easy to give words to our thoughts. Yet I must know what eats you . . . Maybe I've wronged you. I need to know.' He stood back, placed the rifle underneath the bed and stood leaning against the wall with thumbs of both hands tucked in the belt of his trousers. He looked saddened by the forlorn appearance of his friend.

Mandla stood up very slowly and sat perched on the edge of the bed. His body remained crouched, his hands rubbing into each other as he said bitterly: 'I've killed the dog!'

'I don't understand,' replied Mzi. He heard the words all right but their meaning escaped him.

'Batata is dead!'

There was no joy in Mzi's voice as he asked: 'Where? How did you do it?'

'Mofolo, in a house in Mofolo. I used the stick I carried in my lumber.'

'But how can you be sure it was Batata? And he's dead?'

Mandla livened up: 'He can't survive! I caught him napping. The blast was too powerful not to have killed the dog!'

199

'Was it Batata?'

'I saw him, I know his car. Batata is dead! Aren't you happy?'

'Happy?' echoed Mzi in mockery. 'I want to scream for joy, I want to jump,' he said walking like a wild animal in the room. 'How can I? You are not saying you left the dog dying at your feet. You scooted away after throwing a stone and a stick of dynamite in the house. Do you see what I mean?'

Mandla stood upright, shoved both hands in the pockets of the lumberjacket and spoke softly, leaning on the bed now: 'I can understand how you feel brother. I've cheated you of the climax of your mission. I've robbed you of the nation's gratitude!' He stopped, pulled one hand out of the pocket and pointed a finger outside the window: 'The people out there will not proclaim me the hero simply because I killed Batata. They will say our children have rid us of the hated man — at last. If that doesn't satisfy you remember this: I didn't do it out of choice. I walked into a chance and grabbed it. It was a risky business because it was still so early. As things stand I cannot be sure no one spotted me or the car. It was risky for me and for Papa Duz.'

'What about me?' asked Mzi cynically.

'No one knows your papers, so no one can know your face.'

For the first time Mzi laughed drily. He was proud of his disguise in the land of his birth.

Mandla perched on the bed once more. A dark mood descended on him. He said: 'I suddenly find myself with mixed feelings over this. I have a bit of regret in my heart. Something tells me I've dirtied my hands. Killing is evil, it is dirty.'

'You must be larger than yourself,' put in Mzi. He was looking through the window into the darkness beyond. 'At such times you don't have to think of who you are but where you are going. It doesn't matter what other people think of you . . . I mean I don't matter in this case. You've done the job. I must take it. Batata is dead. You have earned yourself a place in history. Mayibuye!' yelled Mzi, clenched fist in the air.

'Amandla! Power!' answered Mandla.

Mandla dropped on his back on the bed: 'I want to turn in,' he said.

'This early?'

'The body is a measure of my time this evening. Besides what's there to be done tonight?'

'Mission accomplished, eh?'

Mandla began to undress for bed. The temperature in the room was falling rapidly because the highveld temperature in winter oscillates between extremes of hot and cold.

'I want to look at the machine outside, who knows I might be required to run you out of the country any minute.'

'You must be joking!' said Mandla unsure of himself at this point all the same.


Major Hall sat up straight at his desk, fingering a file in front of him. Presently he let sail across the desk a snap-shot picked out of the file. Boysi didn't touch it. He looked at it and remained sullen. The print was Mandla's. No doubt about it. Hall began to shudder like a feather in the swirl of a whirlwind because the words he wanted were stuck in his mouth. He managed: 'I-I-I want that boy.' His mouth twisted, so did his face. But Boysi made as if he didn't hear the cop.

'Where is he?'

'I don't know,' said Boysi shrugging shoulders.

'L-Look here,' said Hall pointing a menacing finger at Boysi, 'I don't think you understand. A-a policeman has been mur-murdered. a . . . a . . . police station b-b-bombed . . . two-thirds of you must take the blame . . . serious charges . . . I know Mandla was there.' (The word Mandla took a lot of Hall's breath because it was one of those lateral sounds he found an ordeal). He paused briefly. Then went on: 'I want you to co-operate with us.'

Boysi's eyes didn't leave the cop's face. Simultaneously the face of Willie Meyer was now superimposed on Hall's. This was it, he told himself as he began to contemplate his situation. Roy, Bongi, Snoek, the lot, all appeared before him. Power! Amandla! Power! Amandla! he heard them scream in chorus. Now more than ever before he wished they were all together in the room with Hall. To his strange new presence appeared the blurred vision of Mandla. He couldn't explain why the focusing on his leader was so blurred. 'Bajita, there's work to be done. No time for food,' said Mandla. The words rang clearly but the leader's face was behind a mist in the mind's eye. Boysi winced as if in pain. Edmond Hall sat forward and enquired: 'W-what's the matter? Sick?'

It was an opening Boysi could have seized. Yet he replied: 'I am well.'

'Boysi,' said Hall in a fatherly manner, sitting back in his chair, you are young and I know you are intelligent. You want to be something in life: a doctor, a lawyer, a businessman. Something! Somebody in life. Don't be a fool, man. I offer you a scholarship to an American university, not just a bursary. I'll pay for your books, fees, clothes and I'll guarantee you handsome pocket money. That's my offer. You don't want to go on struggling. Why? When these things can be arranged for you in a very discreet manner?'

Mandla's face played tricks with Boysi. He was aware the Major's offer related to Mandla. He searched for his eyes in the mind as if seeking approval from the vision. But the blurred face was not helpful. Instead he heard Hall say: 'Today a man is a man according to the style of his life – the spacious house, the big car and the job one holds down, these are the measure of a man today. You, like many of us, were born to live a full life.'

Major Hall shifted in his seat and continued: 'Let me tell you something from my early days on-on this green earth: I was driving home after 'chayile' time. I saw a caravan not far off the road, you must have seen one yourself, isn't it?'

Boysi grunted something like 'Yes.'

'Eddie take a chance, I told myself, turning off the road to the caravan . . . you see, these gypsy women, they are like our sangomas. They'll tell you a lot about the future – just for a small fee! Anyway, the gypsy holds up my palm and says: "Policeman, you have a great future ahead of you. Everybody's going to be proud of you because you will do something great for your country." That was a long time ago. Those days I was an ordinary constable with poor pay. So you see, what I need from you is not for myself. I don't need a promotion, as many people think of us. The country needs your support just as I need it myself. We have almost solved the Jabavu Police Station case. We know Mandla was there. And you, not. What we can't figure out is Mandla's knowledge of explosives. Working with the little information he got from the local high school, how could he produce a bomb very much like the ones Russians teach saboteurs? How could he?' After a pause: 'Do you see what I mean?'

'Yes.'

'We know Mandla never went for training in Zambia, Tanzania or Angola. So how did he know the formula for the explosives?'

'I don't know.'

'You chaps talked about these things, right?'

'I don't know which things.'

'Formulas, explosives?'

'I wasn't there.'

'I didn't say so but you must have heard talk about these things?'

'Not in my presence.'

'Mandla went out of the house alone on that evening, didn't he?'

'I don't know. I didn't see him.'

'The SACB and the Race Relations told you people your schools were inferior, they didn't teach you enough science and maths . . .'

Boysi kept silent.

'What I mean is teachers were organised for you by the SACB and Race Relations.'

'We went for classes at Race Relations.'

'And the SACB paid the teachers?'

'I don't know.'

'Oh, you don't know that one? Well, I can tell you a lot but not now.'

Again Boysi looked Hall in the eye as if to say: Telling me!

Hall stammered: 'Th-this chap R-Roy, he is one of you?'

'Yes.'

'He says he was No. 2 to Mandla.'

Boysi looked hard at the Major. He wasn't sure of his answer. The officer's information was disarming. Lest he be caught out later, Boysi said: 'Yes he was.'

'He was with Mandla at the Police Station?'

'I don't know.'

'You heard Mandla did the job?'

'Yes.'

'So Mandla was there? Who else?'

'I don't know.'

'You are sure of Mandla?'

'Yes I am.'

Boysi was surprised to see Hall stand up suddenly. The man seemed satisfied as he went to fetch a pink and yellow coffee flask. It had been standing on one of the steel cabinets in the room. Next to it was a provisions box. Hall collected a cup as well from the cabinet. He left behind the saucer which goes with the cup. Only when the hot coffee trickled into the cup did he begin to say something: 'You must be tired, eh?'

Boysi answered with his mouth shut. He was puzzled by the new turn of events. He found himself dry in the mouth as if in anticipation of a cup of coffee.

'Mine is sweetened from home,' said Hall putting the cup of coffee near Boysi. He poured another cupful for himself into the lid of the flask. And added: 'Some people are very clever, imagine using the lid as a cup also. Smart, eh?'

Boysi was slow to sip the coffee. He was aware of the changed atmosphere and wondered why.

Taking his seat again, Hall said: 'The next step will be for me to draw up a statement with this admission on your part.'

The word admission wasn't new in the world of Boysi. But its legal meaning escaped him. All the same he puzzled the whole exercise. The signing of statements he had heard of before and this he came to learn wasn't a good thing to do in the presence of police.

Presently it dawned on Boysi why the change of attitude on the part of the cop: the coffee, the admission, the signing of the statement, all these in sequence jolted him. He began to realise his blunder. His admission of Mandla's part at Jabavu Police Station was a terrible mistake, he told himself as he sipped the coffee very slowly. Its blackness lacked taste for him. From sweet bitterness, the coffee became plain flat as if made of distilled water. The blurred vision of Mandla became swirling smoke in the room.

Now the Major became suspended in space: eyes, mouth, and jutting chin. It seemed the cop's face was curling up and up before him. He didn't know what was real and to ascertain his own condition Boysi put the empty cup on the desk. It made a thud on the wood causing Hall to stammer: 'Ca-careful! What's the matter, aren't you well?'

'Sick!' said Boysi. Then he pouted his lips as one does when about to puke. His body convulsed while he held one hand to his stomach.

'What's the matter?' asked Hall. Clearly he was unhappy with the new situation. The reports of detainees dying mysteriously in the company of policemen were too many in the daily press for him to have his own name linked with such a strange death.

'C-can I c-call you a doctor?' suggested Hall. He was on his feet: 'M-maybe you've been upset by the co-coffee. Too sweet, maybe.'

Boysi was almost calm at this point, but his eyes were glazed. His mind refused to focus on his 'sin', which the policeman would not appreciate in any case. Why? Why? Why? he asked himself.

He hiccoughed. And kept one hand on his lips.

Hall pressed a button on his desk and while waiting for the door to open he said: 'I'll give instructions for the district surgeon to visit you straight away. You should be all right later today.'

A warder came for Boysi.

He experienced a numbness of the body as he walked drunkenly to the cell. Even on the way he tried to picture Mandla but failed. He couldn't recall his exact words to Hall as he gave his friend away. He thought the interrogation was simple and straightforward. How was it that he became trapped to the extent of giving away an admission of guilt against Mandla?

The prison door shut him into a nauseating presence. He couldn't stand the 'fruity smell.' He collapsed on the bundle of blankets, his nostril clipped by two fingers. He couldn't tell when he passed out.

# 13

Dr Kenotsi hurried to close his surgery, not because he heard the latest in the Soweto saga but because another matter occupied his mind. For a full ten minutes he tried to shake off a man who came regularly for his injection.

'Okay baba,' said the doctor on his feet, 'Okay baba, I will see you tomorrow.' His hands waved vaguely toward the exit door in his bid to be rid of the patient. But the patient seemed oblivious to hints. He stood looking at the doctor admiringly. The doctor took off his white dustcoat, hung it on the door and prepared his medicine bag. The man stood by patiently, shifting narrowly to give way to the doctor as he moved from point to point.

Dr Kenotsi was ready to go. The patient grabbed the medicine bag mumbling something about helping the doctor as he locked up.

'Baba—Father, you may go now I think I'm all right.'

'It doesn't matter dokotela,' said the patient cheerfully, 'I hurry, hurry home, what for, I doesn't do no nothing this, so little bit little bit of time here with dokotela means no nothing,' the man chuckled. Dr Kenotsi chafed under the collar. There wasn't much time left to the next engagement and here was this man being sociable.

Dr Kenotsi did the unusual. He went to the car to have the bag deposited and be rid of the man. Normally he would reach his car parked in the yard only after locking up the gates fixed outside the door for security reasons.

When the bag was in the car, he thought, cheerfulness laid thick on his part might ease the break with his patient.

'Thank you very, very much baba. I must hurry now . . . Good night, neh?'

The patient heard the doctor's words as if in a spell. He stood looking at Kenotsi, hands rubbing together his warm heart. Then the telephone in the surgery began to ring. The two heard it at the same time. At that moment the sound jarred Kenotsi's ears. He didn't want to answer it yet there was within him a voice which said the call may save the life of another dying person. He looked frantic as he rushed back into the surgery.

'Hello,' said Kenotsi into the mouthpiece. His voice was quiet, his spirits seemingly dampened: 'Can I help you?' He was always taking precautions . . . 'Yes that's me all right . . . What?' exclaimed Kenotsi as if in that moment he'd been jabbed with one of the needles in his surgery . . . 'Who's speaking . . . a friend of the struggle . . . I don't know the voice but it really doesn't matter . . . where's he, did they catch him? . . . oh . . . oh . . . thanks for telling me, brother . . .'

He rang off, stood riveted where he was, puzzling the meaning of the latest development. Before his eyes stood a painful realisation: the children's revolution was sucking him into its core irreversibly. For once he was hesitant to set foot outside his consulting rooms. He stood leaning on his working desk, one hand under his chin. A fear entangled his mind and body so that the hand under the chin began to shiver. He put the offending hand in the pocket of his trousers. There was relief flowing with his blood. Thereafter he acted swiftly: locked up the place and got out of it. Thank God! The patient was gone.

His ride in the street was slower than he wished, what with the streets of Orlando decorated by potholes, he seemed to be crawling. So was a little car tailing him from a discreet distance. Knowledge of it would certainly have shattered his frayed spirits. As it happened he was fearful but kept going to fulfill the evening's engagement.

Dr Kenotsi reached a red brick house extended decently with painted corrugated iron sheets, without the slightest suspicion of being followed. Here he knew the routine: dart out of the car, push in the double gate and drive in and close the gate before tap-tapping on the front door. He did all this. As he waited for the door to be opened for him, he searched the shadows within sight. For him at that moment a fear lurked in the darkness.

The contact who housed the recuperating Keke was himself a man of few words: he was so soft-spoken he could pass for being docile. When the medico appeared subdued on that evening, he took this to be a result of the day's fatigue. Nor did he show signs of being unduly disturbed when the doctor passed on the news heard on the telephone. The mood in the room became heavy with sadness. Each was anxious to know how the event might have happened. But the words never ended the speculation.

Keke appeared. He was greeted by the doctor with a grin. There was no way to know Keke's reaction because his whole face was swathed with bandages, leaving tiny slits around the eyes and nostrils.

'How's the big boy today?' asked the medico. He was trying to lift his own deadened spirits.

'Better, sir,' mumbled Keke his voice muffled by the bandage.

'Happy to be going home?'

'Yes, sir.'

'Don't you think it's risky going home?' The voice belonged to the contact who was no longer sure of the move in view of the latest news. Kenotsi remained silent and it was left to Keke to make his stand.

'I want to go home,' he said. He sounded sad.

'Are you sure?' put in Kenotsi.

'Yes, sir,' he lisped.

The contact went to the front door, opened it and stood at the edge of the little stoep taking in the immediate surroundings. He saw the car parked in the shadow of the gum tree but didn't give it a second thought because there was a house nearby.

'All clear,' he said waving a hand. The medico followed by Keke came out of the house and hurried to the car.

Once in the street, Kenotsi felt a pain jab at his stomach. He was driving slowly, his eye scanning the environment. When he crossed the bridge between Orlando East and West he felt a relief he couldn't understand. At the same time he told himself he hoped never again to take the kind of risk placed in his hands that evening. Once he was jolted in his seat by the appearance of a kwela-kwela from the opposite direction. He was tempted to break the latest developments to his passenger but decided it wouldn't be fair to the patient. So they drove in silence. Late as it was, there were still a number of cars on the streets. Some passed him, others remained on his tail until they turned off along the long stretch leading to Dube Village, the black middle class area.

They arrived at Keke's home without the slightest hint of the danger in their lives. Keke's father and mother opened their arms to their injured son. The scene was quite moving, tears streaming down Keke's mother's cheeks.

It was within the warmth of his mother's arms that Keke thought of Mandla and the other members of the group. In a way he missed the company of the others now that he was home. In particular he wanted to know the whereabouts of Mandla but fell short of asking the question in the midst of the prevailing home spirit.

Suddenly there was a thud of feet in the yard; there was a hard rapping on the front door and the quiet lately descended on the home of Aunt Bettie was shattered.

Colonel Kleinwater was devastating once more: 'Tog mense, excuse my coming in like this. It wasn't a special trip. I came to Soweto to investigate the murder of one of my men, Sergeant Rampa, and I thought I might drop by.' As he spoke, the house filled with policemen in uniform and in safari suits. He went on: 'Doctor, your game is over now. As you well know a man in my station needs no proof for his action. Please accompany me to Police Headquarters. Keke, I'm very glad to meet you. Please come with me.' Turning to Keke's father he said: 'I'll probably need you tomorrow for clarification of one or two points. Stand by!'

Dr Kenotsi couldn't believe his eyes outside the house. There were no fewer than half-a-dozen police cars for his detention.

Word spread round Soweto like a fanned veld fire that Dr Kenotsi was arrested. The mood of the people became rotten. Many spoke of killing informers because it was so clear someone gave away the medico.

NEWS ITEM
SOWETO WAKES UP TO ANOTHER SHOCK
PROMINENT MEDICO DETAINED
NO COMMENT SAYS POLICE SPOKESMAN

'They came for me at the dead of night; they knocked on the front door, on the front and side windows; they played their torchlights on all windows; they said they were the police. Luckily I was working all night. Dan Modise came past Bara on his way to work. He told me all this. I thought I should come straight here. I am frightened; I am confused!' It was Sis Joyce speaking, seated in the sitting room at MaNhlapo's place. She sat feet crossed, her hand holding a handbag on her lap. She looked disturbed as she related her experiences to Mandla and Mzi.

'Cowards!' said Mzi.

In the silence that followed she went on: 'Dr Kenotsi was picked up at Keke's place last night.'

'Last night?' exclaimed Mandla.

'No doubt they'll link him with Batata's death,' said Mzi.

'How terrible!' cried Mandla.

'Batata dead?' said an anguished Sis Joyce, 'the paper says it's a Sergeant Rampa . . . Here, I've got this morning's paper in the bag.'

Mandla spread the paper so that he and Mzi read at the same time the big bold black letters: 'Death of Another Policeman.' The report referred to him as a medium height, slightly built youth. The story said it was the diabolical act of a desperate youngster. It added a claim by a senior officer to the effect that an early arrest of the culprit was expected.

Mandla handed the paper over to Mzi. Suddenly he changed complexion and sighed sorrowfully. It was obvious the news was unpleasant. The silence in the room was broken by Mzi:

'So Batata is still alive?'

'Yep!'

'And it's back to square one?'

'Ya! . . . but not exactly, because they have Kenotsi and Keke.'

'That hots up the trail.'

'Right all the way.' Mandla spoke with a feeling which gradually became heavy. It was as if for him a moment of painful truth had arrived. He said with emotion: 'I killed the wrong guy. I've dirtied my hands spilling the blood of a man I hardly knew . . . oh, I feel lousy,' and he began to move aimlessly around the room. 'I'm rotten inside of me!'

'Take it easy pal, one cop is as good as another. Don't take this so badly, you are not to blame.'

'You don't understand. If I knew the driver of the car wasn't Batata I definitely wouldn't have gone through all that . . . Try to understand the sorrow I've brought to many hearts.'

'Don't be sentimental!'

'I'm not. I've killed the wrong man!'

'A dog, not man!'

'Oh! You don't understand. I am guilty for the murder of another person, a person I didn't want to destroy. I must pay the price,' declared Mandla.

'Pay the price, what do you mean?' asked Mzi. He was looking hard at the figure of his friend standing near the front window, looking out into the street.

Mandla watched the scene in the street with a faraway look in his eye: the winter sun remained a promise at that hour. A few clouds dotted the sky; the air was still, yet the people he saw rushing toward Dube Station seemed to be propelled from behind. Some walked briskly, others trotted up the incline to the station. He couldn't guess their thoughts but he was convinced each carried a purpose in his walk, each wished for a survival attainable by this rush to the station. He wondered about his own survival in the midst of that crushing moment. So many people seemed to turn by the twist of his little finger: Dr Kenotsi, Keke, Roy, Sis Ida, the lot.

And in his presence Mzi, indifferent to petty feelings, as he had once said; Sis Joyce, fragile and scared as only a civil servant can be. Mzi asked him a question whose answer was sealed in his heart, for somewhere in his make-up he knew his life had very few options. He could go to jail or simply disappear from the scene. And the killing of an innocent man wrapped up the decision for him. He turned to face his friend.

'Today I shall quit!'

'Quit?' asked Mzi scandalized by the thought of it.

'I can't stand myself around here anymore.'

'But you'll be going with the self you hate,' said Mzi.

'I hate myself because I am dirty. I go away to have cleansed this dirt.'

'You are playing into the hands of the enemy . . . They'll say . . . they'll say you escaped the consequences of your actions.'

'As you say, it will be the enemy saying so. Believers in the cause will understand I needed my batteries re-charged.'

Mandla went to perch on one of the seats in the room. He continued: 'I am a very small part of the struggle. Today I stand on a pinnacle I never dreamt I would occupy. Mandela, Sobukwe, Xuma, Lembede, Luthuli, Dube, Thema, Moroka, even Tshaka, Moshoeshoe, Sikukune and Gaika are my fathers and forefathers. And they are your fathers and forefathers. They are the forefathers of Sis Joyce here. The place I leave will be taken by another one as great or greater than me.'

'So your mind is made up?'

'By my low spirits, brother. I am worn out. For weeks and weeks I've known nothing less than the battering of my spirits. I've seen flames rise and mingle with the smoke of burning municipal offices, banks, clinics, post offices, beerhalls, cars, kombis and buses. I've heard the yell of triumph, the grouse of sorrowing voices. My own voice is hoarse with the shouts of promise. I thought we'd won. But the cops have come and we were left to pick up the dead; to wail with greying mothers and fathers. Now I face myself at this hour as a murderer. Do you begin to understand? I can't go on. I must quit! I quit to quit again wherever I'll be going, for this is where I belong.'

'What happens to Sis Joyce?'

'Sis Joyce?' Mandla said as if he came out of a reverie. In the interval he'd been looking into his situation, the presence of Sis Joyce had meant nothing to him. Mzi apparently convinced Mandla he could now find the time and the energy to look at the current circumstances: 'We have friends. I think she can join Uncle Ribs in Botswana. Are you ready to go, Sis?'

'I don't know. It seems one can never say: I am ready! One never leaves the country completely, so one can never be really ready to go. When you say jump into the car, I'll do so. How's that?'

'Good enough!' answered Mandla.

All three remained silent.

'I'm sorry to have given the impression of not being sympathetic,' said Mzi. 'I know I'm selfish at times. I didn't want you to go because you are part of me. I'm gonna miss you, brother.'

'I know.'

Again there was a pause, the moment filled by the heavy beat of anxious breathing. For at that time each person in the room stood poised to take a leap into the unknown dark side of life.

'How will you make it to the border?' asked Mzi of Mandla.

'I'll use whitey,' said Mandla mischievously.

'But seriously, how will you make it? Because I can chance the drive.'

A smile played on Mandla's face as he said: 'I know a guy who works for whitey as a salesman, he can drive me out there. You see, he sells maize all over the Transvaal. I'll be part of the merchandise.'

'And Sis Joyce?'

'No worry. The same guy will arrange with his colleagues to do something for her. The problem now is how she'll collect her personal belongings. She can't go dressed as a nursing sister.'

'Easy,' said Mzi, 'MaNhlapo will go to Dan's wife and Dan's wife will walk casually to her neighbour's house and do as told. Simple, man.'

Turning to Sis Joyce, Mzi said: 'Is this not right Sis Joyce?'

The moment was brief but it seemed like eternity when Sis Joyce suddenly tightened her face muscles, changed her sitting position and said: 'How terrible! I must sneak out of my birthplace! Hayi mnta kanantsi—child of so-and-so, I can't see any other way. We'll ask MaNhlapo to do as you suggest. Hope she'll agree.'

'Oh she will,' said Mandla, 'She's one darling!'

'Shoo!' exclaimed Sis Joyce, 'I thought my husband was mad to leave the country! These people press us down like a finger pressed into an eye to force someone to give in to something . . . Hayi this is bad!' she said slapping her two hands together. 'Freedom will come to us one day. God is no fool!'

Mandla stood up, stretched his arms and yawned: 'I must take the car to bra Sparks for spray-painting.'

'Dead right,' said Mzi, 'I must finish off my job tonight.'

The whirlwind in MaNhlapo's house began to gather momentum as the sun rose higher in the sky. Everyone in the house entered the stage of action.

The ant hurried on the floor of the cell toward a point he didn't see. It stopped suddenly, retraced its steps, crawled up the wall, zig-zagging in its hurried movements but then it came to a stop again, climbed down, touching the floor very smoothly. Roy wondered about the way it was able to do as it pleased in its surroundings; he wondered about its freedom of movement and the purpose behind its hurried step. And he thought of the wasting of his young life.

It was now a countless number of days since he had been in deten-tion. No one spoke to him, not even to say hello, let alone to ask how he felt. In all that time he never opened his mouth. It got so bad for him in jail he wished they would interrogate him. Very often he heard screams come from nearby rooms; at times he heard thud-ding blows as if someone was being beaten up. Invariably there would be a pained yell for help and a limp cry. Those noises marked a reality for him. Yes, the noises and the trips to the ablution block where he would fart and pee a tiny miserable liquid as he took a shower.

He lost count of time, knew the day and the night by the amount of the noise: the intensity of all sorts of noises increased by day and became only crying sniffles at night.

When he meant to sleep, he would just pass out because a con-scious effort resulted in frustration. On occasions he would remem-ber the advice of his uncle: count the number of sheep entering a kraal. At first he thought it worked but there came a time when the sheep became countless in number.

Mornings were no less frustrating. He hated the coarse and dirty blankets and sleeping mats meant to be his bedding. They provided the minimum comfort in a cell but were a horrible reminder of his imprisoned life.

Roy worried about his own sanity. Often he checked himself in the process of chasing a fly around the cell. He did it to kill time; he did it to measure the flexibility of his reflexes because although he was allowed time to exercise alone, he was no longer sure the walk in the prison yard and the stretching of arms up and forward and sideways did any good to his body. He did it for fear of his sanity

212

which he told himself he couldn't afford to lose. For Roy thought he was no longer sure whether or not he was himself, in control of his full senses. Lately he sensed a numbness of his body and he feared this was a sign of his loss of mind.

The second time he watched an ant in the cell, he believed himself sick. There was in its varied movements something it transmitted to his body, resulting in the twisted feelings he experienced: sometimes joy, sometimes an inexplicable pain of his legs. He was quite sure the delirious sensation was a failing of the mind. The ant was a small innocent object on its mission in his surroundings but watching it made him delirious — how come? Why did he smile at it? At what point did the smile begin? Was it not proof he was gradually becoming a moron? Wasn't it?

The door of his cell opened and he heard the warder say between his clenched teeth: 'Vandag jy kak Kaffer—You shit today, Kaffir.' The words reached Roy as if along a long tunnel. They held no fear for him. Nothing like that. Instead he was mildly excited. Leaning on the wall as he did, he didn't care a damn for the man standing at the door and demanding: 'Kom—Come!' He was too weak to respond with speed. He was too muddled up to focus instantly on the warder's command. Roy sighed, changing the weight of his body from one leg to the other.

The warder rushed in and pulled him out of the door, saying with his twisted lips: 'Jou verdonderde aap—Bloody ape! Vandag jy praat—Today you speak!'

'. . . You must look at me carefully,' said the man seated behind a small table. He spoke in a rough voice, his r's in Afrikaans seeming to be torturous: hard and grating. He went on: 'They call me "Praatnou" and it is for a good reason,' he said, eyes emitting cold fire.

Roy looked at the man's brow. He could not help noticing it because it stood out like a mountain. There were a number of scars running from one end to the other of it. Indeed there was a suggestion in the looker's mind that the scars on the nose were a continuation of what started on the brow. But the brow was too awful, as if a sharp blade cut it up wildly and it was stitched together roughly just so that the man could lay claim to a brow like everybody else. The result of it all was this cliff overlooking the eyebrows and the scarred nose.

'Bullshit me once and you won't know the hole through which you entered the earth.'

The remark was enough to stiffen and anger Roy. He looked hard and hatefully at the cop but showed no other acknowledgement of the man.

'Toe nou, what is your name?'

'Roy Metsing.'

'When you answer me you must remember we've got your god together with Ke. . . Keke,' said Praatnou, referring to a note before him. There were a number of files on the table; some opened, others shut.

The mention of Keke with 'a god' disturbed Roy. He feared Mandla was the god. Yet how could he ask for an explanation from the cop? Roy played the tip of his tongue around his lips. He bit these wet lips as if to hold back the crush of emotions building up in him.

'What's your leader's name?'

Roy was annoyed further by that one.

He couldn't understand the game played by the interrogator. He was convinced the man was playing a game with him but what the game was he couldn't tell. He remained staring at the cop.

Praatnou was swift and devilish. He shot up from his seat and yelled, pounding the table: 'What's the matter with you? Can't you bloody well hear I'm talking to you? Jy's verspot hey? Is Mandla not your leader?'

'Yes,' said Roy quietly.

'Why keep quiet when I ask for his name?'

'I didn't understand.'

'Kak—Shit! Jy lieg jong—You lie, fellow! . . . Why did you bomb the police station?'

Roy had waited for this question and others for a long, long time but when it came it sickened him. Quietly, confidently, he said 'I wasn't there!'

'You lie!' shouted Praatnou, 'Mandla couldn't have done it alone!' You were the number two according to our information from your colleagues. Who else then?'

'I don't know. I wasn't there!' said Roy with a raised voice.

Praatnou hurled himself into action with lightning speed. He made as if to go to the door, swerved suddenly towards Roy swinging his left arm and slapped him hard on the left ear. The blow was sudden, it was swift and it caught Roy unawares. He was sent tottering in the room. Before he could regain his balance, he was kicked on one shin. He doubled up, was picked up with a well-timed upper cut jerking his head violently upwards. A karate chop on the back of the neck crumpled him on the floor.

'That's black power for you!' gloated the cop, towering over Roy. He went on: 'Stand up! Stand up! Swart gat!' Pain and stubborn defiance kept Roy inert on the floor.

Two kicks on the back couldn't impress on him the gravity of the moment. He remained unmoved. Praatnou pushed his foot under Roy's body and tried to turn him over. The degradation of the act was more than the humiliation meted out to the young black boy. The cop gave up and walked to his seat. He was shaking his head to place back in position the mane on it. In addition he brushed his hair into place with both hands. As he sat down he said over the fallen body of Roy: 'You are going to talk, my boy.'

Minutes went by before there was any communication between the two. While the cop fidgeted with files on the table, Roy struggled to get to his feet. His pride was too much to be on the floor but the reality of his physical condition compelled him down there. He dragged himself up to the point where he was able to kneel, powerless.

Praatnou seemed to delight in having achieved this little concession from the stubborn black young man. He said: 'Listen to me. There's no point playing the toughie. We know everything about your group. You don't seem to understand when I say your god and Keke are in our hands and they have talked. I'm merely trying to verify a point when I ask who was with Mandla at the bombing of the police station. You don't seem to understand that the beginning and end of your crimes against the security of the State turn around the criminal act of bombing that station. You've got to tell me the truth. With whom was Mandla?'

All the time Roy was struggling to get onto his feet. He heard the last words of the cop while on his feet. But he couldn't stand upright because there was a pain on his side, the result of kicking. It jabbed at him now and again as if it swelled up and down. To blot it out he kept one hand in the area of the core of pain.

'I'm going to ask you once more,' said Praatnou menacingly: 'Who was with Mandla?'

'Uncle Ribs,' blurted Roy through sulking lips;

'Who is he?'

'A black brother.'

'Black se moer!' shouted Praatnou banging the table. 'I want the man's name!'

'Mr Mbambo.'

'Mr Mbambo indeed,' sneered the cop as he wrote the name down. He asked again: 'Where is he?'

'Dube.'

'Oh, he's one of them, those better muntus who want to be white people. The Government does him a favour, puts him in a better class house and area and he stabs the law in the back. I don't know why we bother to improve the lives of these ungrateful people. Gots! you are all the same.'

Roy stood crookedly in front of the table, his one hand still pressed on the sore spot on his body. He swore he wouldn't give in to the physical and spiritual onslaught of his person. To this end he invoked the image of his father's fathers to give him strength. By this time his body belonged to someone else because of the numbness of its sensitive nerve centres. He could hardly recall the length of time the grilling took place but it did feel an eternity.

For his part Praatnou sat at the table, head in hands. Roy wasn't to know his ordeal of the moment was shared by the cop as well. After extracting the name of an accomplice at the bombing of the police station, Praatnou experienced a let-down. It was something strange, something which came upon him every time he sensed pain, especially when he inflicted it on others. This was a truly extraordinary experience, which surfaced whenever he touched his scarred brow as he did on this occasion. And it all started with a car accident a couple of years earlier. Then he was a young recruit in the police force. In the exuberance of the moment he was driving a police vehicle with another young colleague as passenger. On a stretch of road he attempted an antic typical of a paranoic mind. Of course the vehicle rolled and rolled until it settled on a dented hood off the road. The vehicle was a mangled piece of iron and chrome. The passenger died instantly with his neck broken; Praatnou hovered between life and death for days, inheriting the scars on his brow. But he lived to boast: 'Ek is 'n boer ossewa—I'm a farmer's ox-wagon'. Yet he was made to remember the pain caused to the relations of his colleague and each time he was surrounded by a painful situation it battered his spiritual being so that he was himself so tired he would have to rest and if he so much as touched the scars on his brow, the fire of life and the will to live were dowsed.

Roy was surprised to hear him say almost pleadingly: 'Stand against the wall man, you are crowding me.'

The student leader couldn't hide his relief. The wall was a solace he longed for all the time. And standing there as if it were made for him, he felt a whole weight of burdens unloaded. Only the recurring sensation of the pain on his side remained. Thank God it wasn't so sharp either. So he waited, wondering what the cop planned against him.

He wasn't to guess long because Praatnou said into the mouthpiece of the phone near him: 'Jannie, come and fetch this dog!' The
cop's will had collapsed.

Roy was led away, tired and feeling those bodily aches known to a
tortured person. In his heart was a joy and a sense of triumph. He
told himself he didn't care what they did to him, one thing was
certain, he wouldn't give in to their bullying.


**14**


Mzi arrived quite early at his hiding place: the gum-tree overlooking
the church standing almost opposite the house of Warrant Officer
Andries Batata. The Cortina was parked in the next street, hugging
the green hedge so that any casual looker would get the impression
the car owner was visiting the house hemmed in by the hedge. Mzi
had studied the habits of the occupant, old man Mthembu: sharp at
8 p.m. he shuffled to the front gate to lock it up and soon thereafter
the houselights were snuffed. Mzi knew it all.

The freedom fighter was dressed for the occasion: balaclava over
his head and a brown overall. In this guise the winter's nippy air
meant little to him. He felt nothing of the cold but heard the quiet
rustle of the huge tree against which he was leaning. He stood there
as if unconcerned with the house across the street: one foot on the
ground, the other touching the tree with the sole of his shoe. On his
breast was the AK47 automatic machine, cuddled like a baby. He
waited patiently at first and to kill time his mind went back many
years in time: he had been walking down one street in Queenstown
when he had seen a group of men, faces forlorn and eyes wearing a
distant look. They were herded together, waiting at a street corner:
arrested for pass offences. A sense of burning hatred had filled his
chest immediately because he had felt with empathy what those men
knew in their hearts. Young as he was he had dared the cops to arrest
him. No one approached him and he had walked on, feeling the
bitterness rise up in his blood. Every step he took away from the
source of his unhappiness was treading on a consciousness he wished
to avoid. He was to see more sights like that one many times. And he
came to know it was the lot of his people all over the country.

His mind broke with the past about the same time as he saw
house-lights die in the neighbourhood. He didn't know the time but

it felt like an eternity. But Mzi was not bothered, for this night was for him a special occasion: a date for the fulfilment of the mission to Soweto.

The night became icy cold and to avoid the stiffening of his body he began to swing both arms in turn and to mark time in the shade of the huge gum tree. Mzi was a self-assured person and the exercises undertaken were done with the recklessness only Mzi was capable of showing. But this was his night and he acted as if a voice told him so much. And it was also evidence of the impatience of waiting.

It was in the still of the night when the lights of a car suddenly blazed with horrific effect, turning the dimness of street lights into a glare. Without seeing the car Mzi knew the waiting was over, but being a trained operator he bided his time before taking his position for action.

Batata got out of the huge car and stared up and down the street and at the dingy church with its tall gum tree. It was habit more than fear that prompted him to do so. The massive man opened the big gate to drive in the car. Mzi watched him with a sneer on his face.

Inside the house Irene Batata woke up to receive her husband. Lately she found it difficult to sleep soundly while her husband was away. And any noise in the vicinity of the yard turned her into a bundle of nerves — the aftermath of an attempt to set their home on fire and burn the family alive.

On this night she heard the crunching tyres approaching the yard, the squeaking of brakes as the car stood inside the yard at the garage door and the raking of the big gate as Batata began the final closing up of the iron gates. Irene went over these things as if it was a rehearsal. She waited for the front door to open, convinced at this point that nothing could stop her husband's entry into the house. Nonetheless her waiting was tempered by an anxiety she couldn't explain, as if she should call out to him to hurry before an inexplicable disaster befell him. Yet she remained in bed comforted by the knowledge of being wedded to a brave man, a man armed with a revolver or two.

Warrant Officer Batata stood locking the two sides of the big gate. It was the moment of moments for Mzi. He opened fire from the deadly weapon, sure of the damage it would cause regardless of the point of impact. Batata never knew where the hail of bullets came from because he was riddled all over his body even as he lay gasping his last breath.

Mzi disappeared into the night as house-lights came up from the neighbourhood, one by one. The only words to come from the terrified lips of Irene were: 'Nkosi yami—My God!'

The mission was accomplished.

The first barking shots from the automatic rifle sent old man Mthembu scuttling back into the house. Minutes before he had been up because the call to the toilet in the backyard was irresistible. Coming out of the loo he spotted the vehicle in front of his yard. It was the Cortina huddled by his hedge, empty. His first thought categorised the car as stolen and a matter for the police. At that hour of the night and dressed as he was, trousers and white vest, the matter was for attention the following morning. He noted the registration and was in the process of cramming the details of the model when the night's silence was shattered by the firing of a rifle not so far away. Old man Mthembu read *The Star* at times and considered himself literate and therefore still very much useful to the community. His life was important. He hurried into the house and remained in the darkened kitchen long enough to puzzle about the rifle shots, so powerful, so rapid and so near.

For Mzi the coolness and precision of the final note of the mission to Soweto seemed to evaporate with every passing moment. First he couldn't explain to himself why he took a roundabout way back to MaNhlapo's. Secondly, he couldn't drive into the yard at the very first attempt. Thirdly, inside the kitchen he bumped and hurt himself with every step forward he took, as if the house was suddenly cluttered with furniture.

He sat on the bed wanting to relate his achievement to Mandla, and felt a pang in his stomach at the thought of his friend, now skipped. Something appeared to have gone out in the completion of the mission. But hell, where? he seemed to ask of the darkness. He pumped a fist on the bedding and stood up. Where was the AK47? He couldn't recall bringing it into the house and again a twitch of fear gripped at his stomach. Then he remembered it was still in the car.

The cold night air swept through his flesh because the balaclava no longer covered his face. It was a welcome experience for his disturbed state of mind. He was being knocked into sanity. He knew this as soon as he played the muzzle of the rifle around his nostrils, for the smell of fire still lingered. The feeling of triumph returned, releasing him to a calm if somewhat jerky sleep.

Elsewhere the rhythm of the night acquired a fresh impulse to its sagging beat. The breath and fury of the law huffed and puffed over the sleeping multitudes of Soweto as Colonel Kleinwater arranged the night's events with military precision. Seated in his car at the scene of the act of protest, he directed operations.

From behind drawn curtains the residents of the street where the Batatas lived cursed the turn of events. Many braced themselves for the harassment galloping toward them, for although they didn't hear the Colonel bark commands they saw his men move on the double. And that meant only one thing: hell was let loose! With it came from a number of lips a curse on Black Power.

All routes leading out of the neighbourhood of Batata were manned heavily so that the houses within the cordoned off area were virtually under siege.

Night looked like day as house lights went on in all the houses in the neighbourhood.

The operation was clinical: two heavily armed men darted into the yard, dashed to the backyard and remained there until their colleagues had completed their search of the house with a toothcomb. While four waited to enter the front door two more waited at the front gate.

As time was an important factor for the success of the operations, anyone considered slow to react to the bang on the door had his blood chilled by the words: 'Come on, open up! Police!'

Inside a house the cops turned man and furniture alike upside down. They shook up the snoring inhabitants, hurled up mattresses and blazed torchlight underneath beds. They yelled for hidden explosives and cried out for the dagga-smoker, screaming that they would catch the skelms. No, the people did not know the skelms and when the oldies asked for explanations they were swept aside as if by grass-brooms; they were told to mind their business.

Major Hall sang one chorus line only: 'Where is Mandla? Tell us!'

As the search progressed inexorably the cops seemed to lose their focus: they spoke of a skelm at one point and skelms at another. And it became clear they did not know whether they were looking for one or more men. Perhaps it was for this reason that Major Hall clung to his obsession with Mandla.

It wasn't until Captain Brand smiled coldly at old man Mthembu that the cops began to speak of a major breakthrough.

Old Sarah opened the door for Brand's men, after Mthembu complained of a weakness of the body. But Mthembu came to the scene when he heard the cops speak of a shooting in the neighbourhood.

But first Brand said to Mthembu: 'Ya old man, where is the dagga hidden in this house?'

Mthembu's sense of humour seemed to have remained in the bedroom. He was glum with his eyes fixed on Brand. Brand smiled and said almost playfully: 'Come on, man, show me where you've kept the explosives . . .'

'Explosives?' queried Mthembu.

'Bombs!' said Brand.

The word was magical. Mthembu heard the sound of gunshot reverberate in the cold air outside. He recalled the car in front of the house, how he had hurried into the house scared. The explosive sounds and the cops were placed in sequence. In the silence which followed Brand was reading the signs of relief on the old man's face. He pressed his advantages: 'A man of the law has been killed and you heard the shots. Everybody heard them . . .'

'Who's killed?'

'Warrant Officer Batata,' said Brand.

'Oh no,' cried Sarah.

Suddenly a policeman pushed out a man from one of the rooms of the house. He was half dressed. Brand turned to face the new-comer: 'Toe nou,' he began as if in salutation, 'what have we got here, the man we want? Who are you?'

'Amos Ngubane.'

'Are you the old man's brother?'

Mthembu chipped in: 'He's the minister of my wife's church!' The cops looked at one another their eyes telling tales.

'Where's your pass book?' asked Brand of the minister. It was an embarrassment Mthembu couldn't grind under his feet. He spoke pleadingly: 'This man is innocent.'

'Yes?' said Brand mischievously.

'I was outside when I heard shots fired, many shots . . . I was looking at a car, standing in front of the gate empty.'

'When was this?' asked Brand.

'An hour ago.'

'What?' yelled Brand, his eyes bulging. 'Did you say an hour ago?'

'Yessir.'

'And it was empty?'

'Yessir.'

'Where was the driver?'

'I don't know.'

'Come on think hard, one of our men is dead!'

'He was not in the car.'

'What were you doing outside so late?'

221

'You see, sir, this morning, I mean yesterday morning I wake up and I feel my stomach is wrong, sir, now I drink this thing for the stomach.'

'A laxative?'

'Yes, yes lexington, so now I go to the lavatory and I come out and I see this car in front of my gate. Empty, the car is empty.'

'Did you jot down the registration?'

'I did, I never want the police to say I stole the car. I keep the number plate here in my head . . . I was going to report to the police first thing in the morning . . .'

'But there is no car outside now. You'd better write down the number on a piece of paper for me.'

Old man Mthembu rummaged in the house for pen and paper and came up with an old exercise book. He tore off a whole page to use for the number puzzling over the fact that the car had disappeared. He began to write TJ14 . . . and got stuck. 'Was it more than three numbers?' prompted Brand.

'Six, I think,' said Mthembu. Brand sighed with grief, so did Sergeant Strydom next to him.

''Strue I have it here,' said Mthembu pointing at his head but disappointed with himself. Then he said: 'Wait, I think there was a 2 and a 0 . . .'

'Where?' said a dejected Brand.

'No, I don't remember. I must be true, I don't remember,' said Mthembu in utter resignation. 'But I was going to report to the police.'

'What kind of car was it, big or small?'

'Small.'

'Model.'

'Cortina, old fashion.'

'Are you sure?'

'Cortina, old fashion, white or grey. I'm not sure.'

Brand pounded the table shaking the candle light on a flower pot. He exclaimed: 'Gots! Sarge, we've again missed the bloody skelm!'

'Looks like it meneer.'

'Are you sure of the Cortina?' asked Brand once more.

'Yes, I am.'

'There you are!' moaned Brand, 'missed a second time. What bad luck on me! Sarge, better take these two men to the Moroka Police Station and let each sign a statement.'

'Do we keep them there afterwards?'

'No, Sarge, I'm inclined to believe the old man. Let them go Sarge, we can always call on them if necessary.' Brand turned to Mthembu: 'Don't do anything silly like skipping to Botswana or Swaziland. Stay put here until we tell you you are free to go as you wish, okay?'

To no one in particular Brand said: 'This is a major breakthrough. I must tell the Colonel immediately of it.'

Sarah remained alone in the house to ponder why her man's tongue ran so loose in the presence of the cops. He could have played dumb and remained mum. That way he would still be sharing the bed with her like so many other men in the same street. Her light went out.

It was late in the night although Sis Ida couldn't tell the time. The winter night pinched her cheeks with an icy cold hand as she was brought to meet Praatnou. At this point she couldn't remember the number of interrogations involving her nor was she able to focus on the various faces of her interrogators. The experience alone was enough to be a torture: a harrowing of her spirits. At this juncture she seemed to have no care of what to expect of these sessions: they could kill her if they wished.

There was something horrible about the rough, tough brow of the other person. And the result was that no warmth, no confidence flowed from the man. Sis Ida despised him because he tried to instil fear in her by keeping her in this cold silence and his hard look from his cat-like green eyes.

At long last Praatnou said: 'Ida, today you are going to die.' The man's hands formed a noose in the air as he simulated a choking figure. To emphasise the point he said: 'Do you hear what I say: today you die!' Then he added: 'An eye for an eye! Your buddies have killed one of us. So now, I must begin to repay the loss of that man. He was a wonderful man, an invaluable man. I don't know if the force will ever find a suitable replacement.'

Sis Ida remained silent but the news of another policeman killed settled badly with her. She sat with her hands on her lap, sad. For she was aware the life of the detainees would be definitely more unpleasant as a result of the happenings beyond the prison yard.

She sat in solemn silence, numb from the realisation that she was now at the mercy of the policeman, a man burning green hatred. So she waited, resigned to what fate had in store for her. Suddenly the man half-rose from his seat and screamed: 'Where is Mandla, jong? Where?'

'I don't know,' said Sis Ida quietly.

Praatnou stood up hunched, his hands remaining on the table. He then jerked one drawer open and brought out a towel. 'Are you going to tell the truth or do you want to see yourself die?' said the man between clenched teeth, his brow furrowed.

'I don't know where he is.'

'Surely, you must know his friends and his relatives. How could you hide him in your place if you knew none of these?'

'I speak the truth.'

Praatnou was holding the towel in his hands, stretched out. He walked toward Sis Ida, eyes fixed on her. For a moment she didn't know what to do, didn't know whether to look at his eyes or the towel. Both points were terrifying. The man acted swiftly, aware of his advantages. He swung the towel into Ida's face, catching her flush, on her broad features: her eyes cried, her nostrils tingled and her mouth tasted the wetness of the towel. She was still dazed by the blow when she felt its chilly coldness wrapped round her neck and a strangulating pull closing her throat. The force of it made her struggle on her feet as she tried to free herself from the threat of death. For the first time since her detention, Sis Ida saw herself staring into the wall facing her as one stares at death. Her effort to free her encircled neck seemed to be futile, as indeed it was, because everytime she turned and twisted the otherwise soft towel dug painfully into the flesh in the neck and made her pause. And in the silence she heard only the hard breathing of her assailant. And in that silence she said a prayer once more for her daughter and her grandson. Such was the nearness of death for her. At a point she couldn't recall, he loosened the grip on the neck, aware he had triumphed over her because she had long ceased to struggle free. He seemed to be gloating as he said: 'Kom nou—Come now, talk! Where is Mandla?'

Sis Ida's heart was filled with bitterness, her eyes with tears. She bit her lips to hold back a torrent of emotions wanting to gush out in a scream. Instead she said with feeling: 'Why do you want to kill me?'

'Where is Mandla?'

She gazed at the man, overwhelmed by her own impotence yet aware her strength was not yet sapped out completely, because they were still looking for Mandla; they were still beguiled by black magic despite their laws and their guns. Mandla was still out of their hands; she was comforted by the thought of it. She remained quietly defiant and mum.

'I have asked you a question!' said Praatnou angrily.

'I don't know.'

He said, walking to his side of the table: 'You are making things difficult for yourself. The other people have told us a lot about you. You know too much and an "accident" about your death would remain an accident however much the world howled!' From the drawer he brought out a piece of wire and said: 'This and the towel can finish you off immediately without any trace of evidence. Just remember that one. Where is Mandla hiding, who are his friends, who can give us the clue to his whereabouts? We want the murderer.'

Praatnou began to wrap the towel round the stout piece of wire. He went about the job with callousness, not once looking at Sis Ida although aware of her fear for what he was preparing for her.

Sis Ida cleared her throat because suddenly she experienced a constriction of the throat. She was at that point in time resigned to death as her fate. There was no hope of rescue, not at that late hour within the confining walls of the interrogation room and in the presence of a man who looked as if he was happy to laugh at her fears.

Praatnou snapped. That was all Sis Ida could recall later because she never saw the signs of transformation except that he seemed to sag on his feet, slapped the wire and towel on the table and sat on the seat with hands covering his face. They rested on his brow as if it were the source of his new act. She watched the man agonised by what he couldn't verbalise in her presence. Gradually she began to feel a triumphant aura sweep over her as the other person seemed to go through a painful experience of sorts. Then she felt sorry for the cop. It was a natural feeling of human compassion. There was nothing she could do to help alleviate the pain whose source was not visible to her.

Sis Ida never knew how the female warder came to fetch her away. She left the room with mixed feelings: happy to leave behind her the fear of death instilled in her but sorry for the poor plight of her assailant. Once more her large-heartedness was revealed for the law to see, but no-one seemed to see her as a human being.

The cell was cold, bone-crushing temperatures making of this night one to remember. Sis Ida couldn't sleep easily because her mind searched for the face and name of the cop said to have been killed that night. However, she was overpowered by fatigue, and sporadic sleep.

The telephone on the desk of Colonel Kleinwater began to ring. The Colonel let it ring. He stretched a hand to drag towards him a flask colourfully decorated with red and green floral patterns. The phone jangled and jangled. He let it go on. For him the flask contained relief in the form of piping hot black coffee made by his wife earlier in the morning.

The phone continued to ring and he ignored it as if aware of the message through the wire. He was tired and moody after the events of the past night so that the noise on the desk, and the hurried feet along the corridor of someone intent on treading the shiny floor with four-pound hammers instead of cow-leather, tended to thud off his chest and all this was terribly annoying to the officer.

Someone knocked on the door, pushed his way in and declared: 'Excuse me, sir, but I thought there's no-one here!'

By this time the jarring noise had ceased.

'O.K. Japie,' said the Colonel. Then he continued: 'Jong ek is moeg—I am tired! Those bloody terrorists have cost me lots of hours of sleep. And then comes the telephone on top of it. Nee jong, I am tired!'

'Jammer—pity Colonel,' consoled Brand. 'I am myself dog-tired. But I swear, meneer, ons vang die bliksems—We'll catch the bastards!'

'You think so?'

'I'm sure!' said Brand confident of himself. He was thinking of the number of times bad luck had robbed him of success: Dobsonville and the night at Mthembu's place. He was happy to recall these occasions when he was proved to have been on the right track but cheated by fate. And as he thought of fate he told himself it was not always cruel because one out of ten times it gave success to those who tried doggedly. It was the once-in-a-while chance he hoped for and his whole sense of being depended on it.

'Want some coffee, Japie?'

'I wouldn't mind it at all. Actually I was just this minute thinking how I missed this morning my hot black coffee. . . but I'm sure we'll catch the skelm responsible for all the trouble we've experienced these days!'

'Where do we begin?' asked the Colonel obviously unimpressed by the confidence of his colleague. 'I hope you are not pinning the chances of success on the description of the car seen by the old man. You know as well as I do the car might have been stolen property!'

Captain Brand stood facing the Colonel arms folded across his breast. He unfolded them to take a sip of the coffee, otherwise he would cut a miserable figure in the presence of his superior. There was something he felt receding from his grasp as if by divine intentions. And it was the thought of forces working against him which set in motion the frustration sweeping down through his body. His mind was still engaged with this unseen force when the Colonel revealed the challenge facing the investigating unit: 'Just how many people are we looking for in your opinion?'

'One,' said Brand. He let the word come out in one gush of air. Nor did he add to it — so confident was he of his answer.

The Colonel sat with back bent. But when his colleague put down a simple but emphatic reply to the query, he sat up. It seemed he positioned himself to fire more shots at his colleague.

'What makes you think so?'

'I don't know. It's a mere hunch. I believe the escape of Mandla to Botswana is a red herring. Someone is trying to divert our attention, he's trying to deflate the gusto with which he knows we approach our work.'

The Colonel rose to his feet. The topic was important and heavy. He might find the energy with which to tackle it once on his feet. So he began to pace whatever area there was in his office in search of the mystery of the killing and in search of the energy with which to resolve his problem.

Pretoria was always impatient for replies. This made the searching by the Colonel an urgent matter.

He flopped into his seat once more and said: 'No, Japie, you are wrong.' He sagged further down in the seat and continued: 'It is clear to me that we are dealing with professionals; we've entered a new era in the fight against communism . . .' The Colonel did the unusual: he yawned. He looked the part as he said: 'Ag, I wish I could retire to my farm, Vergenoeg. I am tired.'

The telephone began to jangle. 'O My Here God—O my God, can't they leave us alone.' He stretched his body forward to pick up the receiver and in a low, dull, unfriendly voice said: 'Ja Môre—Good Morning! Wie praat—Who is it?. . . Ag, man, what do you want? . . . What does your baas pay you to do? Do your own investigation! I have no comment to make. None whatsoever!' With that he banged the phone into its cradle. He turned to the Captain and said: 'These press chaps can be annoying . . . what were we talking about, by the way?'

'Our success,' said Brand.

'Success, Japie? I don't see it.'

'There's the break-through at Mthembu's and the information from Keke . . .'

'You have absolutely no ground to believe we are looking for one person. There's the report of Mandla skipping and Andries gunned down . . . How can you speak of a break-through when the kaffir doctor has not said anything? You can't go by what Keke tells us. Who is Mzi? He knows nothing of him save the fact of working with Mandla. But we must first catch Mandla to know more of Mzi. And where is he? Skipped! Nee, Japie, as I see this whole case, we are back to square one . . . unless . . . unless we set an example with one of these people . . .'

'You mean . . .?'

The Colonel took on a conspiratorial stance as he said: 'Well, we do not want any scandal about our methods. You see, these things can be done with a bit of discretion. I don't want our chaps to take the law into their own hands. There must be decency in everything we do. We must avoid do-gooders like that piccanin from the press, what's the name now?'

'Was it Thami?'

'That's it!'

'I'm all for starting with those chaps. We've got to silence the press. They spread the agitation . . .'

'Japie, listen to me . . . let's say we will hurry slowly in these things. I think we need to press for more information from that No. 2 chap. What's the name?'

'Roy.'

'I hear he's a hard nut to crack.'

'Stubborn as a mule.'

'Suits our plans. He's perfectly right for what we've been talking about . . .'

Captain Brand leaned on the Colonel's desk with both hands and said quietly: 'I'm going to ask Sergeant Strydom to set the ball in motion.'

In turn the Colonel replied quietly: 'I don't care who does the job but remember my advice: hurry slowly!'

## 15

Mzi woke up into the unfriendly frigidity of his room. The whole house was silent, breathing the loneliness of lost inmates. He was aware of a certain depression sweeping over him; his sense of belonging dissipated by his lonesomeness.

His mind was made up: he would quit the house and Soweto without bidding MaNhlapo farewell. A fighter wasn't expected to be conscious of such niceties. She would understand, that's how he explained himself to the four walls of the room.

Where to go? It was all very well to say he was quitting Soweto. But where to? He packed the paper bag with the AK47 and the bunch of flowers. The sight of the ready-made paper bag reminded him of the train trip from Park Station to Soweto. He saw the huge black old lady seated with him, heard her make enquiries about the paper bag. Would someone become curious again? A lot of water had passed under the bridge since that occasion. For one thing shots had been fired from the automatic rifle and no doubt the cops would have picked up the cartridges from Batata's yard. The rifle was almost like an albatross to him. But it was also his only true companion. There was no way he could survive escape from the country without the aid of the weapon. That was his belief.

He began to pace backwards and forwards; the room was too small to allow enough movement for his thinking, and the weight of the decision he had to make demanded he walk about the room. His problem was to decide whether to run for Queenstown, or another part of Johannesburg.

His home town was tempting. His parents and friends were out there. But they would treat him as the prodigal son. After an interval of ten years he wasn't sure of his friends. Trust no-one, believe in no-one. The words rang in his ear, crystal clear and as cynically as they were uttered in Dar by one of the bigwigs in the Movement. No, he would have to steer clear of Queenstown. Soweto was all right so long as the heat was not building up; it was all right because his face meant nothing to most people and his name was faceless to the members of the student group and the law. Why, even MaNhlapo and Sis Joyce could relate to him as long as they were in the same house with him. When they were with others he was just another stranger without a history, without a people. And it suited him fine. It bothered him though to leave MaNhlapo without a single cent for legacy. But there was no way he could help it. He was penniless himself. He would have to see Ann for assistance — only this once. Something happened in him as he pictured Ann. He tried to suppress the thought that he wanted her as a woman. Yet he acknowledged the fact did exist.

He went to stand near the front window in the sitting room to gaze at the scene in the street. At that hour of the day the street seemed deserted. There was none of the rhythm and pulse of the early hours when Dube rushes to the station and the taxi rank. Instead he saw a mongrel saunter along the street, a hen peck the earth — this brown earth salted by the blood of the youth of Soweto. He saw it was quiet out there and he heard in anticipation his feet eat into the crunchy earth.

The house became creepy. There was something about it which made him want to leave immediately. For a brief moment he asked himself why he was no longer comfortable within the house. He wondered how long it would take before the cops got onto his trail. Much as he told himself they could never catch him, he became fearful of remaining in the house.

The chilled air was repressive, driving him out. And yet he was aware that for him there was no way in which he could stand outside in the yard to bask in the sun. He wasn't like the people he saw walk up and down the street. He was different, he was a freedom fighter. The cops would nab him. Sure as hell they would!

By this time it was mid-morning and time to take a final decision. He performed a strange ritual: he went back to the bedroom he had shared with Mandla; he touched the bedding and the iron railing and stood away from the bed, clearing his throat as if to address it. Yet he said nothing, his eyes filled up, his chest crammed with emotions. Suddenly he grabbed the paper bag and walked into the sitting room. Again he stood briefly in this room taking in the sparse items in it, and then stepped into the kitchen where he repeated his farewell function.

At last he was closing the outside kitchen door: quietly and gently as if conscious of a sickening sensation. As he walked past the small car parked on the side of the house, he tapped the bonnet gently and let a finger touch lightly on the hood. He experienced a burst of mixed feelings. Once out of the gate Mzi was so oblivious to his surroundings, he didn't bother to look up and down the street to check if his way was clear. He strode straight up the incline to Dube Station.

The station platform was relatively quiet. And waiting for the train wasn't particularly exciting. In fact it bored him stiff and to kill time he played a few times with the peak of his cap, sometimes bending it upwards or drawing it over his eyes like a thug. It amused him, this military cap he wore with such cheek.

The train arrived. The second trip by train held no joys for him. His mind was wracked by the decision he couldn't take. At that moment there was no other place in his mind but Ann's office. It was as if he hoped Ann would be the solace of his worried mind.

Park Station was like a dead place, so different was it from the last time he alighted from the train. It was strange to see ghostlike people sauntering on the platform. He wondered how much they were affected by the dying spirits so commonly seen in Soweto those days. He thought the effervescence of activity and vitality he had seen many weeks earlier as he arrived on the Pietersburg train was missing. Ah, Johannesburg, he mused, was an uncaring city. So very different from Soweto. Here machines were run regardless of whatever happened in Soweto. Yet the umbilical cord ran from one place to another.

The day loomed large outside Park Station. It lashed out at his eyes with such force that the mind was left dizzy. Such was the experience of Mzi as he trod the streets to Braamfontein to meet Ann Hope.


'I'm rather disappointed with Mandla and the turn of events in Soweto. Not once did I think there would be so much callous bloodshed. I know there's desperation among the people, I know it too well but why would Mandla want to kill so many police, first Rampa, then Batata? He's too young to take on the sins of this whole world. God! I feel outraged.' Mzi watched Ann Hope as she rattled away. . . . He was never given a chance to put in a word, not even edgewise. She let go her pent-up feelings as soon as she was able to do so behind the closed door of her office. She took him by surprise and in his troubled state of mind he was thrown off balance and remained silent to let the frustration of the woman run its course. When she paused Mzi was the more surprised with himself. He didn't let go his own pent-up feelings. It seemed he was a victim of a certain disintegration of his personality. He allowed the charged atmosphere to simmer to a standstill of sorts.

All the while he watched her; he tried to find a spot in her agitated nature which he could appeal to for the help he needed badly at that very moment.

The room fell into a quietness. Mzi touched tentatively the hard heads of the flowers in the paper bag placed on the floor next to him.

231

He held one group of petals tightly, releasing the tension gripping his young body.

Their eyes met at the point when he was about to say: 'I need help; I need it badly.'

Ann pulled out a cigarette from a pack lying on her desk. She lit it feverishly. 'You need help, you say,' she repeated.

'Ya! . . . Soweto has become too hot for me, and lonely,' added Mzi.

'Why didn't you quit with Mandla? You could have gone to Swaziland . . .'

'I am of no use outside the country yet. I don't want to retire at my age, what for?'

'What can you do in the country? If Soweto is hot for you, the whole country cannot hide you!'

He looked at her with distaste, this woman from whom he hoped to receive help. And it was to hold back the violence of his own tongue that he kept quiet for a while. Then he blurted out: 'I must eliminate the only informer I've come to know: Noah Witbaatjie.'

'So you want to kill?'

'I didn't say so: to eliminate I said.'

'What's the difference?'

'As I see it, an eliminator fulfills a function. He destroys for a purpose larger than himself. There's nothing selfish about what he does because it is a job he discharges.'

Ann blew out a huge cloud of smoke filling the room with her breathing. She put the cigarette in an ashtray, and wrung her hands as she said: 'You know something? . . . I've often wanted to quit this lousy country and return home. Honestly I have . . . I saw the start of the Soweto demonstrations and I said to myself: at last it is happening. The giant was waking up after all. Those kids warmed my heart; they shamed their parents, as often happens all over the globe. But when certain acts of violence crept into their programme I began to wonder; I became fearful lest the good start go to waste. And now? I've despaired, I've lost the faith and admiration in my heart. Last night's act was the last straw. I cannot see myself forgive Mandla for the string of killings attributed to him. What will become of him? A murderer all his life? Oh my God! Can't someone see he'll be destroyed by the specks of blood on his hands? Now you say you want to eliminate Noah. What for, do you want him to die a martyr?'

'He can never be; he's a weed I want to pull out of society like I did Batata.'

Ann shot up on her feet: 'Batata! So you killed Batata? Oh what a shame. You've made your own life unbearable!'

'Listen man,' said Mzi, he felt trapped in Ann's office and in his desperation he ground his own person under foot. He was in a rotten mood as he continued: 'Why don't you pick up the phone and tell the cops to fetch me from your office for killing Batata? If you feel that bad about what Mandla and I have done you have this last chance to even up things with your conscience. Go ahead, call the cops!'

For a fleeting moment Ann looked beyond Mzi to the door. But never at the telephone on the desk. She wouldn't admit she was scared of the black man in her office. Instead she thought she pitied him. Aloud she said: 'I am no turntail. I have always believed in the justness of the Soweto demonstrations. I cannot at this hour turn my back on the kids however much I disapprove of certain of their leaders.' She paused to recover her breath. Then she went on: 'Anyway, you came to see me for help. What kind of help do you want?'

Mzi watched Ann take her seat again. He didn't know what to make of her; he was unsure whether to put his faith in her hands and risk his life, or what. She noticed his silence and in an effort to egg him on she said: 'I can understand your silence. You don't trust me.' She said it with sadness because there was something about the black man she admired. She wouldn't tell herself it was a thing whose deep-rootedness couldn't be reached in a superficial fashion. To reach it she would have had to place her life in his hands. But after the altercation between them distrust reigned. Neither could open to the other.

Again their eyes met, melting the bitterness of the past few moments. Mzi told himself there was no real choice before him. Either he asked for Ann's help or walked out of the office into the snares of the police. Soweto was out of bounds. He spoke tentatively: 'I am not so sure of myself. You say I can trust you. I don't know if I have a real choice because I need your help.' He noticed her eyes were fixed on him. So he let his next words come out quickly: 'I need your place to hide . . . it won't be for long, just a couple of days.' He was by now wringing his hands. 'I'll find myself another place in the meantime. Ya, that's it. I've said it.'

A certain sense of balance collapsed in Ann. To harbour a fugitive from the law was the last thing she ever thought of doing. She feared the law would certainly cancel her work permit if anything went wrong; she saw herself in confrontation with her senior, Ian Taylor, for the threat to the organisation; she imagined the consultation she would hold with her lawyer and his remonstrations with her for an ill-conceived idea. She felt trapped by her own words for she had given her word that he could trust her. She remained silent, looking down at an imaginary figure on her desk. He saw it all, the turmoil of her mind and wondered if he was fair to her. His strength of character which had seemed to evaporate earlier returned, and he was willing to face the huge daylight outside Ann's office and with it the consequences of his actions. He said rather quietly: 'I don't think you need feel forced to go through it all, I mean if you are not sure you are doing the right thing hiding me, you don't have to do it. I came to you because I saw possibilities of being a step ahead of the law, of recharging my energies for the next point on my programme. I hate to embarrass you, believe me Ann.'

She uncoiled: 'You don't embarrass me at all. I must admit to a temporary shock but it's over now . . . I know I want to help . . . I can . . . I don't have to tell anyone about it. I don't have to discuss it with anyone. After all it is my right to do as I please at my house.'

'Oh.' His eye was fixed on her.

'Come,' said Ann getting to her feet, 'let me take you away now, I've had a quiet morning around here. I'll nip out quickly and be back before anyone notices my absence. How's that?'

'Suits me fine,' said Mzi picking up the paper bag and holding it under one arm.

Both slipped out of Pharmacy House quietly and headed for Ann's place in Kensington.


The upshot of the resolution taken by Colonel Kleinwater and Captain Brand touched Roy like icy water on the body on a winter morning. He was surprised to be dragged out of his cell, frogmarched amidst unprintable curses to an office where he found himself trapped by the presence of Brand, Strydom, Praatnou, Matlala and Ndlovu.

Something told him immediately he would have to prepare for an assault on his person. The brief sojourn in detention taught him never to look beyond a specific encounter with the cops. In other words he accepted whatever fate awaited him in the hands of the police. It didn't take long to give him a taste of it: whoop! whep! whoop! Hard, painful powerful blows landed all over his body. He didn't know how to ward off these attacks.

Praatnou yelled: 'Where is Mzi? Come on, tell us!'

When Roy opened his eyes he saw the Captain standing in the far corner of the room leaning on a steel cabinet munching sandwiches. Strydom chipped in: 'Look my boy, you are now alone. You stand alone because your brothers have told us a lot!' Strydom turned to Matlala: 'Show him this morning's paper!' Roy's mind was still fuzzy but he was clearing up rapidly and was able to read the headlines stating Mandla had skipped the country. Coupled with the killing of Batata the report had the effect of unsettling him. Without Mandla around it looked as if the battle was lost.

In the confused state of his mind, Roy heard Praatnou say boastfully: 'The heat is on boykie, everyone is saving his skin. You must tell us where to find Mzi. Do it quickly or you are dead!'

That's it, the threat, decided Roy. He made up his mind to show the policemen he wasn't scared of death. He sealed his lips.

Praatnou screamed: 'Tell us, where is Mzi?'

Roy remained silent.

Strydom said: 'It costs you nothing, kaffertjie, to speak.'

Roy was stung. He said: 'I don't know him.'

Ndlovu pleaded: 'You are in trouble my friend. The officer here (referring to Captain Brand) wants to know the whereabouts of Mzi, that's all. If you don't talk then you will be in serious trouble.'

Roy remained unmoved. He glared at Ndlovu as if about to spit at him.

Praatnou leaped towards Roy and held out one of Roy's arms. But Brand said to Praatnou: 'Leave him alone. Leave him alone ou maat.' The Captain stood away from the cabinet, one hand resting on it. He addressed himself to Roy in a not too aggressive tone. He said: 'Do you see the walls of this place . . . black! They are black like you are black . . . and the ceilings? . . . white! Like I am white. As you can see for yourself the ceiling stands on the walls. I stand on you my boy, Roy. I stand on you like every white man stands on a black man. There's absolutely nothing you can do about it . . . And let me tell you something else my boy: you can sulk, pulling your face to be as ugly as a toad, you can do fok all about it! You are in our hands to do with you as we please. The law is on our side. The white man in this country makes the law, he interprets it.' The Captain was by now blood-red with anger. He pointed a threatening finger at Roy as he said: 'It will take you people a thousand years to reach where we are. Remember that one: a thousand years before the black man catches up with a white man in this country. You can repeat my words to the press. I don't care! Do you hear me? You can tell your press brothers what I've just said. I don't care a damn!'

Brand pulled open one of the drawers of the cabinet and brought out something which Roy didn't see properly. What he could make out of it as it was hurled to Strydom, Matlala, Ndlovu and finally to Praatnou was that it was made of coloured cloth. The two black cops rushed at Roy each holding out his arms as Praatnou nestled the legs of the bermuda pants on Roy's neck. Strydom spoke quietly: 'We don't want to hurt you but if you don't tell us about Mzi anything can happen.' The noose on Roy's neck tightened, Praatnou hissed threats and hurled curses.

Brand didn't seem to want to witness the final enactment of the resolution. He went to the desk in the office and began to pull out and push in the drawers. Each time he would appear to be rummaging through the papers in the drawer.

The minutes tolled by: these were counted off by the harsh and hard noose gripping the fragile neck of Roy.

In a desperate attempt to flee death, Roy wriggled his body and was able to free himself, first from Ndlovu and then Matlala. Strydom stepped forward to reinforce the might of the cops. No sooner was he near Roy than he found himself the target of an infuriated and embittered young man. Roy lashed out with both hands, landing one fist on the cheek of Strydom. It was sudden, it was forceful, it rocked the middle-aged cop, causing him to stagger backwards a step or two.

Brand didn't see the blow. He inferred it had occurred. He yelled in a shrill voice: 'He fights back! Show him who's the boss!' The command was unnecessary. The other men acted in unison. Praatnou regained his grip round the neck with bare hands; Strydom recovered from the shock quickly enough to enter the melee; Ndlovu and Matlala threw themselves into the fury of the law with bodily onslaughts.

It wasn't long before the inert body of Roy lay still on the floor, dead.

The office became smelly, sweat churned in the air as if it had been sprayed. The men felt hot on this winter day, they were heaving and panting from the heavy duty performed on this fateful day.

Brand said the only thing to be spoken under the charged atmosphere: 'I don't want anyone to say anything about this. I will personally report this development to the Colonel. We cannot have a man of the law assaulted the way this boy did before all of us. Koos, see that everything goes smoothly.'

'Ya, ou maat,' replied Strydom.

The end for Roy was sudden. So it seemed. The lesson was played out for others to learn and shiver.

## 16

NEWS ITEM
DETAINEE COMMITS SUICIDE BY HANGING HIMSELF IN
HIS CELL. NOTHING MORE TO SAY, COMMENTS POLICE
SPOKESMAN

At the same time as Roy was caged in with the other men of the law, Sis Ida sat watching Colonel Kleinwater sip boiling hot coffee in his office. He sat crouched, eyes fixed on Sis Ida. She wasn't able to see the date but the bold lettering jolted her. She wasn't aware this fluttering of the heart was designed by the man with whom she shared the office. The way he sat, the way he looked at her, was all part of the manipulation. She was being driven to the very unhappy situation which made her look hapless and forlorn in the company of the officer.

The man began: 'Gots Ida, today I feel as if I shouldn't have been here. Rather I should be miles away from this place . . . And you know something,' then he swallowed more coffee and said: 'a lot depends on this meeting with you. 'Strue's living God, this meeting is in your hands Ida!'

Sis Ida wondered about the game played by the Colonel. He spoke so simply, so sadly, as if he really needed her sympathy. But her mind drifted also to the paper. What was it they said about Mandla and Batata? The urge to read the paper grew strong. And this made her reaction to his words difficult to verbalise. She heard him speak but it was through an opening which didn't allow her to see through the words. The sound of his voice merely confused what lay in her breast. So she remained mum where at another place and occasion she might have reacted with words of her own.

Colonel Kleinwater pulled the newspaper nearer to him and let it face Sis Ida. She held her breath as she read about the escape of Mandla and the death of Batata. Huh! she sighed. The officer didn't allow Sis Ida to read the story through and this added to the confusion in her mind and spirits. As always she had this motherly instinct which would explain the sorrow touching her heart at the news of the death of Batata. For Sis Ida the taking of life was a matter of concern and it was for this reason that she exclaimed when she read of the news. And the knowledge of Mandla's escape placed side by side with the report of the killing blunted the joy she would otherwise have experienced for his safety.

The Colonel pulled the morning paper that Sis Ida had been reading away, to reveal another paper on the alleged suicide of Roy. The news was stunning: she closed her eyes briefly, bit her lips to suppress the charge of emotions to her heart and eyes. When she raised her hand to cover her mouth the officer took this to be the cue to impress her with the purpose of the meeting: 'You must begin to understand the gravity of our little meeting; it is a point of crisis for me. You see, I have a mission in Soweto: it is my job, my duty to clean up Soweto of all the vermin in that place.' He paused, pulled out a cigarette from a packet standing on the desk and lit it. Between clouds swirling up between him and Sis Ida, he continued, his voice raised slightly: 'Of course you realise this makes your own position very poor. The law is going to fall on you very hard, you face serious charges. Look at it this way: municipal property has been destroyed; Government property has been destroyed and the lives of a number of law officers have been taken. And every one of these deeds was conceived in your house. There's absolutely no doubt about this. And don't forget the little bomb blast in your own house. A lot went wrong in that house, I'm sure of it . . . You know you are in serious trouble? . . . I don't think you are aware . . . it is also my opinion that if the Attorney-General sees fit to do so he can place charges before the court which will earn you the death sentence; remember lives have been taken in many cases where you are obviously an accomplice. And the hangman in Pretoria is never unwilling in such cases.'

Sis Ida had long dropped her eyes because she had tried in vain to search from the Colonel's eyes the reason for all this talk. If Mandla was no longer in the country and Roy was dead, what more could she tell the police, she wondered. The confusion in her mind was made no better by the long-windedness of the officer nor his silence about Mzi. She thought the law was still ignorant about the existence of that name and she didn't see it as her duty to mention it, however tenuous her own position. She couldn't shout down this man of law; she couldn't stand up and leave the man's office in a huff. A detainee is as good as a prisoner, she told herself as she reassessed her situation. Yet she could also do nothing about her glassy eyes because her chest was full, so full she was only a fraction away from tears: such was her frustration.

The Colonel's voice trailed away: 'I think you are wasting your time here. I think so. A person as strong, as popular and active as you has no business to be in prison. Think about it . . . Don't allow sentiment to fritter you away; you could be doing so many things; you could be with your family, in your own house. Gots! Ida, don't be childish. You could be as free as Mandla, do as you wish like Mandla. Tog, I know you didn't mean to cheat the law, you were used to protect law-breakers. Now they talk, they tell us these things. Why not you, hey?'

Sis Ida couldn't contain herself anymore. Involuntarily she heard herself say: 'What must I say?'

'Where is Mzi?' asked the Colonel. It was a simple straightforward question placed before Sis Ida as simply as the papers she was allowed to read briefly.

Sis Ida wondered about the roundabout way he arrived at this point. For previously her interrogators were blunt and short. Impressions to influence her were created in response to her replies but this time he seemed to take pains to prepare for this juncture. She tried to figure out why he did it. Could it be that he was convinced she knew the answer or was he taking a shot in the dark and therefore had to be cautious? But his mixture of threat and persuasion wasn't just for fun. It suggested she was known to be one person with the necessary answer. Sis Ida concluded that someone within the group was a squealer. She was determined not to fall into the trap. She declared: 'I don't know Mzi. I've never seen him.' With those words uttered she began to search her mind for the truth because she was no longer sure if her answers were right. Some reference point in the faculties of her mind might confirm the veracity of the claim. But her mind was blank. She experienced a black-out she couldn't explain or understand. She waited for him to react to her reply which could reveal for her beforehand the man's reaction.

He was swift and deadly, he shot up and pounded the desk and screamed: 'Don't talk bull! We know all about you. You sit there like an innocent, God-fearing little girl mouthing a lot of lies! For months you've harboured criminals sought by the law; you've given refuge to a trained communist saboteur and now you want me to believe you don't know Mzi. Gots! Man, you must be thinking we are bloody fools that we haven't charged you so far. Don't stretch your luck too far! Tell me where is Mzi?'

The Colonel took a step or two away from the desk, stopped, and stood glaring at Sis Ida. This time it was her turn to react. She saw the burning fire flashing from his eyes and felt her own impotence in his presence. Fear of death sent a pang through her stomach. She was aware the man could do as he wished with her, the world wouldn't know and wouldn't do much beyond a sigh of resignation.

Sis Ida remained mum.

This time the Colonel stamped his foot on the ground and yelled: 'Are you deaf?'

'No'

'Then answer me for Christ's sake!'

Sis Ida became aware at that point of the monumental task facing her. How was she to convince the policeman of the truthfulness of her answers? For her Mzi was a name, as he was for the rest of the group. Yet anything she said would be hard to believe, as evidenced by the man's attitude at that point. She took a plunge: 'I am telling the truth. I don't know Mzi. I heard his name mentioned by Mandla.' Sis Ida paused because there was something heavy on her chest. She had to heave it off. She continued: 'I heard they met at Mr Mbambo's place. That's all I know.' She felt a bit better.

'Why didn't you tell me so before?'

She kept quiet.

'In any case I knew it already. But where else did he stay?' He was gentle again.

Sis Ida dropped her eyes and looked at the open palms of her hands. And then she locked the fingers of her hands together. For the strain of the revelations wrung out of her was hard to bear. 'There is a person I heard mentioned once. I don't know her: Ma-Nhlapo. She lives in Dube.'

'She was picked up this morning when we found the car we've been looking for all this time. But like you she claims she doesn't know where he's to be found. You must tell me of his friends, his relatives. I want to know even the distant relatives. I want the culprit's full name. Surely he had a name other than this Mzi. How is it possible that no-one can give us a rough description of this man? Was he tall, stout or short . . . black or light in complexion? Surely somebody must know this. Didn't he have a girl-friend or something like that?'

'I don't know. I never saw him.'

Colonel Kleinwater sat down. He said to no-one in particular: 'We must have a break-through soon otherwise how can we go on with our investigations? This man is dangerous!'

There was a pause during which Sis Ida could hear the thudding of her own heart. She felt hopeless in spite of a certain sense of triumph. Wasn't she part of the struggle? Wasn't she to be delighted because her own people outwitted the law at times? Yet her reality at the time was the fact of her detention. She was scared by the idea of being a prisoner, not knowing what the end would be because already one of them had met an untimely and inglorious end. She

240

always found the company of an interrogator unsettling. The cell was better but these offices and rooms where one faced the unpredictable moods of the interrogator scared her stiff. Even the pauses when silence reigned made the passage of time an eternity. When at last the Colonel spoke, she was a bundle of nerves ripped apart by the fear of an unknown fateful outcome. She heard him as a voice echoing through a dark tunnel: 'There's nothing more I can get from you. I'm afraid you and your friends will be detained here indefinitely. I think you will begin to realise the seriousness of this matter. . . Anytime you wish to add to what you have already told me, be free to come forward. Your stay here depends on the satisfactory information you can give us. That alone will determine how long you remain a detained person. Think about it.' He pressed a switch on the side of the desk. Not long afterwards the door was opened by a warder who took Sis Ida away.

Sis Ida fell on her knees in the cell and closed her eyes. Her chest was full and she needed prayer to relieve her emotions. But she couldn't hear the words of her heart.

NEWS ITEM
SOWETO COAL MERCHANT HAULED IN. TENSION GRIPS
SOWETO. NO COMMENT SAYS POLICE SPOKESMAN

The combi in which Ann and Mzi drove to Kensington was inscribed on both sides: 'Christian Brotherhood'. The trip itself was an exercise in endurance for both persons. Ann held the steering wheel so tight that the blood around her knuckles was drained completely, showing them up to be ghostly white. Now and then she looked into the rear mirror as if expecting someone to be tailing them. Mzi sat back in his seat exhibiting no signs of care. Even the paper bag at his feet was allowed to swing from one point to another on his side without arousing his concern. The trip held some fascination for him: the scenery along the streets, the richness of the foliage in each cottage, brought out the difference between the legacy of the location peach-tree and these sights — much more could be derived from the trees in the white man's suburbs. Once the combi stopped at some red robots and a white man looked at them. As both vehicles pulled off, the man yelled: 'Hey!' at Mzi and made a vulgar sign with his fingers. Mzi was quick to retaliate, to the embarrassment of Ann, who simply said: 'What rudeness!'

But it was the huge lettering of the news poster which shattered

241

Mzi's apparent peace of mind. It read: 'Soweto Coal Merchant Hauled In.' Instinctively he read in the name of Papa Duz. He asked Ann to buy the newspaper but she replied that a copy was delivered at her place. At the same time she suggested that the paper bag be placed on the back seat. But she held back the reason for wanting this because she didn't want to upset him by admitting the shuffling noise irritated her. Mzi assured her he was comfortable with the paper bag at his feet, whereupon she smiled awkwardly at him and continued the trip.

Mzi couldn't recall a previous occasion when he had sat in a vehicle with a white woman. And he thought the uniqueness of the event was witnessed by the many eyes looking at them as if they were actually commiting a sin in motion. At one point Ann jokingly suggested that Mzi should take over the wheel. For Mzi the fun on the road was endless. Not so for Ann. She appeared to have the smiles on her face bouncing off the surface of her skin because one minute she would be smiling, the next she would be dead-pan as if the trip pained her.

At last they reached Kensington. Ann's house was an old white-washed building, without a garden. It looked as cramped as the houses in Soweto. Ann was apologetic about the appearance of the house and she tried to make a joke about the bunch of flowers protruding from the paper bag and the fact that she had no garden in her yard.

Mzi didn't hear Ann apologise about the old furniture in the sitting room. His eyes sought the evening newspaper and when he held it in his hands, he remained on his feet running his eyes on the front page story of the Soweto coal merchant arrested for collaborating with the children's revolution by supplying cars used in their missions. Gradually his whole being collapsed under him; his strong body became weak and he found himself seeking the nearest place to sit. He just sank onto a divan, eyes fixed on the paper. When he finished reading the first time the urge to repeat it was so compelling he went over it again. What he read, slowly, as if counting and itemising each word, struck a gong in his mind. For the first time he found himself fearing for his safety in a very intense way. The loud clanging of the jail gates clapped his ears; it was a sound which jarred the emotions. He told himself emphatically that they would not catch him: 'I would rather die,' he said into the huge sitting room.

Ann came back from her bedroom, perched on the divan at a point away from Mzi and said: 'Well what will you have for a drink?' She put on a broad smile behind those words.

'I've got to leave!' said Mzi. His face looked hard and drawn, his brown eyes were burning with the intensity of his feelings. He was looking at Ann as if she were an enemy of long-standing.

Ann was breathless. She noticed the sudden change in his mood and was affected herself: 'What's the matter, is there anything wrong? . . . Something in the paper I suppose?' She held out a hand to receive the paper from Mzi.

He didn't resume his seat after handing the paper over to Ann. She read the story of the coal merchant rapidly and looked up to say: 'So this is it, the net is closing in swiftly?'

'Can you take me to the Swaziland border?' Mzi said it without hesitation because his self-confidence had returned.

Ann's reaction was long in coming. She was caught between two unwelcome situations: the desire to be helpful and the fear of arrest for harbouring a fugitive black man.

'What about the office? I didn't tell them I'm going away and if I don't show up tomorrow they'll be worried.' Ann saw a succession of tragic events unfold before her eye: panic by her senior, Mr Taylor; the house being stormed by police; the curious looks of her neighbours as she and Mzi were led to the dozen or so waiting police cars; appearance before a hostile court; prison and the cancellation of her work permit and loss of face and revenue. It was through a confused mind that she heard the trailing voice of Mzi. He spoke freely because he had nothing to lose, she told herself.

'Phone the office and tell them you left because you were not feeling well. No-one saw us leave; they must believe a person in your position.'

'What about the appointments I had in the office for tomorrow? It's such a pity to have to disappoint the people coming all the way from Soweto . . .'

'Get your priorities right Ann. Mine is a matter of life and death. If the cops find me here you're sunk,' said Mzi bitterly. 'You don't want that to happen.'

'Of course not! . . . When do you want to go?'

'Now!'

Ann looked at him and found his face cold and unfriendly; she stood up and turned her back to him. The shadows in the street began to lengthen and although she wasn't able to say how the wind felt outside, she recalled there was a nip in the air because the winter evenings were decidedly unpleasant. Her mind sailed across the long, winding road to Swaziland. Then she experienced a twitch of the flesh as she imagined the road blocks set up by the police at such times. Mzi could be a risky cargo, that much she had to accept, and she felt inadequate for the trip. It was to escape the anguish of revealing her thoughts at that point which made her turn to face him and say: 'I'm going to make myself a cup of tea. Would you like to have some?'

'And your decision?' said Mzi.

She left in silence for the kitchen, leaving him alone with his problem. He went over to the divan where he picked up the paper to read it over again. This time he hurled it back to the divan and sauntered to the kitchen.

'I suppose I've become a necklace round your neck which you never wanted to wear.'

'Honestly I wish you'd stop saying such things.'

'I hate myself for being with you. Believe me I do. It just doesn't make sense . . . Look at it this way: I came into the country to get rid of the people's enemy, Batata, and this has landed me on your lap in Kensington. Why? I seem incapable of escaping the clutches of the white man even when he's not in my direct line of action, but why? Why?'

Ann poured hot water into two cups with teabags and shoved one towards Mzi who picked it up from the table. She said: 'I don't believe I'm qualified to say this but since you've asked for my opinion I'll say it . . . The trouble about this country is that everyone wants to step on the head of everyone else. The people haven't learnt to be in step with each other . . . Come, I must speak to the office.'

A little while later, Ann emerged from the bedroom and said: 'Well if we have to go, we'd better start now. I'll need petrol and we must buy provisions along the way. Are you sure you want to go like this?' asked Ann sadly.

'There is no other way . . . I've never had choices, not in my life.'

As if to belie the argument, Ann lingered on the kerb wondering which way to take out of Johannesburg. Then quickly she let the combi roar down the street to Broadway Avenue and the Witbank highway. She clung to the inscription on the combi: 'Christian Brotherhood', making it the one bond between them which would carry their hope of success on the escape route.

For Mzi the flurry of his exit from the country was in sharp contrast to the quiet dignity of his return many weeks earlier. His hope was embedded deep in his heart because for the exile there is always the eternal light burning for home-coming. For him there would be a second coming. His faith in the thought was enshrined . . .